PRAISE FOR *THE YOUNG DESIRE IT*

'This story of a boy's first love is one of the truest and most beautiful things that has been written by an Australian.' *West Australian*

'A first novel of exceptional interest and originality. Few characters in fiction have been more completely or beautifully portrayed.' *Spectator*

'Evokes the hot Western Australian landscape with rare force...A pastoral charged with the awakening of desire, like spring.' DOUGLAS STEWART

'Amazingly brilliant.' *Liverpool Daily Post*

'A beautifully written story of a sensitive boy's movement towards adult love.' *Sydney Morning Herald*

'A frank plea for the freedom of youth...Mackenzie proves himself to be a writer of outstanding ability.' *Mail* (Adelaide)

'Sensitive, vital and erotic.' VERONICA BRADY, *Australian Dictionary of Biography*

'It transcends by its sincerity and freshness the bonds and difficulties of its genre and subject.' *Bulletin*

'*The Young Desire It* presents the adolescent boy's view with power and poignancy.' *The Times*

'Groundbreaking [and] intensely personal.' *Dominion Post*

'A beautiful account of a young man's move into adulthood.' *Examiner*

'[Mackenzie's] masterpiece...Exquisite sexual tension... How did [he] get so wise?' PETER GOLDSWORTHY, *Monthly*

'Extremely impressive...a novel to be welcomed back to Australian literature's available past.' OWEN RICHARDSON, *Age*

'Mackenzie [is] a missing link in our literary tradition. The family tree burgeons at his return.' GEORDIE WILLIAMSON, *Australian*

'Splendid...distinguished by a rare sensitivity and an impressive ethical and psychological wisdom.' ANDREW RIEMER, *Canberra Times*

'A staggering piece of fiction...a true classic, a work by which all others should be judged.' PETER CRAVEN, *Australian Book Review*

KENNETH IVO BROWNLEY LANGWELL 'SEAFORTH' MACKENZIE was born in 1913 in South Perth. His parents divorced in 1919, and he grew up with his mother and maternal grandfather on a property at Pinjarra, south of Perth. He was a sensitive child who developed an intense love of nature.

At age thirteen Mackenzie was sent to board at Guildford Grammar School in Perth. His experiences there informed his first novel, *The Young Desire It*, published under the name Seaforth Mackenzie by Jonathan Cape in 1937. The author was just twenty-three.

The novel drew praise from *The Times*, *Spectator* and *Sydney Morning Herald*; the *Liverpool Daily Post* called it 'amazingly brilliant'. It was awarded the Australian Literary Society Gold Medal.

By this time Mackenzie had studied law, worked as a journalist and moved to Sydney. There he met the leading lights of the literary scene— among them Kenneth Slessor and Norman Lindsay—and married. He and his wife had a daughter and a son.

Mackenzie's subsequent novels were *Chosen People* (1938), *Dead Men Rising* (1951), based partly on his experience of the Cowra prisoner break-out, and *The Refuge* (1954). He also produced two volumes of poetry.

Kenneth Mackenzie's last years were spent mainly alone, in declining health and battling alcoholism, at Kurrajong in New South Wales. On 19 January 1955 he drowned in mysterious circumstances while swimming in Tallong Creek, near Goulburn.

DAVID MALOUF was born in 1934 and brought up in Brisbane. He is the internationally acclaimed author of such novels as *The Great World* (winner of the Commonwealth Writers' Prize and the Prix Femina Etranger), *Remembering Babylon* (winner of the IMPAC Dublin Literary Award) and, most recently, *Ransom*. *The Complete Stories* won the 2008 Australia-Asia Literary Award.

ALSO BY KENNETH MACKENZIE
Chosen People
Dead Men Rising
The Refuge

The Young Desire It
Kenneth Mackenzie

Text Publishing Melbourne Australia

textclassics.com.au
textpublishing.com.au

The Text Publishing Company
Swann House
22 William Street
Melbourne Victoria 3000
Australia

First published by Jonathan Cape 1937
This edition published by The Text Publishing Company 2013
Reprinted 2013

Cover design by WH Chong
Page design by Text
Typeset by Midland Typesetters

Printed and bound in Australia by Griffin Press, an Accredited ISO AS/NZS 14001:2004 Environmental Management System printer

Primary print ISBN: 9781922147509
Ebook ISBN: 9781922148544
Author: Mackenzie, Kenneth, 1913-1955 author.
Title: The young desire it / by Kenneth Mackenzie;
introduced by David Malouf.
Series: Text classics.
Dewey Number: A823.2

CONTENTS

Sketch of Kenneth Mackenzie by Norman Lindsay.
© *H. C. & A. Glad.*

A Perilous Tension
by David Malouf

THE YOUNG *Desire It* was published in London in 1937 by Jonathan Cape. The author, Kenneth 'Seaforth' Mackenzie, was not quite twenty-four. He had begun the novel at seventeen. 'Five weeks of solitude,' he tells us in a dedicatory preface, 'saw the making of the whole thing.'

Like many first novels, *The Young Desire It* draws on the author's own experience. Mackenzie grew up on an isolated property south of Perth, and until he entered Guildford Grammar at thirteen shared the company only of his mother, a younger sister and a few household servants. He was left to roam, barefoot and as he pleased, in the local countryside, whose changes of light and weather he seems to have taken, like his protagonist Charles Fox, as aspects of his own nature and feelings. This accounts for the intensity of the book's nature writing, which is more disciplined than anything in Lawrence who is clearly an influence, but also more inward and passionately lyrical. Charles's first encounter with society, in the close, intrusive and sometimes threatening form of a boys' boarding school, accounts for his puzzled outsider's view of his fellow students and teachers. What is not accounted for in so young a writer is the authority with which he tackles the book's disturbing and potentially sensational material, and the assurance, in the rhythm and cadence of every sentence, of the writing. We recognise the phenomenon, but it is rare, in the precocious genius of Stephen Crane in *The Red Badge of Courage*, in the young Thomas Mann of *Buddenbrooks*, and the even younger Raymond Radiguet of *Le Diable au corps* and *Le bal du Comte d'Orgel*. Mackenzie and *The Young Desire It* are of that company.

The novel has two points of focus.

One is the school as a social institution: in this case an English-style, all-male boarding school in what is still, in the twenties, an outpost of empire, an establishment devoted to the making, through classical studies, music, sport, and very British notions of manliness and public service, of young men.

The masters are imported Englishmen, the students for the most part country boys who have grown up close to the Australian bush and to Australian values and traditions. They are lively and well meaning enough, but from the masters' point of view uncultivated, even when, like Charles Fox, they are also sensitive and talented.

In the course of the book the whole order and ethos of the school is tested by the suicide of a wounded, yet highly effective and revered headmaster.

It is worth recalling that at this time most boys of fourteen or fifteen were already out in the world earning a living. A good part of Charles Fox's impatience to be done with school, and free, is a belief that he is being held back from life, though he also acknowledges that he knows little of what life is. He has till now been a kind of 'wild child' uncorrupted by society, armed only with 'a dangerous innocence' and unaware of 'the necessity for doing evil'. How he comes through—whether in fact he does come through—is the book's other and major concern.

On his first afternoon at the school he is sexually assaulted by a group of older boys, on the pretext of confirming that this pretty boy is not really a girl. What Charles discovers here, as a first line of defence, is a quality in himself, to this point unknown because unneeded, that will more and more become the keynote of his emerging character. This is resistance, which over time takes different forms in him, not all of them attractive. Resistance to others, and to events and influence; resistance to his own need for affection; a growing hardness that will protect him from being 'interfered with', and allow him the freedom—it is freedom of choice that the young so ardently desire—to be himself.

Several moments of revelation mark the course of Charles's adolescent progress, some of them so deeply interiorised and undramatic as to appear, by conventional novelistic standards, unrealised: a common complaint against *The Young Desire It* is that it is a book in which, as Douglas Stewart puts it, 'nothing happens'.

Another way of putting this would be to suggest that Mackenzie, in a quite revolutionary way for an Australian writer in the late thirties, is doing all he can to preserve his narrative from any whiff of the 'fictitious', and himself from any temptation to the fabrications of 'plot'. What interests him is not what happens in the world of events but what happens in Charles Fox's erotically charged sensory world, where he is confronted at every turn with situations for which he has no precedent. It is Mackenzie's determination to stick with the interior view, and the bewilderments of young Charles Fox, that make *The Young Desire It* perhaps the earliest novel in Australia to deal with the inner life in a consistently modernist way. Patrick White's *The Aunt's Story* is still a decade in the future.

The most significant of Charles Fox's discoveries is his meeting, on his first vacation at home, with the schoolgirl Margaret.

Essential to this is that it happens on Charles's home ground. The mystery of the occasion is bound up with the secret, half-underground quality of the place, with low-hanging pine branches, damp pine needles, misty rain, and the fact that it is grounded in the boy's sensuous inner world means he can take for granted that what is so shatteringly 'final' for him is equally so for the girl. It is this that makes 'impossible' for Charles the next significant moment of the book, when, back at school, Penworth, the young classics master he has formed a bond with, kisses him.

Charles has suffered a fainting fit in the school gym, at the sight of his friend Mawley's twisted ankle. When he comes to he is in Penworth's room, on Penworth's bed, with Penworth sitting on the bed beside him clasping his feet in his 'broad hands'. Confused by this but not yet anxious, he allows himself to be drawn into a discussion of his dreams, then confesses his ignorance, beyond the crude schoolboy facts, of what such dreams might mean, and of all sexual matters. The kiss that follows turns the boy's confusion to alarm. He is in no danger, he knows that. This is a proposal, not an assault, and anything beyond this is to him an 'impossibility': he has already had his revelation with Margaret which is definitive and of another kind. What concerns him is how he should act so that his response, while clearly a rejection, will also allow him to retain Penworth's affectionate interest, and Penworth his self-esteem. The man is gently reassuring: 'It's all right, dear lad...Don't be frightened—I shan't hurt you...Were you frightened of—something that might have happened?' But it is the boy who shows the greater care. 'I may not know it all, but even if I am so young,' he tells Penworth, 'I do know that you're unhappy; and if I could help I would.'

As Mackenzie has observed earlier, this is a school 'where many of the boys are old for their years and many of the Masters seem young for theirs'.

It is the delicacy with which Mackenzie negotiates the difficulties here that is remarkable: the way we see Penworth; the way Penworth sees himself; the extent to which the narrator stands clear of judgment.

On Charles's first night in the dormitory, Penworth, as duty master, has stepped in on a scene of bathroom bullying and is surprised, when he tumbles Charles out of a laundry basket, by the shock to his senses of the boy's nakedness. What the moment uncovers in him is entirely unexpected.

Later, after the 'hard, clumsy kiss', the scenes between the two are full of tension, but of different kinds, though they spring from the same cause: loneliness in the proximities of communal living, and an uncertainty in the school's culture about the distance that should be kept between masters and boys. On Charles's side there is his unwillingness to hurt Penworth, but also his own need for contact: 'the goodness of having such a friend, so quickly in sympathy...was a warm glow in his heart'; on Penworth's a growing confusion at 'the warm desires, complex, multiplied, and ceaselessly relevant to his awareness of the boy'.

Later again, disappointed and out of control after he has trapped Charles into revealing his secret—the relationship with Margaret—Penworth moves on from formal schoolmasterly banter and accuses Charles, in front of the whole class, of being one of those who set themselves above the rest 'because Nature has by mistake given them pretty faces and pretty ways, and has further erred in making them aware of her unfortunate gifts'. When Charles, as ordered, comes to see him afterwards and gives way to 'childish hysterics', Penworth finds himself 'enjoying the curious sensation of his secret shame and elation, and above all enjoying now that supreme and most godly power, the power to comfort when his dramatic sense permitted comfort'.

Penworth has had his own revelation, a dark one: 'He could not see the anguish he had brought into the boy's face without seeing also that it was as true as his own pretended coldness was false and cruel. Yet the pain he watched gave him a surge of—was that pleasure?'

There is not much Australian fiction, of this or any other time, that ventures into such uneasy territory, and works so powerfully there. Penworth, weak, inexperienced, emotionally undeveloped, out of place in a country so unlike his own, painfully devoted to 'that eternal tenant of the mind, Reason', but increasingly vulnerable to passions that he recognises from his classical studies but has never expected to be touched by, is the book's most complex character and in some ways its most complete achievement. He is awed by as well as attracted to Charles Fox, whom he recognises, for all his youth, as nobler and more manly than himself. His angry disappointment has less to do with Charles's rejection of his advances than with his realisation that this boy, at barely fifteen, has already come to what he himself yearns for but has still to attain: that perfect communion he had hoped a relationship with the boy might at last bring him.

There is disappointment for Charles as well. He preserves his relationship with Penworth but is increasingly wary of him. More significantly he sees in the man a likeness now to his mother that makes him distrustful of her as well: a quality in someone whose affection he has come to rely on that is not pure care but a wish, under the guise of care, to steal from him his life, his youth. For the first time he applies to his mother his newfound resistance, and she in turn warns him, in terms that are chilling in their prescience of Mackenzie's own future, against the man who has abandoned them both. 'Your father,' she tells him, 'always went to extremes. If he was happy, or miserable, I always thought he was too much so. He let himself go completely…It made him drink to forget; and drink took him away from me—from us. Took him away from you; that's what I mind most.'

The question that arises is less the degree to which Mackenzie is drawing on his own experience for Charles Fox—that is clear—than how far, in the writing, he moves away from it.

The Young Desire It is a third-person narrative but of a peculiar sort. By settling on a single consciousness and a deeply interior point of view, it becomes in effect a first-person narrative in third-person form. At least, that is how it begins. But fifty pages in a new perspective is introduced, that of Charles's classmate Mawley. We never quite enter into Mawley's consciousness as we do Charles's; his is an observatory rather than a reflective intelligence. But one of the objects of his scrutiny is Charles himself, and while Mawley never becomes either a fully developed character or actor in the book, he may, in the end, be its real narrator.

It is Mawley's accident in the gym that causes Charles to faint, and Mawley's need to remain in the school sick bay over the vacation (while Charles is engaged on his second meeting with Margaret) takes up a good part of the middle section of the book.

Each evening Mawley is visited by the headmaster, and in the shared isolation and loneliness of the empty school a kind of friendship develops between them:

> It was impossible not to be drawn closer under the kindly shadow of his great personality; he did indeed seem young, with the essence of youth, with all its ability to feel, quick and deep, the drama of fortune's ceaseless mutation; without youth's clumsiness of thought or speech to divide Mawley from him. The boy's sympathy was not of embarrassment but of what, thought he in his pride, was genuine understanding.

This is an ideal version of a relationship of which Penworth's approaches to Charles are an unhappy distortion. The confidences offered when the headmaster

settles on the edge of Mawley's bed, which are intimate enough, stand in stark contrast to the exchanges
between Penworth and Charles that lead up to the kiss.
On the last of his visits, on the eve of his suicide, the
headmaster speaks of love and the responsibilities of
the lover. 'Once,' he tells Mawley,

> when I was young, someone said to me in
> reproof for some thoughtlessness, 'You must
> learn how easy it is to hurt those you love...'
> Then, I believed that; afterwards I found that
> it was not true, for it is easiest to hurt those
> who love you—those you yourself love may not
> be open to harm from you, according to the
> measure of their regard for you. But if they in
> turn love you, then beware.

In the early forties, Mackenzie, writing to Jane
Lindsay, offered this version of his time at Guildford
Grammar:

> When I was at school I, being angel-faced
> and slim and shy, was apparently considered
> fair game by masters as well as certain boys.
> The boys were at least honestly crude in their
> proposals; but the masters—young men whom
> I thought very mature and wise—had a much
> better technique. They wooed the intellectual
> way, just at the very time I was beginning to
> comprehend something of literature and music,
> and so was most gullible. Again and again, like

any simpleton, I was tricked, only to realise that what I had taken for special interest in possible intellectual promise of mine was not that at all.

This was written nearly fifteen years after the event, and after a good deal of disappointment and disintegration; Mackenzie is in some ways making excuses for himself. But the important point is that the bitterness of this account is nowhere to be found in his novel. He goes on:

> My whole psyche was shaped by those years— first living with women only, then living entirely separated from anything womanly, and with my unfortunate appearance and the fact that I had a boy's soprano singing voice and was Chapel soloist (another cause of disgusting molestation)…All these long-drawn-out circumstances conditioned me mentally, emotionally and—I don't doubt—sexually.

It is true that Charles Fox at the end of *The Young Desire It* is no longer so innocently open and attractive as he was at the beginning. We may even see in him the makings of a man whose course of life is to be 'difficult'. The last glimpse we get of him is not quite optimistic.

Seen through Mawley's eyes when he returns to school for his second and final year, Charles seems easier with the world, or so Mawley thinks. Mawley does not know that in another of his secret places Charles and Margaret, with 'the air stretched to a perilous tension, ready to split and shatter, ready with the whole world to burst into flame', have consummated their love, not as errant, under-aged children but 'by the blind volition of their own single will'. They have also parted and may not meet again.

Mawley is puzzled by Charles's anxiety over the letter that is waiting for him and, when it turns out to be from Penworth, by his indifference. In the book's closing sentence the melancholy, as Mawley sees it, of the late-summer afternoon, is translated to Charles: 'Mawley, on looking up, observed that instead of unpacking he had remained sitting on the edge of his bed, his face expressionless like that of one who thinks steadfastly of something past and irrevocable, upon which great happiness had once depended.'

There is sadness here, and a poignant sense of loss, but none of the anger and aggrieved self-pity of the Lindsay letter.

The Young Desire It is a miracle, not least in that its wholeness, its freshness and clarity, seem magically untouched by the damage that casts such a shadow over Mackenzie's later years. Among Australian novels it is unique and very nearly perfect, a hymn to youth, to life, to sexual freedom and moral independence, written in full awareness—and this is a second miracle—of the cost, both to others and to oneself.

The Young Desire It

It is now opportune for me to thank you publicly for this book, which is really yours. It was written because you suggested it, and also because you made it possible for me to give all my mind and all my time to the difficult task of writing prose. If it has virtues, I claim them, as I must claim its faults; but its actual existence is greatly due to your kindness.

I had already told you that, though this story of Charles Fox is broadly true, the names and characters were, of course, all strictly invented by myself during those five weeks of solitude which saw the making of the whole thing. So we are not doing anyone an unkindness in setting down much that is—or should I say *was?*—true. If you do read this book, and like it, I shall feel doubly assured in offering it to you in friendship, and in gratitude.

Kenneth 'Seaforth' Mackenzie

'To be free to choose is not enough. Though the young desire it, they cannot use that freedom, but must be forced into the decision of choice by good or evil circumstances which while they can perceive them they cannot control...'

Michael Paul, *The Anatomy of Failure*

When he was fourteen, Charles Fox was a smouldering, red-headed fellow, a friend of nobody, slow but tenacious in his tempers, rather proud and not without courage. Most noticeable, perhaps, was that gentleness of which in a year his fellows at the school had removed the outward sign, and a dangerous, angelic innocence which, among them, quickly set him apart, not upon pedestals, but as one of that very contemptible social order, of those who see no necessity for doing evil.

Innocence appears to be as tempting to the gods as it is to sub-Olympians; like the perfect and unbroken face of a pool to one who has a stone in his hand, tempting in its complete freedom from the splash and ripple of character, and as immaculate as a mirror. Charles met the mortals and the immortals in his fifteenth year. It must have exasperated both to observe that nothing could teach him to deceive, to hide his feelings, and to want to hurt. He had already grown close to the earth, and his innocence, apparently angelic, was earthly and fruitful, not easily to be corrupted.

In the late afternoon of a day in February, that hottest of Australian summer months, when a brutal sun stood bronze above the river flats which you may see from the dormitory windows of Chatterton, Charles came to the School with his mother, walking from the railway station to the gates by a private path across a burnt, untidy field, overhung with Cape lilacs that still drooped, dusty and melancholy, in the late heat of afternoon.

It was February, with three more months of summer yet to come. The private path at each step breathed up a soft orange dust that hid the polish of his shoes. Across a road at the farther side of the burnt field the dark old wood of the School gates threatened him. He was afraid. In the lower part of his belly fear kicked and pulsed like a child in the womb, ready to be born; but it was fear of a disorderly kind, born of ignorance. He knew nothing of what life was like for a boarder at a reputable Public School with a name for sportsmanship, gentlemanliness, manliness and the classics. Nor did he know that the experience of it would be coloured by his own round head of reddish, curling hair, his red lips, his green eyes turning hazel, and an innocence which his mind reflected in his face.

His fear, disorderly and ignorant, found an outlet simply in regret for that life which had run its course and was now, as he walked beside his mother on the dusty path, coming quietly to its end. His mother herself symbolized it. A world where he had been left alone, happily free from the understanding and the companionship of any mind or heart; free and unscrutinized, with the greater part of each day given over to his own decision, in a world peopled and filled by himself in an infinite variety of disguise. That world had been chucked to the devil by a useful and necessary maternal decision, in which he had no part.

The preparations for his entry into the high life of the reputable School (governed by the Board of the Council of Churches, rich and very holy) interested him enough to lend him a little courage when he was not alone. Freedom had gone suddenly; he did more things at the request of other people than he had ever done, it seemed, in his life. There was a visit to the city, where he was measured for new clothes by a powerful Scot, lame and charming, who turned him round and about as if he were a piece of furniture, and made his mother smile at him as though, now for the first time, they shared some trivial secret. For a week afterwards the names and appearances of a dozen city shops remained in his mind, together with a growing uneasiness of self-concern, which invaded his body like a disease, and made nightmares of his dreams. He began to pay the penalty of his own sensitiveness, and was often miserable. He had always been of an excitable temperament, liable to sudden emotional excesses; and now, on that short, endless walk from the station to the dark, sweltering School gates, the unpleasant excitement did a final triumphant battle with his defiance, and a lot of tears gathered in his eyes. Fruits of that victory. He began to press them away quietly with his knuckles, trembling and white.

'Charles. What's the matter, Son?'

His mother's voice was as calm as ever. She did not lack affection for him; but, like the rest of her emotions and the arrangement of her own busy life, it was methodical and without evidence of heat.

'Nothing,' he said. 'It's all right, Mother.'

They walked across the blazing roadway.

'That's right,' she murmured, kindly enough, giving his hand a quiet grip between her coolly gloved fingers. 'This isn't really a prison, you know.'

He had once said he feared it would be. But now her sense of method and procedure was at ease. And the gates swallowed them, like the blind open jaws of a dead shark, sinister and smally cathedraline. They had passed through. Freedom and innocence were, for Charles, left outside.

It happened that the name of the Headmaster at that time was Fox. Charles knew this—his mother had told him, hoping to surprise and arouse in him some positive interest—and while they waited in the carpeted ante-room which opened into the august study he tried to take his mind away from troubles in his lower viscera (a new natural urge was threatening muscular control) by thinking of the scene which would present itself if this Fox were, unknown to them all, his own father, whom he did not remember. But in his imagination his mother would not come to life, nor soften and cry out; he could hear no passionate exclamations from her firm, straight lips, see no impulsive gesture. Such a gesture, even in his imagination, would have surprised him and seemed, to memory, foreign. Also, the face of this man hidden in the room into which a young boy had just been taken was the wooden ageless face of a young village policeman whom he had once seen mounting a bicycle outside the baker's shop, and whom he had, by some undiscoverable association, thought to resemble his father. Meanwhile, the trembling in his guts persisted, and he moved his hands and feet restlessly.

His mother was looking steadily in front of her, out beyond the open windows to where water sprinklers turned rhythmically, with faint sounds suggesting music, above clipped lawns. There was a melancholy murmur of doves across the tired afternoon spaces, and from quadrangles and corridors came the voices of boys. The voices were happy and shrill; but for Charles the whole forwardness of life had stopped upon a deep, uneasy pedal-note of suspense. In the ante-room there was a restless quiet. One or two mothers, coming late as he had done, were nervously preening and eyeing their boys, smiling at them, talking in low voices, seeming to find some sort of relief in touching their young, as frightened birds do with their broods. A big woman, badly dressed and intolerably nervous, with a heartbroken affection stiffening her plain face, looked from the pert child beside her to the other lads, and back again, and again at the others, with obvious fear. Words seemed to issue silently from the slight movement of her lips. Her own boy was a merry, ugly youngster; unselfconscious and as alert as an animal, he stared about him, and once put out his tongue at a fellow who was gazing fascinated at that large wreck of a woman from the cosseting shadow of a well-dressed, expressionless parent.

With new and anguished consciousness Charles noticed these things, and was aware in the back of his mind of the doves' moaning, the cheerful cool greenness of the lawns already in shadow, and the green sharpness of boys' voices piercing the afternoon minutely. The heat of the day was easing a little, but a new building across the road beyond the lawns burnt red, each of its bricks a scorching coal as the sun caught it full and brazen from the upper west. A faint smell of wet earth came wandering into the breathless room, and the hairy leaves of cotton palms lay like opened fans on the tired air. In spite of the heat in the room Charles felt cold, and kept wiping the moist palms of his hands down the seams of his new breeches. His mother seemed unable to move, until a Master came out with smiling, conscious impressiveness from the study, and asked her to take 'this little man' within. That Master's face had fascinated Charles since the first time he had issued forth in his black rustling gown. There was an amazing expression of ruthless and petty self-importance in its features, which were classically exact and would have been perfect, had they not seemed too small. When he bent his head and stooped gracefully, looking sideways across his nose, away from the person to whom with exquisite friendliness a small, delicate ear was inclined, and holding the folds of the gown in against his loins, there was revealed a pinkish tonsure of mathematical perfections in the middle of his crown, and from its decisive edge the dark hair was brushed away all round. The impression of his head, and of the face with its carven eyelids and lips, suggested a subtle parody of the head of

10

an Apollo as sculptured by an ancient master. This was not Charles's thought; he only felt dislike trying to force its strange presence in among the muddled feelings and merciless physical sensations which were threatening him with nausea.

They went in the wake of tonsure and billowing gown. He noticed numbly that the door was edged with spongy green baize, and opened and closed silently, with a delayed conclusion sighing on the action of a vacuum stop. Once inside the room, he saw only the bent head and shoulders of the Headmaster across the illimitable orderliness of a great table, and felt cooler air that smelt of books.

'This is my son Charles.' His mother spoke without emotion or pride; the stillness heard. Startled, he saw the reduced god's-head already non-existent behind a small desk; this is my son Charles, the stillness insisted for one moment.

The Headmaster's face was cavernous. The scar of what must have been a dreadful head-wound, deep enough to receive now the ball of a man's thumb, throbbed like a ceaseless ache above the left temple. Beneath strongly-arched brows, bold and bony, shadows held the eyes that were as though drowned in them. High cheekbones dragged up the skin tautly from a square jaw, and below a nose whose shape suggested humour and kindness, the lips, of which Charles was fiercely conscious, set in a straight, shadowless tension. Later in life, thinking of the face of this man whose rule over him was so short, he realized that the whole face expressed a struggle with pain—the pain of a stretched mind as well as of the body. At this time it was

11

a face that merely surprised him, but not with terror or awe, by its living darkness.

'Well, Charles Fox,' the Headmaster said, standing up and leaning over the table to take his hand, 'you and I have the same name. We should get on well.'

It was said with great simplicity. Charles tried to speak, gave it up, smiled nervously, and felt his face distorted beyond smiling. His mother was looking at him, unaware that for a moment the man's dark eyes in their sunken shadows were turned from the boy to her, and that she was summed up, roughly and with broad correctness, and dismissed for ever.

'I'm sure he'll do what is expected of him,' she said, slowly and clearly through her smile. The words had a corrective effect on Charles, who took his hand away from his mouth. There was too much unexpected sympathy and kindliness in the Headmaster's tones.

'I'm sure he will, too,' he said. 'And I think we've got all we want about you. You will have to work hard—the sort of work you will have here will be to a great extent new to you. Just now I am looking for scholars as well as for all-round fellows. You might be one of them. You might make a name for the School as well as for yourself. Mightn't you?'

He spoke with quiet authority. Charles, looking up, nodded his head speechlessly, straining into the other's eyes that seemed to burn with an illusion of systole and diastole urgency in their darkness.

'Yes, you might. Tell me—what have you thought of doing when you finish with school?'

'I don't think he knows,' Mrs. Fox said at once. 'He's so young, of course. And as he hasn't known a father...'

The Headmaster smiled down at her politely.

'Well,' he said to Charles, 'you come along and see me one day, and we'll talk about it then. Now find your way to Chatterton House, and have a talk with Mr. Jolly. He is your Housemaster; he will take care of you.'

'He's so young,' Mrs. Fox said again, rather less certainly.

'We'll see that he's all right, Mrs. Fox. They soon find their way about. And his examination board reports are good. We like boys who have done their previous study privately; they usually prove themselves good workers. Of course, there's more to learn in a school like this than letters only. We have ideals of conduct.'

He put one hand on Charles's shoulder, looking directly at him as he spoke.

'They have to learn our methods, and get used to a regular full-day time-table.'

Charles felt the firm hand removed from his shoulder, and heard him say again, 'We'll see that he's all right. You have nothing to worry about. The finest young men in the country come, many of them, from here, I'm glad to say.'

The words echoed in his mind until he found himself passing through a laughing, moving crowd of boys towards the portentous gates. His mother's gentle farewell did not embarrass him; indeed, he scarcely knew she was going even when her cool lips and hands were removed from him; he was thinking despairingly, there in the hot blue shadow of the front quadrangle, of evening on the river at home, with its perfect loneliness, the coolness, his own naked body rippling the green water, the stars coming out in a sky of dark and burning blue above the dry grassland, and the peace of his solitude. This was the hour when one went down to bathe, as the sun sank and the air lifted on a promise of night, and bitterns began their first shadowy flights. This was the hour; the very hour.

Behind him, as he looked after his mother walking away, the boys shouted and milled in and out, laughing with one another, full of the cheerful energy of apes. The finest young men in the country. Charles thought he would be one of them, and envied them what they did not have.

He turned about and began to walk, looking under his eyebrows sideways to see if anyone were noticing him. The boys thronged and chattered, shouting out across the quadrangle to one another. There was in the air a noisy gaiety that felt unreal; they laughed and tumbled, yet all of them seemed to be waiting for something, for a command or the startling authority of a bell. High above them the milk-pale sky fainted with summer; sunlight on the roofs was thick and red. Under the covered porch that went between a low brick building and the older part of the School, a Master stood bracing his shoulders back against a wood-and-brick pillar, and a half-circle of boys about him yapped and fidgeted like terriers teasing a young bull. This Master's face was a smiling, leathern mask, brown and dark beneath a soft lick of black hair on his narrow forehead, lean but not ascetic; the flat cheeks were creased from the genial depth of his ready and scornful smile, and a mature irony sat easily in his twinkling eyes. Charles heard only

14

the sparrow-like 'Sir' of the boys round him, until he suddenly raised his eyes and his voice from them to shout at a group engaged in jumping the heavy chains that bound the soft evening green of a long lawn. 'Get away from those chains, you donkeys. You'll break your worthless necks', and his warning died into a dispassionate grumbling. He had not ceased to smile. Charles felt a sad admiration and envy for so much good-fellowship; he thought, it must be like living in your own home, to be a Master here.

He went on more quickly, but was not quite swift enough in his search for a lavatory, for he had not wished to seem to hurry. A group of youths, older and less noisy than the terriers, debouched from a sloping covered way that had echoed the sound of their feet and the tones of their voices.

'Here's one, here's one,' said the youth in front.

'What's your name, kid?'

'Oh, oh, where is my dear mother?'

They had gathered round him before he realized it. They stood silent while he looked from one heavy face to another, into blue eyes, into brown eyes, at lips curled with a certain gleaming expectancy, at hands slowly withdrawn from pockets. He blushed and would have smiled as he answered them, 'Charles Fox'.

'Fox, eh? First-year, aren't you?'

'What—I—yes, I only just came.'

'Well, well,' they said.

'Can you tell me...'

'He's sissy,' one said softly, and they laughed with satisfaction. 'Come on,' they said, 'we'll see if you're a girl too.'

'We're the girl-catchers, boy.'

They took hold of him roughly by arms and neck, and he began to struggle.

'No, no. I don't want to. Please.'

They growled, cheerfully. 'Monty, you old bastard, get hold of his ear. Get his ear, go on.' He felt a hot red pain flame into his head, into the very bone, and down his neck. He meant to free his hand to strike down that other hand.

'Wait,' he said. 'Let me go. I'll come. Let go. I will come.'

'You'll come all right,' Monty said, still twisting his ear, and the others laughed loudly at that. 'Go on, he couldn't, he couldn't. Let's see, here, give us a try.'

'Don't be rude,' one said primly. 'Lots of time, don't fiddle with him.' They issued from the hot dimness of the covered way into blood-red sunlight streaming through glass. Their heels clattered on concrete; Charles was blinded by the direct red glare.

'In here,' said one. 'Old Jolly's busy with a few upstairs. He won't come down for another year.'

'Please,' Charles said, 'it's Mr. Jolly I want to see.'

'You'll see him all right,' he was told. They panted and still laughed among themselves as they hoisted him up on to a table-top in what seemed to be a large classroom. 'Pull those doors across,' Monty commanded, his face red and excited. 'Don't want everyone to come in, do you?'

The folding doors were closed; the classroom was half its previous size. Charles, with the irrelevance of excessive fear, was irritated and puzzled by their laughter. They stretched him out on the table-top, held him there, and began to unbutton his breeches.

There were tears ready to fall from his screwed-down eyelids. 'I don't want to…I told you, I told you…'

He was cut short by a flame of pain that ran up his arm. The blood came pelting back to his face, from neck to brow. He yelled, and bit at the coarse, salty palm that was pressed in haste over his open, twisting mouth. They hit him with the backs of their hands; some one took off his shoes while he struggled there on his back, tasting the salt of skin on his flattened lips. A new and crueller devastation of pain gripped him from the loins upwards. He did not know what was being done to him. They spoke no word, breathing heavily while he fought and strangled cries in his throat.

'Go on, that'll do for him for the time being', one lad, who had leaned against the white wall, watching, said at last.

'Yes, better let him go now, you chaps. He might faint.'

They took their hands off him at length, and he lay choking and sobbing with laughter, snorting through his nose with a fury of breath, laughing brokenly. His body sank back from the dizzy heights of pain to which it had soared; his hands fell open. He got down from the slippery table-top, white in the face and trembling convulsedly. They stood round watching while he tried to fasten the buttons of his clothes, putting his hand up often to his neck and collar, brushing his dishevelled hair with hot fingers, in great shame. Their eyes shone, as though with divine inspiration, above the brilliance of their smiles.

'Next time come quietly,' said Monty, a tall, heavy youth, fair-haired and with clear, small eyes. The cruelty in their relaxing faces made Charles speechless. He had never before seen human beings so closely.

'Let him go for the time being,' the boy leaning to the wall said again.

Charles tried to hold his head up. He kept putting his hand spasmodically to his hair.

'He's sissy all right.'

'Now go and see old Jolly and tell him all about mother and father.'

In time he found himself alone again, at the foot of a flight of dark wooden stairs leading up to a half-landing and twisting back and up again. On his right hand, double doors opened into a bathroom. Even in there it was hot. He went through. Save for a terrible memory of living faces, there was nothing in his mind. He leaned on one hand over the urinal, pressing his palm on the cool white porcelain before him. There he waited a long time, until the burning tension of muscle relaxed. In the lavatories he washed his hands and face, trembling still and putting into his movements unnecessary, half-controlled energy. Then he went out and up the stairs.

On the landing it was possible to hear clearly the shouting and laughter that rocketed about the quadrangles. The door in front of him was closed. He looked about, and realized that a few boys of his own age were standing in the half-shadow of the dark red and white walls. He would have to wait.

On his right hand a door stood open upon a long dormitory. White beds side by side in a double row were divided by a stretch of bare wooden floor; he had never seen so many beds; his own present insignificance began to dawn on his consciousness. With the walls, the bare polished floor, the white ceiling, they swept away in an exact perspective to a large window at the far end. Windows lined one wall, high up; the kindly green of virginia creeper broke their sharp glassy lines, reminding him of the kitchen windows at home. There on his left another dormitory stretched away, another exaggerated perspective of intense whiteness; and a door opened on a wide balcony where one line of white beds immaculately faced the red sun sinking beyond the wide grey river flats with their fringe of trees. His eyes ached for colour; but on that floor there were only the dark surfaces of woodwork to relieve so much whiteness.

While he looked dazedly from his right to his left, the others watched him, and spoke in low voices among themselves. Through his heat and confusion he heard one whisper, 'That's my brother's dorm. He says I can go in there. That's his bed at the end.'

'Your brother a prefect?'

'Aw—what do you think! 'Course he is.'

Charles could see their faces clearly now. To his returning awareness they were the same faces he had seen gathering round him downstairs—good-natured, excited, expectant, fair and dark alike; their eyes and teeth shone dully in the reflected light from the west. He began to believe, without understanding why, that he was like them— one of them. Of course. But he had no prefect brother; the reputable name of the School had scarcely a meaning for him, until that afternoon. Its honour, the understood code

19

of behaviour that its scholars as young citizens carried with them carefully into the world, were not yet his honour, or his code; but they were there, perceptibly filling the place; they were in the attitudes of boys to Masters, of Masters to boys—'This holy place is ours; this is the hatching-house of all that is decent in the country's men. Betray it if you dare.' His mother had said, when she told him of her intention to send him, and he had protested from the darkness of his incoherent intuition: 'But Charles, it makes all the difference to your success in the world, if you've been to a good Public School.'

'But I don't want to succeed.'

'Oh, son, don't say that. You don't understand. And you don't know what it's like, after all.'

He was already learning.

A sudden mild roar of laughter sounded strangely lunatic out of the silence behind the closed door; as though an officiating priest were to laugh before an altar. The small boys outside became silent, too; Charles could feel the pounding beat of his heart. The door opened, and a lad backed out hastily, red-faced and smiling. The others pushed one another forward, each one determined not to be the next to walk into that unknown room. They crowded round the fellow who had just come out.

'What's he like, Wilson?'

'Pretty decent.'

'Sounds a bit cracked, to me. What's he laughing at?'

Charles, helpless before the expectancy in their looks, found himself facing the afternoon's third ordeal. They watched him go through the door, nudging one another, hooting softly after him. 'Who's that stupid cow? Looks a bit sissy to me. D'you reckon?'

They judged him, but without much feeling one way or the other; while he himself stood by the table, resting his hand upon its cool edge, hardly daring to look the Master in the eyes, yet not daring to look away.

Mr. Jolly appeared to have been suitably named. When he took from his lips a tumbler of weak whisky-and-water, his eyes, blue, piercing, droll as a sly clown's, were revealed beneath leaf-brown lids. He was a tall man, with the eager, inquisitive stoop of an avid scholar; his nose was very long, and was fairly set off by a lock of flat, grey hair that curved inward above his left eye, giving him a mildly distracted appearance; and below that long, inquisitive nose, that looked to have smelt out every secret contained in life and books, his wide, well-made mouth curved sardonically back into flat, grey cheeks. But for his eyes he would have seemed old; but they had such a knowing droop in their upper lids, and were yet so bright and open, that his face had an essential youth still untroubled, and you would think that his greatest concern was to locate and pin down with a long ironic forefinger everything that savoured even faintly of a jest on which he could exercise his mind.

'Well, well,' he said as he put the tumbler down, 'so here's another. I no sooner rid myself of one than here's another.' His voice was husky and sly, but not unkind. 'Could you by any chance tell me how many more of your kind are beyond that door?'

'I don't know. The Headmaster...' Charles began.

'Yes, I know. And let me tell you, young fellow,' he extended a forefinger that matched his nose in length and shrewdness, 'a finer man is not governing a school at this time. Not here nor anywhere else in the country. Not in the whole world.' He growled in his throat, and his bold glance strayed to the book-shelves beside him. 'And yet the Board, the damned confounded Board...' As his eye met Charles's accidentally, he growled again and cleared his throat.

'Well,' he said abruptly, 'what's *your* name? Smith? We've too many Smiths. Jones? Same with Jones. Now come on, old chap, what's your name?' He pleaded huskily.

'Charles Fox,' said Charles, whose mouth had been open to speak while he was talked over.

'Charles Fox what?'

'Charles Fox—that's all.'

'Now listen to me, old man. In this school your name is "Charles Fox, sir". D'you see what I mean? "Charles Fox, *sir*".'

'Yes, sir,' said Charles, his face twitching nervously. Mr. Jolly looked at him with great care, his stare blue, humorous and unfaltering.

'Old chap,' he said huskily as though with deep emotion, while his eyelids drooped a little more heavily, 'you've got a lot to learn.'

He let this ride home upon that bold gaze, while Charles repeated his 'Yes, sir.'

'Yes,' he said. He became animated again, turned over papers with his long, inquisitive grey fingers, and finally took a sip from the half-empty tumbler.

'Well, Charles Fox sir, you're in my House. Your

dormitory is Dormitory B—the fifth bed from this end.' He gestured to his left. 'One two three four five. H'm. Now make yourself familiar with the rules. Rise at seven; bath; breakfast at seven-forty-five. Etcetera, etcetera. Yes. Dinner at twelve-thirty; tea at six. Line up for meals with the other members of your House—the best House in the School; a statement which you will be careful to refrain from questioning, from this moment until you leave it. H'm. Your evening preparation begins at seven-thirty and ends at eight-thirty, when like the other young puppies you will come rowdily upstairs for evening prayers in Dormitory B. Evening devotion. We take it for granted that your Church is the Church of England. That is, we do not question such things. All dissension must be kept to yourself. Yes. After prayers, make your toilet and get into bed. No fooling in bathrooms—no noise—quiet conversation you will find to be an excellent recreation while in the dormitories. Get to know your fellows; but no dog-fighting, or I shall make it my business to find out all culprits and chastise them personally. My canes are in that corner by the door. Let us hope you make no closer acquaintance with them.'

He stopped abruptly, and his eyes left their staring to wander once more over the book-shelves, as though if they might they would drag him after them, hands outstretched to select.

'Yes, sir,' Charles said.

'Yes,' said Mr. Jolly, gathering himself back into his chair. 'Now you just listen to me, old chap. We know nothing about you here. Your job is to teach us, just as ours is to teach you. You teach us to like and respect you;

we'll teach you something above all price. I mean knowledge. We may even teach you a little wisdom, though your
associates will teach you more. Keep yourself clean. We all
know what healthy young growing boys are, and we try to
help you as far as that is possible. There are some things
gentlemen do not do.'

He gazed blandly at the wall beyond Charles's head.

'There are some things we punish with expulsion, just
as we punish other things with caning on the behind, others
with cancellation of exeats, others with lines, and others
perhaps with a mere reprimand.'

As he intoned this huskily, his expression became
impersonal and lofty, and he pointed his long nose at
Charles, looking down its each side, his eyes bulging a little
beneath the shells of their lids.

'Cleanliness first, old chap...That's all.'

Charles backed awkwardly towards the door. He
wondered what Mr. Jolly would say now if he could have
known what happened downstairs, twenty minutes earlier.
He had no wish to tell him of it. It was not Mr. Jolly's
business to know what happened to new boys, nor what
went on in their minds and hearts during their first days
at the School.

His hand was upon the brass knob when Mr. Jolly
looked up with difficulty from his book-shelves. Recol-
lection wiped the amorous glaze from his blue eyes as he
observed Charles.

'What did you say your name is?' he asked huskily.
Charles did not see the mild twinkle in his regard.

'Charles Fox, sir.'

Mr. Jolly laughed, and to the sound of the laugh Charles backed out, flushed but smiling twistedly, as the boy whom he followed had done. A need for action sent him rapidly through the little group of sneering, interested lads by the door, and got him down the stairs. In a pile of luggage at their foot he saw his own trunks, draped with the new travelling rug his mother had given him. As he stared, and struggled with a fresh impulse to fall down and give himself up to despair, the sharp, arrogant nagging of a bell fell swollen on the hot evening, and some one yelled, in an excited voice, 'Tea!'

At the long refectory table on the dais sat the Headmaster and some of his colleagues. He was almost exhausted from the strained excitement of the first afternoon of term; the restraint put upon him by continually meeting, considering, summing up and remembering nervous new-comers had laid a weight upon his head and dragged down his lips and his shoulders. But he made it his business to smile as he looked blindly down the long, uproarious dining-hall, where twenty new boys were having their first experience of a meal in Hall, and as many others, transferred this year from the Preparatory School a mile away, were assuming a loud equality with older boys, brothers, cousins and their friends. Social adjustments were in progress. To-morrow, when term officially commenced, there would be more of it; with the return of those eminent ones who allowed themselves to arrive as late as midday of the first day, the growling tolerance of this evening's atmosphere would be keyed up sharply with something sterner, something (for any who would have dared to say it of the School) more brutal.

On his right Mr. Jolly sat pointing his nose attentively at his plate. The exhausted lock of hair hanging over his left eye gave to the downbent penitence suggested by his attitude an air of sly and solemn rakishness. When he raised his head to speak to the Chief his nose swung across the vista of the Hall like an accusing finger—phallic and hortative had it not been for the dispassionate flatness of the nostrils. He glared round the weary lock of hair, growling.

'Noisy little beggars. During the holiday this experience was never quite out of my mind.'

The Headmaster smiled with his thin shadowless lips.

'They look quite a promising lot, Mr. Jolly.'

'The same lot as last year's, sir. The same as the years' before last year.'

'It may be,' the Headmaster said quietly. Under the waves of sound that cannoned against the pulp itself of his tired brain, he had little say. Like a man dangerously afloat in a sea, his concern was to swim to the safety of something as firm as silence and solitude, and into that harbour of sleep from which unhappily he put forth each morning. The hollow scar above his temple measured the beat of his heart. From habit he held his head high so that it should not be too much seen.

There was little to be said among them all at the long table. Two younger masters, side by side on the Headmaster's left hand, were laughing and pretending to make merry over their holiday experiences. Like most of the staff, they were Englishmen, graduating from Oxford to the divine Parnassus where schoolmasters seem—to their pupils at least—felicitously to dwell. These two young men, by nature alike and scholastically as opposed as the poles, had a doubly strong bond in their age and their memories of England, passionately green still in their green minds, at such an intensifying distance from Home. Even in the circumscribed world of the School, where they were encouraged and never deterred in their England-my-England cult, they sometimes felt themselves alien; but each would have scorned to admit that he was anywhere aware of a national personality in the boys he taught, and made Common-room jests about, and privately feared. The suggestion that their 'little wretches' were wild with the raw, crude strength of a young nation beginning to feel its horns they would deftly and politely have turned aside with a laugh or an oblique, comparative reference to their own Old Schools and the fellows at Home.

So now, as they sat in state above the little wretches—who could trouble one's self-esteem even at mealtimes—they did not allow themselves to acknowledge their noisy presence, and would not acknowledge, in their own hearts, that after a summer holiday in the south this, the inviolable temple of their cult, seemed very empty, very lonely, and pervaded with that sense of personal frustration which they spent their waking hours denying. They were laughing together, Penworth rather bitterly, Waters with mild and childlike simplicity; they were talking of the sea, of the sharp sunlight, of girls and young men—secretly a little proud to think that for a time at least they had so successfully made their own involved, tradition-haunted personalities seem

27

blithely akin to those of the simple, vigorous young people they had played and romanced with.

The boy next to Charles, a lad from the Preparatory School, dug him in the ribs.

'That's Penworth next to the Head. You wait till you get him in class.'

He had heard a boy opposite him talking in the same way about Penworth, and could repeat it now with an appearance of authority. Familiarity with the clipped jargon of speech that became the School made him easy.

'The Bad Penny, that's what he is. Always turning up in the wrong place. And sissy too. Had my brother shot for six, smoking down the slope.'

Charles, choking over bread against which his throat was dryly rebelling, raised his eyes from his plate. Fright and wretched foreboding (he had heard discussion about something they called Initiation, which took place in dormitories at night) had made him feel sick again. His mind had not yet returned to a proper and natural functioning; thoughts of his mother in the train on her journey home troubled him incoherently: life itself seemed to have stopped suddenly, and as suddenly to have sprung up again into a nightmarish madness. So when the sensuous, pale, mask-like face of the Junior Housemaster, whose elbow every now and then brushed apologetically against the sleeve of the Chief as he turned to Waters, floated dimly before his eyes in the rusty-red light in which the dais swam, he could not see it, and it meant nothing; but he could feel yet the impact of that boy's elbow with his body. He peered before him. Waters's face, composed it seemed of childish spectacled eyes and a loose, pouting, kindly mouth, glimmered pinkly in the ruddy light; two blank circles resolved themselves, as he turned smiling, into the thick convex of lenses.

'After all,' Penworth said, bending his head and looking up under brows for ever arched delicately, 'what's a holiday for? I should be sorry to have to come back here with nothing exciting to think of.'

'Oh,' Waters mumbled, turning his lenses on him, 'I think you exaggerate, old man. Personally,' and he peered with a myopic smile down the Hall, 'I find all the excitement I want here. And a bit more.'

'We played the César Franck at Batty's the other night,' Penworth said with deliberate, bland irrelevance. 'I thought it went pretty well. But I must say I'd like to have been staying on with you.'

'Why do you play the fiddle?' Waters said vaguely. 'You know it's bad for you...I say, I believe I can see a promising lad down there, Penworth. Have a look: fourth table from us, facing this way, third from the end. See him?'

He always tried to see more than he could, and had a happy faith in his ability to read in a boy's face obscure promises of future scholarship. His heart was too kind.

'Yes. I see,' Penworth said briefly. 'That's Wilson senior. You struggled with him all last year, if I remember. And the year before.'

'Oh,' Waters mumbled. 'I thought it was a new face.'

Penworth laughed. 'Need we talk shop so soon? After all, there's always to-morrow. And you surely know by now that there's no such thing as a new face in this place.'

29

As though apologizing for an inflexion of bitterness that characterized much of his conversation in the School, he turned to the Headmaster with a polite question as to his health.

'All right, really,' Dr. Fox said. 'I had hoped to have more time in the vacation; but you know what it's like—there's a lot to do. I resume here feeling tired, still.'

Penworth heard more than a little weariness in the careful precision of his speech.

'I understand, sir.'

'We should have a good year this year. And by the way, you have quite an interesting-looking lot in your House.'

'Is that so, sir? I only got in in time for tea.'

His words spurned the cold meats lying untouched on his plate, eloquent witness to the state of his mind.

'Yes. You're a sensitive fellow, Penworth...'

He interrupted. 'Thank you, sir.' His smile tried to express humility, but was twisted still.

'...Well, there are one or two of the new lads who will need some looking after. You could give them that. Unobtrusive, you know. There's one chap who looked quite sickened with fright to-day. A fellow with the same name as my own. Fox. He is in your House. It might be as well to keep an eye on him for a week or two.'

'I will,' Penworth said cordially, his mind already away.

'Glad if you would. One or two others, too, perhaps; you will not find it hard to recognize them.'

He set his teeth suddenly together, so that the muscles at the back of his jaw bulged, hollowing cavities in his long cheeks. His hand passed briefly over the brown, hairless dome of his skull.

'There's the Head—see—he's doing it now. Watch. No—wait on, you'll see him do it again in a minute. Once he starts he can't stop. Dobson reckons he's going off his nut; his father says.'

'Yah—Dobson's old man!'

'No, but—you look.'

Charles felt another indigestible dig in his side. He looked up towards the fading red haze of light, and saw the gesture that so delighted the boys.

'He's waiting for the hair to grow.'

'Hair nothing.'

'Oh, he is! He had it treated with electricity in the holidays.'

'Electricity nothing.'

'Oh—you shut up, Carrol, or I'll give you a smack in the mouth.'

'Me fat arse.'

'So it is.'

'Right-oh. You wait till after.'

They yelled at one another over the length and breadth of the long trestle tables, whose rough white cloths were already made homely and comfortably stale by marks of spilt tea and jam. Charles, having at last for very despair overcome his fear of meeting their eyes, looked about and realized that no one was watching him. Opposite his seat on the hard, polished form sat another lad whose plight seemed similar. He was a plain-faced, freckled chap, the same whose mother's face had twisted with such heart-break and bewilderment, in the Headmaster's ante-room that afternoon. Charles, out of the quietening confusion of his mind, brought up a memory of him there, pert and alert. There was some comfort in seeing him so near, and in the thought that someone else who was not merely a name was in a like condition to his own; for in his ignorance he supposed that everyone entering the School for the first time would be searched for signs of girlhood, would be put on a desk-top and taught new degrees of pain and shame.

'What's your name?' someone said, with a sort of threatening reserve; and at this reminder that they were not one big happy family, the others nearby became silent and watchful, and only the voices of the prefects, seated at top and bottom between their favourites, went murmuring and laughing on.

'Bush,' said the freckled one promptly, looking boldly about from one to another.

'This chap's name's Fox,' Charles's neighbour said. 'Isn't it?'

Charles nodded, his eyes wide opened. A wit spoke up from the scrutinizing silence:

'Ever see the fox go into the bush?'

That was well received, with howls and jeers and approval, and the storm of chatter broke again. Charles, who had looked bewildered at their delight in the quip, yet felt pleased with it if it had made them all start talking again like this. Bush was looking across at him, grinning nervously but boldly enough, and he smiled back and turned his eyes away.

'Listen to them,' Waters said, peering and sweating above his empty cup. 'The very devil of a row.' His plump pink face creased in a cheerful smile. Despite bouts of homesickness and mild despair of being able to do his work, he always looked cheerful, frown and gloom though he might. The beaming moons of his massive lenses betrayed him everlastingly, in secret treachery with the pouting geniality of his mouth.

'Let's go out, shall we,' Penworth said; and after making their excuses to the Headmaster they rose and self-consciously walked out one after the other, giving slightly at the knees in a walk they had salvaged from the wreck of a life that had had Oxford and rich green lanes and the open downs and a mellow, ageless confidence for its setting.

'I want to get this confounded collar and tie off,' Penworth said when they were outside in the shadowless evening light. 'This damned country—a man can't even eat in comfort.'

Silently, they let that general protest cover all their melancholy and rebellious feelings at being back at work once more. Penworth said he would go to his room.

'Get my pipe,' Waters mumbled, and shouted after him: 'I won't be a minute, Penworth—come along as soon as I have my pipe.'

A sudden angry ray, that seemed to have lingered after the sun was gone, struck Penworth violently in the eyes as he turned into the hot darkness of the covered way, going towards his room. He cursed it, and went back to a light-switch which controlled the lights in that passage. It was hot, and in the stillness beneath the everlasting seethe of crickets in dry grass a shrill whine of mosquitoes irritated his ears. He damned everything because there was nothing definite to damn. Along the edges of the river flats the trees drooped their grey leaves; the bark on their trunks looked to have been cracked and warped by the summer's heat. A bad beginning, he thought, for February, which was certainly the worst of the summer months. The sound of a far surf was still in his ears, and he forgot the whine of the midges, imagining instead the salt taste of the water still bitter and clean upon his white, thick skin. And now—this! Barren, he thought; chaotic under its cheap veneer of system and public-spiritedness; and with a Chief who did not look as though he would hold out much longer. Any change there would upset the whole of that routine which was so difficult to achieve, and so comfortable to follow, freeing the mind at set times as a good dog is freed from the chain to caper here and there and lift a scornful leg at the statelier and more ancient facts of existence. Such as the morale of the School, and sport, and keeping up appearances, he thought, swirling into his hot little room as though he already had a gown gracing his shoulders and billowing urgently behind him.

There on his bed was the smaller suitcase, with its raised top exhibiting an almost feminine neatness of packed clothes inside. The larger one was on the floor. Leaning back against the solidity of his working table, he kicked the big case with one foot, and it slithered heavily under the bed. Across the grassy square outside his window the noise from the dining-hall came monotonously, in a high-pitched drone; he listened, and stared at his chaste and narrow bed, with a case on it, and a case under it, and the mosquito net at its head cascading down on the pillow. A smell of stale smoke and ink and old books lay still in the room. His table had been dusted; red ink and blue were in their proper wells, and his pens and pencils, many more than he needed because each had the key to some part or other of his little history, lay before the inkstand—as stale as last year.

The shrill singing note, varying no more than a quarter tone, thinly pierced his listening. A few mosquitoes had gathered round his head and hands, coming in from the damp lawns outside because he had blood in his veins, just beneath the surface of that thick, fine-textured skin. He cursed and started up from his leaning position, crossed to the light-switch, and then took up a spray that stood on the dressing-table at the bed's foot. His savage pumping spread a vapour of kerosene and chemicals on the hot air; a most sterile smell, dispassionate and unreal, overcame the odour of his old pipes and old books. When he put the spray down again, he stood looking at the still, speaking face of a girl half-smiling through a silver window. Then he stood the photograph up as it would stand for the next thirteen weeks, turned his back to it, and in the utter wretchedness of his heart began to set the whole room to rights and to put away everything he had brought back with him, methodically, carefully, with a kind of blind, meticulous hatred restraining all his movements.

A sudden roaring scrape of seats became an audible silence, with one voice saying certain indistinguishable words. He mimicked them furiously: 'For what we have received may the Lord make us truly thankful.' Out of the fullness of my belly do I cry to Thee.

The noise of talking broke out more vigorously than before, full-bodied now with the tramp of feet, as though that pause for grace after meat had acted as a dam before a lusty river. One minute later he heard the thunder of feet racing up the covered way. He cursed, without ceasing to unpack. Sharp-toned voices began to bring down a rattle of echoes through the House; they seemed to stick in his flesh, like inflexible arrows. It was a relief to hear Waters pummel on the door softly with his fist, and to hear him say mildly, 'I've some whisky here; thought we might celebrate our return to felicity.'

Beyond the dark blankness of the door, steps and voices tore the evening to shreds.

The first week of his new life was to Charles a nightmare of endless days. It had a nightmare's excitement and a nightmare's horror expressed in longing for safety and for sleep. He thought, at the end of twenty-four hours, that his only times of peace would be the hours he spent behind his desk in the classroom, and the hours lost in sleep. Only by exercising or evacuating his mind could he hope to reduce its unease and misery to some condition approaching normality; and exercise it he did, upon such foreign studies as languages and the sciences which he was told he would need to study if he wished to make his school course properly progressive.

Within forty-eight hours, with very little sleep to assuage the intolerable thirst of his heart salted by memory, he had begun to show that defiance which grew in him until it finally characterized him among his fellows, as they in their own ways were characterized by other excesses. Such defiance usually arises from perfect unhappiness. With Charles it was so. The pain within his breast at length seemed to him to have become a physical suffering, such was its intensity. After the first seconds of half-consciousness as he woke each morning, it leapt up with the pain of a wound touched unexpectedly. He turned himself away from it, urging his mind to sleep again; it would be another hour yet before the dormitories were roused to their first full noise of life and increasing haste. He looked at the lines of huddled bodies covered only by sheets, stretching to his right and left, and opposite. The air was still cool, eased by the fading night; in the unreal light of summer dawn those sleeping bodies were real enough, to him, and expressive, it seemed, of a dozen different kinds of thoughtlessness, selfishness and passion, even in sleep. He did not wonder whether he should ever cease to be afraid of them. They were there, tangible, potent, liable at a word, at the clamour of a distant bell, to become mobile and cruelly dangerous. They were there. He had no eminence from which to regard them as part of the young manhood of a nation, none of age's aloof idealism nor of philanthropy's deliberate blindness; he was one of them, and already it seemed to him that he was like them. He thought of the first occasion on which he was treated not as a vulnerable curiosity but as a boy; the few moments of secret relief made him almost hysterical; it was like a dream, and ended as abruptly as a dream, and he awoke sharply to the old awareness of his isolation.

Charles was built slim and not tall, but his arms and shoulders were as strong as those of a colt. Riding in the hilly country of home had strengthened his back and given his chest depth. This was belied by the round smallness of his head and face, which his curling dark red hair—the ungentle gift of early puberty—softened and made yet more delicate. For this he was marked down at once, and had his names among the other boys; but fear and defiance, coming to the aid of inexperience, taught him how to use his clenched hands when, on his first night in the dormitory, he was driven to fight. That condescension of Fortune faced him abruptly in the direction in which he was apparently destined to go, as long as he lived in the School: it taught the others that, though without doubt he was fair game for their baiting and might always be shouted at from a distance, derisively, he was not safe to tackle single-handed, since obviously he did not know what he was doing. Two or three might beset him at once, with right and morality on their side; otherwise, since he seemed not to care how bitterly he fought, it was most comfortable to leave him to himself, and to be content with miscalling him and making him as frequent a jest as was possible.

This unspoken compromise in his relationship with the majority of the boys remained to him unknown. His first fight was indeed the first fight of his life; the shock was so great that when it was ended, with the honour technically on his side, he had to retire to a private place, for his instinct warned him urgently how fatal to him would be the revelation of such incredible and bitter passion. There he remained, schooling himself to silence;

and when he had washed his face and was back at his bed-side they looked at him more attentively than they had done, and the captain of Dormitory B came and spoke abruptly to him:

'You can't fight in the dormitories, you know. I'll punish you next time, so don't do it again.'

He had the tone and expression of a man speaking to a slave; as he turned away he winked at the others, and they began to talk again, breaking their interested, expectant silence with ready laughter. The Junior Housemaster passing down the aisle between the beds caused them to still their jeering.

'Oh—Mr. Penworth, sir! Sir.'

'Hallo, sir. Have a good holiday?'

'I bet you're as glad as we are to be back again...'

They turned their attention to him; Charles, left alone, was not aware of anything curious in the attitude of the young Englishman towards them, of them towards him. He was too shaken still with the shock of physical combat. It was something so unknown to him, so far beyond his present imagination, that he could only regard it with a horror of which he was scarcely master. His body still burned from forehead to knee; on his face the marks of fighting showed red, where the struck flesh was still angry, and his hands felt as though they had been scorched by their brutal contact with something so unknown and awful as another human body. Desperately he tried to seem at ease in the control of himself; he took a book from the top of his locker, and lying on his bed used it as a screen between his eyes and theirs, pretending to read.

They for their part were engaged in a new conflict of a kind they did not understand. This was no simple, primitive battle of muscle and bone with muscle and bone; it was not concluded in minutes of time, for it was that sort of sublime struggle which death ends only because to most the dead have no arousing power. Even its sublimity was not apparent. There was merely a young Englishman being pleasant to a group of laughing boys. The new-comers in the dormitory took no part in this; they retired as much as possible from notice, looking side-ways sometimes at Charles with secret suspicion because he had probably set in motion some mildly lethal mechanism which would not be likely to discriminate. So he had no sympathy—unless from the boy in the next bed, a lad named Forrester, plump, bewildered and clearly fair game for any tormentor, with his shining brown cow-eyes inviting more disgraces.

Penworth walked slowly down the aisle between the immaculate beds, hands in pockets, knees loose, lips wide in a quizzical smile, eyes sardonically watchful beneath the delicate stressed arches of their brows. The wave of unformulated antagonism spread out behind him; he felt it, and was angered, yet satisfied. His tolerant good-humour (after three whiskies with Waters downstairs) when he spoke was reflected back to him from them drunk with their own numerous youth; each party looked down a little upon the person and the character and the mind of the other. It was a very public gathering. They smiled with the sincerity of cats.

This, thought Penworth, is a great Public School, run according to the English tradition; and it's no more English than the country itself is England. When I am about, their voices are polite and their manners are good—or if they're not I have to tell them so, and can punish them for their mistakes. When there's no one like me to make them self-conscious, what must happen? What must it be like among them?

And he realized that he had no more idea of their emotions and passions than they had of his. To him they were, and would always remain, crude, unchangeable young animals, who had never seen an English spring or an Oxford dusk; they were looking forward, but he looked back, for ever.

To them, he was a foreigner whose speech they happened to understand. They watched him as the men on their fathers' farms and stations watched any young English novice, hiding their smiles or not, as whatever courtesy they knew prompted them. The pure, cultured accent of his voice was always strange, even though they learnt to imitate it. They paid a high price in money for that accent, and for his knowledge of dead languages and their living tongue; he belonged to them, and to their successors—a necessary appurtenance; when they left the School to become, by passing through those dark gates, men, he would remain, and remain a teacher of young minds with a little brief and nominal authority over young bodies also. But he would remain as a stranger who talked of Home and meant that shape on their maps which they recognized as England, a place in which they believed, without imagery or emotion, and which few of them would ever see.

41

With the oldest boys, prefects and classical scholars of the Sixth, he had a rather better standing. He once confessed, when he was older and the School was not much more than a memory, that he felt, when among them, as if he had suddenly found himself back in his Oxford Common Room, among young graduates of his own age.

'My own age,' he repeated carefully. 'Not my own tastes, of course. But according to our standards at Home their general intelligence, and their worldly intelligence especially, were well above their years. Of course there were crudities. Of course. But they knew what they wanted from life, and you felt they were going to have their way. I thought at first it might be some contemporary characteristic, something to do with their generation, you know. But I realized—it's a sort of shock, even now—that after all their generation and mine were really the same. The difference was hemispheric: climate and culture and tradition. And then, of course, I smoked a pipe and drank whisky, which made me feel very much their senior. It was quite deceptive, all that. I don't even quite get it now. If I had read more Latin and Greek than they would ever hear of, that didn't concern them. But it did concern me. It was part of my manhood; they were young ruffians of boys. Yet—somehow—I never quite believed that. Couldn't.'

That was the kind of confession a man makes when his emotions are no longer involved with what he is considering. At the time, and in spite of himself, his emotions very surely were involved, in a way he could not understand. Regret for the past combined with fear of the present and uncertainty as to the future, prevented him from observing himself objectively, even for a moment. Perhaps to have said he feared the present would have been to put it too definitely. Yet there was certainly fear of some sort at the root of his dislike for the boys, the School, and the country which had borne them all. Even the stomachic geniality brought about by a few whiskies in his room downstairs, conversing amiably with Waters, could not dissipate it.

However, he paraded in great style, feeling the indefinite, angry satisfaction that always stimulated him when he walked among them and felt them move out of his way. At the end of the dormitory the new Captain of School, a choice cricketer and a good classical scholar (one of his own creations, he thought pleasantly) sat on the House captain's bed quietly conversing. Penworth went to shake hands with him. He was, among the boys, a hero; and as a hero he was a fellow to be reckoned with, even by an aloof and scholarly Junior Housemaster.

'Well, Fairfax?' Penworth said kindly; and asked him another question in Greek, which made him frown and laugh.

'I'm afraid the holidays have made me forget all that, sir.'

'Oh well. Soon pick it up again, you know,' Penworth said confidentially; and there was an echo in his mind of his own voice querulously suggesting to Waters at the high table, 'Need we talk shop so soon? After all, there's always to-morrow.' And here he was—the habitual pedagogue already, eyes, voice and smile hinting yet deprecating the intellectual intimacy implied in his words. This sort of intimacy was inevitable with Fairfax and uncompromising after all.

He discussed holidays with him, thinking secretly as he watched his lively, good-looking face that he was probably as mature as any of his own younger companions of the south coast summer; and as himself—almost. They talked of cricket prospects, and of the new year's eight. Fairfax would row stroke again...

'Stroke bene factum,' said Penworth suddenly; and having with such coy suavity put himself once more in the secure, austerely amiable position of a classics Master conversing with a very promising scholar, he stood up, nodded, and walked away.

'Oh, he's really not bad,' Fairfax said, replying to some warm criticism of the House captain's. 'It's our own fault if he seems like a stranger.'

Penworth went downstairs. Waters was sprawling back in the big study chair, with his feet up on the table, holding a full tumbler in one hand, reading with myopic concentration.

'How are the little ones?' he asked. 'Why aren't you drinking?'

'You forget,' Penworth said severely. 'I'm on duty. As for the little ones—you'd better come up and see for yourself.'

His own room seemed to him wretchedly apathetic and empty. Light glared boldly from the porcelain-shaded globe, picked out sharp highlights on inkwells, pens, glasses and the polished table top, and fell with a blind angularity upon the floor and the white walls. Shadow was as sharp as the light. He stood for a moment staring at the childish top of Waters's lowered head.

'Keep them. I don't want them,' Waters mumbled kindly, and went on peering at his book. Penworth moved uneasily about, lit a full pipe, and leapt upstairs again with pretentious alacrity. Mr. Jolly, tall, lean and greyer than the shadows, with his nose pointing down like a jester's finger, waited for him above.

'Nice crowd, Penworth. Fiends. Horrors. Like a whisky?'

They went into the Housemaster's room, which was of the same size as his own, with the furniture placed, of necessity, in the same way. But on the shadowy table a reading lamp shaded with a green shade cast its cool light demurely downwards. In that light the tumblers, the decanter, the frosted soda-siphon looked all more attractive and living than Waters' plain fare. Penworth thought, I must have a reading lamp.

'There's a fellow here the Chief suggested me looking after,' he said cheerfully. 'Chap named Fox. Do you happen to have seen him, sir?'

Mr. Jolly growled at the tilted decanter. 'Yes. Yes. H'm. Nice little lad. Not so fiendish as most of them seem to be. Damn them. Yes. Fox. A little coward of a fellow, but very friendly. Pretty-faced, you know. That may be why…We shall need to keep an eye on him; that sort can get mucked up fairly easily, in my experience.'

His bold eyes, that never betrayed the thoughts behind them, moved from the glass in his hand to the pale, sensuous face of the young man, and rested there steadily. They drank their drinks. The cold soda buzzed in Penworth's throat. Mr. Jolly, humming and growling, raped his dim bookshelves with one majestic glance and remarked that, as it was the first night of renewed purgatory, they had better drink again.

'How do you think the Chief looks?' he asked abruptly.

'Well...he might have had a bit more rest,' Penworth suggested, as though it were a question.

'The best Headmaster in this country, my friend. The best—not a doubt of it.'

This reminded Penworth of those times when he and Waters and the rest of the younger men had discussed the possibility of Mr. Jolly's appointment as the next Chief. He considered his senior's exclamation of faith, understanding well that something more than simple charity had made it empty of any tone of hopeful expectation. There was sympathy and superb pity in Mr. Jolly's voice as he spoke.

'The best. And you are right, old man—he needs a rest. Did you notice him at supper to-night? Worn out already. Damnable. And the confounded Board...Well, I wonder whom we shall have next, that's all. I mean to advise him to retire as soon as he feels he may.'

'I can't imagine him doing that,' Penworth said thoughtfully. 'It means too much to him, being Head in this particular School, seeing every day how much he's done for it, and what he hopes to do.'

'Ah yes. He may never feel justified. He may not. But I would'—Mr. Jolly leaned down suddenly and almost took a volume from the massy shelves. 'I would, I can tell you.

God knows…I may even be able to, one day. I hope so. This is no life, my friend.'

'Why,' Penworth said with some embarrassment, 'you might be Head yourself. No one is more suited…'

'I!' Mr. Jolly said fiercely, and the rakish lock of hair dashed itself across his left eye against the protuberance of his nose. 'Why, my dear old chap, I'd no more take on that job than I'd—than I'd burn those books.' His eyes bulged, turned to the books, and softened passionately. 'No. Not I.' He growled a laugh. 'Don't you young bloods go getting ideas of that sort.'

Penworth walked down the aisle between the stark white beds. Laughter, cries, murmurs of familiar talk filled the dormitory. They were getting ready to go to bed. He felt restless. From the bathrooms came a sound of stamping feet bare on the concrete, and muffled echoes of some sort of horseplay. He walked slowly back, through the double doors, past the stair-head to the bathroom doors, which were closed. Some one was being put through the inevitable ordeal of going into the big linen basket that should stand by the entrance to the water-closets. When this basket was half-full of stinking socks and soiled linen, it was considered an ordeal of the higher senses for the initiate; when, as now, it was empty, all who went into it came out sore and bruised about the face and elbows and knees, from hard contact with the stiff cane sides. Penworth could hear the heavy breathing and difficult laughter of the boys who were bouncing and trundling it about on the concrete floors.

'Here, you young monkeys,' he called, and opened the doors. 'Back to your dormitories. Jameson! Drake!

You—what's your name—Stand that basket up, will you? All of you. Take that lid off and get out.'

Abashed, but not frightened—for it was, after all, the first night of term, an angry gala night—they straightened their backs and tried to compose their expressions to suit this expected intrusion. The shine of their eyes and lips, as they withdrew themselves from their high enterprise, was animal, provocative, brutally attractive to Penworth. He hardened himself against it, and stared coldly.

'Out you go, all of you,' he said tersely; and they went out, to loiter about the door, watchful and loth to lose any moment of sensual excitement. Their hot bodies were tense in the half-light. Over the top of the basket a boy's red, terrified face turned dully from them to the Junior Housemaster's pale, sardonic mask.

'What are you doing there?' Penworth demanded automatically. 'What's your name?'

'Charles Fox, sir.'

'Oh.' He stared. 'Well, come on—get out of that basket. Go back to your dormitory. This sort of thing isn't allowed, you know.'

'It's not my fault,' Charles said loudly, fighting back a strong urge to scream and tear the flesh of faces with his hands. 'It's not my fault at all. Why do you blame me? It's not my fault.'

This surprised Penworth greatly, both the reckless passion of the boy's eyes, and his own sudden nervousness. He was used to a deference which, even if it was only superficially respectful, at least seemed more than skindeep. Subdued laughter hovered about the doorway behind him. He swung round, whisky-fierce, with the haughtiness of embarrassment.

'Get away from that door, and shut it.'

They went away, grumbling and laughing. His hot stomach seized on the laughter's insolence, and in a fine temper he turned upon Charles.

'Look here, young man. One of the first principles of this School is politeness to your masters...'

Charles, shaking his head from side to side, trembling and stammering, saw the world as a nightmare that whirled a little, swayed and surrounded him.

'It's not my fault, I tell you. It's not. It's not.'

There was no insolence in this defiance, anyhow, and Penworth, becoming a little calmer, understood.

'Come on. Get out of that basket,' he said gently.

Charles's face went white; then blood reddened it; then it paled again. He stopped shaking his head.

'I...I can't. Sir...I can't, sir.'

'Come on,' Penworth said, roughly hiding his changed embarrassment. He took the basket by its thick handles, and lowered it fairly gently to the floor.

'Oh,' Charles said.

He sprawled out of it, white and naked upon the concrete. Penworth stepped back not understanding his sudden agitation. To Charles, whose body was hot, marked by the hard cane of the basket, the floor felt awkwardly cool. He put himself upon his feet, still flushing and paling by turns. Until this night, since he was a very small child he had never stood naked before anyone's eyes. And certainly Penworth's eyes were on him. Certainly they were. He tried to hide his nakedness. At length he turned his back. Penworth looked at it, and felt some strange sensation of pleasure and shame course through him, dissipating all that was left of his censure, as heatless early sunlight dissipates frost on the grass.

He laughed shortly.

'Where are your clothes?'

'They took them away. They've got them, sir.'

Penworth strode to the door. The boys, of course, were still there, silent, listening, with curious smiles of pleasant anticipation. He scowled.

'You young fools. I thought you'd have had more sense. You've frightened the wits out of the boy. Haven't you any sensitiveness yourselves? Think—and do things more carefully. If you must do them. Where are Fox's clothes? Who has them?'

They saw that he had suddenly become very angry. Anyone who affronted that sort of mood in him would, as most of them knew, be fiercely punished. The pyjama suit was put into his hands, and they went away. Only in their dormitories, where they urgently told the story, did they venture again to laugh.

'Don't go into the bathrooms. Penworth's there, and he's mad.'

'Jesus, he's mad.'

'With that new kid.'

'Fox, the sissy.'

'He's not mad with Fox. Mad with us.'

'Jesus, he's mad.'

They knew it was Fox's fault.

Penworth gave Charles the pyjama suit. The boy's white skin had faint red marks upon it, round the shoulders, burning and fading. He put one hand on it, very briefly. It was as fine and as soft as a girl's skin.

'Put 'em on,' he said. 'And go along to bed. Don't you worry. You'll be all right.'

His kind, quiet tone gave Charles another shock. He began to cry, and Penworth, who became filled with a mild sentimental grief when he heard it, pretended not to notice. He picked up a towel that lay knotted in a corner. The knots were huge and thick, and loosened easily enough.

'This will be your towel,' he said at last, holding it at arm's length. 'Wash that dirty face and go along to bed.'

Then he went out hurriedly, leaving the doors wide.

In Dormitory B the House captain, who presided also over that dormitory, was still sitting on his bed talking. Neatly folded clothes, books, and a scatter of other possessions, lay about on the white coverlet. He was a short, fair young man, popular as Fairfax was popular; but he was no scholar, and he suspected scholarship.

When Penworth came along to him he sat looking up at his Junior Housemaster with calm indifference. His eyes were blue and piercing, with a catlike quality of remote concentration pointing their undisturbed stare.

'Just keep your eye on that young chap Fox for a time, will you, Bourke?' Penworth said at once. 'I don't mean coddle him. But see that he doesn't get too rough a time.'

'Very well, sir,' Bourke said shortly.

'You see,' Penworth went on, with a certain craft, knowing where the House captain's heart was affected, 'it doesn't do the House any good if it has some one in it liable to behave badly. That lad is completely strange to this sort of life. We'll have to do things gently; teach him how to be a credit to the House.'

He relaxed a little, feeling more sure of himself as calmness returned with the deliberate exercise of his mind. He was thinking rapidly.

'You see,' he said with a smile, 'it's up to you older chaps to see that there's no nonsense in the House. Most of you know more about the younger boys, as human beings, than the Masters do. That lad Fox will have to learn to be a good sport, like everyone else. But...you see what I mean?'

'Yes sir. I see.'

Bourke's eyes looked with more tolerance after him when he had turned and was walking away, sneering at himself for having talked such horrid nonsense. He hoped he had chosen the best way to make things easier for the boy, even if his own integrity, as he saw it, was affected.

Charles came in from the bathrooms feeling that it mattered little and made little difference where he was, what he did. He made a pretence of busying himself, and tried to set his locker in order. Article after article, as he touched it, and looked at it, reminded him so sharply of home and that former life that he was inwardly tortured beyond belief, and eventually the noise and light and movement about him became unreal. The unfriendly stares and low-spoken remarks of some of the boys he faced with the blind defiance of complete grief. Nothing mattered—neither where he was nor what was done to his body. The very worst that could happen had happened already, he knew.

Penworth did not leave Dormitory B until the lights were put out. He walked up and down, aloof, condescending, amiable, his sensual full lips moving softly as he smiled or spoke. Beneath their wide arched brows his beautifully-set eyes appeared now to observe all things with disinterested tolerance. At Charles he did not once look, and Charles at length ceased to expect that. The lights were put out. Penworth still walked through the dormitory quietly, like a darker shadow upon the darkness.

When he went out for the last time, noise welled up freely again, and the remainder of the evening's entertainment was begun. Long after it had been stopped by Bourke and the other prefect, Charles lay awake. In the village, half a mile away, a church clock told the hours as the hot night dragged on. At last, in the peace of imagining himself at home again, with all this as a mad dream, he was asleep.

Looking back on his own first days and earlier weeks in the School, Mawley, who knew him better than anyone at that time, saw more and more clearly what the experience must have been, as recorded by Charles's too-sensitive consciousness. There were few things against Mawley. Superior schoolboy cousins had coached him to be ordinary; and, having attended schools before, happily enough, he was no doubt ordinary, secretive, full of deceits and self-deceits already. In spite of this Mawley's was not an easy initiation. Therefore it was possible to perceive, afterwards, something of the desperation with which, in an instinctive awareness of imminent but still unrevealed decisions, Charles at that time faced what he thought was life.

Among the mass of boys there, he was in fact like a person from some remote land that had been civilized without sophistication. He was a visitor from the very real country of childhood, and from that innocent demesne in it which all others of his age there had left, long ago. His innocence was only ignorance in that he had never been schooled to guard against and suspect his fellows; and that was only because he had been unfortunate enough not to have to do with other human beings, other than his mother.

His mother, who had passed her thirty-fifth year when he was born, was still to his unready vision not a separate personality from himself. He could not see her except as one who had been unvaryingly kind, unvaryingly remote, concerned, he believed, as completely with her own methodical life as he was with his life of solitary dreaming. He had never felt youth's alarm before the objective regard. If he had thought of their relationship at all, he would have imagined them as two who lived in a single harmony making neither gesture nor demand.

Now, in the first intensity of loneliness and unknown self-consciousness, he felt a longing for her presence, as though he might have found great comfort in losing himself in her, not with the positive shows of affection but as passionately and negatively as if it were indeed possible that he should be drawn back, from this life, into the perfect and impregnable existence of the womb. He perceived for the first time, emotionally, her importance in his own life, and for the first time consciously desired to be with her. It was vaguely evident to him now that, after all, his way of life had been of her choosing; without seeming to decide, she had made his decisions for him; he had been first in her thoughts. That in her which to many had appeared as coldness had never been coldness to him. Lying wretchedly awake in the hot night, he thought of her face and hands, the assured movement of her strong body, her eyes calmly regarding him. Something in the face of the Junior Housemaster had reminded him of her; but he could not think what it was. That man was a stranger to him, though he had been kind; but she was no stranger. She had too often soothed him to sleep when he was a child, and now it was the annihilation in sleep that he so fervently desired, when in the incomprehensible strangeness of a life worse than bad dreams he found himself faced helplessly with his own individuality.

He wished himself away, back in his room under the eaves at home, secure from this new, uneasy necessity of decision and self-knowledge. In the light of the candle her face, delicately etched with the lines of fifty years of life, would reassure him, as it had always done, of her unfailing power to comfort and cure him. Wide-eyed in that long room full of the stir and stillness of human creatures dangerously asleep, he fancied himself looking up into her grave eyes, her composed lips pencilled now with shadow by the steady candle flame, the powder-grey fall of hair on her shoulders, while her cool right hand was stretched out to rest on his forehead with the quiet insistence of a command, though she did not speak.

She had always been kind. He saw that he had trusted her, now, when she was not there to guide and command him; and he imagined that he had consciously loved her, when with her the world he had known and loved was parted from him by such a translation into strangeness. He wondered what he would do. Unknown to himself, he desired her dominion, and, lacking it, was as though lost. The experience of unhappiness was as strange and passionate to him as would be the first experience of conscious love.

Penworth said nothing to his senior in the House, nor to anyone else, of what had happened in the bathroom, but it came often to his mind. The curious pleasure he had felt when he saw that boy's white body, and when he touched the firm skin of his shoulder, would have seemed more strange than it did had he remembered it clearly; but there remained most vividly in his mind the memory of a bewilderment, of the same bewilderment with which a young man for the first time considers the revealed body of a woman—something of fear mixed sharply with the intense admiration of desire sublimated beyond material imagery. The great business of those following days and weeks would have erased even that from his mind, if he had not seen and spoken with Charles more often than he had expected. Greek and Latin classes, as well as the innumerable brevities of House routine, brought them frequently together; and, though Penworth was ready enough now to oblige the Chief, he was careful, rather for his own sake than for the sake of the boy, to prevent himself from showing any unnatural interest in him.

Charles's defiance grew as he slowly became aware of everything about himself that was different from others.

He knew, without understanding why, that there was this difference; indeed, he could not have helped knowing, when in a dozen ways each day it was made very plain to him. He heard himself called names whose meaning he did not understand, but which, from the way they were mouthed, he could recognize as the shrewdest insults. Before long, he found he could face such callings; it was physical insult that he most horribly dreaded, and this he also invited by the unabating defiance with which he bore himself. Fortune had given him strong hands, and the instinct to use them in his own defence, but against a number he was, of course, soon powerless.

The dark complexity of this sort of life became increasingly dreadful as day followed day.

That February was a hot month, hotter even than an Australian February might be expected to be. Every afternoon those who were not listed for practice at the nets went down to the river which wound between its double line of trees beyond the wide scorched flats where the dairy herd was pastured. On the flats the grass was changed from gold to a bleached grey in the weeks of merciless sun. It frayed and split, seething with cicadas and insects that kept from dawn to dusk the sibilant waves of their immortal susurrus; and this sound, filling the whole world, became an unheard background to all the noises of day in the School; even at night, taken up by the crickets, the song never ceased and the air was mad with it. Sunlight was broken up like glass by the polished dry threads of stem and leaf; the grass fell flat, more than dead, and only patches of water-couch, defying the blinding heat, showed dully green about the hollow places, and spread in a scarred covering along the edges of the exhausted river.

The thick, fleshy odour of sweating mud hung in the air here. Even the river reeds, that marched like an army in the shallow water and stopped only at the sides of the platforms, and clustered by the slipways of the rowing sheds, were yellowing and breaking. When a breeze oozed warmly and fitfully down with the current, they knocked together and rattled secretly, until it seemed that the lazy ripples whispered in that swooning air. The boys came noisily down, under the care of an excellent old athletics master who sometimes made coarse army jests, and the place was shattered and outraged by their shouts and laughter. They were the blessed of the earth; they were lords of this tarnished stretch of original creation that spread flatly and wearily in the brassy light. To them, newly let out of the close afternoon heat of classrooms shuttered from the sun, it was heaven to be down here, half a mile away, with only Old Mac—lean and long like a ramrod, with silver moustaches stabbing at the pallid sky as he threw back his head to laugh—to watch them and listen delightedly, with his deafest expression, to their merry, dirty little jokes at one another's expense. On top of the distant declivity that fell down to the flats lay the School, empty now save for exhausted Masters taking some sort of ease in their shuttered studies; the red brick buildings shuddered like a long mirage in the fierce light, and through the smoke-grey tops of trees the tiled roofs pressed flat against the flat sky of the south-east. That skyline was all flatness, a poor enough backcloth against which, each afternoon, the hilarious comedy of these water-babies was played. They never looked that way. In front of them the greenish water stretched, a hundred yards to left and right of the platforms, forty yards across. Its surface was as still as a glass—something to be broken again, something to play with, to feel, to taste, something no cooler than milk cascading over shoulders and half-naked bodies as they plunged thirstily into its slow, invisible current. The soft clean odour of the water, that suggested river mud, leaves, and the secret smell of water-rotten wood, clung about their hair and bodies afterwards, reminding them of the coolness as they sat over their studies in the heavy evenings.

Charles went down. He went with the rest, running helter-skelter as madly as sheep down the ramp, down the baked clay of the slope, slowing to an eager walk in the white grass of the flats, damp with sweat already, swinging towels, singing, whistling, laughing jealously at those who, in spite of the heat, ran on before them. He had a vague idea, born of the labour of thought at night, that perhaps his one protection from further bodily shame would be to keep among them. The more people there were about him, he thought, the less likely it would be that he would seem conspicuous, a target for their eyes and their words. The first days had been busy with a confused shifting from place to place; rolls were called, scholars had given them the blank time-table forms which they filled in according to the course of their studies. Masters stood on daises, explaining, asking questions, sweeping in and out in their billowing black gowns, referring this boy and that to another classroom or another Master. The continual cry of 'Silence, please', still echoed warmly in Charles's ears as he walked in the sun. No one had taken much notice of him; he wondered if it would last.

Evidently he must stay at the place, at least for a time. If he were to write at once to his mother, carefully explaining why he disliked it there, and asking her if he might not come away, he knew what would happen. She would explain, just as carefully, that he was only homesick, and that he would find how different that life could be, later on. He was strange to it yet; there had not been time for him even to guess at what it was really like. He must face difficulties like a man, and try to get on with the other boys. He must not think of coming home. It was the best school he could have been sent to; it would mean a great deal to him later in life to have been to that school.

He saw her firm handwriting on the face of the grass; he foresaw all that she would say, and within his mind argued, passionately, incoherently, and pleaded with her, but perceived that she was stronger than himself. Turning away from her, he wondered what else there was to do.

There was death, a word he knew. The image of her face expressing unhappiness came into his mind. It was not to be thought of that he would die, and escape that way. He did not want to die; it meant an end, it meant a nothingness, and now, since he had been at the School, his instinct to live had received such encouragement that it had crystallized into clear imagery. He passionately wanted to go on living: but it would be necessary, for happiness, to live in a different place...

But there was no different place. Home was closed to

him by his departure. If he ran away from the School and went to live in the hills near home, either he would starve, or someone would certainly find him, and then, as he knew, it would all begin again.

He considered these ideas clearly, with great seriousness and feeling. No experience in his life had yet suggested to him how little he had learned of living. With animals and the land, and with trees and birds, morning, noon and night as his constant companions, life was easy. There were dangers. He might fall out of a tree, as Johnny O'Neill had done two years ago, and be injured. A snake, hiding coldly in the dry grass, could kill him at a stroke. If he were lost for long in the hills in summer, he might starve and die. But life was easy to live; no natural danger could approach the awful horror of the danger of human beings. That was so dire that he could not understand it. He was entirely without understanding of deliberate evil; his mind could not grapple with it—not yet.

It was evident that, until he had found some resources of his own, he must stay in the School. He cast about in his mind, but could see no other thing to do. And he wanted, too, the fine satisfaction of learning. In his life he had read little; a few works of natural history in other countries, descriptions of the lives of foreign peoples, and merry stories of English Public Schools had, after the earlier tales of adventure, made up his occasional reading. He knew a little of the writing of a few poets, and understood the emotion but not the meaning of their works. The desire to know was coming to life like a fire in his heart. He wanted to learn. Now in his innocence he perceived that to live lost in the country he knew, with learning to nourish his mind and the earth to gladden him, was the finest of all living. Desire and fear were only now beginning to wake within him and take over their predestined rule of his whole life. Their germination and first conquests were confusing him at present with a chaotic unhappiness.

His first attempt at protective subterfuge began. He decided to go swimming. He knew how to swim.

There were other new boys going down. They walked mostly alone, while the second-year lads and the rest, whose speech and manner made them seem to belong for ever to the School, went in their own groups, ragging one another happily, laughing like girls. They were already at home again. There was talk of the crew to be selected, and of the two cricket teams.

'And the swimming,' one said happily.

'Yes. What about the new kids? Who will be picked?'

'Yes. Little Miss Fox will be picked, for sure.'

They laughed joyously. Charles walked on, looking at the white grass.

'Yes. What about that big chap that came a day late?'

'The white-headed chap?'

'Yes. Thomas. What about him?'

'Go on. His name's not Thomas.'

'It is Thomas, I tell you.'

'You lying bitch, Saunders. It's not. Thomas is that thin bloke with the ugly mug like yours.'

'All right, Peterson.'

There was a scuffle in the grass, and the two boys who had been arguing jumped to their feet again when they observed how far they were left behind. Grass seeds clung to their clothes and in their hair.

'Watch this,' said Saunders, and he set off at a run.

Charles felt a sudden weight, like a house, strike him and take him heavily to the ground. They laughed as they watched his surprise; their laughter was not unkind. He got up, smiling, and walked on with the straggling last few, smiling still from nervousness, smiling defiantly though no one noticed him. Anger, fear and a growing relief made his heart beat madly. When they were at the dressing-sheds he undressed himself as though nothing had happened. The boy next to him was he who had sent him sprawling. He asked Charles if he could swim. In a low voice Charles said he could.

'Just as well,' Saunders said. 'This water's deep. Where you from?'

Charles told him, looking at him straight, wondering what was concealed in the suavity of this attention.

'Down there? I've been there for the winter hols.'

He said nothing more, and soon went out. Charles, finishing his change slowly, struggled to understand why a boy should trouble to make him look ridiculous before everybody, and then speak naturally, almost kindly, to him. Loneliness flowed in his mind like a cold wave.

With his thin towel over his shoulder he went out into the more blinding light, and was in the water as quickly as might be. Within a minute he had been ducked under and kicked down two or three times. That was Saunders.

'Thought you said you could swim,' he said to Charles. 'That's not swimming, paddling round like an old tart in bed.'

He went away, hoisting himself through the water strongly. Charles made the mistake of getting up on the diving platform, and was pushed in again. He clambered up, and was pushed in a second time. One or two boys, standing to watch with water running and dripping over their bright faces, laughed delightedly. Some one shouted, 'Oh, let the kid alone for a while, can't you?' and the scorn in that remark demanded a punitive attack on the speaker, and Charles was for a time left alone. Later Old Mac called him.

'You, sir. You, there. Come along here.'

He turned and received a solid push in the back that sent him stumbling at a run. Old Mac looked down from his stiff height with his usual fierce kindliness.

'You swim, sir? By gad, eh! But damned badly, sir. Damned badly. However, you seem to me a likely sort of fellow. Get into the water.'

Charles had five minutes of ceaseless criticism, delivered in a terse and level voice from above him as he swam past half a dozen times. He was shown the action of a racing crawl, and how to use his arms, racing-style. 'Come back. Knees together, knees together. Better. Elbows in— so. Come back.' After that he was passed on, and left to himself. Not knowing what was expected of him now, he went out into the channel in mid-stream and tried to practise what Old Mac had shown him; and there he remained until he was exhausted, trying not to remember the quiet happiness of days spent in the river at home. When at last he came out, the hot sunlight on the bank was gladdening after so long in that unbuoyant cool water; it thrilled up his legs and his naked back, and he lay in a sort of dazed lassitude, watching the drops fall from his flattened hair to the short, bristling points of the grass. Only when a handful of mud was vigorously rubbed about his head and ears— and, when he turned over, into his face—did he remember where he was. It was necessary to go into the water again, loudly derided this time. While he was still in, Old Mac blew his whistle.

He waited till the last boy had clambered from the water, and followed slowly. Old Mac watched him, took him by the arm, felt the muscles of his shoulders, his thighs and calves. Charles suffered the squeezing pressure of those dry old fingers easily; they were dispassionate and purposeful. Finally Old Mac straightened his back, wiped his finger-tips on his towel, and fixed a hawk's stare upon Charles while he did so.

'You're hard, sir,' he said. His parade-ground voice was capable of many modifications of volume, few of tone. When he spoke quietly it was an echo from a far parade-ground.

'We may soften you. Not impossible. Properly trained you may swim well. You may be of use to the School. Keep that in mind. Make it an objective, sir. Hope to be a credit. All right—dismiss.'

From habit he broke the last word into two contrasting syllables, the first long, the second short, a breath hissing through the silver of those arrogant moustaches that scorned his kindling eyes.

Charles went to the dressing-sheds, and got into his clothes quickly. He was among the first to start walking back towards the School, across the flats. The air was less burning now and the light not so brutal; his legs and arms felt weak, tired by the unresisting fresh water, and a growing lassitude spread like drunkenness over his whole body. Before he had reached the red upward slope and the wooden ramp descending it, a wish to sleep made him pause and stumble once or twice.

At home…

At home, yes, he could have slept now, had this strong urge taken him. He could have slept, and have been up and abroad till midnight after it. Swimming at night, in the river that ran past the house, was nothing like this. It was a dark paradise of silence. The deep voices of the bitterns did not break the surface of night. But he could not go home.

He sighed, puzzled as deeply as ever by the strange difference of this new life.

'You may be of use to the School. Keep that in mind. Make it an objective, sir. Hope to be a credit…' And Mr. Jolly had said, 'Keep yourself clean. Cleanliness first, old chap.'

And Mr. Penworth had smiled and comforted him with the tones of his voice.

It seemed to him very unlikely, and even impossible, that he should ever understand it all.

Very quickly, and without apparent trouble, the School fell into the rhythm of the year's routine. The Headmaster interested himself in everything that was being done. Within ten days he knew every face and seemed to know each boy by name, and to be familiar with the course of his studies

and with his athletic possibilities. Day after day he made
a tour of House notice-boards, at the same hour each
afternoon. Once a week he conferred with Housemasters,
and with Formmasters on the same day. He was familiar
with the entire working of the School, not only with what
was happening in field and classroom, but with its domesticity also; a Matron and a nursing sister reported to his
study twice a week, the one on kitchen matters and the
running of the staff of servants, the other on the health of
individual boys.

His own teaching staff wondered, privately and
between themselves, in the Common Room, in studies, at
the long table in Hall, how he was able to keep up this practice of knowing everything without ever seeming to intrude.
He never appeared in a classroom, and they liked him the
better for that. It was an open secret that the governing
Board was opposed to many of his ideas, and gave him
neither peace nor quarter at the monthly board meetings.
And of his health they wondered even more. Even the boys
understood its uncertainty; they sympathized, for they liked
him well, though they were ready enough to make jests at
his expense. Their opinion, when they thought of it, was
like Mr. Jolly's, that no better Headmaster could have been
entrusted with their precious fates.

After a collapse during a service in the Chapel, at the
beginning of the previous November when the summer was
gaining vigour, no one expected Dr. Fox to continue in his
duties. He appeared to understand this, too, and in his own
quiet, friendly way he took pains to let it be known that
there would be no change in the office. No one understood

the anguish it caused him to remain in the School as its Head, nor the joy it gave him to be able to remain; he knew that though those at the bottom of a social order may show their feelings without needing to take care, any confession from the highest could shake the whole structure, and would so shake it, indeed, almost as completely as the admitted possibility that a new Headmaster might be needed to take his place.

For this reason he continued to supervise the conduct of the School, without relenting towards himself. Had he realized that now he was being watched, by boys and Masters alike, for the first signs of relaxation and physical relapse, it is probable that without haste, but without hesitation, he would have renounced his charge at once, and have retired to that quieter and less strenuous sort of life which he was beginning most seriously to need. It is probable that he would have done this if he had known that even that gesture of his, that unconscious setting of his lean jaws and passing his hand over his brown, bare cranium where the hollow scar measured the beating of his heart, was watched always, by everyone. He hardly knew he was doing it; no one ever told him, and the inward pain more often now grasped his brain like a hand.

Since he was not aware of this continual watching, he went on with his strenuous duties, and because he was so outwardly serene and so competent the School hummed as pleasantly as a hive of bees in the sun. Those who came close to him during his term of office there realized afterwards, as they looked back to consider his quiet kindness and understanding and the unchanging patience of his courtesy, how fiercely he must have struggled to hold up the mask which he was so often and so bitterly tempted to put aside for ever.

At the time, neither his friends in the School nor those who knew him outside could have guessed. He was the same as he had always been and would always be. The School was increasing in size under his care, and this gave to his thoughtful silences a naturalness which inwardly they had not.

The smoothness of this routine at first confused and then solaced Charles. He felt for once the charm of being part of a lively machine in action. Life was being arranged and explained; for the greater part of the day he knew, and each of his Masters knew also, where he should be and what he should be doing. The intervals in his time-table added the needful imagination and romance to this mechanical weekly repetition. He was not allowed to forget his first fear, though custom and the familiarity of his presence among them had permitted him to modify it somewhat. His defiance secretly sustained him. Though he pretended to be like them, he did not care. To the rest of his fellows he was an aloof, incomprehensible creature; because they did not understand anything in him, he remained what he was to them—potentially dangerous, in no active way perhaps, but as the living personification of certain forces which were strange to them. As ordinary people do, they feared strangeness; and what they feared they were prepared to hate, keenly, without knowing that this hatred had its origins in nothing more devilish than a difference of temperaments. They took refuge in that frankly expressed contempt which

Charles himself could not understand. He countered it with a helpless defiance, and made rare attempts to reconcile them to himself, not yet realizing that it was his own self which he must reconcile to them.

One thing altered his life somewhat in its exterior form.

At the end of his fifth week, just before the Easter holiday, the Headmaster sent for him to come from his second morning class. Charles went quickly, feeling a pleasure that would have astonished the others, who had been taught to dread these sudden summonses to the Big Study.

Dr. Fox was sitting back in his chair, looking alertly at the door as he entered. Charles took one look at the hollow scar pulsing, and one swift glance around the room before he found himself being commanded by the man's deep shadowy eyes.

'Sit down, Fox,' the Head said pleasantly. 'I want to talk with you seriously about yourself.'

Charles sat on a wooden chair against the wall. From his table behind the door the Master with the minute classic features and the pink tonsure rose and walked out like an automaton, his gaze rigidly before him. The room was easier when he had gone, Charles thought.

'I have had unusually good reports of your work,' Dr. Fox said at once. 'You will remember what I said when I met you first—that we like scholarship and hard work as well as prowess in sport. Do you remember me saying that?'

'Yes, sir,' Charles said.

'Well, I want to talk with you about that again. The reports your Masters have given me are very good, as I said. I feel sure you will like to know.'

Listening to the deep quiet of his voice, looking into the dark eyes he could with difficulty see, Charles felt a rare, growing exhilaration as his contact with that calm personality, that powerfully masculine effluence that wished him well, was sustained and strengthened. He said, hesitantly, how glad he was.

'I am sure you are. Now I want to make a suggestion. Don't make the mistake of supposing it to be a command; I should be sorry if you did that. I want to suggest that you let us put you up into the Intermediate form, the form you would normally have been in next year. You understand how your course of study is made out here. After two years, as a rule, you sit for your Intermediate examination certificate, and so go on to another two years, after which you take your examinations for Matriculation.'

Charles followed him in part only. It seemed he had just been told, but not in so many words, that he would be in the School a year less than he had expected.

'If you agree,' the Headmaster was saying, 'to go into IVA now, we'll be glad to trust to your own judgment, and we'll have faith in your ability until you convince us that we've been too hasty.'

A slow smile broke the shadows in his bony face. His eyes shone brilliantly in the darkness of their caverns.

'Don't hurry to decide. You will find the work there much harder. It will mean some extra study for you; there will be a lot of catching-up to do.'

'Yes, sir,' Charles said, smiling himself in his swift joy.

'I find that in English and other languages you are particularly able. In Mathematics, however, there is a danger.'

71

'Yes, sir,' Charles said quickly, 'I'm not very good. But I should like to...I mean to go up to IVA, sir.'

'Wouldn't you like to find out how far ahead they are, and think it over?'

'No, sir. I'd like to go up.'

'Very well. Now there's this...You seem cut out for a classics course; that is plain to me. In IVA you can dispense with your science classes, since you need only five passes for the certificate. If you dare to work without a margin, I should advise you to give up Greek for this year, and pick it up again later. That will leave you three languages, and two mathematics. Think you can manage with those? Three languages including English.'

'Oh—yes, sir. I'll work hard.'

'Very well, Fox. You can start in IVA after the Easter holiday. Let me see...you will be fifteen about now, sometime?'

'Last week, sir.'

'Good. That's all, Fox. And good luck.'

As Charles was going out, he called him back.

'To show you that you have done well—and can keep on doing well—let me tell you that you are only the fourth boy in five years whom we've put up like this. That should help you to keep going.'

'Yes—thank you, sir.'

'How do you like it here?'

Charles started to speak, stopped, changed his mind again, and said, 'I'm getting used to it now, sir. At first I hated it, I'm afraid.'

Once more the Headmaster smiled.

'That often happens. But remember that, as the saying is, life isn't all beer and skittles, even for the worthy. Often the more you try to do right, the harder life seems to hit back. Anyhow...you may find that out later. Well, that's all, Fox. Go along now.' And he said again, 'Good luck'.

A minute later, leaning back in his chair, he set his jaws till the muscles knotted at the base, and passed one palm heavily over the brown bare dome of his cranium. The hair growing at the back and the sides of his high skull had once been black, but was now very grey. He sighed and shut his eyes for a while, trying to turn from admiring the boy's youth and wakening life; it was becoming increasingly hard for his mind to change from one matter to another, such was the flogged intensity of its concentration; and to deal with every human being as he wished to deal was, each week now, more deliberate and conscious an effort.

The letter Charles had that day from his mother told him that there had been more rain. It was the third lot of rain since January, she said; and she remarked, too, 'when you come home next week there may be mushrooms. It has happened once or twice before, mushrooms at Easter. I know how you like picking them.'

That brief mention of mushrooms, put there, he knew, because it lengthened out a paragraph a little, brought from his memory a most vivid image of the Far Field in autumn, when the grass was always cropped bare round great worn patches of dark clay, and the earth itself in those bare places had begun to shine and live again, after the first rains. It was a beautiful soil to peer into: the smooth surface, baked in months of summer sun and trodden almost to a polish by the hard little hoofs of sheep, would crack and soften with the moisture, and dry again on the surface in the humid heat that followed the earliest showers. The grass was greener after rain had washed it; it began, within two weeks perhaps, to renew the buds the sheep had nipped when everything was dry; it lay flat where they had trodden and pressed it down, and stooled out, clinging as closely to the earth as a cloth. In the wide treeless spaces there the wind came past, in the autumn, as fresh as spring. He imagined the shapes of birds, far off, flung into the sky above a grove closely planted for shade, crying loudly with a remote sound like a triumphant '*Ah!*' full of sad finality, as though for months they had foretold the breaking of a bad summer and the renewal of the earth's life.

Here the first mushrooms appeared, breaking through inches of half-softened crust from the moister warmth beneath, just as if for their pulpy round heads it was no feat at all. They came up in a night; they seemed to come even as he walked about stooping with his knife to take them up into the basket; against the darkness of the earth they shone like moons, and the pink flesh of their secret under-sides was wonderful to see...

He was enraptured, remembering the spaciousness and freedom there, among the rolling fields that rose against the sky in uplands from which he could see the hills five miles away, covered with a mist like the bloom on plums, and as purple and dusky as plums in the soft distance of evening. Without his knowledge, the agelessness of those lonely places made him understand in some degree how

brief and immaterial his own life was. He looked upon a
world that had not changed and was without knowledge
of time, and was himself the product of change and of
unreckoned thousand years. As he grew more at one with it,
there were moments when its timelessness became his own.

He was enraptured, remembering it. All through
the following days it haunted his mind almost beyond the
doors of sleep. The urge to express something of it which
he could not grasp, something darkly reflected in the mirror
of his passion for it, became so great that it seemed to him
like a physical sensation, a trembling of his very heart. In
the School he went about as though he were walking in a
dream, and his uneasy fears and uncertainties did not rise
up in him as he became aware of the others of his kind
there. There was excitement among them; they were going
home, too. He thought that must mean to them the delight
of freedom from the ceaseless yes and no of that life they
were leading.

By a sympathetic coincidence, just at this time
he chanced to look into a Shakespearian play, during
the apathetic quiet of Sunday afternoon in the Library. The
work of that poet was almost unknown to him, except
for two or three set plays. *Julius Caesar* he was reading
with desultory interest in class. Now for the first time the
curious fluency of the style, uninterrupted by a Master's
comments, caught his attention like a clear voice suddenly
breaking silence in the big, badly-lit room where he stood;
and he read on, and came to a sentence that turned his lips
in a smile of delight.

'A babbled of green fields...

He read it over again. Who babbled of green fields? he wondered. The type was small and worn; he took the volume over to a window that opened into a well where the light was better, and stood there, turning back to find out who it was that babbled so. Some person called Falstaff. It was not a name he knew. An index at the end said, referring to the name—'Sir John F., v. *Henry IV* and *The Merry Wives Of Windsor*. F. was one of Shakespeare's most famous creations, and probably the most popular during the Bard's own life...'

Charles was ready to imagine himself, that hot silent afternoon, babbling of green fields in the rapt incoherence of death.

The librarian gave him the volume, and he took it outside. The mid-afternoon sunlight was still and scalding, blinding like a fire too closely peered into, yet as dull in colour as brass. He went quickly up the concrete path to the Chapel; under the shadow of the south side boys were lying about on the grass, too lax to make their usual happy noise, or to play. They sprawled on their bellies in the shade, or lay looking upwards with narrowed eyes at the white heat of the sky, chewing pieces of grass while they talked and argued as incessantly as ever. Some of them called out after him; Saunders, who lay on his back with his knees drawn up, turned his head lazily.

'There's a swim this afternoon, Foxy. Coming?'

'I might,' Charles said shortly. He was in haste to get out of the sun.

One of the half-doors was swung back, and he went in quickly, without troubling to listen to what they had to say further. Inside, in the vestry, there was a coolness; the creamy stone and the oak looked fresh in the sudden shadow. Sunlight fell in long broken blades across the dimness in the spiral stone stair that turned up from the right-hand tower base towards the organ loft. Here, to his embarrassment, he came upon his music master, sitting on the lowest choir bench with his elbows on the rail and his face smothered in his fingers.

'Oh—I'm sorry, sir,' he said.

'It's all right,' Mr. Jones said, looking up and feeling for his spectacles. When he had put them on he looked again at Charles, who remained at the entrance to the loft, in hot uncertainty as to whether he should withdraw from what he knew was an intrusion.

'Oh, it's you, Fox,' Mr. Jones said. 'What are you going to do here?'

'I was going to read, sir.'

'All right. What are you reading?'

Charles showed him. As he came close he saw with great confusion that the organist's hectic thin cheeks were wet in places, under the eyes.

'Ah,' Jones said. 'Well, you couldn't do better than read Shakespeare in a lovely place like this. Away from—away from interruption.'

'I'm sorry if I interrupted you, sir,' Charles said in a hurry. 'The light in the library is so bad; I thought I'd—I'd come up here.'

'Stay, stay,' Jones urged him, kindly. 'I was going, in any case. It's too hot to practise...'

Charles believed he heard him add 'in this damnable country' under his breath; but he was smiling, although the smile was rather rueful. He had a charming quick smile with a whimsical sharpness and twist in it, suggesting a happy wit, which he had. From the low opening into the stair he said, turning back, 'I'm going home. If you care to come over to my cottage in an hour, when you'll have finished that, we could have tea together and talk about it. Mr. Penworth is on duty; I'll see him on my way.' He went on down the stair without waiting for an answer; and when he had disappeared Charles heard him call out in a voice that strained at light-heartedness, 'My wife went back to England yesterday, so there'll be no one there'.

And yet again, above the clatter of his own descending heels, he said loudly from below, 'She couldn't stand the climate...' and in a moment there came up the fading sound of his feet going quickly away down the Chapel path.

The echo of these words died in Charles's mind when he began to read. It was hot in the loft, though the long blinds had been drawn down over the tall, narrow windows whose leaded panes, farther up the Chapel, broke into fragments of sullen gold the sunlight slanting in. Charles unbuttoned his coat and his waistcoat, and stood leaning against the northern wall. In the silence of the great vaulted roof his heart beat heavy and slow; the seductive, strangling murmur of pigeons floated down from the belfries above him. After some minutes these sounds too became the silence.

Perhaps half an hour after he had started to read *King Henry the Fifth* there was a noise of feet coming lightly but slowly up the narrow stair. Charles, however, was so concentrated upon the page that not till Penworth had spoken twice did he look up. Then, when he realized that he had heard him speak once already, the blood came quickly into his face, and he began to stammer out an apology.

'Well, and what are you doing here?' Penworth said in a friendly way, coming to stand by him. Charles let his strong broad fingers take the book out of his hands.

'H'm; you're not doing any harm reading that, anyhow.' Penworth was pleasantly decided, and Charles felt again how well he liked this cultured, easy man, who could make even Greek syntax seem a matter for smiles and small excitements.

'What do you think of it?' Penworth asked. Then he laughed and said, 'No—don't bother; schoolmasters spoil things when they start asking questions. And this is Sunday, anyhow. Read it and enjoy it alone. Nothing is nicer.'

He sat down, and Charles remained where he was standing, feeling happy that he had been surprised in such a way by such a man. Penworth was looking up at him, cocking an eye under the fine arches of his brows. From the bays of his wide temples Charles could see how the hair was already receding, as though into the bays of a coastline a tide were being sent.

His smile was weary and pleasing at first. Then, as he talked and looked at Charles, it became deeper and more lively. He confounded the heat...Charles listened to the colourful cadences of his voice with half-unheeding content; he was still wrapped in unfinished thoughts about the play he had been reading, and parts of it came into his mind surprisingly, and were confused with Penworth's idle words.

'...just between twelve and one, e'en at turning o' the tide: for after I saw him fumble at the sheets, and play with flowers, and smile upon his fingers' ends, I knew there was but one way; for his nose was as sharp as a pen, and 'a babbled of green fields...So 'a bade me lay more clothes on his feet...just between twelve and one, e'en at turning o' the tide...'a babbled of green fields...'

Penworth ceased talking abruptly.

'You weren't listening,' he said; but his smile smoothed the abruptness of the words.

'Yes, sir—oh, yes, I was listening,' Charles said, feeling his face become hot. 'But that play too...it...'

'...kinda gets yer, eh? As your friends outside would say.'

As he said this Penworth quite carelessly put out his hand and gripped Charles's leg firmly above the knee. His palm was warm but dry; Charles hardly noticed it in his relief at not being thought rude. The gentle fingers slid slowly upwards under the short trouser leg; they touched Charles like moths, in sensitive places, for hardly a second, and then as slowly slid down again. Penworth had not spoken; he was looking into Charles's eyes, and smiling. His smile was in his eyes, too, as though turned inward to deride himself. He withdrew his hand and let it fall upon his knee.

For a moment the silence was hot and intense. Then

Penworth stretched his arms up, and pulled his head back, yawning so that the skin creased down his flat, healthy cheeks. He still looked at Charles, sideways, and raised one eyebrow as though he would have said, 'Well, what fools all of us are'. Charles laughed. He had already forgotten the caressive touch, which had seemed almost as dispassionate as the touch of his own hand upon a sheet of paper.

'It makes one wish to live like some rich Greek of centuries ago,' Penworth said, when his yawn was ended in a gasp of breath. 'This climate of yours, I mean. To bathe and hunt and go to the games, and in the evening walk about in public places, and converse like men. That was the life. But different ages, different conventions. Different moralities.' And he added darkly, 'Intelligent men must work like any slaves, with starved souls'.

He stood up, sighing. 'I suppose you don't trouble about what I mean. Why should you? Anyhow, we can't put the clock back as far as that, can we?'

'It's a pity we can't,' Charles said, in sudden enthusiasm. 'It's a pity—yes, it is a pity. Did they have boarding schools, sir?'

Penworth laughed, a barking, Alma-Mater, wit-appreciating laugh.

'Well—not of this sort. Why, don't you like it here?'

'No. At least, not very much, sir. I do like it when you talk to me like this, though. It makes me alive again.' He realized as he spoke that Penworth had been speaking to him as though to an equal; and, perhaps for that, he felt in some way an equal. In what way that was, he did not understand. Well, he thought, it will not last. To-morrow morning I shall have to pretend that I don't know him any better than anyone else does.

But he was wonderfully heartened by such kind friendship, which was not feigned, as he knew very surely, and clearly hid no intention of doing him bodily insult.

Penworth put an arm round his shoulders and rocked him gently to and fro.

'Like it, do you?' he said quietly.

Charles felt tears suddenly burn his eyelids, and knew his face was flushing, as it did in any strong emotion.

'Yes, sir.'

Penworth looked for what seemed a long time into his eyes, with a steady, searching gaze, holding him closely with one arm round his shoulders. The pupils of his eyes were dilated darkly, as they might be in the passion of rage, or fear.

He pulled himself away miserably. A moment later Penworth had gone. There were sounds of people coming up the other stairway. He could hear the light tenor tones of the Master with the sculpted features and carven eyelids, making some small and very quaint remark. He went to the stair. Penworth was gone.

The feeling of tears was gone also. It would be good to go out through the heat of day, to have tea with Mr. Jones, now, in a place that looked like a home.

Charles's knowledge of world-creation had come to him from hearing read aloud parts of the Old Testament, which taught him in untroubling words that God had made the world in six days, and in the seventh had taken his ease in the front garden of His own creating; so that Charles imagined God as a full-bearded and venerable patriarch, and had never voluntarily approached the problem of creation to resolve it for himself. His thought was still largely shaped in immature and incoherent imagery; he knew, and was learning more widely, what things were pleasant and what were not; and the pleasant and unpleasant were gradually extending the scale of their degrees into subtlety and complexity, as he learned the positive and negative of life. As yet he was perhaps only looking through the spacious doorways of that real world where thought, conscious and deliberate and urgently objective, is exercised at large. The problem of God and of the world troubled him not, though its imagery was rich and pleasing.

If his knowledge of world-creation was mistaken but conscious, his understanding of that act of man-creation wherein lies our destiny was neither conscious nor existent at all. He supposed that man was an animal and did as they do, if he thought about it at all. His idea here was barren of all imagery and without warmth; he had watched creatures of the fields making sport in the gusty wind and sunshine of the brief spring, and understood that they did as they were supposed to do, and that it was good that they should. Once, when he was a few years younger, an older cousin, whom he seldom saw, one day watched a bull and a cow together in one of the fields near home, and, as he smacked his lips with all the appreciation of an enthusiastic connoisseur, he told Charles that so it was men and women behaved. To Charles at eleven years of age this was so obviously a fantastic fiction, and an unpleasant clumsy idea too, that he knew he was being deliberately lied to, and dismissed the whole thing from his mind with the thought that Dick, his cousin, was far from being grown-up yet, and therefore not likely to know. But as he himself grew older he understood that there must be some sort of physical agreement between all male and female creatures, including humans; but of what kind it was he still had no knowledge; so that his idea of love's physical desire and imperative intercourse was without an image, though love itself, as an extraordinary passion, he admitted and, in some Ariel-like, heavenly way, understood. From love of food he himself had progressed to love of colour; from that love to a joy in colour and form, and so to a love of life itself as it evidenced itself in colour and form. If, therefore, he should meet some girl who in colour and form mirrored the evidence of what he loved it might be supposed that he would love the reflection.

But as yet he knew nothing of this.

However, during that hot summer, and more noticeably since he had lived among boys and listened to the manly and experienced images in their talk, he was frequently aware at the back of his mind of a tightness in his own loins and a warmth there, as though some hot flower were about to break from the green bud, or some ripening fruit to burst and scatter rich juices through his whole body. Had this already happened and been assimilated into his widening self-consciousness before he came to the School, he might have made easier and happier progress through his first terms there; in the haunts of his untroubled solitude he might have explored his mind and body freely, secure and timeless.

His misfortune was to make the greatest of all discoveries, to become aware of his own manhood, in the School itself; and sleep, that had been his refuge and innocence, was now his concern, and for a long time haunted and troubled him. From those deepest depths some mysterious succuba flung him face-upwards into a dark and bewildered consciousness, and hot night bore down on him. The seconds-old memory of dreamed conflicting forms stretched repetitively in a chaotic perspective, confounding him; but in a while he fell asleep again, now tired and without thought beyond the innocent conviction that he had passed through a unique moment in that still dormitory. He may have been right.

So it came about that he took home with him a warm and lively secret, as well as a complete edition of the Shakespearian plays; two of the greatest discoveries of his life, happily made, and in his mind to be contemplated as one would contemplate the vast shores of a land unknown to the world, with wonder and longing. The Shakespeare he bought in town, during the time between his arrival from the School and the departure of the south-bound train in the late afternoon. The city was in a gloom of heat that broke in thunder and lightning, with a few wrung drops of rain falling like sweat from the straining sky. In honour of some occasion, flags were showing from the Post Office when he passed it after leaving the smoky darkness of the station; they hung lifeless, sultry flames of colour against its dusty stone, stirred now and then by gusts of wind from the north-east. In the dark unnatural glare of the afternoon, people's faces were green-white when they turned upwards

85

to the sky as though in the fear of superstition; after the thunderstorm the air was still, and heavy traffic rumbled like the minor tone of drums, ominous and incessant.

Charles found his way after a time to the shop where some of his books had been bought. Here he was able to get the Shakespeare, complete in one volume of frail-looking India paper with red-cloth boards, for what seemed to him a small price. There was enough money left to make him consider what he might buy for his mother. Books were all about him, and in a confusion of titles he tried to think what she would like; she read many things, but he could not remember her choice nor decide upon her taste. Above a card printed THE LATEST FICTION spread long lines of bright-coloured volumes. He knew none of the authors' names; but after a great deal of hesitation he chose one of those, glad to be able to leave the shop at last and get the dazzling madness of dust-jackets out of his sight.

It was nearly time to catch his train. He walked back to the station as quickly as was possible in those crowded streets. The thunderstorm seemed to have increased the heat; his collar was sticky and perspiration made his shirt cling to his ribs. He thought how good it would be to get home again, after such noise and turmoil, after all those weeks; and his heart beat heavily and quick, as it had been beating since the beginning of the last morning class before that rowdy dinner in Hall. All that seemed very far away from him; yet it was with him, having already made him part of it; when he walked in the streets the School's badge on his hat and his grey coat pocket marked him out, labelled him and gave him, in the bright eyes of every schoolgirl, a degree and a background.

He found that he, too, was looking out for that badge. Several times boys he knew had passed him; once or twice hats were raised, as was proper in women's company, but they seemed not to look at him as they did it, and he supposed they must have seen him first. Once three merry-looking lads, one of whom was Saunders, called out to him as they swung past, upright, manly, busy giving the School's good name a polish up in the public memory. 'Hullo, Foxy!' He turned his head to answer, but they were gone among the crowd.

At the station there was much bustling about and shouting. He redeemed his suitcase and ran along a platform. That might have been the train. He asked a porter.

'Over the bridge, son—number six and you'll need to hurry.'

Charles thanked him breathlessly over his shoulder as he ran up the stairs. There it was. The rear end of a carriage was opposite him, and he climbed aboard. Along the corridor there was someone in each compartment; he hesitated, and hesitated again, and finally went into one. A corner seat welcomed him, and as he sat still, breathing quickly from so much haste and excitement, the rare smell of leather, smoke, burnt coal and a general humanity hung all about him. He began to feel calmer. When the train pulled out, gathering speed securely, he undid with hasty fingers the string of his parcel, and took up the book, thinking that never in his life had he known such a moment of rare happiness. Those covers were of red imitation leather; when it was stiffly open the dry, enchanting new-book smell came out from the leaves and conquered the hot odour of the carriage itself in his nostrils. Incredibly free and secure in that little space, he went through the mental actions of reading the words, but was not in them, and for the time they fell dead in his mind. His joy was to be among strangers who neither knew nor cared for him; the few other boys on the train, busy smoking cigarettes in a carriage of their own up near the engine, would not trouble him. These next few days were his; no one was to rob him of them. His heart grew big at the thought, and at the thought of how few they were.

An hour passed. Charles, with the carriage now to himself, continually interrupted his mechanical reading to look out beyond the spinning foreground to the hills in the distance. The line was coming nearer to them; they changed from pale blue to grey, from grey to dull green. Far off, their flanks burned grey and russet in the red evening sun. Now and then he could see the sharp, cool flash of water in the shadow of a valley. As time passed they became blue again, and appeared very remote and lonely in the level western light. Held in the opposite windows, the sun was already running along behind the tree trunks, keeping pace inexorably with the train. There was no cloud now; the heat was easing, but at every stop the merciless *obbligato* of the cicadas, rising clamorously as sunset drew down, made the sudden human voices in that stillness seem false and unreal.

There was a change of train. He found himself in an uncomfortable little box of a carriage, full of the blood-red dregs of sunset light. Another boy followed him in; that was Forrester, whose large and humble eyes reminded Charles of one of the cows that were even then being driven along a dusty road past the station, on their way out from the evening milking.

'Do you mind much, me getting in?' Forrester asked, and Charles felt awkward as he said of course he did not. He stared at the neat badge on pocket and hat-band, and remembered that he too was wearing it.

'I was up in another carriage,' Forrester said. His thick, plump face was red and marked.

'Oh. Did they give you a good time?'

'They chucked me round a bit when I said I didn't smoke. I didn't want to smoke, and they tried to make me; and other things too...you know.'

'You were a fool to let them,' Charles said, surprised at his own unconcern. Forrester had made his explanation in a voice which suggested pride as well as a vaccine humility. Charles looked at him and said nothing more. Unknown to him, that same sort of treatment had already made him resent any mention of it by another. He would not speak of it himself. To have done that would have been to admit his own dislike and fear, which he intended never to do. It was as though speaking of it, putting it into words, gave it a power over him.

Forrester talked on, rather more freely now that they had left the station. Looking at him, Charles remembered to have heard him crying in his bed at night, once, during the first week of term. That again he mistrusted, feeling at the same time guilty for not being spontaneously sorry for him. Why should the fellow cry? What did he know of unhappiness? He was a flabby sort, with round cheeks and round red lips; one who fed himself well, Charles knew; a born butt for the more active minds and hands of others. Friendliness towards him made him become alarmingly familiar; Charles, having once tried friendship, had realized his mistake, which shocked him more than his immediate protective aloofness had hurt Forrester. Forrester was always the same.

The train rattled on, and the sun set in a final burst of heatless ruddy light. Above the orange radiance of the horizon, the sky was a colour of lemons, paling upwards through faint green to blue. The infinite sadness of the bush country at evening came into the carriage like a sigh; silence swept in a wave over the world. At length even Forrester was quiet, contenting himself with a blind gaze out through the open window, which let in a stream of air whose speed gave it the illusion of coolness. Against that western colour all the trees were as charred as though its fire had consumed them. Crickets took up the cicadas' song in a melancholy key that emphasized the vast silence of stopping-places where milk-cans rattled and beside the carriage could be heard the steady rip-rip of browsing beasts; in the east, where the sympathetic light was dying slowly above the line of purple hills, Charles saw the first stars come out.

Suddenly they were in country that he knew. He looked closely. That field, with the trees whose dark evening outlines were as familiar and lovely to him as faces, was five miles from home, outside his mother's lands. The station, then, was six miles farther on. In a quarter of an hour...

He hardly knew how to pass those minutes; his hands felt cold. Forrester began to talk again. He was going right through. Charles became nervously active.

'I get down at the next station,' he said.

'It's an awfully long journey,' Forrester grumbled. 'Will I be able to get something to eat here?'

'Refreshment rooms. What time do you get in?'

'Not till ten o'clock.'

Charles was not listening. Far off across a field he could see a light where no light should be. That was what they called the new farm, where no one had lived for some years. Then he remembered. He recognized its place, and looked to the north. Yes, there were the lights of the big farm; above them set in thick blackness the sky was shell-pale; that lemon-coloured sea of light paled as he looked, and everything began to fade under his eyes.

All the time, looking out till his eyes ached in their sockets, he was building up the country they passed through. On either side of the line it was as familiar and as strange to him as the face of a lover; in the depth of dusk he visualized it as though he were at that moment walking in it and could smell the perfume of it. The low starry lights at the foot of the west had vanished; even as he peered out, the train swung round a bend towards the east, and ran into the gold lights of the station, its brakes grinding. Up in front a valve was opened, and the roar of escaping steam was being punctuated by the clanging of the bell in the refreshment rooms opposite his window. A guard passed along swinging a lantern in the patches of dusk between the lights, calling out the name of the station in cheerful tones that rose and fell above the bell, the slowing hiss of steam, and a final clamour of voices.

The morning after this momentous return, Charles was abroad at dawn. There was a dew—the first dew of early April, the first he had seen since the last spring blossomed passionately into summer. He went down to the river to bathe, alone with the birds that thronged the shadowless light before the coming of the sun. From the cool solitude of the farther bank he saw the tree-tops above him burn red and brighten into green in light that sank down from the middle sky, as the sun rose from the eastern hills. A perfect stillness held him; against the brown and green of the shadowed bank he shone whitely, perched on his log as motionless as a heron. Past his eastward-looking eyes a kingfisher flashed, as blue as noon; upstream it stopped, and suddenly was back, motionless on a low branch a few feet away. He thought he knew it, as he knew every scar and turn of its dead branch. It eyed him speculatively but with great alertness over its long beak, reminding him of Mr. Jolly. His merry laughter vanished the bird to reaches untroubled by such sounds.

He dropped back into the water and swam lazily across. It seemed to him that he must know every yellow stem and green blade of these grasses that overhung the lower platform and spread back from the edge in a close carpet of green which the eternal passing of the water kept fresh. He could see no current; to look down was to gaze into a green mirror that showed him his own pale face framed in the paler sky behind it; he had to force his eyes to peer through to the glimmering floor beneath, touched by the fairy shadows of little fish questing, their heads for ever upstream. The level of this water had sunk since he was last there; it was far down the legs of the higher platform where the spring-board of his own making swung out in space, reflected exactly, twelve feet beneath. Dryness had crusted the slime on the wood of the posts, and it was flaked and ready to crumble at a touch.

When he had put on his clothes he climbed the steps and hung the towel on a line to dry before going about the orchard and the gardens. Even at that hour the air was too still, and threatened him when he listened. Except where it lay in the long shadows, the dew had already gone; with the rising warmth a haze was forming in mid-heaven. He wandered, finding that nothing had been changed except his own regard, which was so keen now. There were still grapes hanging in shadow among the leaves of the vine-trellises, but a sweet, faint odour of must showed that the recent rain had already begun to make wine of them where they hung. On the slope of the orchard the earth was softening under-foot; against its red face the last leaves of peach and plum and apple lay yellow. The whole air was heavy with late ripeness and clung in his throat; bees, come out at the first light, took sugar from rotting fruit and the rare flowers. They grumbled and affected surprise among the grapes, where the small birds outdid them and feasted full, drowsing in the leaves, drunk with autumnal nectar, and opening suddenly their wide bright eyes, ready to feast again.

Charles was drunk like the birds, but with the realization that all this that seemed to him so beautiful was not, after all, part of a dream he had made to console loneliness. When he looked on the reality of all his years, it was that other life which seemed now like a dream making more vivid this light. He roamed about, whispering words to himself, whispering to his own ears things he could not have said aloud. On his knees upon the warm soil faintly steaming, he peered close, and saw the dagger-points of the first new green coming through—tiny pale surfaces, leaves almost invisible stretched to catch air and light, gasping joyously at the ultimate release from the buried seed. A week of dryness would wither them to death; but in this morning light, hazy with the evaporating dew, they drank in life like giants. Consciousness was coming back to the soil after the stunned pause of summer.

Half an hour after sunrise the sky was drifted over with a tissue of haze that deadened light and dulled the edges of the shadows. It grew hot very quickly, and the air stirred with unease. At breakfast, which they took on the low veranda, curtained in by a cascade of dark creeper shot with holes of light and patched with pale flowers, Charles asked about the mushrooms.

'I don't know,' his mother said. 'I meant to ask Mr. O'Neill about them. But I have an idea they don't care for them.'

Charles said he would walk out to the Far Field before lunch. This was at the farthest corner of his mother's own property, which O'Neill, an Irishman of good family with some means of his own, rented from her and worked with his numerous sons, whom he wished to bring up in the land-owning tradition to which, at home, he himself

94

had always aspired. This farm property was set about four-square to the compass; it extended seven miles or more from north to south, and in part six and in part ten from east to west, stopping a couple of miles short of the hills at its farthest eastern boundary. In the angle formed by the abrupt extension from a six-mile to a ten-mile boundary lay the most part of a small property which for years had not been worked. Mrs. Fox had suggested to O'Neill that they might share in the purchase of this outlying farm, and after a noisy council in conclave with 'the boys' he agreed, seeing here no doubt the beginning of his full ownership of the whole property, if the years brought him luck. He was noisy, cheerful and superstitious, with a bad head for whisky but a good heart and enormous hands. It pleased him, who was by nature untidy, that the boundaries of the small new property were clean and made the whole estate compact by its inclusion. This had occurred in the previous year, and the joint owners, being unwilling to take over the working of it at that time, let it to some man whom Charles did not know. The lights he had seen from the train last night shone in the windows of this new farm, and calmly disagreed with his memory of its loneliness.

He walked out over ploughed ground where the plovers were already crying, with their lost sounds of lamentation. As he walked he noticed how clouds had come into the sky, slowly putting out the sun. The air quivered still with the trembling uncertainty heralding rain; a cold wind from the south rose and blew in gusts that searched him to the skin; but when he looked up towards the dazzling dullness overhead, he observed how the surface of cloud closing him in to earth was moving steadily south-east in a high cross-wind that would probably bring rain before night.

It was strange, he thought, how completely that bright dawn could be dispersed. He walked steadily on, over dried clover now, feeling melancholy with the day. The problem of self came on him again, fed and active upon his own melancholy, and he pondered on the surprise of his body's growth and potency. The brilliance of his own dawn had gone like the day's, clouded over by a high wind from the north-west and distressed by a questing breeze of doubt; but he, looking on himself from the too-close standing of immediate experience and with youth's impatient, humourless eye, did not see it so, for the unquestioning true-belief was gone with childhood's asceticism, and he had no simple perspective of faith and innocence now.

There was more emotion than thought in his consciousness as he walked across the pastures. He believed it was the day's sudden change that dulled his mind; he felt his flesh aching as though for rain; and rain would come.

In the Far Field, when he was there, his mood changed. The dead trees stood up stark against the windy sky; time and weather and the passage of fire had worn them down to solid masses undisturbed by branch or twig; that green grass that never seems to want life by dead trees, but thrives on the death it comforts, was thick round the buttresses of the scarred black trunks. Near the farthest fence he found what he was seeking; as he had imagined them, they broke through the softening crust of bare patches, shining like moons against the dark earth. A bold, unnatural excitement swelled in him as he gazed at the smooth white crowns breaking up through the moist virginity of the soil. He put down his basket, and made a wide cast, walking very quickly, to find any other beds that might be there. He was elated, but with something greater than the discovery. It was the trembling elation of secrecy, such as a lover knows when he explores his beloved's body in darkness and feels, in a blind joy, that he will explore the soul of life itself. But if he will, it is not for him then to know it, for his understanding's farthest boundaries are dictated by the assurance of the flesh.

Nor did Charles know, nor trouble to know, the source of his own surgence of emotion. He took in with his cast the soil where there would be patches, found two more and a linking scatter like a milky way tumbling across the grass, and returned to where his basket was. The sky, growing darker, locked him in, in that wild place where the greatest sound was the warlike beating of his heart in all space. He danced on the earth, drumming it with his feet; he fell down and lay spread out on the grass, on his face and on his back, laughing at the eternity of wind and sky. In the distance, above a grove of trees some way to the south, he could hear the birds; when he turned his head, there they were, flung into the sky, flung flat against the rising wind that turned leaves whitely. Their long cries, '*Ah! Ah!*' seemed to triumph, as though they had foretold the breaking of a hard summer.

'Rain,' he said aloud. 'They want rain, and so do I. I want it, I want it. Please, God, send some rain.'

He laughed at his own unthinking prayer, and believed he could feel an answer to it in the wind that was running along the grass, blowing over him where he lay. Peace and his isolation intoxicated him; there was no one else in the world, if the cries of the birds and the secret whisper of the wind in his ears were to be believed. The yes and no of life had mercifully been lifted from him for an hour under a darkening sky. The rise on whose bald eternal crown he lay offered him up like a living sacrifice.

In this ecstatic surrender of himself to all that was good in life, he remained for some minutes without moving, his head turned to one side as though some vision had been too great for him; and the wind played with his curling hair like a woman. That auburn fire that matched the greenish light of his eyes was clearly to be seen in it now, when he moved; in that dark gloom of the sun behind cloud his colour was pale, almost white, and the full, determined yet too sensitive line of nose and lip had their own promise of sorrows and difficulties to come, things of which no one reads in the expurgated textbook of a contented childhood.

In a while he left his contemplation of dreaming distances, and rose with some effort from the ground, as though he were leaving his strength like a garment there. A little way off, the mushrooms glimmered. He did not care so much now. It had been good to lie down and think of all the happy parts of life, such as the secret beauty and chance of dreams. But since they were there, waiting, he might as well gather them.

This he went about to do now, and was in the midst of it, bending to take them up with his knife in a renewed admiration of the deli-centripetal pink of their undersides, when the first heavy drops of rain were flung to earth round him. Instinctively he turned south and was in a moment running as hard as he was able towards the grove of trees which lay dark and solid some way off. That ground had no traps for his feet; he knew the cavities, concealed in the greenest grass, where trees had once been rooted, and the dry sandy course of a stream that rushed that way in winter and before the end of spring was gone again. He leapt from one low lip to the other, laughing aloud as he heard his mother's cool voice greeting him on his return: 'There, son, I told you to take a coat. Now you'll be wet through, child...' and fading calmly away with the familiar words, 'you should do as I tell you'.

Like a fallen curtain, low branches and brown trunks closed after him as he thrust through. They were there for shelter for cattle from summer sun and the boisterous westerly gales of winter, and the ground sloped down to the east, so that to one facing west a skyline cut across the silhouettes of trunks and branches high up. This was a dry and lonely place, with the whistle and sigh of the wind in the dark hill of pine needles all round, sounding like an old man falling into a doze, with a mute, restless air of half-sleep.

The weather was in the south, and only on his side of the grove did the trunks and branches give protection. Looking out from his shelter, rubbing his hands together absent-mindedly as though he had made some good bargain with himself or life, Charles recalled how he had bathed in a blaze of young colour not many hours before, when the day promised to be hot and still. All the bees would be gone from those dark clusters of grapes whose excess of ripeness brewed ambrosia for them; the mirror of the river would tremble in a sheet of grey, dull uneasiness, and the birds, caught in the deep of the morning siesta, would be refuged among the rustling leaves. He watched sheets of fine rain drifting past before his eyes in a long, slow rhythm almost hypnotic to a fixed gaze, closing him in with solitude more surely than stone walls.

To his surprise he realized that there was someone else under the trees with him. There was no solitude. He could hear movements on the crumbling leaves of the floor within the encircling pines. It was dark under the trees, and heavy drops had begun to fall from the branches; but, though from instinct and a constant habit he did not suddenly turn to confront the sound, he knew there was someone there, walking on the leaves like rain.

It was a girl, a stranger. She had evidently not seen him for she was stooping to pull up clothes that had slipped as she ran, and he could see her chest heaving when she straightened herself up again. Her legs were bare, and she had no shoes on; he could see the insteps of her feet in the leaves that sank beneath her. That was why she had been so quiet. When she bent down two plaits of hair, as thick as ropes but softly alive, slid over her shoulders and hung each side of her face which he could not clearly see. His breath was coming more comfortably; he turned himself round, and sat down quietly by his tree trunk to watch, aware of no privacy save his own. It was a wonder who it could be. No one ever came to these far pastures, except sometimes the O'Neills, noisy with shouts and the bark of dogs, to put sheep on, or look at the fences; no one strange ever came. Charles was sorry and at first angered to see a stranger there; but he was interested in this girl because she did not know he was there; and when she moved it gave him pleasure to watch. He sat as still as a rabbit in his squat, not realizing that it might have been kinder to show himself. To him sitting there, the mystery of a human being, particularly a woman, who is unconscious of any watching eyes and has abandoned all protective postures, came as unexpectedly and enchantingly as the telling of some romantic secret.

She was wiping the rain from her pale forehead with the palm of one hand; and when she had done this she dried her hands on the hem of her skirt, which was green and came not below her knees. Charles moved his head and saw her face under the low branches stretched like old men's arms between them. It was a young girl's face, pale, clear-coloured and round; but, above all, expressionless in its unawareness of any regard. To him it did not live as much as those busy hands and white knees lived, clearly in the dimness. He lay low, with one shoulder against the rough tree.

The wind sighed in the darkness of the myriad needles above him. If he had been unconcerned he would have made a fire, just for the pleasure of the flames licking and whispering. His blue cotton shirt was hardly wet, except along the shoulders. He ran his hands over each shoulder and round at the back, feeling the warm dampness. When he looked up his returning gaze came full into the girl's eyes.

She was very white, and her mouth was half-open, as though in a will to speak but without breath. Charles felt a tremor of fear himself, for he did not realize that it was he who frightened her.

'What are you looking at?' he asked nervously, at last; and the sighing silence, which had strained to be broken, turned its face away, reassured by his voice.

She too was reassured, it seemed. With an uncertain smile not yet lighting the dark pupils of her eyes there came a rush of colour flying delicately back into her white face.

'I was looking at you. I didn't know there was anybody there. I'm afraid I—I was frightened.'

In an hysteria of growing relief, she laughed, and the silence paused to listen.

Hearing the low laughter catch in her throat, he said sharply, 'I thought something else had frightened you. You needn't be frightened of me.'

'Of course not.' He could see she was, and it irritated him. They were speaking with the conscious seriousness of children, like diplomats meeting upon some matter of tremendous issue.

'I didn't know there was anybody here,' the girl said again.

Charles said: 'I heard you come in.'

The smile had reached her eyes. She put one hand to her breast.

'My heart's beating like mad.'

'You were running from the rain,' Charles explained. 'You're on the open side over there. Under this tree it's dry.'

She stooped to pick up a box she had put on the floor; and once more he saw the heavy plaits of hair slide over her shoulders and hang beside her face. Then she came across the leaves, bending low to pass under the branches.

'Your top part is pretty wet,' he said.

She shivered a little. Watching her hands touch the thin blouse, he saw that they trembled.

'I tell you what,' he said, standing up. 'I'll make a fire and you can get dry.'

'Oh no,' she exclaimed, and turned quickly towards him. 'This belongs to someone, this place. You oughtn't to do that.'

'It's ours,' Charles cried, laughing with surprise. 'It belongs to my mother. Anyhow, you couldn't see a dry-wood fire on a day like this. The smoke gets lost in the rain.'

He went about, gathering pine branches. Heavy drops fell round him from the leaves; the rain was drifting on the wind like mist, fine and steady. Higher up the slope there was gloom under the massed branches and among the trunks.

When he came back, dragging long light branches with both hands, she was still standing where he had left her, watching him.

'I suppose you think I shouldn't be here, then,' she said.

'No,' he said, 'it doesn't matter. Wait till I get this going.' In a couple of minutes flames shot up yellow among white smoke from the pile of pine needles and broken twigs. He scraped the ground clear all round.

'I was hoping to find mushrooms,' she said, still watching him. His silence seemed to embarrass her.

'Where are you from?' he asked later, when the blaze was merry and had cast off its sheathing smoke.

'Over there at the farm.' She turned her face towards what they called the new farm. Charles, kneeling by the fire, looked closely at her now.

103

'Oh,' he said slowly. 'I didn't know there was anyone young there.'

'I don't live there; it's my uncle and aunt; they live there. I just came for Easter.'

'I'm home for Easter, too.' He was filled with great enthusiasm, all of a sudden. 'Isn't it lovely. Isn't it lovely being away from School, out here where there's nobody at all.'

'I don't mind school,' she said. 'I go to a convent, you see.'

'Do you live there?'

'No, at home with my sister.'

'Well—oh; that must make a difference.'

She said nothing.

'You sit down by this now,' he told her, 'and get dry. That blouse is pretty wet, isn't it? Why don't you take it off, and I'll get you a stick to dry it on.'

He jumped up and went to get a straight piece of stick. When he returned to the fire she was sitting with her back firmly against the tree.

'You haven't taken it off,' he said. 'And that tree will make you wetter still. Look, there's water going down the trunk.'

She looked up at him slowly under her eyelids.

'Why do you want me to take it off? I can't, I've—I haven't got enough on underneath.'

'I don't want you to take it off,' he said. 'It's not me who'll get a cold.'

'Well,' she said, 'I don't think I can.' She looked frightened and defiant, as though she had been trapped into some admission she had not meant to make.

'Well, move away from that trunk then, or you'll get a wet tail as well. I only made the fire so that you could get dry.'

'Thank you,' she said vaguely. With her back to the fire and him she appeared to think for a while; Charles looked at the whiteness of her neck, like pearl, up near the long parting in the hair. Her shoulders bent forward stretched the stuff of the blouse against the flames, and the light played upon her. Only a crackle and whisper of dry wood burning broke the silence of the wind up above them.

Charles's mood of joyous content had gone. Now that the fire was made and there was nothing more to do, he felt gloomy within him, and heartily wished he were alone there. Rain was still drifting past, in long falling cadences he could see the sky was set. It might not stop for an hour. The time, he thought, would be late after eleven, and he was feeling hungry. It would have been better if he had brought food; he could have stayed here all day out of the rain and wind. And a book; how well that Shakespeare would have sounded, read aloud to such a loving silence as this.

'What is your name?' he asked.

'Margaret,' she said without turning round. Aware of a strange tone in her voice, he looked suspiciously at her back. She was laughing. He became tense; his voice was difficult in the moving silence.

'What are you laughing at?'

She laughed aloud now, low and helplessly.

'I'm not. I was just thinking—how funny to be here like this.'

'I don't think it's funny,' he said coldly.

'Well—I wonder what they'd say at the convent? We're not supposed to…'

'I don't think that's funny either,' Charles said loudly.

She began to laugh again. He understood that it was hardly laughter at all; it was a curious stretched sound, too humourless to suggest mirth. It shocked him into speech.

'What's the matter?' he said. 'I didn't mean to be angry. I'm sorry. What's the matter?'

There were tears on her cheeks. Charles, completely bewildered, stood up and at once sat down again, because he did not know of anything he could do that words would not do more safely.

'It's only—that I got a fright—when I saw you first,' she said brokenly, her eyes clinging to his look. 'I couldn't help it. The silence and everything—and then—you.'

'I know,' he said to soothe her, for he did not want to look at her tears. 'It's always like that unless you're used to it.' He cocked his head on one side, meditatively.

'I've heard of men going mad in this country. Mad, mind you, in those hills, with trains going past every day. If they live up there alone—they used to when people thought there was gold—they come down specially to watch the evening train going in.'

The thought had an unexplored darkness for him.

'It makes me shiver,' she said. 'I can understand.'

'It's terrible,' he declared emphatically. 'Even here, away from the hills, you can feel it sometimes. I know; I've been up there in the evening after sunset. But it wouldn't get me into that state, I'm sure. But you ought to see it,' he cried, after thinking a moment. 'All the shadows disappear when the sun's gone. Not a shadow. Just distance.'

He stopped abruptly, aware that the words had burst loudly from his lips.

'Don't shout,' she said.

'I'm used to being alone,' he said more quietly. 'No one will hear. But you ought to see it. You ought to be there alone. It's like magic. You never forget it. Those hills...'

After a time she said, 'It would frighten me. I should be frightened.'

'But that's just it,' he said. 'There's nothing—nothing at all. Not a thing. Only the sound of a waterfall that you can't see.'

'That's just it,' she repeated. 'You wouldn't know, when there was absolutely nothing. Would you?'

He pondered in an abstraction of thought.

'I suppose it's that that used to drive those men silly when they lived there alone. I can't see how, though. It's wonderful. I'm frightened of people sometimes, but never of things...like that.'

The warmth of the scented fire had dried the tears and brought a flush of colour into her delicate cheeks. She was leaning forward, looking closely on him; unexpectedly he saw the serene secrecy of her white breasts revealed unawares, and a flush came into his own face, and his tongue, ready to speak, was stilled. She seemed not to notice; she leaned forward in a pose of thought and unconscious beauty, and it was plain that, whatever her age might be, in her body she was already a woman and sensitively awake.

He, for his part, having looked away from what he had seen, came to think of his own words with surprise. 'Even here, away from the hills, you can feel it.' The plough made no difference—how had he happened to say things he had not known he knew? The words were forced out of his mouth, as though a weight had crushed him; they were certainly his own words, though he could not find their source in his mind.

'Margaret,' he said. 'That's a good name. If you don't change it to silly nonsense like Maggie.'

'I hate that. And even Meg I don't like. That's what they call me. The Sisters call me Margaret.'

'Are you a Roman Catholic?' he asked curiously.

With great and innocent scorn she said she was not.

'No,' he continued, 'otherwise you'd be at a Mass now. My mother has gone to a service. I wouldn't go; it's better to be out here than in a church listening to what you can't understand.'

'Why do you speak like that so often?' she asked him. 'As though you were laying down the law.'

He did not know what she meant, and was confounded by being made to consider his own voice and manner. He had had no dealings with girls and women, except in the laconic relationships within his own home.

'I didn't mean—that way,' she said gently. 'I mean, why do you?'

'I don't know,' he said on a falling tone. 'I'm not used to talking to anybody. I don't even know anybody to talk to. I like being by myself.'

The silence cowered over the fire with them. Wind

and rain went by together, weeping in a key beyond passion.

'Is it me you mind?' she asked at length, her voice sounding to his ears as though drenched with the rain.

'No, of course not.'

'Because I can always go. It's your own place.'

'You'll do nothing of the kind,' he said in a loud voice, and repeated it more quietly. 'You'll do nothing of the kind. You're wet as it is. Do you want to get a chill and die?'

'I wouldn't mind.'

He perceived no mischief in that sober admission. It seemed a very sad thing to say, sadder than the day, sadder than the silence. He almost pleaded:

'Don't say that. You don't want to die. How can you say it? I love being alive.'

The School and its insinuating urge to unhappiness might never have touched his mind. He forgot all that, as though within a few days he would not be back there, turned inside out with miserable sickness for this freedom, as severely as he had been at first. His eyes were bright with tears in his excitement. The girl was looking steadily at him again, and, for the sake of doing something positive, he put more sticks on the fire. They cracked cheerfully as they caught.

'You talk very strangely,' she said. 'I've never known a boy to talk like that.'

The thought of being compared in her mind with other boys confounded him again. She was, he thought, the sort of fair and quiet creature who would know and admire boys like Bourke, or Saunders, or Wilson junior,

109

that sharp-voiced, blue-eyed bully; good sporting fellows, all of them, with mouths already hardening into insensitiveness towards life's better passions.

'Do you know many, then?' he asked cautiously.

She shook her head. 'Only friends of the other girls. Lots of them have brothers. What's your school?'

He told her. To his surprise she laughed.

'They all say you'll never win anything; but I think it's nice, anyhow.'

'Who cares about winning things?' he demanded.

'I know. I don't care either,' she said. 'But boys should. I think I saw you on the train last night.'

'Yes,' he said. 'I was there.'

After that there was silence, while she looked low down under the branches to see if the rain were stopping. Charles watched her, disturbed at the talk of school and boys, but carefully seeing, with a sort of delight that he had never known before that moment, the happy movement that turned her face away, and threw into full view the side of her head, smooth and fair, the one long plait near him fallen and hanging on her knees, and the soft curve of breast and arm. She was very beautiful, he thought. She reminded him, with her effortless stillness, of a sunny day in the hollow valleys of those remote hills hidden now in rain. Such days were always waiting, still and golden but terribly alert, shining like a girl, but as watchful, and as full of disturbing secrecy.

He sank into a sort of dream. Above the dying rustle of the fire big drops and scatterings from the living leaves fell on the dead leaves of the floor, running about like little animals in the shadowless depths. He heard her sigh without impatience. In a while, listening beyond the slow beat of thought, he knew that the rain was going to stop. But the wind went on in the leaves.

Supporting himself valiantly with the iron staff of high and honourable intention, Charles returned to the School at the end of the holiday, and tried to forget the past few days.

Mawley was now in the same room with him, in the same class. Outside there was a red-barked tree whose amidships was framed in the brown-painted window-sashes on the left of the dais; suppurations of crusted and partly reabsorbed gum looked like great gouts of dried blood on that comely trunk, whose upper and lower ends could not be seen, where they mixed with the sky and the earth. That tree, which reminded them of those rich torsos exhumed from Mediterranean soil, deprived by time of the more meditative brutalities of earlier Christians, of all frangible extremities, was there to remind them also of what Mawley heard Penworth call 'the life beyond'. No one who remained sane in the midst of the excesses of their century could look at such a tree and not receive some benison from the high spirit of it. This tree of theirs, which Charles referred to as the wishing tree, because it made him wish himself away at home, grew in a sort of broken courtyard, squared on the hither side by their classroom wall, and yonder by laundries with staff quarters above them and articles of apparel hanging for ever in the windows. (And what a tragic Tantalus life, Mawley thought afterwards, those maids—if maids they were—must have had, living the year long among so many delicate little morsels of itching masculinity!) At this end of that court there was a sports changing-room, belonging to one of the Houses, thought-fully built up between the library windows and the light of day; and down there, at the far end, a line of lavatories soothed the troubled scholastic eye with their dark red and white and black paint.

It could not be described as a beautiful courtyard. Too many walls and windows reminded it that truth is not always beauty. But a carter's lane debouched gaily into it on the left, coming round the laundries in a rutted, undisciplined curve during its few moments of unobserved freedom; and beyond its edge, down the wild tangle of a stretch of slope, young Cape lilacs traced the sky and pointed out the whitest clouds, and in the spring, while their leaves were opening, themselves hung out cloudy sprays of those tiny purple and white stars that so enchant the air of warm spring afternoons. They could not see the lilacs from their seats in the classroom, nor the lavatories, nor the lusty carter's lane embracing the stout laundries like an arm. Their view, in secret moments of inattention or during the permissible pauses for meditation in English or Latin composition, was that sturdy section of red, blood-stained tree's body, and a miraculous depth of sky behind it. From this sky, all the year round, the light came into the room, and, like some wise friend from a class higher than their own, helped while it seemed to hinder their work. Even in dark afternoons of winter, there it was beyond the streaming window-panes, wrapped coldly in cloud through which it seemed still to thrust its blue shoulder.

After that first holiday, when he experienced the novelty of an honest scholar's return to his desk, there seemed to be a change in Charles. Any of them who noticed him at all were aware of it, and interpreted it in their own ways. He sat in the seat in front of Mawley, in that class, and for the rest of the year Mawley's most familiar sight was of his reddish, curly head bent low between his shoulders over the desk, and his right hand, white and bony about the knuckles, raised in mid-air without urgency whenever a question was asked. A graph of his progress in a stern-driven, difficult class might have been made from the increasing number of times his hand went up during the second half of his earliest term, and the first half of the winter term. At first his slim back and broad shoulders expressed all sorts of embarrassments and uncertainties; he had a way of turning his face to the grey wall and staring blankly at it, as though the wall itself had voiced the solemn questions he could not yet answer; or he would run his fingers through his hair, and, as though some spring in the brain had been released, up would go his hand, always without urgency. Others of them strained up, waving hands like flails, or floundered back; he moved slowly and with decision. This was some sign of the self-control which, in a few pathetic weeks of bullying and unkindness, he had been taught. Whatever might move bubbling beneath, his appearance remained defiantly calm. Penworth, himself frankly enthusiastic in certain scholastic pursuits, such as the sleuth-like tracking-down of an irregular verb's movements from infinitive to gerundive, was often thrown into an enchanting fury by the calm of Charles's pale face and hands.

113

'For heaven's sake, Fox,' he would snap, 'at least try to *look* as though you cared.'

Penworth's passions always seemed very innocent. Once, Charles having laughed loudly in sincere enjoyment of some sharp irrelevance, he offered to skin him alive and looked as though he meant it. Such scenes, however, came later, when both Masters and classes were wrought to a sad pitch of nerves by the looming examinations of November, and when the friendship between Penworth and Charles had reached a sad state too. During the first term humours and enthusiasms might be expressed freely, provided the expression were seemly and proper to the manners of the School.

The change in Charles appeared to have come about during the brief Easter holiday. On that cool and clouded Monday he drove with his mother into the village, and they heard a service in the small church planted dimly among great pines, with a scattering of headstones as grey as the sheep feeding among them. He looked with concealed eagerness at everyone in the church, at first, but later devoted himself as sincerely as might be to following the vagaries of the service. He and she left the church with the Canon, to whom she must speak of coming social affairs; they talked of some kind of fête, and he stood by, not listening much. When they drove away in the old phaeton (she would not part with it), there was no one in sight. As they went, the sun came out warmly among great steep masses of dazzling, icy cloud, and shone on the road, and touched off small explosions of light among the drenched leaves of the trees. It was very still, a clear autumn day after the sharp, repeated rain of the weekend. Distances across the shining fields were as clean as though seen through the wrong end of a telescope; the light wind of their passage brought tingling blood to his cheeks; he felt deeply at peace with the world, and put one hand on his mother's arm in a friendly way that surprised and pleased her, though she did not let it be seen. On the way they talked a little about the School, and she told him, for the first time, that the Headmaster had written very well of him and had explained the change in his form.

'Why didn't you tell me when I told you?' Charles asked; but he knew his mother, and when she said nothing he was not surprised. The even thud of hoofbeats on the soft surface, a faint creaking murmur of springs and harness, bore them along, escorting them in their own silence, which neither of them found further occasion to break.

So the holiday ended. On Wednesday he was back again, and life, spreading from that central point of refuge, the white bed in Dormitory B, like a spider web over the School, took on in certain ways a new purpose. But his secret fear, of bodily insult and physical pain, remained as it was in the beginning. His clear, watching eyes, now becoming almost hazel in colour as they darkened with young manhood, kept him aware of all rude intention. Boys are not reticent about their feelings towards one another. Their hatred is as thorough as is their admiration, and they show both with the complete and uncompromising frankness of pagan amorality. Only in the higher strata of the School's society, after boys were invested with prefecture, or otherwise made responsible and partly free in action, did a conscious sense of duty begin to grow like an invisible cataract over the feelings in their eyes. Among the younger ones, who made up the greater number, there was only a keen sense of being alive, of having some ineluctable way to a destination, towards which they must surge as ruthlessly as a mob of sheep, and with very little more deliberate intention.

In himself Charles was hardly aware of a change. His mind was now occupied in considering the tremendous distance that seemed to loom bottomless between a matter-of-fact first-year application to the execution of a schedule of work, and the hard driving toil of the higher class, made continually conscious of itself at work, and with its eyes repeatedly directed towards those ominous examinations. For to Charles, whose greatest schooling had hitherto occupied him never more than three or perhaps four hours in each day, in the governess's room at home, this leaping, urgent butterfly-hunt, for seven and eight hours daily, in pursuit of fluttering facts so many of which looked alike, was at first liable to have driven him to despair.

The Headmaster sent for him once, after two weeks in the Junior form. Charles, made bold by the fear of appearing unable, told him he was already feeling more confident, and would certainly go on with it.

'Never feel it's an impossibility,' the Headmaster said, 'to do a lot of work in a short time. I have an idea that in your own case it will suit your temperament, Fox.'

Charles thanked him, without properly understanding what that meant, and was told that he must consider himself free still to withdraw from his undertaking, and so was dismissed.

Walking away from the soft closure of that heavy door, Charles knew that he would not withdraw. Having tasted both the exhilarations and the despairs of driving his mind harder than it had ever been driven, he could not enjoy the thought of returning to a class of boys of whom many were younger than himself, where all that would be asked of him would be perhaps fifteen minutes of serious thought in every thirty passed in the classroom.

Also, in addition to the set hours of work by day and evening, with their new, unrelenting application, Penworth had offered to give him extra classes during the week, of Latin, and to assist him with the textbook part of English whenever he chose. When Charles told him that Greek was to be discontinued, because of so much essential work, he looked grave and said he was disappointed, and muttered about forcing young minds so that they missed half of what was good in life.

'Anyhow,' he said, 'if you get through all right—and there's no earthly reason why you shouldn't—you can always pick it up again next year. Next year, of course, won't be so hard on you...' And when Charles mentioned the fear he felt about the two mathematics, he consoled him there also.

'You only need a bare pass. Learn all you can, but concentrate on your classics subjects, and I guarantee you'll get through all right.'

In the second half of that term, a strange, unspoken friendship grew between them almost to an intimacy. Penworth, young, lonely and bewildered by he knew not what strange forces of a strange land, took a curious, discontented pleasure in talking to the boy as though he were equal in age and understanding. In time Charles began to feel that indeed he did understand the mind and heart of the man; and when this happened and he perceived it, he put yet more distance between himself and the rest of his company. Had there been time, had the November examinations approaching not acted as an effective brake upon all inclination to spend hours with pleasant unthrift, his tendency to precocity, generated by too much sensitiveness and an unnaturally solitary childhood, might have been sadly forced by the Oxonian aesthetics and enthusiasms of the young Englishman.

Penworth himself would at that time have had great pain to explain, even to his own questing conscience, what were his objects in so cultivating the boy. He knew he wanted to touch him; he knew he felt some kind of complicated pleasure in observing the changing expressions in Charles's pale face, with its steady green-brown eyes and clear red lips; he was pleased, when one of those happy strenuous private lessons was over, to put his own white hand on the boy's touselled, ruddy crown and notice, without appearing to notice, what a fine flash of happiness and gratitude relieved the face below of its intent frown; but he would not have attempted to explain this pleasure, and he took care that the boy should not be aware of it. To this end he allowed himself moments of spoken impatience, sometimes of irritation (more genuine than he knew, and from an obscure cause), and his reward for these essays was a burning colour in Charles's face, and the hint of tears not readily to be shed.

In his own youthful self-centredness he did not at all understand the real power he was gaining over Charles. He was happy to play at an aloof intimacy expressing itself more often than not in subtly allusive quotations from one or other of the dead languages he professed, salting his conversation as young scholars down the ages, delighted at the infinite prospects of joy offered by learning, have salted it; or to enthuse tersely, by gesture and expression and with few words, over some ancient or contemporary poet; or even to discuss at length, as though to himself, in a word-imagery much above the intellectual height of Charles (but not beyond his affectionate admiration) the beauties and associations of certain musical compositions.

All this was as disturbing and as sublimely serious to Charles as the passions of religion or the pangs of love would be. Its evident danger was, in some sort, pardoned by the tremendous ardour it fired in him to learn what he desperately needed to learn—the cold, unsuggestive truths of earlier Latin syntax and accidence, and certain textbook rules of English study and composition. Penworth's sensual, smiling lips driving creases into the flat pallor of the cheeks, his bold, white brow already straightly seamed, and above all his grey eyes in their arched and beautiful setting of brow, lid and nose, all became associated for Charles with irregular Latin verbs and the obstinate eccentricities of the fourth and fifth declensions. They gave particular urgency to the understanding of the prologue to the *Canterbury Tales*, and to the elucidation of obscure word-usages in *Hamlet*, which Penworth joyfully insisted on reading with him out of class, in addition to conducting the whole form through it soberly in the classroom. He was a young man who loved his work. Charles began to have some understanding of the joys and travails of studying Shakespeare and Chaucer with an enthusiast whose Master's degree entitled him to expound richly and with force.

Charles became suddenly happier, during those weeks. He did not notice that Penworth's hand more often touched his, or was liable to caress his head or his knee in moments when the air in the little white study was fierce and tense and attentive. He knew only that he was learning, as he had never learned before, the beauties of his own language and of that from which so much of it had grown. He had the ideal experience of being in harmony with the close brotherhood of Latin and English learned at the same time and in the same way; his heart was full and overflowing, at such times, with the passionless ecstasy of knowing.

Only the memory of the girl's comely face, and the incommunicable secret harboured in her breasts, in the sighing shadow of the grove, came from the outside world to surprise into a surrender his moments of straying thought. The harder his mind spent itself in toiling, seizing, claiming and assimilating the facts that contained fluid essences of knowledge, the more vividly, afterwards, it turned away to receive those thoughts of her. Reacting from the labour of days he made in his mind a wild but innocent life of actions and contacts, as remote from probability as a dream, in its perfect carelessness of experience. Vaguely she took her part in the fantasy of his real night dreams, when his body lay sprawled and still in that double row of sprawled, still bodies, doing its work of sober recuperation for his brain and his mind winging so gladly away in darkness that was light. He had never seen the secret bloom of a woman's breasts before; but, as though schooled by poets and others through all time, he perceived in them nourishment for the mind and foundations on which to build dreams. And the line of brow and cheek, of smooth hair and neck and shoulder, of obstinate knees and straight legs—these in memory took on a large significance of which life must certainly soon try to rob him. With such knowledge of her, the smallest yet, perhaps, the choicest he could have known, his mind in sleep or day dreaming, during a noisy morning recess or under the meaningless glory of a service in Chapel, composed ecstasies whose frailty and unworldliness were mercifully kept from him. In a rare and lonely way he was learning, as those others were learning, with surprise and happiness, to live.

The season turned suddenly that year, more suddenly even than is usual in such an empire of surprising contrasts. At Eastertide the weather had been full of autumnal blood and promise; the sun shone hot but more kindly, the earth was softer, sinking already into a misty half-shadow of palest green. Now the pause came, like a breath held. In the open simplicity of the playing fields there still sounded the crack and hiss of balls sent from the bat on their brief spin down the net; still, on the lower field with its tall pines leanly silhouetted against the western sky, beyond the boundary fence, shouts and exhortations sounded clearly as the white figures moved about leisurely in afternoon sunlight, playing the gentleman's game. But the air that caught up and echoed these sounds was motionless. For perhaps ten days the change hung poised more in mid-heaven than on earth. Mr. Jolly, behind the nets, leaned on his stick and watched a boy he was coaching. His eyes were narrowed in the light; an old felt hat, pulled down at back and front, gave to his lengthening shadow a look of humble rusticity.

'No, no, no,' he said with tired patience. 'Look here— er—Ford my lad. Look, boy.'

He gripped the stick as though it were a bat; his long stooped body became full of springing purpose as he demonstrated the niceties of hitting a fast ball low to a far, far boundary. When he had performed this his eyes bulged and glared unseeingly round the field shining in the sun, as though still in search of the books he spent most of his days loving.

Ford would sigh out 'Oh—I see, sir,' with admiration and proper self-scorn; and once more, having signalled to the little group of bowlers, Mr. Jolly would narrow his cool blue eyes between their leaf-brown humorous lids, and turn on the small boys standing about him a smile mixed in brilliance and weariness, saying 'You see?' hoarsely, without bothering whether they did see or not.

For six afternoons of the week this lazy chirrup of bats and boys sounded from the playing fields. Charles went down whenever he was listed, which happened on such days as he did not have a class after hours with Penworth. He too came under the cool whimsical eye of Mr. Jolly, who used just as much patience with him as he had with Fairfax, the School's first bat, and refrained until afterwards from telling him that he had no eye and no footwork.

'But you have arms all right, old son, and shoulders,' he said with a slow disinterested smile. 'Go down to the end net and let them bowl at you for a bit.'

At first Charles was filled with alarm at such a thought; but he walked down behind the line of nets to number six, where he was unkindly greeted with a few choice obscenities from one or two of the onlookers, who were becoming excited. He tried to appear at ease when he walked round and stood among them; at least, he thought, we are dressed alike.

After a time someone threw him a ball and said, 'Now then, sweet one, go and bowl'.

He thought he must do as the others had done. Taking a run he delivered the ball furiously, but from too high; it came down hellishly short, bounded up and was taken and nipped low and far off its second fall. 'Six, six!' they shouted, laughing at him. No one went after the ball. Finding it, he picked it up and trotted back to the three other bowlers. His turn coming again, he took a breath, ran, and again pitched short and hard, but this time the ball went wide and sank in the walls of net. The batsman, relaxing his tension with a useless swing at it, flung down his bat and stood upright.

'Who the hell did that?' he asked loudly, looking at Charles with injury and anger in his eyes.

'I did,' Charles said defiantly.

'Well, for Chrissake don't do it again,' the boy snapped, and the others laughed.

'I've got to learn,' Charles replied loudly, his face reddening.

'Not on me you haven't,' that boy shouted. 'Go on— clear out of the way, you red-headed maniac.'

Charles stepped aside, seeing that it was useless to argue—useless and, it seemed, somehow indelicate. The others drew away, smiling and looking.

'Let yourself go loose,' one lad told him later on, when they had forgotten him again. 'Don't try and kill anybody. Let your shoulders go loose, and let the ball go when it wants to, and don't throw it hard like that. Watch.'

He took the ball that fell on the turf near him, and withdrew for a run, tossing it with practised nonchalance in the air, as he walked. Charles watched, saw the smooth continuity of run, delivery and the ball's flight, and thought it impossible to imitate. He could not learn that unity of three motions. He did not want to. However, he caught the ball thrown with a careless flick at him, and tried again. Another batsman was at the stumps. This time he did better. The same boy, whose name he thought was Walton, encouraged him by telling him he was improving.

Later Mr. Jolly stood behind the net; Charles happened at that time to have a ball again.

'You'll never bowl,' Mr. Jolly roared mildly, after his second ball. 'Drop that, Fox. You'll never bowl. I'm quite sure you won't. Come along, take the bat and let me see again.' He hooked a wide yawn with the top of his stick; the fresh afternoon air, free of the classroom's melancholy odour of ink and books, was making him sleepy.

Charles went back to the School with one or two others, joining in their talk as they walked or ran under the trees. The dry leaves and twigs of summer's reaping cracked against the soft soles of their shoes; their voices in the open spaces were high and merry. He noticed how the days were growing shorter, and felt the coolness of the evening air on his warm skin. Away in the west, keeping pace with them in magnificent creative silence, the sunset clouds were afloat like galleons in the sky; the sun was gone, but they glowed still, rumouring him in colour and splendour, in lavender and silver, crimson and gold that ached like the fever of love before it faded all to ashes. When Charles looked out from the changing-room windows, while he silently stripped naked for a shower, it had gone; but the mood of release and happiness that had brought him home persisted, and his body's weariness seemed good. Once more, as in that grey morning in the sheltering grove with the unknown girl, life's great beauty was whispered and murmured to his mind from the full tide of his heart, in wordless images of gladness, purpose and content.

He was thinking of the shape of things: the remaining four weeks of term, with a stern trial examination waiting at the end like a not unmatchable wrestler challenging him; four Sunday afternoons when there would be nothing to do but read, and perhaps have tea and talk with Mr. Jones, small, kindly and whimsical, whose conversation effortlessly took him in among its surmises and calm surprises at the inexhaustible beauties of chamber music and organ works, with an occasional revelation about the difficulties of training a choir of boys, and some dreamlike remembrance of working in London or in Leipzig. And then, finally, the May holiday.

125

Strange tremblings in the pit of his stomach disturbed him pleasantly as he walked to the bathroom, where a high-spirited uproar and the sound of water pelting and splashing was too big for that place of brick and concrete, and forced its way out into the echoing dimness of nearby classrooms. He was going to see Margaret again in these holidays; and he was going to work. May, late May, with the fields full of green and tender grass already, and the channels of winter streams beginning to run with a sound that rejoiced the vast night silences like a lullaby; books that necessity was making familiar and dear to him; and the girl made somehow dear by strangeness. He could not remember her face, save as it was colourful and fair; a page of type came more readily to his mind; but that was a face in which the delicate fire of youth glowed with commanding innocence, surrounded by the mystery of the first climacteric's superb accomplishment as a candle flame is surrounded and glorified by its aureole of transparent gold. His heart beat when he thought he could have seen such magic and have looked upon it with open eyes.

Down the stair by the bathroom doors Penworth came lightly. His gaze discerned Charles white in the shadowy hallway there. He went closer.

'Oh, it's you, is it?' he said with a smile. 'I thought it might be. Won't you get cold standing there with nothing on?'

'I'm going to have a shower, sir,' Charles said.

'You look happy. Been playing the Game?'

'Yes, sir—playing the Game.' Charles laughed ruefully. 'I'm no good at it, sir, I'm afraid.'

'Oh well,' Penworth said with a slight inflexion of impatience, 'neither was I. It doesn't matter, perhaps, in the long run. What's made you so happy then? Are you good at something else?'

Charles was embarrassed; he always was when one asked him for an explanation of a mood or an excitement.

'I don't know, sir,' he said in a low voice, feeling that he must answer. 'Just—the day—and life—and everything, just suddenly.'

'Lucky fellow; oh, lucky fellow,' Penworth said in the same low tone, but with great unrestraint; and he pulled Charles to him and held him hard against him. Charles felt for three seconds the heavy beating of that unknown heart beneath the rough, smoke-sweet jacket front, and the warmth of the hands holding his arms; then he was away, embarrassed now beyond expression, almost laughing with surprise. Penworth stepped back, saying in a calm tone through his sudden smile:

'Go on, off you go and have your cold bath, and may it do you all the good the authorities mean it to.'

With a pleased laugh he swung on his heel, strode across the hallway and was blotted out by the closing of his door before Charles could manage a reply.

He himself went into the bathroom and joined the milling, scuffling, shouting groups round the shower cubicles. While he bathed and was teased and jostled and flicked with knife-like pangs from the corners of towels on coming out from the shower, his mind puzzled over Penworth's strangeness. He felt happy every time Penworth showed such spontaneous motions of affection, yet he could

127

not bear to be touched or held by any man; and it was difficult to perceive in himself anything that warranted such gestures which others did not also possess; unless it was that Penworth himself, from loneliness or some other starvation, was beginning to feel for him the affection of a father or a brother. It was all strange and confusing to him, when he considered it as now, striving to make plain to himself the man's reasons and his own feelings. He had known nothing, before those weeks and months, of the precious friendliness of one man towards another; if it had been one of his fellows he would have held himself ready for a sudden change of face; but with Penworth, whom he knew to be old enough to be, without doubt, beyond such foibles and hearty treacheries, he was quite uncertain. Nothing that he had noticed could make him suppose that friendships between Masters and particular boys were natural; and if prefects and House captains and some others did often fraternize with Masters almost as though Masters were their equals, prefects and House captains were often all people of quality and privilege, inheritors of a long social tradition, and vigorous symbols of boyhood's own authority. Himself, he was no House captain, no prefect; he had no franchise, but was one of least positive importance, a first-term boy. It must be that Penworth understood how he differed in many ways from the others, and found in his own vague loneliness a kinship of difference between himself and Charles.

Charles argued this out laboriously, in terms of difficult thought, and was happy to believe it might be right. The belief gave him courage to trust in moods and intuitions of selfhood that were disturbing him more and more frequently; as though with leisure and experience grouped opposite application and learning, he must crowd all possible self-experience into the little true leisure he had. He felt the growth of self in himself; it showed in his heightened and now consciously intensified reactions to the new surprise of beauty in the world; it showed in his persisting defiance towards that unfriendly suspicion with which his occasional offers of friendship were regarded when, in the hope of peace to follow, he schooled himself to blind overture. It showed even in the lessening and final abandonment of those advances; it was hinted, to Penworth and other observers less perceived by Charles, in the deliberate way he applied his mind to work. The bodily miracle that had seen its own fulfilment was becoming a slow miracle of the mind.

During those weeks some enchantment held the season in mid-turn. By the change of shadows in the classroom they knew how the sun moved down earlier in the west; but there was to be seen only the torso of the wounded tree soaring upward in a hard fountain of hope, and beyond it that darkening and incredible depth of blue, navigated more often now by the skyey galleons that fought silent, leisurely battles up there, conquering and overcoming one another while the idle gaze divined them not as ships but as cloud. Then at last, as if weary of such lazy mockery, they joined all together and turned upon the sun great dangerous sides of grey.

The rain began on some Friday afternoon, after a day of revived heat. The sky set firm, and a shower that whispered with deceptive innocence during dinner at noon had so increased and established itself by three o'clock that only the curious melancholy voices of iron drain-pipes, silent since so many long months, made one aware that it was still raining. They played harsh liquid music from every corner and angle of the walls; after a time even their plaintiveness fell upon the ear unregarded, and life in the sprawling buildings went on as it had always done. Notices on all House boards, cancelling whatever arrangements for play had been made, were by most read gladly enough. There was a rush for the library, and a more sober advance by some to the dusty and echoing gymnasium, where Old Mac, straight and iron-faced, waited in his office, cocking a martial eye every so often at the lawns beyond his window, where a small flood was rising and overflowing into the neat paths.

Charles went to see Penworth, who ordered him with moody abruptness to go away and close the door quietly. This surprised Charles, and for a moment caused him a rich pang of self-pity; but from habit he took a firm hold of that softening, smiled to himself, went to the bathroom mirror to see himself smiling, and (such is the virtue of the reflected image) went down the changing-room to undress feeling happy enough. While he was changing he whistled merrily.

Of all the playing places in a school, its gymnasium is perhaps most attractive to the future individualists in that community. There, in the muffled drumming of feet and bodies on matting and mattress and floor, the individualist may step forth valiantly from his wise retreat and exercise himself freely and as he chooses. It is a sort of collection of one-man shows, like a fair, where each young merchant, having once learned something of the trade, sells his own goods for admiration. It is an aloof but lively place; and this might always be remarked of Old Mac, its deity. He lived in magnificent solitude there, issuing forth in close formation at the mid-morning break to command his own armies on the School parade ground, where the Chapel with Christian severity flung back his steely kettle-drum voice in a piercing echo that served to italicize each crisply-shouted command. After that, when all ranks were dismissed from parade, he marched back to his inner realm, a study of perfect control and grace as he walked at a stand-easy pace over the worn grass, training his moustaches ever upward to deny the kindling kindness of his eye.

When it rained he lurked, like a spider anxious to teach a fly the intricacies of the web. He welcomed the rain as something that did its duty in emphasizing his individuality by keeping him indoors in the easy and vigorous atmos-phere of the gymnasium. This day he had not long to wait; under the narrow shelter of eaves they ran to the doors at the side, which he had left open at dinner-time after one fierce glance at the sky. Charles, coming after the others, slipped in unnoticed and joined an energetic group playing with a medicine ball under the gallery at the south-east end.

Later he tired of that, and went to watch the crew at work on the wall bars and parallels. Their great hour was only some ten days off; the papers were already noting form, and beginning their comments; during the coming week excitement would rise to a fine pitch in all Schools, and there would be much argument this way and that. To-day, with the aid of benches, they were at arm-work and leg-work together, naked to the waist and sweating already in spite of the afternoon coolness. Charles stood watching with dreamy admiration the smooth flux and ebb of those flat masses of muscle beneath the sweat-polished skin, noticing how pectoral and dorsal tension rose and fell, with an echo in the wooden squareness of the steadying thighs. He felt proud of having a man's body, lean, smooth and beautiful in action, and proud in being a brother of such isolated, pulsing realms of purposeful energy. A hunger for the rhythm of movement troubled his limbs. In that busy place of honestly selfish concentration he was not noticed much; eyes whose direction he interrupted and shared were kinder, with that blood-conscious kindness of the athlete, the individual, secure in his own body. Charles turned to the horizontal bars, where the shining lights of muscular artistry were gathered. He lost himself in close contemplation of Milltree's grand circles, hearing, instead of the thunder of feet and the slap and drum of the medicine ball, a creaking protest of resinous palms against wood as Milltree sent his arched body flying round, extended full length from the hands as it came head-downwards to the upper vertical, swinging out and down with brutal acceleration, and drawing together from that essential abandon for the retard of the final upswing. The repetition of this rhythm became mesmeric.

It was that rainy Friday that began for Mawley a conscious friendship with Charles. There were several—individualists all, no doubt—who had gathered together to monopolize the springboard and vaulting horse; they had the horse broad-on, and were, with that sober self-examination and approval so good to indulge in in youth, going from short-arm bend to long-arm. The responsive thrust and clatter of the board gave great animation to these serious proceedings, and it was the general excitement, as well as an habitual excess of confidence and blind zeal, that made Mawley forget his feet in the first long-arm, and left him laid out on the mattress with a tendon torn out of the right ankle, in such overwhelming perfection of pain as few are allowed to know while remaining conscious. Lying there, hidden from the others by the varnished broadside of the horse, it was possible to observe with one of those receptive abettors of consciousness, how the great hall had suddenly deserted him, its merry activity unabated but his own place in it closed up and gone. Its white walls became intensely more white; faces and all vanished, but the shouting and the laughter went on, the clatter of the springboard sent invisible bodies thudding over on to that mattress, and suddenly there were Charles's eyes, horrified. Speech at that moment was not in Mawley's power; it was for Charles. Suddenly again, as though consciousness were being released in abrupt jerks, there was his body dancing frantically and his mouth open, shouting, and his hands waving. Something seemed to have frightened him properly, for his face was greenish with pallor; it must have been Mawley's foot doubled unnaturally outwards, lying flat and out of line with leg and body, looking, as he said a long time later, 'worse than murder'. He said, 'I'd rather see a chap dead than lying like that and being alive enough to laugh'. His antics must have been worth laughter.

The next gift of consciousness to Mawley was a dawning sight of the lower bathroom in Chatterton materializing swiftly out of a white blankness, and a foreshortened vista

133

of his own leg and foot extended into a flooding wash-basin. If only there had been blood, Charles thought, it would not have looked so horrible. You could not mistake Old Mac's dry, flat fingers, with the small one on the left hand gripped by a heavy signet ring. Charles's white face, drawn down in a ghastly tension of colour from the slowly turning eyes, was peering; Penworth, terse before animal suffering, let out monosyllables abruptly. Pain, so immediate in its need for exclamation, does not aid coherent speech when it grasps body and heart like a great hand, and stirs the guts with an icy, inquisitive forefinger. But hearing seems to have become minutely acute. Every tremble in Charles's breath, as his heart stamped the action of his lungs, throbbed on the air. Something had greatly shocked him. It must have been that gold and purple royalty which was, ten minutes ago, a happy and obedient joint. Penworth observed its effect on Charles, also.

'Better have a drink of water, Fox,' he snapped. 'Glass in my...Oh, the young idiot. Damn.'

Charles slid comfortably down the wall, moving his hands in blind groping as he went over sideways. Penworth cupped a double handful of water from the flooded basin and flung it into the shrunken whiteness of his face.

'Leave it,' said Old Mac impatiently. 'Upstairs with this one.'

From the bed in Dormitory C it was a surprise to Mawley to hear the turmoil in the gymnasium going on as before, with a crash and clatter still from the springboard and a chinking rattle of rings. Old Mac's hands were neat and orderly, resting on his chest to hold him still, while his voice said, 'Hold still, sir. A nasty fall, by gad', calmly, as though to himself. The pain located itself at last, withdrawing its false rumour downwards. Steps and words rose on the stairs; the School's nursing sister smiled and murmured like a brown dove over his shivering:

'What have *you* done with yourself? Let's have a look.'

Penworth, with drops of water still falling from fingers and wrists, lifted Charles half-conscious from that foolish tumble between wall and floor, and bore him off to his room.

Charles was struggling, saying: 'It's all right, sir, really it is,' but Penworth as abruptly as before bade him shut up. He closed the door by kicking it with his heel, and laid Charles on the bed.

'Now,' he said, and suddenly was smiling. Charles sat up, and at once lay back again; waves of light and darkness still swept steadily into his brain, but that tide was going out.

'Lie still,' Penworth said, and busied himself with a glass and a bottle.

'If this makes you drunk,' he muttered, 'it'll be the open road for me, my lad. What on earth made you go off like that?'

Charles turned his face to the wall, as though to read reason on its white page.

'I don't know,' he began, and then, with tears in his eyes, said sharply, 'It was so horrible, wasn't it? All torn sideways like that.' He hovered uncertainly between tears and a relaxed force of laughter. Penworth handed him the tumbler.

'Whisky,' he said. 'It's a waste giving it to you, but still, you'd better drink it. There's not much.'

Charles swallowed it, and as it fumed in his nose and throat his teeth began to chatter again on the thin edge of the glass. A memory of his mother's face hanging like a calm mask above the light of a candle by his bed, as she said almost those words—'You'd better drink this, son. There's not much'—grew up vividly in his mind. There was her head's great shadow doubled in the angle of wall and ceiling like a torn piece of paper; and her hands coming out of the brown darkness to comfort him after the unwieldy horror of a nightmare. The reek of whisky was something very real, to which from the anguish of the mind it was good to turn.

He told Penworth shyly of this memory, and of others.

'Nightmares, eh? Do you still have them?'

'Sometimes,' Charles said, looking away to think. 'Not often, sir.'

'What sort of dreams now?' Penworth seated himself at the foot of the bed, and took Charles's feet in his two hands firmly, as though without seeing he did it. Charles looked at him suddenly from the pillow.

'I dream a lot,' he explained, 'but in a sort of muddled way. I don't often remember.'

'Your dreams now,' Penworth said thoughtfully, his eyes upon the boy's pale face, 'should be interesting. I wonder...'

Charles felt some relief in his confidence. He told him, in a new assurance of sympathy, of some of his dreams. His unwitting frankness shocked Penworth into looking away, and then attracted him so that he turned his face to

Charles again, his deep pupils dilated, his sensual lips full of passionate seriousness.

'I know,' he said. 'Of course, one doesn't...'

'What worried me,' Charles said gravely, 'was just at first—you know, sir. There is no one to explain. I suppose everyone's the same.'

'Yes, yes,' Penworth murmured, his eyes looking back into his own initiations and experiments. 'All of us, sometime or other.'

'You see, I don't know anything—about that,' Charles explained.

'The shock of discovering your own body,' Penworth began; but he stopped himself. Looking upwards to the grey face of the window he could see the ghost of rain against the sky, as mysterious and vanishing as marks made on still water. Looking upwards, he seemed to be having some inward debate with himself; Charles could see how blind were his eyes beneath the white curve of the forehead above its deeply arched brows. His full lips were moving and trembling with every turn of his thought. He still gripped Charles's feet with his broad hands. Through the near silence of the room floated a sustained echo of tumult from the gymnasium.

At last Charles struggled to ask, 'What are you thinking of now, Mr. Penworth?'

He turned his head sideways and down, looking into the boy's serious eyes.

'Of myself,' he said quietly. 'As usual. And of you. Has no one ever told you anything?—anything about physical development and your own body?'

'No, sir.'

'What about living here? Surely you can't live among these—these boys and not have learned a lot?'

Charles considered his own mind, frowning unconsciously.

'I hear what they say, you know,' he said at length, after Penworth had stared into his face unwaveringly for a minute or more. 'But I don't think I understand...I mean, I sort of know what it's about and yet I—I sort of don't know. That sounds muddled...'

'I understand,' Penworth said shortly, as though he had come to the end of a train of thought which he had been following even while he listened to the boy's difficulties in speaking of his own mind. He was surprised to find that Charles was speaking the truth, and speaking it simply. He neither dramatized his innocence and half-knowledge, nor attempted, as others would have done, to make it seem, without actually saying, that he knew more and was willing enough to talk about it. Penworth, while he was puzzled, and confused also in certain depths of which he was only just now discovering the nature, was turned a little compassionate in his own belief and admiration.

'Well,' he said, 'I'd find it rather hard to tell you everything face to face like this...'

'I'd probably find it hard, too,' Charles said with a smile.

'Anyhow,' Penworth went on unheeding, 'there are things you'll learn; and it's probably just as fair to you to let you find them out for yourself. As the gods see fit. But,' he said, 'don't get into the habit of talking as the other boys talk until you know what you're speaking of and what it all means. You'll only do yourself harm—in your own opinion, later.'

His charity just then surprised and flattered him. He felt driven to it, at first, because he had finally discovered and admitted to himself why he liked the boy as he did. He was, despite his youngness, honest enough and lonely enough to admit that this was a physical attraction, of exactly the same sort as he would have felt in the untutored presence of a girl of the same age. Had he been rather older, separated from his own deeply impressionable boyhood by darker, longer years, he might have regarded with jealous hatred the idea of himself desiring the unknowable body of this boy ten years his junior and a lifetime apart in ignorance; but he was at that time still subjectively familiar with the rules of philosophy and domesticity of the ancients he studied, and, because also desire can reason against itself without for one instant quitting its intention or questioning its present emotion, he considered himself calmly, and, had he been alone, would have shrugged his shoulders, as though to say, 'Well, let it be so, then'.

'Action can wait,' he heard himself murmur; and to the urgent question in Charles's eyes he could not reply for a moment. At last, when the silence between them had calmed to a quietened current of thought, he spoke again.

'You don't need to worry about yourself, nor about those dreams. You are made to grow like that so that one day you can have a wife and children. One day...'

Deserted as suddenly as he had been possessed by that charitable restraint, he took his hands from the boy's feet, reached forward impulsively and took his cold fingers into his own, pulling him up to a sitting position, feeling with a heart-beat of fear the weight of the body communicated to his own back and shoulders, and imagining with rage its warmth and deathly whiteness. When their faces were close together he looked desperately into Charles's eyes, striving with the stubbornness of despair to find in their far depths some response to his own will.

Charles went stiff with the alarm of this. When he turned his eyes sideways, startled beyond thought by what was happening to him, seeing only the stillness and finality of the closed door, Penworth kissed him clumsily and hard on the lips.

The silence of the room roared like a surf in their ears. It was as big as the dreadful silence of his own nightmares to Charles. He could not move; he could not even turn his head more to avoid further contact with the dry eager lips of another man. Slowly his eyes came round. At the uncomprehending alarm in them Penworth laughed shortly, and let his hands slide free; that clipped, low laugh exploded like a long-awaited thunderclap in the still room.

'It's all right, dear lad,' he said. 'Don't be frightened— I shan't hurt you.'

Charles stood up; and he too rose; so they faced each other.

'Were you frightened of—something that might have happened?' Penworth asked, lightness lifting his voice out of the mire of emotional extravagance. 'There's nothing to be frightened of now. Is there?'

Charles shook his head several times, without being

able to speak. He did not clearly know what he felt. It seemed somehow like happiness, but there was a black colour of doubt and regret hanging undefined about it. The goodness of having such a friend, so quickly in sympathy, so spontaneous in showing sympathy, was a warm glow in his heart; but he knew without being told that men do not kiss one another so. It was such an impossible thing that he had never even imagined it; and now...He shook his head. That was the origin of the enormous doubt and the shamed regret he felt; he understood that something had been done which should not have been done, though he did not understand why there was argument against it. Instinct warned him uncertainly that from this moment he would never talk of it, and his own shyness made it impossible that he should turn to Penworth there by the window and ask, Why? For he had been made most conscious, in the last fifteen minutes, of the vastness and danger of his ignorance. The coil of life was about him, and as yet he could not follow it with his eyes, nor sink back in the empowered calm of understanding; he must remain poised, keeping balance deliberately and with effort.

'Here's the damned winter,' Penworth said at length, without turning round; and immediately he asked, 'Do you by any chance know what it is to be as lonely as hell?'

Charles nodded; and then, remembering with confusion that he was not being observed, he said, 'I do now, sir,' struggling to reach the high and windy level of the other's thought. 'Since I've been here, at school,' he said slowly.

'Exactly.' Penworth swung round upon him as sharply as though he had been angered by the words. 'Here,' he said, 'in a place like this—to be lonely; to want some sort of peace; to want love. To be lonely among so many. A microcosm that mirrors the worldly macrocosm—this place. An analogy with life in all the world—so many, and each one alone. If we try to touch each other's heart, it's misunderstood. And, worst of all, we don't understand it ourselves. We're lost; in a crowd it's as though we're... I can't tell you.'

'I do know; I feel it,' Charles said as calmly as he might.

'Well, don't say it so smugly,' Penworth said bitterly; but his stare softened and became warmer, and he said, 'I forgot that you're so young. Why do I talk to you like this? Why should I? I haven't the right; I haven't the right to do it. There it is again: every action and inclination blasted by life's discreet irony. We're always at the mercy of that.'

He came close and took Charles's face between his palms, looking down not now with desire but with something clearer and more assured.

'I can't expect you to understand,' he murmured coldly. 'You're a child. What can you know? For all your pretty looks you're as masculine as any of us—and more than some. What can you know?'

He stared unwaveringly into his eyes.

'And yet—perhaps you're not. If you're not, it's not for me to know—not now.' And he muttered to himself between his clenched teeth, 'I haven't the courage.'

With a gesture as of one dropping something into space he let Charles's face slip from between his hot palms, and stood back from him. To Charles there was nothing deliberately dramatic in this; but to Penworth there was, and he watched its effect reflected in the boy's face, in the unhappy striving to understand and to keep pace with the thought spoken.

Charles made an effort and answered him.

'I may not know it all, but even if I am so young I do know you're unhappy; and if I could help I would. If I can.'

Penworth smiled, but his eyes were steadily watchful.

'Nobly spoken. Nobly said. However'—and once again he changed in that sudden way that so bemused Charles— 'I believe you mean it.'

'I do, sir,' Charles said, and felt once more uncertain of his ground. 'But I don't know what I can do—except talk to you. I do like that. I like it awfully. No one else talks like you.'

He hesitated, and found he could say no more.

'I should not have upset you like this,' Penworth said. 'I should have remembered that you are working hard, and that you can't be normal when you're doing that. I try to solve a physical problem with intellectual co-equivalents and get an answer in spiritual terms; and it can't be done. Anyone could tell you that. It can't be done.'

His smile shone at last in his eyes. He put one arm round Charles's shoulders, rocking him from side to side, gently, as he had done once before, in the heat of afternoon up there in the choir loft. He looked down affectionately into his face.

'You're doing well, too. Now—let's forget about this afternoon altogether. Is that a bargain?'

'Oh, yes, sir,' Charles said earnestly, not thinking whom the bargain might profit because of the full return of happiness and assurance that leapt up within him.

'Right. Now go upstairs and see how Mawley is getting on.'

Steps paused at the door and a fist pounded softly on the panels.

'Come in,' Penworth snapped; and, when Waters put his mild pink face round the dark edge of the door, he turned to Charles from the other side of the room, and said coldly, 'All right, Fox, you can go now. And don't be a fool and faint next time you see a sprained ankle.'

When he had gone Waters came into the room and shut the door with care.

'What happened? Faint?'

Penworth flung away an impatient gesture.

'Young Mawley hurt himself in the gym—pretty badly, I think—and that young idiot fainted in the bathroom. I gave him some perfectly good whisky; wasted it, in fact. You'd better sample it yourself.'

'He's a pretty child,' Waters mumbled amiably, seating himself on the bed.

'He is,' Penworth said, his back still turned. 'That's his misfortune. This is our good luck.'

Waters took the tumbler from his hand, and asked about news from Home.

Charles went for the May holiday feeling somehow out of key with life. The instrument of his mind would not seem to play in tune, even though it was holiday and a time to rejoice in. He took books with him, and set himself to study during the last week of the eighteen days of freedom.

This discontent would lose itself in work, he thought; but in his heart was a child's cry of bereavement at the loss of pleasure anticipated. Margaret, of whom he had thought more and more often in the last days of term, after that discomforting scene in Penworth's room, would not be at the new farm. She was nowhere, in his mind, because he could only imagine her as she had been, that morning in the grove—given to him as a gift by the earth and his own imagination, rich and silent as the land that held them in its mighty palm and gave reason to their being. On the day of the Boat Race he saw her, and she told him then that she was not able to go down. Sitting in his room at home, looking out blindly at the dancing ecstasy of a camphor laurel ravished by an evening of wind and rain, he still felt the surprise of her hand's light touch on his arm as he walked from one place to another, on the windy brim of the Mount, with the river's lake stretched in ruffled grey and blue far beneath, and the eights like insects moving on it slowly. She must have been watching him for some time, though he had not seen her among the little groups of uniformed girls mixing with the boys from the Schools, up there in the wind. She must certainly have seen him, though he had not looked for her there; for in his mind she was still most vividly present in the grove's long silence, out in the Far Field beyond the world, and it seemed that no one else in the world could know her. Yet there she was, when he turned his head as he walked against the cold wind; and when he stopped, unable to speak or even to say her name, looking slightly down into the excitement and frightened pallor of her face in the dark blue of her hat, she glanced about as she spoke, and he too was unwilling that here, of all places, they should be observed by anyone.

'Come near the edge,' she said without smiling; and when their nearness to the scattered crowd saved them from the fear of being conspicuous, her smile came only slowly and her eyes remained wide and dark.

'I'm not going down after all. I have to stay with my sister.'

When she looked in his face again, where there was only the warm liveliness of his joy at hearing and beholding her come in the rich reality of flesh from a backward present of imagination, she repeated what she had said.

'Oh,' he muttered, and ground the sandy turf under his heel, still looking into her grave face. Then the edge of his disappointment showed clearly. 'Oh,' he said again, flushing, shamed in his expectation.

'I'm sorry,' she said. 'It would have been very nice. I would have loved it. But you see, I can't. But I expect next holidays I'll be down there.' She stopped, still poised to go away, like a bird that sees the approach of something strange and will take flight. 'If I come down next holidays,' she said, raising her voice a little against the wind, 'will you be at that place with the trees?'

'I wish you could come,' he said. 'I have to take exams this year. I wish you could have come.'

'Yes. I do.'

'It's a pity you can't.'

'Yes, it is. But I have to stay with my sister.'

He struggled with something difficult to fit words to, and his face showed his great concern.

'I seem to know you well.'

'But we don't,' she said in a low voice, looking at him steadily.

'Well—couldn't I write to you; or something?' But as he spoke he understood that he would not know what to say if he did write; and when she said no, it would be better not to, he agreed and looked away in silence.

'Well,' she said at last, 'I must go now.'

'I suppose so.'

'Good-bye.'

She was gone out of his sight. When he looked again, and saw her standing near, as though she had thought of something more to say, he walked quickly along, behind a hedge of backs and trousered legs, uniformed backs above black stockings, planted square and almost shapeless together in a long jostling line.

'Good luck to your School,' she said with a laugh. 'Can I have a piece of your ribbon?'

He was giving her the whole rosette when she stopped him, putting out her hand.

'Oh no—don't do that.'

'It won't matter,' he said. 'Do take it. Everything will be over in ten minutes, about. Take it. When shall I see you again, then?'

'I told you,' she said in a low voice. 'Next holidays—August. You've never told me your name.'

'Charles,' he said.

'Is that all?'

'Charles Fox.'

So, with the term at an end, the big race lost, as usual, to the School, and eighteen days ahead of him seeming to stretch towards eternity, he found himself at a loss how to order his mind. He was surprised and sad to realize what pleasure it had given him to imagine that that girl, whom now he had seen only twice, would be down there, near his home; it was surprising to think that already, after seeing her once against the quiet landscape he loved so well, he had preserved her there in the sight of his mind and had been in no doubt that he should see her there in the touchable flesh, and listen to the quality of life and silence in her voice, or watch her when she did not speak. No foolish guilt of secrecy was in him to be relieved at the knowledge that after all she would be away, and he and the solitude would lack her; he knew little enough of any kind of love for another human creature, and it had come to be most natural that he should think of her and himself happily together when he thought of his home and that country; for she was the only being who had known him there, and it seemed right that in his imagination she should share it as no one else could have shared it.

He felt that he had now lost something of it, losing her.

Going home from the station, muffled warmly in rugs under the high hood of the phaeton, with Jimmy talking beside him, he peered out into the night beyond their moving golden side-lights. The lamps ran the road through their fingers like an endless wet brown ribbon; above the opposite seat the horses' rumps were hardly to be seen in their quick rise and fall, for the night was windy and the candles in the lantern boxes shook their flames. On his right, Jimmy's face came gradually out of the darkness, the faintly-lit profile of a bronzed mask; from his pipe sparks flew away for a while, until the ash settled. Jimmy, who would have worked for Mrs. Fox if she had paid him nothing at all, had refused to let her come out on such a night; and Charles was for the first time touched with amused wonder when he realized the ease with which that brown little man guided her to her best comfort and safety.

'Well, Mist' Charles,' Jimmy mumbled sibilantly across his pipe-stem, 'I s'pose you're dashed glad to get back home again?'

'Yes, Jimmy,' Charles said through the cloudy darkness. A lacework of rain was flung sharply into his face as they turned a corner into the weather.

'You keep yourself warm now,' Jimmy said with the same mild tone of authority which Charles had heard him use to his mother—a tone no one else ever thought of using in speech with her. When he took out his pipe to chirp hoarsely at the mares, he added with sober, guarded enthusiasm, 'Ah, there's nothing like the country for you kids, Mist' Charles. Nor for us old blokes either.'

The rhythmic smack of the hoofs and a creak and ring of harness made the windy night seem friendly when he had finished speaking. They bore on steadily; the warmth about his knees and the blustering wind hissing and hammering on the deep hood lulled Charles into a dozing half-consciousness full of the clear voices which, when sleep comes first, take bodies to them and are visible dreams. Jimmy's quiet, lively words, expressively commonplace, lay on the surface of his mind, arousing no suggestions in him but soothing him into deeper calm and the acquiescence of an accustomed confidence. He could not have remembered a time when there was no Jimmy.

They stopped at the white gate that was the first welcome of home. He was wide awake at once, but already Jimmy had jumped down, and the rattle of the gate's fastening sounded through the quieter wind as he was hearing a voice echo still—Congratulations, Fox; you are doing well.

'I'm sorry,' he said, when the phaeton had moved slowly through and Jimmy was up beside him again. 'I could have got down.'

'That's all right, Mist' Charles; you was having a bit of a sleep, lad,' Jimmy said comfortably; and Charles, lying back again in his corner with the familiar smell of the worn cushioning about him, saw the rough trunks of the old pear-trees along the drive go past like dark friends in their lanterns' light, and felt the quickened pace of Julia and Jane, the two bays, as they came home. They turned to the left and stopped; the garden hedge stretched back to his right, its wet leaves shining in the light; in the lee of the house he could smell the warm, leathery sweat of the horses, and he brushed their steaming noses with his hand as he passed in front. His mother from the sudden calm light of the open door looked down to him, and asked Jimmy to bring in the suitcases when he had finished with the mares; then she held out her hands to Charles.

'Well, son?'

He was glad that she had not changed, and that her welcome, though it was warm with conscious motherhood, was not demonstrative. He felt he could not have borne that just then. When they were inside, she turned to look at him again, while he took off his things, and spoke almost his own thought.

'You haven't changed, son; but you've grown a lot.'

The passive calm of her voice suddenly irritated him, with a sharp irritation of which he was ashamed.

'Did you think I would have changed?' he said quietly.

He took her arm and they walked up the dark stairs to his room. There was a lamp burning beside the bed; its ring of low blue flame threw upon the wall at the bed's head an elaborate blurred shadow of the guard inside the glass, and upon the ceiling a pale ring of yellow, but gave scant light. She turned it up, and was herself revealed in the mild, still radiance, her pale face sculptural in the dark shadows driven up from cheek and chin, until she looked down into the flame. He stood watching her, and they smiled together; but all she thought to say was, 'Yes, you have grown. I'm glad you've done so well, Charles. You'll be able to work here when you want to, my dear, unless you'd like the governess's room. No one shall interrupt you.'

Jimmy came up the stairs with the cases, and swung them in through the open door, and nodded, and then went away.

'Change your things,' she said, 'and come down.'

He was looking about the room, remembering it even more clearly than he saw it, when from outside the door she said, 'I've made you some soup; I knew you'd like it.' His 'Thank you, Mother', followed her down the stairs.

\

Outside the windows he heard the passion of camphor laurels lashed and laughing in the night, and the melancholy whistle of wind through the bent cypresses; and he stared at the mighty and unreal immobility of his own shadow on the blue pallor of the wall, and realized that after all he was changed, for he had never before felt as he had a minute ago—irritated by her whom he had come to consider so kind. As he stared at that still shape of shadow, the image of the girl's face appeared in it, and in sudden, vague unhappiness he turned abruptly away.

Because Mawley's home was far to the north, he was left at the School during that holiday, and for the other reason also—being confined to bed with dull discomfort for a most constant companion. Letters, more vivid in their unimaginative brevity than any careful and colourful description would have been, made him a picture of the land's agonies in a bad season. There seemed no promise of a break in the drought that engulfed the north-west; they had already given up hope of rain. No one could leave the place.

He was moved to the emptiness of the sanatorium, across the road, where the silence inside and the passing of cars without, day and night long, drew close with the viciousness of a continual taunt. The silence in the dormitory would have been worse; here at least there were young poplar trees at the bed's head, bending and dancing beyond the stark uncurtained panes in a nakedness of spiring twigs against the blue or cloud of the windy May sky. Sometimes people came. The nursing sister brought books; a strange Scots lass, of whom much could be told, came three times a day with meals on a tray; when she looked at the bandaged thing that had once been a smooth and easy ankle she would open her eyes wide and then narrow them, as if a high wind blew into her face, exclaiming 'Eh…! Puir wean', and at last could be made to smile at an imitation of herself: 'Puir wean; puir wean, Mary; puir wee yen.'

Often the Headmaster came across the busy road through wind and rain or wind and sun. He was not away from the School during that holiday; when he came he would sit on the edge of the bed and listen to all sorts of stored-up chatter, seeming always to be interested. That was his charm for everyone, that he gave his whole mind to each person he engaged with—or so it seemed then. He did not say much, during those visits, after his long smile at the delight with which his frequent gifts of fruit and sweets were received; sometimes he would say, 'Read aloud to me, will you?—from whatever you're on now'. But once Mawley made the mistake of starting to recite an Ode of Horace's that had caught his fancy because he could understand its meaning; but before he had sighed out the mock-melancholy 'Eheu, fugaces, Postume, Postume' the Headmaster was shaking his head with a smile. 'No, not that. Try me with Wilkie Collins; I've forgotten him.'

He looked haggard and worried during those two weeks. Mawley thought afterwards, with that passion which pity draws into itself when it is too late to pity, that if they had only known, surely, surely…But perhaps that man knew his own destiny; perhaps it was the secret of his strength.

His talk was sparing, but there was a great sympathy in those companionable visits, and when he said, 'I should

153

like to be young again, sometimes, like you, lad', the boy could nod and smile, not understanding that his wish was as deep as hell, but quite ready to believe and share in the admiration for youth which lay in the face of his words.

It was impossible not to be drawn closer under the kindly shadow of his great personality; he did indeed seem young, with the essence of youth, with all its ability to feel, quick and deep, the drama of fortune's ceaseless mutation; without youth's clumsiness of thought or speech to divide Mawley from him. The boy's sympathy was not of embarrassment but of what, thought he in his pride, was genuine understanding; and perhaps it really was understanding, for his tragedy, great though it was in its stature, had ultimately the simplicity of a child's despair.

His last visit brought him to Mawley's bedside the day before that holiday ended. For the first time he was, it seemed, in great spirits. He talked fully and in a manner that raised his listener upward into a sphere of high enchantment. The boy's own mood of pleased anticipation, concerned with the return of the School and a renewal of life, may have encouraged him, as it did aid the readiness of the other's wits, and colour his imagination together with his words. He seemed not to wish to cease talking, and in the end not to be able to cease, for the torrent of phrase and exclamation bore him on and on, while Mawley dealt with an evening meal, hardly tasting the food.

He was speaking of the great goodness of life, and of its beauty. No matter that it seems cruel, he insisted; it is great and beautiful as much for its cruelty as for its gentlenesses. But it must be lived fully; every waste was beauty lost and perception delayed. And it could be as beautiful in solitude as it could in crowded places.

Men and women, he said, are all more conscious of the will to do good than of a desire to do evil. Even if they do harm it is without full understanding, and so without real intention; and understanding must be taught in schools by men, as well as afterwards by more intimate experiences...

To Mawley this seemed a strange way for that dark and silent man to talk to a boy. Had it not been for the elation he had aroused in him, Mawley must certainly have felt the embarrassment of one listening to a passionate confession by a stranger; but there was a great excitement in that broad, bare room, and the beds widely spaced in a square of barren white promontories round the four walls were as attentive as they both were to what he was saying.

'Some people would say that I should not talk to you like this.' His speech was now carefully exact, but rapid. 'But you are a nice lad, Mawley. I have known that. A little truth will neither alarm nor harm you. Listen to me: take great joy in all you do, however small it seems; make all things honest and let their purpose be kind. Learn to think always that there is no limit to what you can know and understand about the other fellow. What you know now—this day, this hour—can be added to by to-morrow's knowledge. Remember these words. To understand fully you must learn to love fully. See all men as people in a story whose ending you already know, and keep your eyes always on the circumstances of their lives, for it is those circumstances which make them do as they do, though there is something greater than circumstance which makes them what, in truth and honesty, they are. Originally, the human character is beautiful and innocent. Things may change it outwardly. With a hammer you can make a piece of gold into some cruel or ugly shape, but it will remain what it was—gold.'

He was leaning forward, that deep wound above his left temple beating violently. The lean folds of skin running upwards from the corners of his mouth were marked by shadow; in the depths of the eye-sockets his eyes burned, like coals in the eye-sockets of a bare skull, startling and unreal, framed by the fleshless astringency of the jaws and cheeks, and the broken curve of that brown forehead behind which the brain, like a prompter hidden, hung on the tide of his words. Mawley could see into his dark eyes. Looking through the flame of a fire you see the blackness beyond, still and untroubled like an iron intention.

'Do not think I know all there is to know,' he said. 'You, because you are to me only a child, might be dazzled or confounded by my words, and I would not have that. It is man's most difficult task to impart both knowledge and understanding. Remember this: some day you too will learn that there are times in your life when it is not in your power to avoid hurting others. Then do what you have to do, quickly—whatever it is. If it is very difficult, your own courage will pardon much in your deed. But you must know that those who love you will be the better for it; and then, when your mind is made up and you can act, you will have no more fear and no impatience. Once, when I was young, someone said to me in reproof for some thoughtlessness, "You must learn how easy it is to hurt those you love…"

Then, I believed that; afterwards I found that it was not true, for it is easiest to hurt those who love you—those you yourself love may not be open to harm from you, according to the measure of their regard for you. But if they in turn love you, then beware. Everything you do will have tremendous meaning for them.'

He sighed, and silence fell. The dark had already come; but there was light and warmth about the bed from the tall orange cylinders of a radiator on the floor. It seemed as though he, and not the boy, were sick of some great pain; but Mawley could not easily understand what he had been saying.

His voice had been changed by his thought when next he spoke.

'I have been looking at you. You are young and clean. You have a long time to live. Now, in another day, the new term will begin. I hope it will be a happy one—for all of you.'

Mawley said, surely it would be happy.

'Well,' he said, apparently with some difficulty. 'You must all make it happy for yourselves. If many work together to that end, the faults or weaknesses of one, or a few, will not spoil their happiness.'

'But, sir,' Mawley argued, reasonably, 'you will be here too. Or are you going away?'

He smiled and reassured him.

'Yes, I shall be here. I shall always be here. But more depends on you now than on me.'

Drawn back from the dull orange light, his face was dark in the darkness. He stood up and walked to the door.

'Would you like me to put the light on for you now? Or would you rather lie in the darkness and sleep?'

Mawley said he would have it on. The man smiled, wished him a good night, and was gone.

Charles came up the stairs, clattering and stumbling in his haste. When he was by Mawley's bed in the dormitory, the other could see the rain shining on his white face like tears.

'You know, I suppose,' he said dully, and seated himself on the bed's edge. 'What will happen now? I can't believe it. It doesn't seem possible.'

'What did I know?'

'Don't you know?' he said, slowly. 'The Head. He's dead. Last night, in the storm in town, he—killed himself. Good God! When I say it it seems to mean nothing. I can't understand it. I can't. To shoot yourself...'

There was nothing to say that could yet be said between them; they were too young. The whole of the previous evening's scene came back into Mawley's mind quickly and savagely, bitter with sudden self-scorn. They looked at one another, and something stayed Mawley from telling him about it—the inevitable glamour of all secrets, or perhaps merely the wish not to seem to peer too deeply beneath a surface. He was already exhausted. To increase the boy's own distress, he noticed tears on Charles's cheeks, heavy tears bigger than the rain-drops, moving slowly down. Suddenly the great bell of the chapel began to ring, as it rang only on Sundays and on the first day of a new term. It crashed among its own echoes, each stroke hanging crowded on the air and spreading out as relentlessly as a ripple spreads on the face of still water, impossible of arrest. There came, after the first stroke, the frantic beating of pigeons' wings; they were always sent flinging across the day from their refuge in the towers, as though so great a sound had muscular force to hurl them out like a giant. They wheeled through the rain under the grey sky, past the windows against which Charles's ruddy head, wet and ruffled, was outlined darkly.

Trying to divert both their minds from struggling with something they could not understand, Mawley told him of holiday experiences—of Mary, in particular, whose impulsive, speechless love-making in the empty sanatorium (its greatest colour her flushed, embarrassed face framed in a brilliant handkerchief tied over her head) had, until this morning, appeared as the only drama of those dull days. At what was no doubt a frank enough account of actions and words quite unreal to him, he looked startled.

'Did she really do that?' he said. 'It seems horrible, somehow.' But he asked other questions, his face flushing slightly but his gaze steadily refusing to be ashamed. To the whole recital of masculine braggadocio he listened closely, and neither of them could smile at it, after all; for its element of tragedy, a woman's sterility, embarrassed him deeply when he understood it.

'Don't tell anybody else,' he said. 'They'd only laugh.'

After that, it was almost a relief for them to speak of the Headmaster again. Charles evidently felt this death passionately, for some reason not connected with death at all. In retrospect, it seems probable that he had unconsciously idealized the person of the dead man as the

159

manifestation of something symbolized by no other person in the School, instinctively realizing the power, the 'goodness' he would have called it, of that positive masculinity which in Penworth, his closest friend until now, he could not find.

'I don't know why,' he said, 'but it makes me feel lost. If I'd known him well, or...You knew him better than I did. He was such a good man, and so kind to everybody. So strong. Now I can't see what will happen.'

The suggestion that Mr. Jolly might succeed to the office surprised and pleased him.

'I never thought of that,' he said. 'Perhaps he will; do you think? He's a good man, too. But Dr. Fox was so young.' He smiled slightly frowning over a thought. 'Perhaps I liked him because his name was the same as mine. I don't know. That was the first thing he said, the day I came. And now— he's gone.'

He stared at his clasped hands in silence for a while. His eyes were shining when he looked up.

'I never had a father,' he said. 'I mean, I never knew mine. That makes another reason why I liked *him* so much, I suppose. But of course I didn't know him well. But you couldn't help feeling...Could you?'

He was searching his own mind to find why he should incline so to take this as a loss personal to himself. The Headmaster, familiar enough in sight, had been actually a personality cloistered, remote from us, hidden away in a sound-proof room with a green baize door that closed slowly on the delaying action of a vacuum stop; he had used his canes on boys, but there was that in his manner that made such intimate approaches to him causes for pride and a general increase of esteem and self-esteem in the boys punished. Yet that was all. Charles was trying to reconcile with this apparent remoteness his own sudden impression of intimate knowledge of the man himself, and the confusion of his mind added to his feeling of grief.

At last he got up and went out to his own dormitory across the empty landing, putting his cases on the bed and opening the top of the locker. That bell went on booming, every thirty seconds, strange, startling and out of place in his mind, but at one with the day. He was the first who had returned; there was this day of holiday still to end, before classes began in the morning. He looked down the white, empty dormitory, dim with winter.

Oh, he thought; and the tears flowed easily. Lying on the cold whiteness of the coverlet he held his eyes open, staring, and the pillowcase, fresh and smooth, smelling still of soap and steam, became wet under his cheek.

We should have known, he thought. To die like that...

Presently his thought grew calm again. It was the first time death had in any way come near to him, and, with his heart already troubled at another return to the School and shadowed with regret for what had been denied to him in the holiday, such a piece of news, hinted at in the shouts of paper-boys on the smoke-dark station, briefly told in the cable pages of the morning late editions, had so burdened his mind with grief that his thought became confused, and all he could ask of himself was, What will happen now? again and again, as the train plunged through mist and rain and its own smoke, bringing him nearer the School from town. The windows of the compartment were clouded over on the outside and thinly slashed with slanting rain; this and his own unhappy preoccupation caused him to be carried a station too far. There he got out, and with the suitcases weighing more and more heavily on his arms walked back along the main road to the School gates.

The Matron told him he could have dinner at noon in the Hall. Her eyes were red and ugly with crying, and she peered at him between swollen lids, trying to see what he was feeling; but his face showed her only what he knew, and she smiled and nodded and let him go. When the door was closed after him she sank back heavily into her creaking basket-chair, and began to sob again, with the ease and freedom observable in some women, to whom the drama of grief is a rich comfort.

It's the books that make them so heavy, Charles thought, as he took the cases upstairs in Chatterton.

When at length he had unpacked them, he changed his clothes and had dinner. His mother's calm and quiet would have comforted him; he had long since forgotten his momentary irritations, and ached to be home again, and considered with foreboding the long line of weeks stretched forward from that day, before he would be there again, and before he would see the girl. While a staring, red-eyed maid served him with his meal, as he sat solitary in the far end of the great Hall, gazing now at the black beams and struts overhead, now at his plate, he determined to work very hard in the winter term, so that the time should seem to pass more easily; and once more he said to himself that a sense of loss would lose itself in work. But when he thought of Sundays in the Chapel, with no familiar face looking east to the altar from the golden shadow of that pew reserved for the Headmaster and his family, grief came back to him keenly, and he could not clearly see his food for tears.

The term opened like the second movement of a symphony, slow and pitched in a minor key. Work, said the Common Room notice board tersely, would proceed as usual, and after a special service in Chapel all classes would sit at once.

As though nothing had happened, Charles thought, marching down the wet path with the rest of his House. As though in a haste to forget.

He was readier than all others to begin work and thought again, for he felt he must forget this death whose obscure significance troubled him so. During the delay that preceded the entrance of the Master taking them for an hour of mathematics it was strange to hear the quiet in that long grey room, which would on any other morning have been in an uproar of raised voices and thrown books. This morning boys looked at one another with almost guilty expressions of sobriety. They were for once not drunk with their own irrepressible youth. Groups sitting and leaning by the windows talked among themselves, with self-conscious quietness; their eyes were bright but tremendously set in seriousness above the healthy colour of their cheeks and lips hanging on speech. Charles laid out his books for the hour and crossed in front of the dais to join them. He stood in silence while they talked, sometimes looking at the urgent mobility of their young faces, sometimes letting his eyes take him out through the window, past the tree's upward-soaring strength of trunk and branch into the breaking sky beyond. In his mind, going ever and ever back over events up to this moment of troubled pause, there still haunted the thread of the last long *'Amen'* of the choir poised up above the darkly packed bays, between floor and vault; he followed it as it floated like a breath down the white length of the chapel to the altar, held and preserved, as it faded, by one sustained pedal note from the unseen organ. As though in a dream of peace the service had ended.

He wondered what happened when a man died; whether there was indeed peace for the body whose life had rushed out like a man from an empty house, and for the brain in its weariness; whether something neither darkness nor light came quickly and finally down over all. His mind, used to small, pathetic deaths in the fields and among trees and beside the ceaseless life of streams, made no suggestion to him of a survival beyond the last passion of flesh and tissue. The act of death blocked his view now like a wall; and a fear that was no fear of death, but was the desolate fear of one who sees a symbol torn down and destroyed, made him long for some deed that would reaffirm manhood.

At last the Master came in, staring ahead darkly, conscious of expressing sorrow in the careful sternness of his impassive features; conscious also of being watched in every movement. When he had reached the dais and mounted it, he turned about, and, after allowing himself to puzzle them with a brief, keen smile, composed his face firmly.

'Good morning. Now…Where did we stop last time?'

He could feel, as he dragged them through the fifty minutes of that first interminable period, that they were in no mood to work; but like a master of hounds he hallooed them on, wondering meanwhile what was happening in the Masters' Common Room.

Mr. Jolly was there, slumped in a chair, his head down between hunched shoulders, looking like a large sick bird. From the grey depths of his silence he watched the younger Masters; his eyes bulged slightly and his long nose pointed to the floor in the middle of the room, like the muzzle of an unhappy dog; a rakish lock of hair hung across his left eye dejectedly. He knew what they were thinking; it was what he thought himself, and what he deeply feared.

I'm damned if I do, he said loudly in his mind. I'm damned if I will. If the Board insist—then for six weeks, until they find another man. I'm too old. One House is enough for me; I'm damned if I look after a whole school-ful. They can find a younger man. I'm too tired.

An ageing man's sorrow, without the passionate quick-ness of leap and fall that younger hearts feel, was rising in his mind, a grey tide, steady and without rhythm or cessation. He sank more deeply into his chair, and turned his eyes to the fire prattling and whispering joyously in the hearth. This was the saddest thing he had ever known, he thought, cursing himself as he had been continually doing, without bitterness but most deeply, for not having been active to help that man while there was still time. He had not thought—that, he told himself, was a great sin, not to have thought, not to have been in his observing and his thought as solicitous as the other had been for them all.

He sighed, without much emotion. At sixty, he thought, a man understands too much and feels too little, and takes all comfort for granted.

After he had sat still there for some time, he heaved himself up out of the chair and went out into the dark corridor whose only lighting came from the School Common Room to which it led. He looked towards the Chapel, and in a while noticed that the rain had stopped. Hunching his stooped shoulders, looking like a tall grey bird ruffling its feathers, he stepped out into the stillness of the day and moved up the Chapel path, slowly, as though he were tired. At the doors, which still stood open after the morning's service, he paused, looking in without sight. Then he turned on his heel suddenly, his hands thrust down into his pockets, and made his way across the parade ground between the mirrors of its little pools. The day was grey and still, as though waiting to rain again; from the main porch the too-familiar clamour of a bell rang out upon the air. He remembered that after this break he had a class, an hour with the Sixth, and at the thought of the effort of commencing work again he groaned gently and stopped to stare at the wet grass.

Charles, coming through the outer door of the changing-room, saw his tall figure stooped against the sky on the edge of the slope. He walked up to the far end of the flat field, where trees were gathered thinly along each side of the boundary fence, overshadowing in places the black surface of a road beyond. The earth was soft under his feet; with eyes that were accustomed to observe each movement of growth he saw the bright green spears of the

166

grass standing like the lances of a tiny army upwards from the soil's clinging darkness.

Life had been arrested by this common calamity. So it seemed to him; for the steady forward movement of his mind through time and youth had been made to pause once more by something which he did not understand. Wandering aimlessly along under the trees, letting the twigs crack and bend beneath his feet, he wondered if life were to be understood, or whether it was not till a man was old, too old to be any longer a part of the world's beauty, that understanding came to him as a compensation. This thing had made the idea of death seem for the first time fierce and positive. He had never before thought of it like that; it had been, if he considered it, calm and negatively conclusive—the lowering of a curtain when something was ended, not the terrific, violent, significant climax of the play itself. He could not understand his own feelings, that made him shiver and close and open his hands; not consciously in his mind did he associate himself nearly with the man who had died. But the shock and grief of such a positive dying was forcing him to substitute, in the vision of thought, his own mind and body for the body of the man now dead; he saw his body wandering distractedly at the bidding of its mind seeking some peace and extinction; he saw it lying dead on a cold floor, heavy and broken, looked at curiously or with horror or anguish by eyes that moved and lived, told of by tongues that still could speak.

He had lost the symbol of a necessity, but this he did not know. He felt only a dull pain in the incessant contemplation of the idea of death; and it was indeed incessant, though a more obedient part of his mind had guided his hands and taken him through that period of study not long since brought to a close by the monotonous bell.

He opened his eyes widely, and looked at the grey roof of sky above the still leaves overhead. Only a few yards away was Mr. Jolly, halted in his walking and staring at the ground with eyes that bulged slightly above the thoughtful pointing of his nose. He appeared to have forgotten something which he was trying now to remember; as Charles watched, his shoulders shrugged and his head sank low between them. Charles moved away, but Mr. Jolly called after him, calling his name. He turned and went back.

'You were back early, weren't you, Fox?'

'Yes, sir.'

'Always report to me when you come back early, old chap. If you were to take it into your head to go and—commit suicide, now, no one would know.'

The extraordinary harshness and vibration in his voice made Charles redden and avoid his eyes. Mr. Jolly looked again on the ground, as though waiting for some more lively reply. At length he raised his head.

'What am I saying?'

His tone was husky, as always.

'I'm sorry, sir,' Charles said.

Mr. Jolly nodded his head soberly. 'Always report to me. What in God's name brought you back early, Fox?'

'I've been working at home, sir, and I wanted to—to get back so that—so that...'

Mr. Jolly gazed boldly at him now. 'Well? "So that" what?'

'So that I could settle down straight away, without getting put out by—coming back, sir.'

'I see. Does change upset you, son? You oughtn't to be upset at your age—er—at your age. Well, I can tell you there are some changes coming now...' He stopped and pointed his nose at the ground, a grey dog who has lost its master. 'Don't you young devils start thinking you'll have an easy time of it with me. And what's more...'

The lines on his forehead and cheeks deepened as he spoke; his eyes looked with melancholy slyness from their leaf-brown lids drawn fine with wrinkles, and long rayed creases from their outer corners made them seem to smile. Charles studied his face nervously, and waited, watching his eyes move from side to side as though spying out an eavesdropper among the slim rain-dark trunks.

'Well—go along,' he said mildly. 'I don't want to have anything to do with any of you—you toads.'

His face creased in a smile round the jutting sombreness of his long nose. Charles knew his habit of using strong epithets with that brilliant smile; it was as characteristic as the lock of hair over his eye suggesting past revelry, and just now it was very reassuring. He withdrew from there.

Mr. Jolly, left alone, ceased to smile, and with sadness making the day more grey for him pondered on the intractable divergence of inclination from knowledge of duty. When he turned, raising his eyes from the leafy earth and seeing the School buildings across the wet field, with Chatterton, his own House, jutting out from the main buildings towards him, he scowled, and his blue full eyes looked fierce but without cruelty. By the time he had sauntered gloomily back, and was once more walking down the chapel path towards the porch where the bell hung, he knew what he would eventually do, for the School and for himself. He growled in his throat.

With Mr. Jolly as Headmaster they felt at ease, particularly those of them who were becoming panicky already at the nearer approach of the examinations. He was familiar, even when his new authority caused them to look more closely at him as he passed, even when he was no longer 'Old Jolly' and 'Jolly Roger', but 'the Head'—masculinity personified. He was not changed; his hoarse voice still drawled in the Sixth, and murmured behind the closed door of his room in Chatterton in the evenings; if he looked more tired and growled more often, it was not the School who noticed it. A change of Headmasters is acutely felt in a School where many of the boys are old for their years and many of the Masters seem young for theirs. Had a strange man come among them just then, the tension between Masters and boys might have been so heightened that useful work would have become impossible—just as impossible to the insensitive, who would not have noticed the tension in the air, as to the sensitive, whom laziness made the others imitate. Innumerable small changes would have set their small fishpond seething; the withdrawal or substitution of habitual understandings between the Masters' Common Room and the Big Study would have been irksome to the conservative-minded Englishmen who frankly disliked changes even in their least interesting classes; even the different and suspicious personality of a strange man would have sent the School into a slight hysteria of nerves and self-consciousness.

As it was, nothing like this happened. Mr. Jolly, new to them as the supreme arbiter of their destinies there, was familiar and well liked as a man. Such a calm settled once more over the life within and about those tall walls of ruddy brick that Charles, whose lost symbol was thus replaced, was hardly aware of the growing pains in his own mind, and worked steadily through the winter term. He did not go home for the usual mid-term week-end because he was unwilling to be sheered off even for a day from the straight course of his purpose, or estranged even for a day from the atmosphere of overseen study. Instead, he spent much time in the library, reading and making casual references which might somehow concern his work; and, as Mawley was now going about nimbly on crutches, they walked together in the afternoons, moving up and down the parade ground near the edge of the slope, slowly because he had a regard for crippled movement over the uneven ground there. Those days, from Thursday until Tuesday, were cold and fine; coming like that in the middle of a stormy season, in the middle of a term trumpeted in by the passion of a great man's despair, they were halcyon in their brilliance and calm. Charles, deeply sensitive to all weathers, felt this, and as he walked through the pallor of afternoon sunlight looking out over country stretching for ever westward below him, he rejoiced in the elemental peace that lay in earth and air and drew a veil of misty blue over those green distances. The hard and brittle outlines of summer were gone from all things, and in his mind a like

171

sharpness of definition was being softened by experiences of which he had had no thought in the solitude of his life before. The coming change of this in him was perceptible; the very virginity of his mind was a reason why every new impress made upon it by circumstance and thought should stand out so clearly; he was so lacking in the armament of pretence and habit, so open to surprise, that not to show his feelings or the struggle of his thought would have been unnatural, and impossible except in the presence of his own fear. In his suspicion the body could die innumerable small deaths of insult and outrage; and that was the only thing he feared. Before such a suspicion, every unkind intention is a deadly one, every physical insult a mental agony of shame. He was not a physical coward, and would at that time have undertaken many things which to others might have seemed fearsome; but in such action he was the master of his own body, not the victim of foreign impulses which, because he was so far from understanding them, seemed full of evil power. At no time could he imagine himself laying hands on any creature to do hurt.

In that way he did not change; but a striving for tolerance towards others, unnatural and rather too solemn at his age, proved his growth and hinted at decisions not yet faced. He was new to the action of objective reasoning, and spent time trying to put the increasing complexity of his feelings into some ordered arrangement of thought, because he felt, with a blind instinct still, that only from conscious and clear thought could clear action spring. Already, being in the dawn of manhood and guessing at manhood's responsibilities of choice, he was forcing himself to abandon instinct for reason as the one guide to action. How it would have pleased Mr. Jolly to observe this effect which life at the School was having upon his mind, no one can now know; without doubt he would have applauded Charles's intention even while he deprecated the young man's seriousness.

Serious he must have been in the ultimate privacy of his mind, but he was gay and happy enough during those days of early July sunshine, full of hopes about the progress of work and still intoxicated at times with the old wine of learning. Penworth was among those who remained at the School, and he came out one afternoon and joined this promenade, bare-headed in the sun like Charles, blinking and smiling as he swung along leisurely. The misted soft-ness of the landscape spreading out beyond the red height of the slope moved him like a gentle intellectual laxative, mildly, and as he looked at Charles shining in the sun with a fire of youth and beauty he talked of his own boyhood, and made a loose enchanting picture of lanes and woods wet with spring rain and brilliantly in leaf again, and went over the names of the flowers he knew caressingly; or there would come into his mind some almost undiscovered inn come upon during a summer walking tour, where in good self-conscious undergraduate style he had eaten bread and cheese, drunk red wine, and composed carefully impas-sioned verses, imagining himself as fine a fellow any day as Parson Herrick snoring over an empty claret jug in the half-light of a summer dawn, with a guttering candle on the table by him. Talking of Herrick took his mind to Parson's Pleasure...it was unlikely that Herrick ever swam in anything as weak as water...in those days they left water to its proper function, which was chiefly to define the outlines of land, good and firm beneath the feet, or to make pleasant sounds of exhortation when one was courting a lass; they had no far-fetched, pagan bathing-cult nonsense...

Charles suggested the Greeks, a civil and civilized people who bathed continually. By the droop of Penworth's eyelids he knew he had reminded him of his own words, in the choir loft, that hot summer afternoon. Penworth was smiling, and began to set upon him with apparent serious-ness, arguing that a nation could be highly cultured without taking to water.

'Like the English,' Charles said delightedly.

That, of course, was different. That was a matter of latitude and longitude; this climate, now, was a purely Greek climate, different altogether from England's. It was a Greek country, probably; some thought the immortal gods had taken refuge here. After what? After Rome and Egypt invaded Greece and set the seeds of a crop of fruit-vendors and professional immigrants who would possess this country as they had possessed America.

'There's for you, my red-headed acolyte.'

The air grew colder. They walked up and down more quickly. Over beyond the dark trees of the river channel the sun had gone down; from the edge of the slope it seemed as though the far horizon was raised in air by the pale force of light beneath it. The shadows disappeared. Charles, in the quiet melancholy of that hour, remembered the hills of home, shadowless and mysterious as the last light of evening swam up to their crests and swept on into the high

sky of dusk. He remembered telling the girl about it; and his
heart beat heavily with happiness at the thought of being
there with her, standing invisible on the hill-side together,
while from the darkening depth of the valley a night chorus
of frogs froze the chill air.

'You're very quiet,' Penworth said. 'Want to go in?'

'No, sir,' Charles said.

'What were you thinking of? Or,' he added with an
effort at jocularity, 'ought I to have said, "Who are you
thinking of?" '

'I don't know, quite...'

He felt inclined to tell him about that day in the grove,
to see what he would say, yet for some reason he hesitated.
As he looked back now on it, the whole adventure, which
no amount of work nor stress of subsequent experience
could cause to fade in any remembered detail, became
startlingly clear in its beauty. He heard the wind sigh and
toss in the pine needles, and as he watched her bending
towards the little perfumed fire, towards him, in a still pose
revealing her breasts' warm and secret pallor, the heavy
drops from the wet leaves above still fell like little animals
on the dead leaves beneath. Things he now remembered
surprised him, for he had not known he saw them. The
growth of manhood, becoming stronger in him, sought
them out as tangible things on which to spend its adoration.
He was suddenly conscious of the strength of his desire. The
white fullness of her two knees, where the stretched skin
shone dully over the flesh beneath as she leaned back from
looking into his face; and the brownish smoothness of the
backs of her hands closed and twisted towards the licking

taper flames—unbelievable nakedness in such outstretched hands, and in her knees like ivory cut across by the green hem of the skirt. The fire was mirrored minutely upon her eyes, hiding whatever might have been passing across their depths; in the dry, healthy paleness of her lips quiet lay, and slept there. He tried to imagine what they would look like when she herself was asleep; but all he could see was their upward urgency and softness, as they would be beneath his own when she desired him to kiss her.

A wedge of restless pain was hammered between his ribs by the insistence of such thoughts; he flung his arms wide, presently helpless, and the back of one hand struck Penworth lightly.

'What now?' Penworth said, and in the dusk his voice sounded strange, as though he had been uneasy in thought since he last spoke.

'Oh, I am sorry,' Charles cried, embarrassed by what he had done, surprised not to be alone.

'Well, you didn't do me much harm. What made you do that, child?'

Charles said dully, 'I don't mean to be childish,' which made Penworth laugh and put his arm round his shoulders, leaning no weight.

'Perhaps you're not so childish after all,' he said soberly. 'I gather you were thinking of some young person, like yourself; and your own inability to come, as it were, to grips with the more difficult noumena of loving made you fling your arms out—throwing the problems away, to enjoy the joys.'

Charles looked round at him, but could not see any

expression on his face in that dark light, though the ironic disapproval in his voice was clear. During his disturbed silence they heard the lowing of cows down below them in the milking shed, and a man's voice, as quiet as the light of his lantern, speaking to the beasts as he clapped the bails to behind their horns. An occasional clatter of cans made the evening seem more still; a train had rounded the bend beyond the station, and silence came down conclusively after it.

'Now,' said Penworth sharply, listening to sounds and silence. 'Was I right? Here is the only perfect moment for a confession. Speak now or be silent for ever.'

His voice had a light sting of sarcasm whipping his words.

Charles laughed nervously; it died in his throat before it could reach the stillness in which they were.

'I didn't think of it as love,' he said.

'All the more reason why you will now that I've suggested it,' Penworth said lightly and with a faint note of scorn. 'That is part of my duty, you remember—to crystallize emotions into thoughts; to tidy up thoughts that have been allowed to grow too long without pruning; to focus the eye of reason...'

Charles described how he went home, and told him of the grove and the mushrooms and the day, stumbling often at having to speak for so long without pause and the quick stimulus of reply. When he told how he had seen the girl suddenly, Penworth was more attentive, and he could feel him listening; but in his own growing preoccupation the other's lack of sympathy was not apparent to him.

'She was wet, so I made a fire. She thought I shouldn't—she didn't know, you see, that it was my own place. So I told her. And then she said perhaps she'd better go, she had no right there; but it was raining. She couldn't go. So I—I made her sit by the fire, and she kept looking at me in a very strange way, as though I'd done something to her.'

'Perhaps you had,' Penworth murmured, tightening his arm to make him walk more slowly; for as he had spoken his steps quickened with his heart under the sharp reality of words.

'Well, we sat there till the rain stopped, and then we went away; we went home.'

'Did you tell each other your names and talk about yourselves?'

Charles remained oblivious to that faint, disappointed scorn.

'No—well, I asked her her name. But we didn't talk much.'

'Silence speaking more than words, eh?'

'It wasn't exactly that, you see. But you can't go asking a—another person questions and poking about and—can you? when you don't know them...'

' "Her". Mind your grammar, you young ass, or you'll be at the mercy of any intelligent female.'

'Her, then. Well, you can't do that. At least, not all at once. Anyhow, I didn't want to; I didn't want to know anything, not then. It was just something very surprising, that's all, and strange, too, to see her come in like that, not knowing I was there, and not minding. Of course, it was my mother's country; I mean the Far Field is hers, and the

178

grove and all—oh, I'm so glad. Life is wonderful when you're there. Anyhow, I said she might get a cold and die, and she said she wouldn't mind. She would though...'

Penworth's prompt laughter had almost a sneer in it.

'Of course she would. Well, what then?'

Aware now of the unsympathetic effect of his words on Penworth, who appeared not to approve of the idea of girls, Charles kept his silence while they turned at the far end of the field. Against the dark sky the scattered lights of high windows were golden and arid, suggesting to their minds the emptiness within those walls.

'Come on,' Penworth said impatiently. 'Tell me the rest. We shall have to go in to tea in a few minutes.'

'Well,' Charles said slowly, 'that is all, really. We looked at each other for a long time.'

Penworth let out his breath most dramatically, in a whisper which Charles did not hear.

'So at last the rain stopped, and we went home. The fields were all wet, and you've no idea how good they smelt.'

They walked very slowly, in silence. Charles felt the warm weight of Penworth's arm about his shoulders, and could smell the faint tobacco-smell quietly treasured in the rough cloth. He wanted to move away from that manly arm, but did not like to seem willing to break the spell of silence borne on by the slow rhythm of their steps.

Penworth had been deeply and curiously affected by the simplicity of Charles's words. 'We looked at each other for a long time.' The thought irritated him strangely as though this boy were deliberately frustrating some ambition of his. He knew of such looks. He had once seen a great writer at a crowded undergraduate party in Oxford. There was a girl at the party, someone strange to him. She sat on one side of the room, and the poet, the lion of that gathering of young *illuminati*, was against the other wall, with young men and women about him, chirping and chattering like a lot of birds; but once their eyes had met they could not look away from one another. So lively was the talk, so young and important that gathering, that for a long time nobody noticed; but the poet became more silent, and though he smiled and seemed to listen to what they were eager to say about his work and his ideals, he now looked like a man burningly athirst who sees a pool springing in clear silver from the rocks of barrenness, where he dare not try to reach it because of the spell of weakness its presence put upon his flesh. And she, too, felt the anguish of such an ecstasy; her face leaned towards him, and in that crowded room she leapt to be possessed.

But in the picture which Charles's words had brought into his mind there was a troubling element of innocence. Perhaps, he thought, these two children, opening like flowers together in the sunshine of the body's life, had already taken each from each a virginal purity which, if they were to adore one another with their bodies also, would make such an act binding not only upon the flesh but upon that high spirit which suffers earthly experience both as an ennoblement and as a bondage of chains until death. He knew that in its first surrender of self an immaculate body has put upon it a mark as deep as a brand to the very bone; a mark which no later surrenders, even without number and to the whole fullness of variety, can erase or alter.

The thought of such a surrender, with its appearance of triumph, now discomforted him greatly. God knows, he thought distractedly, why I should worry. It's none of my business. The boy's an impetuous fool, like everybody else in this damned place.

He repeated that to himself, and removed his arm from about Charles's shoulders, expressing to himself by that gesture of renunciation a disinterest in which he had not the power now to believe. Here was this youth, beautiful, conscious, almost his own creature, intellectually at all events, and apparently ready to fall happily in love with a girl. He felt, suddenly, the danger of defeat in what had seemed to him a contest where his own triumph was sure; and from silent condemnation of Charles his mind turned to exercise itself bitterly in generalizations condemning mankind; until finally it returned to Charles.

'Well, I dare say you'll get over it, Fox.'

Charles heard the bitterness in his voice, and instinctively added to it the removal of that manly arm from his shoulders; but the sum of this addition he could not see, though he felt its content of disapproval.

'I'm sorry, sir, if it's been boring you to talk like this,' he said with shame. 'I didn't mean...'

'Boring!' Penworth laughed. 'Make no mistake. It's been most entertaining, I assure you. Most illuminating.'

He spoke lightly, knowing well the superior power of levity as a destroyer of sensitive antagonists.

'I'm sorry, sir,' Charles said again, and was unhappily silent. He wondered what he had done to annoy him; he had seemed so ready to hear, and now here he was—angry;

or at least not interested any more, as though laughing at such confidence. There slowly awoke in Charles that which Penworth had never before aroused against himself—that defiance he showed to all others. He felt unhappy, struggling with it yet knowing himself to be in the right. And Penworth refused to speak.

Better for this boy, he was thinking angrily, to be made wiser by some married woman, like the rest of us; made ashamed of his own clumsiness, his own youth, his own manhood, when the thing is done, and comforted and forgotten and allowed to forget. Better that for the price of a little shame and self-disgust he should buy peace and the sort of freedom that will make the rest of his life his own concern...

As they walked, he tried to put aside such troubled and troubling thoughts, telling himself that they were hardly pertinent to the passing sentimentality of a boy-and-girl affair of first love. These two would of course become parted by the tide of youth's life, and would forget, as everyone forgot, the surprise and the harmless passions of childhood dreamery. But the magic of his vision lingered like a perfume in his brain; once more he was abashed by his own damnable desire for the whiteness and innocence of the boy even then by his side, sharing this silence with him as it could share other silences less obsessed by such longings.

In the darkness he drew in his lips between his teeth, biting upon them and made desperate by their folded softness. The tip of his tongue found their smooth warmth; he closed his right hand hard round the rough bowl of the pipe in his pocket, taking between his lips a thirsty breath of the cold air lying against his raised face, to cool his throat and steady the quickening pace of his thought.

'Here we are,' he said, with deliberate curtness. 'And in two minutes the bell will go for tea, so you'd better get a move on, or you'll miss your soup.' It was in his mind to say also, 'And forget about the nonsense you've been talking', but instead he turned abruptly and walked away in the darkness.

There were several Masters staying at the School, and half a dozen boys, whose table was by the swing-doors leading to the kitchen. The Masters sat at the dais table, looking down the Hall, pleased with its emptiness.

From his seat against the wall Charles saw Penworth come in, his pale face marked with a frown under the mild light of globes high overhead. He sat between Waters and another, and it was some time before he began to join in their talk. His still face, seeming not to move as he took the food before him, was like a yellowish mask; only now and then, when they spoke to him, did he turn his head sharply to one side or the other, wiping his lips almost nervously before he replied. But in a while he began to smile, and before long there were loud shouts of laughter from that end of the long dim Hall, which made the little group of boys first look astonished, and then break into a merry conversation among themselves, with a great deal of argument, in which with an effort Charles joined.

He was still confused from the experiences and the atmosphere of the evening, upon which his thoughts had woven a pattern of colour and feeling as he urged memory to feed imagination; memory as much more rich now as

183

imagination was ready and fruitful after Penworth's words about love.

Sitting there making himself break silence lest he should appear too deliberately isolated, he thought uneasily how strange Penworth had been while they talked together, and wondered whether having learnt of this surprising and lovely encounter, he would ever do again what he had done that day in his room. He had changed a little since then, though; until this evening he had become more easy in his looks and his informal speech, and now Charles's words and his discovery in them must help to set a seal upon that change after all, so that they could perhaps talk together as two men should, without either of them being troubled by the fear of finding in his own words some evocative overtone of remembrance or suggestion. Perhaps, he thought, all friendships should begin with something as regrettable and clumsy as that.

Going about it in his mind, he even felt ashamed of his inclination to withdraw from the warm weight and intimacy of that arm about his shoulders, telling himself that it was indeed childish, and showed his ignorance of how varied can be the meanings of one small thoughtless gesture.

But Penworth's sudden coldness remained in his memory, and he could not find complete contentment.

Later, as he came up the dim covered way and passed the empty unlit classroom on the ground floor, he heard from Penworth's room the reasoning of a Bach prelude, played with smooth, incisive bowing, marching upon the air like a philosophy; it reminded him how, during a dissertation one afternoon upon the effect of music on the mind and thought, and indirectly upon action, Penworth had amused him by describing how, when he found the content of his own playing degenerate into sentimentality, he made himself abandon all other compositions for a long study of Bach. He smiled now as he passed that closed door and went quietly up the stairs, pursued by the slow exhortation of the strings. This must be another period of discipline. Penworth believed that music known and remembered affected action; take the best, he said, and play it to yourself alone. Charles wished, as he walked into the dark dormitory, that the music rooms were open; he wanted to explore again some Beethoven slow movements, for that was his mood.

When he came down the stairs the words and actions of the music, which had haunted him above, still soared into the night. He sat on the lowest stair, shivering with cold, and held his face in his hands to listen. At last a pause came, and the rustling of sheet-music promised something further. The flow of his thought stopped and circled as the music ended; it hovered in question round the violin's silence, and was suddenly bound, and freed in a great leap, as the instrument's voice started in a key of passion and with hot emphasis the fourfold opening theme of the César Franck sonata, designed and sensuous, like a flower.

Charles had never heard it before, and so could not know why it was such a favourite with Penworth. He sat and listened, troubled now beyond belief, until the ultimate joy of the canon released him, and he could go away.

By the time the August holidays fell due there were signs of the final breaking of winter, although not until after the September gales would lovers of the hot sun begin to think of summer. The term ended in a mood of strain and excitement; the School went into the spring vacation, and there was none to feel sorry that two-thirds of the time-table year had been put by. The third term remained; it hovered dangerously in the minds of many, and Charles, whose mind was stretched and tired by those weeks of unceasing work, felt afraid but dared not let himself relax in the acknowledgment of fear. Mr. Jolly sent for him to come to the Big Study on the morning before classes were formally ended.

'Well, Fox,' he said, leaning over the great wilderness of table and clasping his hands together on its edge. 'What are *you* going to do with yourself in this holiday?'

'I thought—I don't feel quite sure, sir,' Charles said. 'I did think I'd better go on working a bit all the time.'

Mr. Jolly turned his full eyes to left and right; the lids drooped slyly as he observed the back of familiar books; he cleared his throat and growled to himself.

'Well, that's what I wanted to ask you, old man,' he said hoarsely. 'It's no good you going and getting yourself overtired before the examinations. It's absolutely no good. On the other hand...'

He glared amiably at Charles, and his mouth twisted in a smile that creased his face like laughter.

'On the other hand, my lad, if you let go now you may find it damned hard to pick up again. You have worked hard; I wouldn't have thought you had it in you, son. But you've got it, all right. Now. As from the first week of next term there are—let me see.'

He took a calendar from a drawer and turned it over inquiringly with nose and forefinger. The lock of grey hair joined in the search.

'Er. Now there will be nine weeks from the beginning of next term until you sit. The last week or so is for a general revision of the course; there's always a Master with you, but you'll be mostly left to yourself. But any questions, always ask, old son. And if you want any extra hours besides those you're having now...'

He put away the time-table and leaned forward again.

'I can see you're a likely lad, Fox,' he growled. 'Don't be a fool and get excited over this examination. Don't think it's a matter of life and death.' He glared. 'If I had my way there'd not be any examinations. But I have an idea you can get through all right. And then you'll not be asked to work so hard again. Only I want you to do your best and get through. D'you hear?' he said loudly, 'you're going to get through.'

With a smile suggesting great satisfaction he sank back into the chair, his eyes still on Charles, who was also smiling. He knew Mr. Jolly's growling manners, and they made him want to laugh.

'Well, there—watch your step, er, Fox. Watch your step,' Mr. Jolly said finally, and waved him away.

But when he was at home, installed in the quiet of his own room, unease grew in him like torment, and his heart beat heavily as he looked at his books and thought of the grove and Margaret. That place would be alive and murmurous on such a day; the pollen from the russet pine tips would lie like incense on the air; and she would be there. From the garden hedge the cold, intoxicating perfume of the pittosporum flowers assailed him perpetually; the flowering was early, and in the close masses of leaves cream-coloured clusters of blossoms thickened each day, and sweetened the sharp air always. Beyond his window the wattle-tree still piled its treasure of decaying gold; its perfume was heavy on the air, too, and it murmured alive with the bees. He struggled against this earliness of spring, and could not get his mind in order. Down in the garden his mother was talking to Jimmy; it was a day of warm, still sunshine out there, and the roses were as hot as the faces of amorous girls. Lassitude lay drowsy in his flesh, as though sleep were wooing him; but the chill of night lingered still in the room, where the sun would not shine until noon came round and found him there bent over the pages.

He walked to the window. Jimmy was at work with a weeding tool in one of the long beds which would be later a high sapphire splendour of delphinium; his mother stood near, watching, and the rich mild sunlight fell across her head and shoulders with such a golden reflection from earth and air that there was no shadow in her averted face. Her slender hands looked enormous and ludicrous in thick gloves of cotton; a pair of scissors dangling from her right wrist swung slowly and caught the sun on their gaping blades; it flashed into his eyes and was gone. He waited for it to come again; it was like the secret illumination of a thought.

'If it comes again,' he said, 'I'll go.'

He closed his fingers and felt the sudden moisture in his palms. The scissors swung more slowly, and seemed to stop. He wondered if she would move. If she moved, if the scissors were taken away so that the sun could not flash from them into his eyes, he would stay with the books and note-books until lunch-time. He dared not move his head. Slowly the wide blades turned, and a low, faltering glint of light ran down one of them like water. Surely that was the sun's own acquiescence in his desire to go? The glint of light had been hesitant; he remained there, staring down into the garden's green and red, not even realizing that his mother had moved away until he saw her face bent and grave above a cluster of pale roses far away, by the low wall shadowy with moss. Against the darkness of the old brick her head in sunlight shone silver. He wondered how old she was, and was glad that age could be so clear-cut and peaceful.

When she saw him coming across the garden in the sun she straightened her back, beating those big gloves together, looking at him. His hair was dark and unruly; the light slanting blindly across it showed how ruddy it had become. She regarded him gravely, unable to tell him how close was his likeness to his father, though she felt the blankness of a remembered grief when she saw it. There was just that same high and defiant carriage of the head in the man who had begotten him. She looked at his mouth and eyes, but did not recognize them, for they were her own.

Charles said: 'I think I'll take Danny and go out for a while, Mother. I can't seem to settle down straight away.'

He looked at her and then away at all the garden about him, green and flowered and springing in its growth. The sky above the green, gold and pink of the camphor laurels and the deep darkness of the cypresses was brilliant, like water; there was no wind, and a madness of bees made the wattle-tree, blazing at a corner of the house, seem to swoon with the weight of its gold and abounding fragrance. None of its silver leaves could be seen now, so heavy was the tumult of its flowering.

'Look at it,' he said. 'It's never been so covered in blossom.' She looked instead at him, and his words said so much more that she too became happy, seeing his happiness. Understanding between them had grown up in his absence from her; but it was still impossible that they should test its strength with words. Their silence contented them both. She could in no way have talked intimately with him, and she doubted, as she was now made aware of the growth of his body and the conscious activeness of his thought, whether she was doing right in leaving him to learn for himself the interpretation of life in the flesh and in the spirit. It seemed to her at that moment that she would be wiser to know more of him, lest chance should rob her of his fealty. She was a woman who smiled but could not easily laugh, who would listen rather than talk, even among her friends. To her son she was as familiar and almost as unknown as he was to her; but because they had trusted each other even in imagination they had found no need to look deeply into the hidden springs of such confidence. So now, seeing him ruddy and happy in the sun before her as she looked up again from the roses she was touching, she could not inquire of him why he should seem to glow so vividly; but she observed it, and suddenly mistrusted it in him. He was not like that for her sake, she well knew.

'I was watching those scissors while you were over there with Jimmy,' he said, laughing so that she smiled at the rose between her hands. 'The sun shone on them, and I said, if it does that once more it'll mean I may go out instead of staying here. And it did; only very slowly, as though it meant, Now, Charles, just this once you may.'

She wondered whether it were simply gladness at being home that made him chatter so. It was not like him, and she watched him closely. He was swinging from side to side on his heels, with his hands in the pockets of his woollen jacket. She saw that he had put on the heavy shoes he used for walking, and she said without looking up, 'Why don't you walk instead of riding Danny? I think you're too big for him now, too; you'd better ride Julia except when we're using her. But why not walk?'

'I think I'd meant to, all the time,' he said; and before she realized that he had gone the gate in the sweet-scented hedge thudded to behind him, and she could hear him going down the drive, the quick crush of gravel under his feet dying away as she listened; until at length the latch of the white gate rattled faintly, scarcely to be heard in the nearness of the bees.

Across the road young wheat shone richly in the sun. He broke some as he walked through; in his mouth the fat leaves gave up their sweet thick juice, and he crushed it out and swallowed it, until there was only a quid of rough fibre left. It was to taste the very soil and air whose essences the sun was transmuting into sweetness. He walked on quickly, down the bare centre furrow the drill had left; the sun shone, and the green field was still and brooding and alive.

It took him almost an hour to reach the Far Field. There too he saw now the young green in all things; even the undying grasses about the dead boles of trees were thickening, and in shadow the dew still lay on them coldly. He was dazzled by the sunlight from the turf. At the boundary fence, near where the mushrooms had come up, he saw that the next field, belonging to the new farm, was also under crop, though not so forwardly as the O'Neills' sowing. Too much lime, he thought; not much could be done with it; but farther east there was good soil, near the broad rich rises before the hills. He found that this limestone country was the dearer to him for its hard openness and the massy roll of it up and down, like an ocean swell. Even the spare outlines of the dead trees made the sky seem nearer and more deep; they stretched themselves like giants in their endless sleeping, black against its eternal blue.

Through all this conscious welcoming of it, he knew that his mind was awake towards only one beauty, and when he looked again towards the east, where the new farm was spread, invisible beyond the trees down in the flat hollow of a valley's issue, he expected to see the girl moving there; and the expectancy was in his very flesh, so that he trembled. But he did not see her; there was no one there, and the only movement was the faint upward shifting of blue smoke, hardly visible, so blue was the air there; the only sound a far crying of birds, and, a mile or more away nearer home, the remote echoes of men and dogs busy with sheep. From north to south his eyes searched the familiar eastward land, and then, when he knew that no one moved or stood there, he turned to the right and walked towards the grove itself.

The sun, his shadow said, stood at some time after ten. Under the trees marching up that slope the shade was very dark, and the coolness of night clung still about the rough trunks. He parted the pine branches and went in, brushing from his hands the scented dust of pollen that fell at his touch. So great was the depth of the shade after the brilliance of earth and sky under the sun, that for some moments he could not see more than the broken patches of green light on the farther side. A cold sweetness of pine needles slept on the air, and as his eyes were used to the change in the light he saw where the sun was making pools of dark gold in the dead leaves of the floor, though their downward falling was hidden, so that they seemed to lie there by chance.

Here was the earth where he had made her fire. The leaves were over it, but pieces of burnt stick came to light when he stirred the place with his foot. He looked about and listened, and at last called, 'Is anyone here?' in a low, trembling voice which, breaking the long silence of his thought, sounded strange and unlikely, very loud. Only a bird answered him, by springing upwards out of the leaves with a short cry, almost a cry of pain, which, because the silence was wounded by his own voice, he felt his mind echo. There was no other movement, and no human answer.

If I sit down, he thought, I shall be able to see out there, and see the grass in the light. So he sat down where she had sat, bending his head to look beyond the roof of branch and leaf. There was the grass, motionless in the sun; and above the humped shoulder of a hill a piece of pale sky gave depth to his low view. He leaned back again.

Probably it was of no use to wait. On a day like this the dimness under the trees did not seem desirable; she would wish, rather, to walk about in the sun, or lie face downwards on a grassy slope and feel the warmth of the air weigh on her till she fell asleep. She would not come.

Quickly making himself assured of this, he walked round the grove restlessly, bending to pass under the branches stretched out to stop him. There was no one there. He knew there never would be again, now. His longing for her rose like a fever, increased by the certainty of that knowledge.

Perhaps, he thought calmly, she has not come down at all. How would I know? It would be possible; she may not have come.

It was possible that she had not come; it was possible, too, for him to learn yes or no; but he was unwilling to go across the fields to the new farm until he had asked his mother whether she knew the people there. He would find that out this day, and when she asked him why he wanted to know, he must tell her. He heard his own voice asking, and her question when she had answered him; he saw her face lit up softly by a lamp on the white table-cloth as she watched him and listened; but he could not think what she might say, for it seemed to him that there was nothing to be said. And after all, it would be at noon, when they took their meal on the veranda at the side of the house, in the air; there would be no lamp, but she was watching birds chase the bees out of the wattle-tree's great yellow pile, and listening to him; and of course there was nothing for her to say. He imagined the scene very clearly, and suddenly, surprisingly, was afraid of it.

Before he left that place, after waiting for half an hour in the certain knowledge that no one would come, he took a folded sheet of paper from his pocket, and wrote on it in pencil the name of the day, Friday, and the time, and finally a question: *Will you come to-morrow at eleven o'clock?* This paper he pinned to the bark of the tree, fixing it there with two splinters of wood. Then he went out into the sun, remembering that sudden fear of his mother; and because of it, and because too the place so held his imagination, he was in no haste to return home.

There would be visitors in the afternoon; his mother was playing with a bridge four, who visited one anothers' houses regularly. By the time he sat down, she had had her luncheon; for he had purposely been long in coming home, going through to the old farm to see Mrs. O'Neill and her small granddaughters on his way. These children had made him play with them; they had an endless game under the olives and lemon-trees growing round the old white house, and when he had left them, and walked along the river bank towards home, he felt happy.

He had his meal quickly, and went up to his room, so that he should not see strangers in the house; and there he remained, forcing himself to work out algebraical formulae and close, stale problems in trigonometry, forcing his eyes upon the paper until the afternoon waned and faded, and the sun set. Emily, who liked him but could not understand

why he talked so little, brought in tea when she had served
the others downstairs. He woke from the blind concentration of unfriendly study sufficiently to remind her of
an old jest which had come to have some new humorous
significance between them; and she went away thinking of
him, thinking he was 'a funny kid' but easy to get along
with—not like some she'd known, she thought darkly,
tossing her head in the plain pride of untroubled chastity.

The tea grew cold in the cup while he stared at the
wall, struggling with the slight bewilderment of awakening.
In time he returned to his work, driving himself at it stub-
bornly. When at last the light shrank and drained like a
pool from his window against the sky, he got up and lit
the lamp. In the room it was cold; as the flame drew up
from blue to yellow it spread a fog over the glass, and he
thought, watching it fade, that something had happened to
him even in that day, and wondered what it was. Somehow
his mother had become more real for him, and in a sense
less reassuring. To laugh at love for the sake of peace was
inconceivable, not only because of his youth, but because
he had not sufficiently associated with his own kind; he
had not learnt that sort of laughter yet, and was still arro-
gantly unknown to self-disgust. While he stared at the
crystal clarity now of the lamp glass, and wondered at the
change in him, wondering not objectively but in a personal
bewilderment like pain's, he heard his mother call him from
below, and knew that the house was once more still and
at peace, with the strange voices gone from it. He turned
down the lamp, judging the twist of his fingers from habit,
without thought, and went out of the room.

Over their dinner table by the fire that evening he observed his mother's face closely for the first time in his life. It was hard for him to read there anything but the associations of his own mind; but he saw, or seemed to see, that she was, in a passionless and rather tired way, beautiful, and that her eyes on his face were expectant, as though she too were looking at him with the attention of some search. He thought, she knows I have changed. He wondered what she would think, and was sure of one thing: she would treat him with seriousness. For already the life of those two terms at the School had made him aware of the shattering force of laughter upon the mind's delicacy, and now he would have dreaded it, for to laugh at him would be to laugh against the girl; and from that his thought shrank.

'Why are you looking like that, son?' she asked him, causing him to draw his vision back through its distance, and to realize that he was still staring at her calm, lamp-lit face.

'I was wondering this morning who are the people at the new farm,' he said. 'Do you know them?'

'Yes,' she said, 'I know them. Their name is McLeod; middle-aged people, only a man and wife; no children. Scottish people.'

The question which all day he had been expecting was not asked. A sense of incompleteness, of something yet to be said before he would be free, made him speak again, after a moment's pause to steady voice and mind. He told her, with difficulty, why he had asked.

'Oh,' she said, when he had ended; and as though something had thrust them apart, they leaned back in their chairs under the impact of the silence, looking at one another, waiting for further words. When at last she spoke, the unfamiliar sadness of her voice, coming to him like that at the end of a strange, troubled day, made him once more consider her, now with a new compassion.

'Does that make you feel happy?'

'Yes,' he said slowly. 'Oh, Mother—I don't know—yes, unless...'

'Unless?' she said. 'Tell me.'

'Unless—I was going to say, unless it doesn't make you happy. And even then...I don't know if it's exactly happiness. I don't know. I don't know what it is, or what to think.'

'A mother is happiest,' she said deliberately, 'when her children are happy.' In the sudden emotion at her heart she saw how plainly she had lied; and she realized, with a force of shame and half-withered longing that because she found him like his father she desperately wanted to keep him from—her mind ventured on the words dully—from other women, and from love. It had been her belief that he would think of her before all, and now she knew her belief was mistaken, her heart betrayed by its own desires; she knew that her words had been a lie, spoken to ensnare his feelings. So she repeated them, looking at the fire beyond the white line of the table's edge. She said also, 'You will have to learn life for yourself, son. You have to go through these things; every boy does. But try, do try—not for my sake but for yours—try not to let them seem too serious to you at the time.'

They looked at the fire. He was glad he had spoken,

for he believed that now, as always, she would let him do what he thought best, without restraint.

'Your father,' she said, 'always went to extremes. If he was happy, or miserable, I always thought he was too much so. He let himself go completely, and it told on him in the end. It was bound to. I knew it. It made him drink to forget; and drink took him away from me—from us. Took him away from you; that's what I mind most, you not having a man to grow up by. But I think it's all right now; you don't need—you're old for your years, and manly enough. Only, you see, I don't want you to be like him—I don't want you to let yourself go like that—to extremes. You see, son, it does make people unhappy afterwards if they let themselves go. Too much.'

She had not looked away from the yellow merriment of the flames while she spoke, so that he could not see her speech in her eyes; but it seemed to him that her repeated words, 'to extremes', had some meaning for herself particularly, deeper than he could reach; and he wondered uneasily for a while what she had intended him to understand; but the silence came warmly down on them, parting them again, and his thought, not fully set at rest by the way she had spoken and looked at him, clung about her words. She made him think of Penworth—each had seemed to argue with him, and again his defiance was touched.

But when they spoke at last, it was of other things, though all the time now he was striving to remember what the girl's face looked like; for to his surprise he had forgotten it, and retained only his own emotion at the thought of her, which now haunted him.

She spoke of the School and his work.

'Don't work too hard, Charles; I'm sure it's not good.'

'I've got to get through,' he said mechanically, making an effort to return to the room. 'Mr. Jolly thinks I can. And Mr. Penworth...'

That suited his mood, and he began to talk of Penworth, telling her what a good friend and teacher he was, forcing himself to forget the change he had noticed since that evening of the mid-term holiday. In the enthusiasm of talking, as his feelings, held down long, now found an oblique outlet in words of praise, he did not notice Emily clearing their little table and returning it to its place by the door. The familiar peace of the room encouraged him, and took from his mind the uneasy shadow of secrecy that had been there all day.

But when he lay in bed, feeling the sheets grow warm about his body, wonder and hope and fear returned a little to trouble him, and it was some time before he did fall asleep, with his face still towards the stars gathering so whitely in the window.

She was there when he came.

She lay on the grass, as he had imagined her yesterday, in the full light of the morning sun. He looked, and believed. Black shadow lay beside her, from shoulder to heel, and she seemed not to have seen him; his feet were quiet on the grass. Looking at her body stretched away from him in that unconscious and chaste abandon, and at her fair head rested motionless on her crossed arms, he felt his heart leap with a final shock of amazement and relief, and also with fear. Something sudden and strong urged him to go away unseen, now, at once. It came up swiftly within him, and in it was the knowledge that he would not go; whatever strange vision of a future already accomplished had for one moment said '*Go!*' was itself gone. He stood still, trembling, flushed and pale at once; and as he felt this violence and tumult shaking him, a freed, observant part of his mind, an isolated and perfected consciousness, recognized the paper she was holding under the curled fingers of one hand, and said calmly, 'She has just now found it'.

He stood without moving, a few yards from her, once more watching unobserved. She was not as small as he had thought; stretched there on the close grass she seemed near his own height, and with more bodily fullness. For the first time he was looking at her, at the girl herself; and he ceased in a while to be afraid, for he knew now what was in his heart, as he had not known before. The sight of her did not merely solve the complexity of thoughts of her; it vanished them, and he thought of her no longer. Her stillness seemed forgetful, not dangerous; he was puzzled how to break in upon her now, and bring her out of the dream in which she lay. She was not asleep; he could see that, for her fingers closed and opened sometimes on the bent piece of paper, and there was wakefulness in the still attention of her head on her arms. He felt a great impulse to shout, to throw his voice like a stone into that stillness, but at last all he did was to walk close and say 'Here I am'.

She turned to raise herself on her elbow, looking at him calmly over the curve of her shoulder. Such calmness made the rage in his heart seem odd and foolish;

but he still trembled as he knelt down on the warm grass near her.

'I knew you were there,' she said.

She was smiling, and the smile was brilliant in the black dilation of her pupils.

'Here I am,' he repeated. 'It's great fun to see you again.'

Hearing that it was great fun, something simple, made them both easy, and they could talk without effort. As he chattered, with nervous happiness, of holiday and work, he did not see how closely she looked at him.

'I came yesterday,' he said later. 'I suppose I was too soon. I suppose being in a hurry to see you again...It's a long time, isn't it?'

His gaze besought her. She did not answer it, but said quietly, 'I've often thought of you. It was so silly of me, that day; but really, you did give me a fright. I was frightened. Doesn't it seem stupid now?'

They could not say each other's name, knowing the intimacy there is in a name spoken; but there was no need, for the sky, and the light, and all the quiet of earth in that place knew them well already. Charles looked at her, and she at him; he saw her more and more clearly, as though he had touched her face with his hands; and he thought that never again could he forget the steadiness of her eyes and the pale warmth and fullness of her lips in repose, as she listened to his idle, lively words—a mouth so quiet and gentle that peace might have slept in it, and innocence haunted its still curves. He did not know what he was saying, though the words leapt quick and conscious to his lips, and she appeared to follow where speech led them.

'Well—what shall we do?' he asked, after a short silence had shown them again each other's single, unknown identity. 'Would you like to see the place? I could take you to the old farm if you like; but we don't live there, you know. No; we live there—over the hills and far away. But you can't see it until you walk to the top of this slope. Come, and when we get up there I'll show you.'

He was on his feet, holding out his hands to help her; but she got up from the ground without seeming to see his gesture, and smoothed her skirt down about her knees. He saw she wore shoes, but no stockings; her skirt was longer, and the dark green of it was the green of the ribbon bows that swung at the ends of her plaited hair as she moved. Looking at the careful tying of those bows, he tried to imagine her doing it, turning her head sideways as she plaited the shining hair in her fingers, tying the bows with blind, habitual little movements. He thought he could imagine it.

They walked round the end of the grove, looking briefly at the shadow within, and followed its flank up the rising ground. He was filled with complete pleasure and surprise to find her beside him, when he looked sideways, and to feel her easy walk and the happy backward fling of her head which made the fair gloss of hair flow downward from it. When they were at the top of the rise he stopped and looked at her straightly again.

'Now. It's like being on the top of the world up here, though it's really not so high,' he said, throwing himself down to feel the height and the isolation more keenly. She too lay down, propped up on her elbows, but able, at a turn of her head, to see the far westward deployment of the land, the green or brown fields, and trees standing up round and small on that lowered plane of distance. The high place held them up towards the sky. A light wind brushed their turned faces as they looked, mingling its coolness with the warmth of the sun on their skin.

'See,' he said. 'That's home, over that way. It's a bit south of us here, and more than three miles off. Over this way, there's the old farm, less than a mile from home. And here are you, behind us; so it's a sort of quadrilateral triangle, a tall one.'

'You make it sound like geometry,' she said. 'I don't like geometry.'

'I do it every day, but I don't like it much either. I'll be doing it this afternoon.'

'What,' she said; 'in the holidays? Will you?'

He told her how hard he was working. It seemed not to surprise her.

'Why do you do it? Do you have to?'

'I want to get away from the School as soon as possible,' he said, 'so when the Headmaster—it was Dr. Fox—he asked me if I'd like to and I said I would, and I was glad. That's why I'm doing it. I want to leave School as soon as I can.'

She looked at him curiously, and then smiled with her eyes on the grass between her fingers.

'I remember. You said that before.'

'And you said you didn't mind being at school.'

'Well—I don't. But I'll like leaving when the time comes.'

She might have been looking into the future, and the dreamy content of youth's optimism was reflected in her face; but he knew she was thinking of herself only, and he felt alone there, where never in his life he had felt alone. He stared at her hands playing with the short grass, stroking it as though it were an animal's coat, and as he stared he reminded himself warmly that, after all, the future life of both of them was still far away, and at present there was all the holiday left for them, and other holidays later, perhaps; yes, surely, surely; so that the present might stretch away beyond sight. When he insisted to himself that this was so, his discontent began to fade, as suddenly as it had cast a shadow over him, and he was able to turn to her again, and to find in the dreaming promise of her face only his own happiness.

'Do you like being here?' he said.

She lay on her side warmly, where she could watch him. The curve of her body from shoulder to knee, the relaxation of her pose, were so vivid in his mind that he felt her weight on the grass as though it rested upon his own arms.

'Yes. I like it.'

'You look so lovely lying there,' he said, and tears came into his eyes. 'I must say it. It makes me so happy to be here like this. Does it make you happy too?'

His voice trembled like the trembling brilliance of her smile.

'Yes,' she murmured, as though they might have been overheard. 'Why do you say things like that?'

'I don't know.' He shook his head, blinking at the cool tears. 'What does make me? I don't know what does. But it's true.'

'You're funny,' she said seriously. 'You say things nobody would think of saying. But I don't know. You see, I've never known any boys.'

'And I don't know anything about girls.'

They looked at the grass, their two heads, red-dark and fair, bent together under the weight of the day's light. Minutes fled away, and neither of them spoke. While they listened to their last words, a long enchantment seemed to have fallen upon them, as though this were all a fairy tale, his green love and her knowledge of it, and that in her which might now be gathering together for a response to him; as though they, the people in the tale, were also listening to its telling.

The cool breeze dropped, and the air between them and the high sky was still. All things paused, listening. When they slowly looked up it was at the same moment, as though someone had called them each by name; and they looked into each other's eyes, and found they were not able to speak, nor even to move. At the heavy summons of his heart Charles felt the blood drain from his face and head; and like an echo to this silvery spreading faintness a deep colour rose in her throat, her lips, her cheeks, and even to the golden pallor of her forehead, so that her eyes were dark, as if she had been afraid, or in pain too great to cry against.

They could not look away now. His heart beat so mightily that he thought the earth itself was thrusting up against his ribs. The colour came back to his face when it ebbed from hers, leaving her dangerously white, and still the spell held them, and still they could not look away from each other's eyes, as though some force too rare to be comprehended had lifted them up from a foothold security, leaving them in a space without time. And now they were falling, unable to drag their eyes from one another as they fell swiftly through that space; each the one hope of the other, the one fear, the one vision and the one reality. As they fell they reached out hands to comfort one another; and when their hands touched and clung, the power and the spell were abated, and with his fingers coldly about her wrist Charles let his head fall upon his arm. He could at last close his eyes, feeling as though he had almost drowned.

True worldly innocence must have just such an effect upon the source of love, the first springing desire, as has self-imposed or inevitable restraint, transforming the libidinous upsurging current to something rare, as exquisitely as a fountain's jet transforms its abrupt force of water to beauty. So it must have been with the world's giants, men who in the negation of bereavement found a vision of heaven concealed, with the key to it in the unquenchable thirst of their bodies, and the ultimate belief of their minds.

In just such a subtle and powerful way did Charles's innocence of mind transform the experience of that morning, even at the moment of its happening, into a conception and promise of heaven. He had been unconsciously preparing in his mind for such an episode, and its effect upon him was like that of a burst of thunder to one who has watched the lightning and waited. When their hands touched and he felt the clinging comprehension and compassion of her fingers within his, and the spell between them was at last eased, he was seized by an exhaustion of the body and the mind, as leaden and blind as that which comes upon a man who has hung drowning in the sea, and who suddenly feels land under his feet, and drags himself up into the arms of the shore sand, to lie there not knowing he is there. To such a man the tide seems still to sway and suck at his body; even when he lies upon the hot sand of the beach he feels the rhythm of the waves, dreamy and merciless, swing under him.

So Charles felt as he lay with his face hidden in the crook of his elbow, while his left hand still clung desperately to her warm wrist and she did not draw away. So she may have felt, for she continued to look towards him while the sun fell warmly upon her, and the light breeze, rising again as if impatient of the moment gone, stirred the softest hair at her temples and between the smooth swerve of her plaits where they parted upon her neck. He did not see that her eyes were dark still, and as heavy as though he had possessed her bodily, and not only with that white flame which she had lit in his mind. Even though she was young, she was a woman, lacking that complete innocence which Charles did not realize was his; but in her face there was a candle-light purity as well as the richer illumination of accomplished beauty, suggesting that love would be strange to her, as it was to him.

Penworth had not so wrongly imagined them; but this first step towards some complete consummation seemed almost to have overshot its mark, leaving them helpless, as if dead, and threatening to make coarse all other experience. This silence was the unthinking silence of perfect surprise. They were unaware even of the pledge which that long, desperate look had made between them; only at a later time would the memory of it act upon them, to bring them together and keep them close.

When Charles opened his eyes he saw she was looking upon him still, and wondered if she had moved at all. He took his fingers from about her wrist, and for the third time, as he raised his head to lean on his hand, their eyes met, without smiling.

'What was that?' he asked, breaking the silence with difficulty. 'It was like a dream. I don't know what happened.'

'Neither do I.' She answered him in the same low voice.

They looked at one another with wonder and curiosity, like strangers oft-reported who meet for the first time and see each other's face. The sunlight on them made them beautiful, and he was again almost frightened at the youth and loveliness he saw in her. Her head was averted from him, and she was looking down at her hand on the grass.

'You held me very hard,' she said slowly. 'Look. The marks are still there.'

When she held out her hand he took it, and saw round the wrist the white imprints where his fingers had clung to her like the insane fingers of a drowning man. Laughter at last came into his throat, and caught there and choked him. He trembled, and she saw it, as he supposed from the concern in her eyes.

'I'm all right,' he said.

'You're still holding my wrist.'

'I want to, Margaret,' he said, and was glad he could use her name now, as a seal upon the community between them. 'Let me hold it.'

She laughed briefly and released herself from his fingers. An unhappy shadow lay now in the depths of her eyes. Seeing it, he sat up and asked what was troubling her.

'Nothing,' she said. 'Only that I have to go now.'

'Go?' he said loudly, and fell silent again, thinking. 'I suppose you must. Oh yes.'

He shook his head quickly.

'And I must, too—go to my silly books, and spend the afternoon working when I—when I…'

She smiled, and again the amazement of their alliance spoke between them.

'You make me laugh. You speak like a very grown-up person; and yet I know you're not.'

'I don't care,' he said.

She begged him not to speak so loudly.

'Don't they stop you at School?'

'I don't do it there,' he said more quietly. 'And you listen: I don't care'—he spoke almost in a whisper—'how old I am or not. And I have to go and work, and I want to be here and have you here to look at and talk to. Now—was that quiet enough?'

He was excited to see her blush as she looked at him.

'I think you'd like to be here too,' he said. 'It's a pity we can't live life as we want to.' He flung his arms wide.

'It's so beautiful to live; but it seems difficult too. Most of the things we want to do we can't, and the other things we must. I don't know. But to-morrow…'

She looked up quickly.

'Not here—not like this.'

'Why?'

'Hush—don't shout, Charles. Not to-morrow.'

He looked at her, suspicious and unable to speak for a time. Her eyes pleaded with him.

'Why not? Aren't you allowed?'

She shook her head.

'It's not that. But—not to-morrow, Charles. Don't you see? I can't; you know I can't.'

She seemed to be pleading with him, but he did not know why. Her soft pleading, which could not find its words, made him quiet.

'Tell me; tell me why. I'll understand.'

'Well,' she said, 'after to-day, how can I? It wouldn't be the same. I mean—I must think. Oh, how can I tell you?'

'I don't understand,' he said patiently. 'Tell me what. Try. You seem as though you've gone quite away, now, and I know you haven't. You seem older than you are.'

'You're impatient,' she murmured, so softly that he could hardly hear her. 'If you had something given to you— and you wanted it very much and yet you didn't know till then you wanted it—wouldn't you—wouldn't you have to take it away all by yourself, and...'

He understood, but his face was dull still with the pain of disappointment.

'Yes, I see,' he said. 'But—why? Why away from me?'

'I must think,' she repeated. 'You've started me thinking.'

He said nothing, looking at her face, expecting her to go on. She turned away from him.

'I don't often think,' she said at last. 'Now you've made me.'

He moved nervously, and felt the short grass prick upward under his palm.

'How do you know you don't think?'

'I don't think,' she repeated with slow obstinacy. 'I don't want to. I'm not like you. You do, I know. But I don't. It upsets me if I think; but now you've started me, you see.'

She said this simply, as though it were too clear to be in need of argument or explanation. Her eyes upon his face were soft and kind, but still the unseen shadow hung restless in their depths, and he felt that it had shaken the union between them, threatening it. To him her impulse to be apart from him was not clear at all; he could affirm it to himself in his mind, but it was not clear, for it was against the way of his desire. Nor did he understand thought as something separated from living, from the actual daily experience of the senses; to think of thought as thought, as something that could proceed now and in an hour be turned off, like water from a tap, was beyond his conception—so far beyond it that he could believe it possible when she said it, though he could not understand. While she was by some instinct guided to a conclusion and a determination, he, who tried now to follow in her flight with the faltering tread of reason still half-dormant, came far behind her. So, as he had said, he was bewildered by her ageless assurance; and the effort of thought troubled by emotions made him weary and sink beneath a gusty sadness that worried at his heart, while the sun shone warmly and her beauty, so near and perceptible to him there, was as remote from his touch as the beauty of a portrait.

'Why must we think, either of us?' he cried; and the breeze seemed to pause and listen, just as she turned her face to him from looking blindly away into the day.

'Can't we just live, without thinking? It spoils everything. I was terribly happy, and now I feel sad. And you're sad too. Everything's sad, because it's spoiled. Everything, everything.'

He hid his face in his arms.

'Don't be sad,' she said. Her hand, stretched out to touch his head, was quiet and burning in the light; the fingers lay close together, calm and full of sleepy peace, with thin pencillings of shadow between them curving at the knuckles and running past the delicate cloudy pink of the nails. He, however, did not see this, for while he felt with troubled joy its weight pressing upon his hair, his half-closed eyes were wandering among the huge points and buds and trunks of the short grass an inch away from them. He did not want to look at her now, for she was near again.

When he turned over on his back, keeping his eyes closed, her hand remained upon him, curving over its down-turned palm, and lay lightly across his eyes. If he opened them he saw a dim colour of flesh, with light coming sharply in under the edges; it smelt warm and alive, as though her naked body were against his face. By moving his head a little his lips were brought to touch that warm, intimate place where the foreign skin lay living over the artery in the palm, so that they trembled upon her heart itself. She let the weight now of her hand and arm rest on his mouth, and her whole body was still. Under them the earth seemed to surge upwards with the renewal of its growth in that season; he felt it pulsing beneath him, but that was the working of his own heart; and he felt her hand resting upon him, her heart beating mysteriously in the hollow of the palm.

'Nothing like this has ever happened,' he whispered into her hand; but she seemed not to have heard, nor to have felt the movement of his lips on the skin's velvet roughness. The sun fell in a stream upon his closed eyelids. Proud and brilliant in the height of its noon, the day was all about them.

The holiday passed in rain and sunshine. Charles, shut within the stillness and easy familiarity of his room, worked in the afternoons. During the week of rain and storm that followed the great clearness of the first weekend, he remained there alone, and sometimes at night went up again when dinner was ended, leaving his mother sitting by the fire in the big room downstairs, whose wide windows faced east and north. She was always busying her hands in something; when she had finished writing letters or sewing, she did patience games, sitting up very straight behind the little cards laid out neatly in their ranks, slowly twisting the gold bracelet on her left wrist while she considered what next to do. It seemed to make no difference to her whether she succeeded or failed in getting a patience out. He longed for her to show whether she cared, for he became, in that week, impatient under his own restraint; it was doubtful whether she even thought about it, for her mind seemed to be far away from the dull green baize and the coloured problems of the cards. If she looked up and saw him there, observing her silently, his book face-down on his knee, she smiled; but he had no idea of what she was thinking, and would not have asked her, nor would she have offered to tell him. This wordless companionship exasperated Emily every night, and when she took the hot milk in to them she never failed to break in upon it with some chirped exclamation of surprise, and a few challenging remarks as she put down the tray and straightened up again to wish them a good night. Her cheerful voice sounded loud and vigorous across the pool of lamplight on the table.

It rained steadily during that week; in the room, with its lamplight and firelight and dark drawn curtains, the sound of rain at night was comforting: it beat in gusts of frail fury on the windows at the north end, where shadow lay on walls and floor, beyond the light; and when such a storm ceased, as abruptly as if the whole sky were clear again, the clouds all gone, they could hear the laughing trickle of water on the earth outside, the mellow chuckling run of drain-pipes, and over all that great silence which night rain leaves behind it. Charles looked at the fire, and thought of the drenched country-side stretching from the windows to the east, cold and murmurous with water under the silence of the returning stars; and when the north-west wind rose again, waking him perhaps from sleep in his room under the roof, he felt it blow across the flat top of the rise out there, and toss the trees of the grove shaking free a ceaseless scatter of drops that fell on the chill dead leaves of the floor, while night stood still, blow how the wind would. He saw the top of the rise desolated with peace beneath the white stars.

He was at first unhappy and distressed during those days, fretting with impatience against the weather's assurance of his loneliness, and anxious, too, for his mother to speak of what she now knew. Work helped him to forget the passing of time; and in the mornings he took his thick shoes and a coat, and went out walking, pleased to feel the softness of the soil underfoot and the coldness of the grass heavy with rain, but impatient at first even in his pleasure, and discontented with what had seemed beautiful. Trudging through the still fields, with a wet wind cutting across his face, he thought of nothing but the girl; over every moment of that sunny morning he went, again and again, finding it each time more lovely, and more unlikely, until he began to wonder whether it had happened at all, and whether the gestures, the thoughts, and the mysterious contact of that helpless look were not the wishes of his imagination. Yet he must believe for with all the reality of pain her memory was in him wherever he walked; it grew in his blood and was borne through his body, so that at night he dreamed of her, and by day her face and her voice, and her eyes more than all, looking at him without release, haunted his troubled mind.

It seemed to him that he had approached near some enormous understanding. In moments of nervous exhilaration he could laugh, when he was alone, to think how near he had come to a great knowledge, and how thinly he had passed it; even in the midst of work, which he attacked with a new fury of purpose, the page would blur and vanish as he stared, his pen would halt and its dark ink dry on the nib, while he looked into her face that now was there where paper and words had been, returning his look with darkened eyes that could not move from his own.

He did not see that the year's work had been too hard for him, and was already thrusting him up into a condition of unrelaxed nervous tension; nor that the same force of rebellion and dislike for the unnatural life of the School, the very force that had driven him to work so desperately, was now driving him farther, to a conception of the girl from which it was unlikely that he would ever be freed. Already, with him at least, the thing was done. That moment of rare spiritual exaltation in the sun had given him an experience of something which it is not for many to know, but for which all those who have known it strive in the flesh and sometimes in the spirit, to come at it again, to lose their identity in it, and in it cease to exist. They strive, and fail because they strive; the flesh deceives with promises impossible, and the spirit is untutored. Such knowledge is only come on unawares, and unawares is lost again, while the remembrance of what it was remains and grows, taunting with its own futility the yearning of the heart.

But with Charles a first unquestioning simplicity rested, and though he was haunted as men are by dreams, he became happy also. Alone in his room, or at large on the wet country roads and in the fields, he rediscovered his joy in life, and let go from his mind the sense of some gentle antagonism in his mother, not yet realizing that nothing he did escaped her notice now. He had changed in his face;

217

it became at last, beneath its mobility, more tranquil. She observed this also, and for some time remained silent, allowing him to drift back into his former acceptance of her; but at length, when the failure of fine weather seemed not to trouble the rapt inward concentration of his mind, curiosity was aroused in her. Choosing her time, she suggested that he might go over to the new farm for her, for O'Neill had mentioned that the McLeods' cow was not milking well, and she had thought of sending butter, and eggs and fruit also, to Mrs. McLeod.

This suggestion startled him for the first time from his reserve.

'Why?' he said, almost angrily, as though she had roused him from deep sleep too soon.

'I thought you'd like to do it for me, son.'

Something in the way she said that let him see her mind with a sudden flash of clarity. It surprised him, and set him on guard, to realize that she was not happy; and so acute now was his perception that for a moment he understood why. In that instant of understanding he knew also that he must harden himself against her, more determinedly than he had against Penworth's franker disapproval.

'Of course I'd like to do it for you,' he said quietly.

She put one hand on his shoulder, smiling still with her fine lips.

'We understand each other, dear. You know how I love you. I want you to be happy—that's all. It's for you to find out how, Charles.'

In those moments of unhappy conflict they were more intimately revealed each to the other than, until now, they had ever been. They regarded each other objectively, he with growing mistrust, of her and of himself, and she with a growing sense of possessiveness. For him the revelation was distressing, and as they stood looking at each other he shuddered to be free of the distress. With an effort he spoke.

'Why do we—What have I done wrong?'

She ceased to smile, and looked away. He had time to observe a swift expression of sorrow darken in her face.

'It's not that you've done anything wrong, son,' she said. 'But you're young, you know, and inexperienced.'

He submitted restlessly to that.

'I'm older,' she said, 'and I know what life is like. The disappointments, the misunderstandings...We must never misunderstand each other, Charles.'

'Oh, Mother,' he cried, with impatience setting an edge to his tone of compassion. It caused her to turn again, but he spoke first, quickly.

'Mr. Penworth—I told him about...I told him. He was just the same as you are. Why? I don't understand.'

'You see,' she said sadly, shaking her head, smiling. 'We're older, Charles. We know. Perhaps you would take more notice of him than you would of a—a woman; because he's a man, dear. It's not that we want you to be unhappy...'

'What is it, then? What is it? You don't tell me; you simply hint at things and seem to want to make me feel ashamed.'

'It's not that, son,' she repeated wearily.

'I wish I hadn't told you,' he said with sudden passion. 'Either of you. It's—it's my own business.' He ended uneasily; her grave gaze turned to him; gravely accusing, she held him a moment with her eyes.

'You mustn't say things like that, my son. It's not fair. It's not quite kind.'

He went impatiently away from her to the windows, noticing even in his excitement that the rain was holding off, and feeling at the same time that if this argument did not end he would cry, or laugh.

'Well,' he said at last, making his voice and eyes steady when he had turned to face her. 'What do you want me to do? Do you really want me to go over with the things?'

'If you want to go, son, I'd like you to, yes.'

Now he did want to go, most certainly. Already, like himself in these last minutes, Margaret might be changed.

'I'm sorry I said anything unfair, Mother. I didn't mean to.'

'I know, my dear. Oh, believe me, I know how one feels...Now put a coat on, like a good man, and get off before it rains.'

She came and put her arms round him, kissing his half-unwilling lips firmly, with a slight, uncontrollable pressure of self-assertion.

'Let's forget all about this. We must be good friends, darling.'

'All right,' he said, with some relief, in the satisfaction of having escaped the commitment of promises. 'When shall I go?'

'The basket's ready now, dear.'

When he left the house, however, his conscience was not easy, and for some time he could not restrain his mind from going over that brief scene of conflict between them. As they had been in May, since that evening by the fire, so they were now. There was something in it all which evaded his understanding, something which he wanted to call his mother's unreasonableness, and put aside, but which made an obscure demand on his sympathy. He felt an anger against her, as he had against Penworth, for he could not see why his absorption in Margaret should provoke them like a sword turned to them.

Never before had he found himself in conflict with those he loved, and his conscience was uneasy, in spite of defiance, and he was sent back hastily to seek a cause in himself, rather than in them. The thought that he might have erred in the conduct of relationships once dear to him made him unhappy now, and in unhappiness his mind turned to Margaret, in whom he imagined some secret power of comfort. After their parting in the noon of that day he had gone homeward swearing he would be there the next morning, in such a hot visualization of their next meeting that he could not believe she herself would not come; but when he woke the bright day and the dreams of night taught him to fear disappointment and mistrust his certainty of her; and in the end he had not gone.

Now, as he walked out by the roundabout cart road that led like a lane between two lines of slim trees towards the hills, he wondered whether after all she had gone there on Sunday morning, and, after that brief but discomforting scene with his mother, was amazed at his own certainty in not himself going. But, when he recalled the sincerity of her words, spoken not to speed but to reveal a conclusion made already, he could not believe she had. She had known what she meant to do, but he had not, and he was still jealous of the power her assurance had over them both. But it was that assurance which he went to seek now, after the doubt forced on him by conflict. What would she have been doing? Surely she could not have spent the week 'thinking'? But, he remembered, in any case the rain would have kept her indoors.

Walking on more quickly, in a renewed hunger for the sight of her, he had her image before him.

From the top of sloping ground, where the cart road faded into the grass as though it had never meant to lead him anywhere, he looked down across a flat field not fully cleared of trees, to where the new farm lay under the grey sky, with the lavender-pale line of the hills behind it. The bare branches of a patch of orchard made a faint cloud against the still trees beyond; in the green-black of orange trees there was a scatter of bright fruit, and a paler mandarin, standing apart, was heavy with it. Farther off he could see the line of the brook's course. He knew those fruit trees well, and the ground about them, for when the place was empty he had often wandered there, even trying to see in through the dusty windows into the strange loneliness tormented, as he imagined, by memories of people who had lived there. There were the bare figs, their thick silvery branches now dark with rain, low and appearing more iron-hard than they were; between them and the naked orchard trees was the orderly green of a garden. He thought he could see the first flowers in the orchard, and knew that within ten days, perhaps, it would be clouded pink and white with flower, flesh upon the bones, before the leaves broke from the bud. Pink and white petals would fall in frail loveliness, like snow, upon the dark red earth beneath the branches, when the sky was blue and the gales came whipping out of the west.

To-day there was no wind, and the sky hung low in unbroken grey above the shoulders of the hills. He went down the sloping field and climbed through the fence at its farther end. Here the road from the new farm ran south-west to meet another that led to the village three miles away. He had only to go along it the distance of one more field, open the gate and pass through, and his journey would be ended.

As he walked on the hard crown of the road it began to rain, not heavily now but in a fine falling mist. The basket was making his shoulder ache; but he forgot that, in marvelling at his sudden calm, as he approached the house. It seemed to him that he must have grown older in this one week; once he would have felt in a trembling hurry to face and pass beyond this perilous second meeting and the equally perilous first meeting with a woman he did not know. Now, instead, he felt at ease and contented. He thought, 'All this is our own land now'. The assurance which ownership gives made his step unhesitant; and he felt, also, that after all he could have come and gone as he pleased, secure in the new realization of his individual being.

After the habit of country people arriving at farmhouses in the morning, he went round to the back door, where the kitchen was. A woman's voice was talking cheerfully away within, and a dull, hearty thumping sound drummed an uneven accompaniment. Charles rattled the wire door, and put down his basket.

'Meg,' said the woman inside, 'there's a body there noo. See who it is, lamb.'

Charles steadied himself against the door's opening, holding the fly-proof screen back with his foot. Margaret's face when she saw him seemed to wake from sleep. He trembled to see it change so, flushing and widening to life again.

She whispered quickly, 'I don't know you'. He thought he must have expected that. There should be no suspicion of her. Her troubled regard increased his assurance; he looked past her and asked, 'Is Mrs. McLeod here? I'm Mrs. Fox's son; I've brought some things for her.'

The same voice said, 'Och, then! Ay, bring um in, Meg. Come in, young man.'

In the low dimness and length of the kitchen he saw first the fire in the stove, and then that big woman, resting her rolling-pin on the pastry board as though it were a baton. Her broad, high face charmed him at once, for the eyes slanted and bore out her clear smile. It was a humorous and kindly face, mobile from much talking and an inexhaustible ability to express surprise; the lines round the sly keenness of the eyes showed how often laughter closed them. She was almost laughing now, her big breasts shaking softly under the closeness of her grey bodice.

'Well, noo! Look at how y've found me! Never mind, laddie. What can I do for y'r mither?'

'She sent you some butter,' Charles said, his voice

sounding slow after the quick tumble and rise of her syllables. 'And some eggs and apples, I think.'

'Och! Meg noo, what d'ye think! Isna that kind?' Surprise once more took her face by storm; she looked almost ashamed, as though she were unduly blessed. Charles put the heavy basket on the table, and went to stand with his back to the stove while she unpacked it, with an accompanying babble of exclamatory talk. He thought he had never known anyone so consciously happy, and so quick to show it. It was not his presents, it was life itself that pleased her. Hers was not the empty talk and laughter of women who spoke without thought; it was the vivid cheerfulness of a heart that had outfaced the hardships of the land itself and was still able to laugh and find life good. No man would have remained serene after half a lifetime spent in suffering the rigours and torments of that country where the wheat belt lay; few women, too, came through such a life without the bitter brown claw-marks of the land scarring their faces and deforming their minds. Her Scottish nature, into which no Highland ice and fire had burned, still shone clearly like the bright colour of her face and the sharp laughter in her eyes; her hair, where the characterful, keen ridges of the cheek-bones met it below her temples, was as thick and heavy as smoke.

He looked from her to the girl, who stood with her back to the long table in the middle, leaning her hands hard on its edge and staring out with expressionless tensity through the open doorway.

'That's Margaret,' the Scotswoman said. 'That's our lamb, noo; eh, and I wish she were our ain too.' She had seen his glance.

'Might you have met her a'ready in the fields, then? Ay—when I was a bit of a young thing like Meg...'

She laughed, and he thought the girl's lips were trembling against a smile; but she kept her eyes away from him, and he could not be sure.

' "When a body meets a body comin' through the rye", f'r guidness sake. Oh, Robbie Burns was a pet of a fella noo. We ustna sing just those verra words—not the words you sing in this country. Ours were a deal more ruid, y'ken.'

She looked him in the eyes and laughed again, holding an apple in each hand; till he felt his face grow hot, and must laugh, too, without understanding her.

'No' y'are to have a cup of tea when my scones are cooked, and y' shall have scones t'it. That was rare kindness of your mither, young man. I wonder...'

She gazed at him; her eyes twinkled like stars beneath their flat brows. The girl continued to look out blindly through the doorway.

'I wonder what I could do for her. Eh, but there's nothing I could do. Did she happen to know our cow wasna milking well noo? And apples! So I shall make old Jock yonder an apple pie to his tea, for he dearly loves such things.'

The quick accent delighted Charles, as he listened to the way it gave life to the casual words of speech. She was busying herself about the room, going from the stove to the table.

'Look at yon,' she exclaimed. 'She doesna say a word a' day, like my old Jock. Ay, not a word out o' them.' She nodded towards Margaret, who seemed not to have heard her, and did not turn her head.

'Perhaps,' said Charles, 'she has nothing to say.' This spirit of cheerful raillery infected him, and made him bold to speak in open secrecy. 'Some people don't even think, do they?'

She gave him a shrewd glance, and the red light from the stove reflected in her eyes like mockery as she bent down by it.

'Y'are a wise young man noo, aren't you,' she said. 'Meg and Jock—they're aye like that; they hardly think a thought, I swear, a' day. What they should do without me, I wouldna like to say just.'

Later, when they were by the table, he sitting on the edge opposite them in a strained attitude that helped him to be calm, he dared to suggest that the girl might come out with him one day when the weather changed, so that he could show her over all the country about.

'Up at the north part,' he said, speaking quickly to carry them on from what must seem a forward suggestion, 'it's much more interesting. It's only half cleared, and a lot of it isn't at all. When my cousins stay with us we always go there...'

The girl's eyes met his as Mrs. McLeod took him up, once more with what seemed a flash of mockery in her shrewd eyes.

'Och, she does as she pleases. Don't you, my bairn? Well then, it might be guid of you t'ask her; and perhaps she'll say "Ay" t'it. Puir soul—she hasna much t'enjoy hersel' at wi' us folks a' the day doing and a' the night asleep.'

He said he would come over when it was fine.

'She's been awfu' silent and mousie these last few days,' Mrs. McLeod said, speaking still as though of a third person absent, in a manner Charles found safe and imitable. 'Now maybe,' she said, 'it's young company she needs. That'll be fine noo.' She looked at the girl as she spoke, and though she laughed with that same curious mockery he could see the pain of love in her eyes, the shadow of tender concern over so much silence in someone so young, standing there with such clearness that he was surprised and discomforted, for no one had ever looked at him like that.

When he was leaving she told the girl to walk with him as far as the end gate.

'Go along, Meg, it'll do you guid. Here you've been stuck in the house near a week, and your holiday too. Put on your jacket then, for it's raining. Though when I was a young bit of a thing like you ones we didna much care aboot rain.'

She watched them go out, and stood at the door, her strong arms still for a moment, folded under the genial depth of her bosom; with great kindness she begged Charles to thank his mother, and then looked after them while they walked round past the house, beyond her view. The rain was light and grey; when she turned away the kitchen's warmth and worn cheer welcomed her.

Charles looked at Margaret, but her face was mostly hidden by the curve of the hat brim, on which a dew of rain already stood, and he could see only her straight nose and her lips, full and pale, seeming to tremble as though she would speak, or smile, but could not. He too tried to find words, but now, with the peril of their meeting past, the safety of speech was forbidden him, while the memory of his mother came close and weighed heavily. From the half-revealed shape of her face he looked up to the black branches of the plum trees past which their path was leading them. There was already a scattered white of blossom on them, and he could see the tight promise of other buds and the brown buds of leaves that in September and October would have burst in a dew of green. Beyond them the flanks of the hills rose upwards into the sky. As he looked over this hazy distance, her voice fell on the cold stillness of the rain.

'Have you been working hard?'

'Yes,' he said. 'What have you done? Have you thought—enough?'

It was difficult, after that, to keep silence, in an eternity of seconds waiting for her answer. She turned to him, and again her face sprang into life and full being as he saw her eyes.

'I've been missing you,' she said. 'I didn't think I—not like that. Perhaps I shouldn't tell you. But I have. I've missed you. I didn't know what to do, and I thought...I thought I'd go away, go home; but I couldn't, I couldn't.'

Her eyes besought him to understand the passionate suddenness of her outcry. He had not expected this; it was as though she knew what had happened that morning, and it wakened him to such a white fury of joy that he was frightened.

'Didn't you miss me too? Did you dream too? I dreamed of you.'

'I wish I could tell you,' he stammered, frowning. The words stumbled on his lips, and lay on the air between them as they walked, slowing their steps in the new darkness of their necessity. He had not been prepared for such words, spoken by her voice, given meaning and weight by that direct, clear look in her eyes which he remembered too well. He had not expected, either, that her last few days would be thrown open for him so desperately, by such words; laid bare of all concealment, with their loneliness admitted in the eager, troubled tone of her voice, and his own presence in her mind and heart confessed. Her calm silence, in the house, had suggested nothing of this; while he looked at her there he had imagined that such a calm was also within her, and that so she had passed the days; and even when her aunt had laughed at her affectionately for having been so silent—she who, he thought, was always silent—his imagination had persisted in describing her as at peace with herself and ready to be at peace with him too. From the surface contentment of his own mind, and from his refusal to look deeply into that future which might hold unthinkable disappointment, he had built this image of her; and now she had shattered it down, so certainly that his very heart, after its leap of joy, was dumb in the completeness of her confusion.

She looked away from his face, and repeated what she had said.

'I dreamed of you.'

'I did too,' he said. 'You have been with me all the time.'

'Yes.'

230

She nodded; he felt her looking at him again, but could not turn to her.

'You know how people like my aunt say "Good night and sweet dreams"? I know now; sweet dreams. I didn't know how much there was in—in dreams; what they could be like. Now I know.'

'Tell me, Margaret.'

'I can't. Not in words, I couldn't.'

They had come to the gate; and, as people do who have walked side by side and are at a parting, they turned to face one another. Her eyes, shadowed by the arch of the hat's brim on which lay a hoar of rain, were shining with tears, that trembled on the lower lids.

'You think I'm being silly, don't you?'

'I should put my arms round you, Margaret.'

At that, and at his vehemence, she closed her eyes, standing there limply and still, and the tears pressed out from under the lids and went heavily down her cheeks. She shook her head.

'Don't, not here. No one must see. No one must know that—that...'

Her mouth twisted with misery and happiness so that she could not end it; but he thought he knew what she would have said. Never had the violent fusion of grief and joy torn a face into such a hot mask of beauty. He dared not look at her deep eyes regarding him; his hand was on the wooden latch of the gate, and he saw how the light rain was dewing the back of it, and how through the paint the whorled grain of wood was showing bare. His hand was now a stranger to him; he could see the minute drops of water gathering on it, but could not feel them there; they lay on the faint hair and on the peaks of the knuckles where the skin was stretched white. He looked at them for what seemed a long time.

'You must go,' she said. 'Your hair is getting wet.'

The determination following a decision was coming into him as something he could feel and trust. The words of her surrender had given him leadership and the right to speak and command. It was she, he felt now without shame, she alone who greatly mattered to him. He looked up at her frankly.

'When it's fine I'll come,' he said. 'The first fine day. We can go out—out that way. Somewhere. I know it all.' He waved towards the north, confident and alive within himself, alive to her and to his own stronger manhood.

'How long will it be?' she said.

'It ought to clear in a few days. I know this weather.' He talked on, quickly and eagerly, until her face became calm and she smiled. Tears had come easily; so much thought, and the experience of unknown passion, must have wearied her mind to that helpless surrender which with tears and passion she had admitted. Now she wiped her cheek with the back of her hand.

'I can't come here, you see,' he explained. 'I mean, I wouldn't like to come often. You know. But Margaret, don't be miserable. Look here...'

He made her look up.

'Don't be miserable. Think how good life is, and how soon—think about me, and I will about you. Don't cry.'

'I'm not miserable,' she said, shaking her head.

'No. Think of me, and I will of you.'

'And dream. I can't help that.' She tried to laugh.

'Yes, and dream too.'

'I wish I could sleep all the time,' she said. 'Sometimes I feel frightened. It can't be true—we're too young. What can we do? We're so young. But oh, Charles...'

She spoke his name softly, as though he were not there.

'Don't,' he said; and his hand, that had seemed foreign to him, was his own, filled with his whole body's consciousness as its fingers rested upon hers.

'We're not too young. Look, I tell you, we're the happiest people in the world. Don't be frightened; and don't be unhappy any more. I hate to see you cry. It makes me feel torn to pieces.'

'I won't cry any more,' she said. 'But just then, seeing you again and not being able to tell anyone, not anyone— until you came—I couldn't bear it any more; and oh, Charles, I did want to be sure, I wanted to see you, to see if you were—like I dreamed you were. And now I've told you, and I don't care what you do, it makes no difference. It all hurts me inside, too, like...'

'But now you must be happy,' he said slowly, in wonder at the passion in her face.

'Yes.'

'Promise?'

'And you promise to come? Don't leave me here, with no one to talk to.'

'I will come.'

He was going away; she looked at him.

'And Charles...'

He waited for her to speak. At length she said:

'You know the other day? It was wonderful, only I couldn't tell you then. It was like a dream. I shall never forget.'

When he opened the gate the warmth of her hand still lingered in his palm. After he had pushed the latch to, not letting himself look round lest he should lose the last image of her in his mind, he heard the soft sound of her steps when she went on past the budding fruit trees to the house. As he walked towards home, the rain awoke and became heavier. He put back his head so that it might fall cold and sweet against his hot face.

At the beginning of the summer term the tension in examination forms was pitched high. Charles's deep moodiness became familiar to any who noticed him, and even Penworth, though he fell into minor furies over it, began at length to leave him alone.

He had come back to the School looking rather tired, and much thinner; and this seemed to accentuate the green light in his eyes and the boldness of his nose and mouth, so that his face, though it kept its softness of expression and its pale reserve, seemed yet to have cast off superfluous delicacy and to have gained something of young manhood's sharpened maturity. At first Mawley did not notice much change in him, because of his own concern with time lost and examinations looming darkly nearer. But the pose of that head in front of him in the classroom, and the fierce frequency of his fingers ploughing through his auburn hair, at length made Mawley curious enough to look more closely at him; and he saw, or imagined he saw, that once

more the events of his holiday must have impressed themselves deeply on his mind; but neither Mawley nor anyone
else knew then what had happened. He proved that he must
have worked fairly continuously by scoring a sound pass in
the short test papers in Mathematics with which the term
commenced; and as this was the first time he had come
well through any such mathematical ordeal, the Master in
charge thought it worth mentioning, and Charles, who had
always evaded with fear and suspicion any public commendation of himself, had to submit to the unpleasantness and
danger of being exhibited to his form as an example of what
sincere purpose and conscientiousness could do. 'Sincere
purpose and conscientiousness' were the Master's own
words; Charles was subsequently laughed at and ridiculed
in a fitting manner, and his reaction to this proved Mawley's
own half-interested suspicions about him; for he fell into
a white rage, and battered two boys soundly with his fists
before a sufficient number could bring him down and prove
further, by the force of numbers, how wretched it was
for any fellow calling himself decent to do work out of class
and try by queanish means to find favour in the eyes of the
common enemy, the Masters. This attack, it appeared to
Mawley now, must have been in ferment for some time, for
Penworth, in spite of his intentions, had fatally shown his
regard for Charles, and even in his loudest and most snap-
ping temper was unable to hold his eyes from kindling with
a secret and not quite tutorial warmth of interest.

So for Charles the term opened; and, had it not been
for the concentration of one admitted purpose, on which he
could not now go back, he would have felt the brief force of

that antagonism more keenly. But in the uneasy excitement of that September, at the beginning of the most broken and uneasy term in the year, he was allowed to keep to himself as he seemed to wish. Training would commence at once, for the big sporting day of the year, when the Public Schools made a serious match of general athletic ability. Before this day, which was usually fixed early in December, the School culled its best athletes, after a morning and afternoon of private competition between the Houses. On the first night of term, before all had returned, lists were made up by House-prefects; and some instinct of self-protection, or bravado, prompted Charles to enter his name for three events, when the first call was made in Chatterton.

Penworth was surprised and disappointed by this; but, after a very pleasant holiday in town, with Waters living not far away to meet him for various social enjoyments which they shared, he had come back to the School in no mood of friendliness towards any person there, since it was necessary to transfer his self-contempt out of the subjective. Even Waters, against the too-familiar setting of classroom and Common Room, seemed far less interesting, and Penworth, now as always greatly at the mercy of his own swift moods, was driven by discontent to write long letters off to England, and to stare at the photograph of the woman's face on his neat dressing-table, and think of marriage as a possible freedom from the persecution of solitude.

He began his final series of classes by delivering, at Charles in particular, a clipped and sharply-worded string of remarks on the necessity for decent interest and quiet, attentive behaviour in form. The boy, still sore and distressed from his trouncing, and by nature not inclined to see in this sudden jeremiad from the dais a good reason for the others ceasing their unkind treatment of him, tried to make a reply, in the last flush of that rage he had earlier given way to; and Penworth, who had now arranged things as he wished them to be, interrupted him promptly to begin a real diatribe against those who deliberately dissociate themselves from their fellows—'because Nature has by mistake given them pretty faces and pretty ways, and has further erred in making them aware of her unfortunate gifts'.

By the time he had finished this speech he was exhausted and in great relief. The Latin class could now continue. Seeing, when he looked up gravely from his book, the expression of miserable bewilderment in Charles's face, he was further eased of his own discontent; he gave him no particular attention during that hour, but before he left the dais, when the echoes of the noon bell were still shaking on the air, he spoke to him again.

'Fox, I want to see you this afternoon, when classes end.'

'Yes, sir,' Charles said.

When the door had swung closed after his flying gown, some laughed and some commiserated with Charles a little. He did not answer them, but took up his books and went out. The day was brilliant now under the high sun, and as he walked across the courtyard and up the covered way, to put the books back in his House locker, he began to wonder why he had ever come back. Before, it had not entered his mind to wonder; now, as he understood with every beat of his heart the gulf and distance that seemed to separate him from all others in this place, he considered why he had returned—why he had not locked himself in his quiet room at home, or run out into the fields and beyond the fields to the lonely hills smoky with blue mist, in those last two days when Margaret was gone and he, as he saw, was alone in the world, without even the comfort of a belief in his mother's expressed affection and understanding.

He looked about. There was the brick, the glass, the wooden floor; there were the open doors of this prison, with streaming sunlight across and beyond them. Voices sounded sharp and clear, voices he now knew well, coming from the stairs, the changing rooms, the bathrooms above; he heard the slither of feet on the floor of his own dormitory, over his head, and words and laughter were in the whole building, so familiar and inevitable that it became unreal to him, and his own mind and body became unreal. He stared at his hand holding up the locker door. If he let it go that door would fall back with a clear smack of wood on wood; if he pushed the books they would hit the back wall of the locker with a bump, a hollow noise, and the inkstained cloth, polished higher by much handling, lie smooth and slippery against his fingers.

'What made me come back?' he asked; and that second voice which was now the eternal tenant of his mind, that voice which was learning to reply to every question he asked of himself, and would never be silent until death put a quiet over all, answered, Reason. You knew you did not have it in your nature to do anything else. Even this is a part of life, though you are unwilling to think that. And, the mute voice added, even this will end.

He shook his head, hearing without understanding, knowing without knowing why he knew. These voices would go on for ever, arguing their ceaseless drama from the proscenium of his brain to the narrow auditorium where his consciousness sat listening. Arguments about his mother's sudden emergence from her former placid silence had been rehearsed and rehearsed there; arguments about Margaret had begun to absorb him passionately; and now once more Penworth, who had been his friend, worthy of admiration and love, was matter for unhappy debate.

The clamour of the bell made him drop the locker lid, and it came down sharply with a smack of wood on wood, and a rattle of the catch. The sudden pause upstairs was invaded by a sense of purpose that brought feet scampering down in a crowd. He went out of the classroom where the lockers stood, and was caught in the jostling throng that already reached to the covered way and was streaming down with a thunder of running.

At the brief knock on the panel, Penworth, who had been staring darkly through the open window and feeling at odds with the cheer of sunlight slanting into the pooled lawn outside, called to come in without turning round. Charles saw his head and shoulders cut out against the trees and the sky; the shoulders sloping dispiritedly, pulled down by the deep thrust of hands into trousers pockets.

'Sir, it's me,' he said.

Penworth brought himself slowly round; his frown remained dark, and the full melancholy of his lips reflected in his eyes.

'It's not "me",' he remarked coldly. 'It's "I".'

'Yes, sir,' said Charles, on guard before this mood.

'Well,' he said. 'What do you want? Did I send for you? Oh, I know—this morning, yes.'

He seated himself in his chair, so that the light from the windows behind him fell thinly on his brown, wide head. Charles once more measured with his eyes the width and height of that forehead, and its deep downward arc of whiteness from temple to temple. His admiration for the sensual beauty of the face would not change, no matter how darkly he was considered. The bold nose with fine nostrils, the wonderful setting of the eyes that could look so cold, and the sensitive, full mouth reminded him of kind words and friendship. Only the chin was small, round and womanish; but he did not see that, for the man's eyes drew his look always.

'So you're going to run races, eh?' Penworth said, after regarding him for some time as though he were a stranger. 'Will that leave you enough time for working with me, or can you dispense with me now?'

Charles stared, and his lips trembled when he spoke.

'No, sir—please don't think that. I only gave my name because—I only gave my name so as not to seem to want to dis—dissociate myself too much—so as not to seem out of it too much, sir.'

Penworth raised his eyebrows, without smiling.

'I see you remember my words,' he said. 'Come here. No, right round the table, this side. There. Now look at me.'

He took Charles's face between his cool palms, and stared into his eyes.

'What's the matter with you? You're trembling.'

Charles said nothing, concentrating his mind on returning that deep look.

'Well,' said Penworth quietly, 'what have you got to say for yourself?'

Charles said: 'Nothing, sir. I just came. You told me to.'

Again Penworth raised his eyebrows.

'I see. You came because I told you to. I see. If I hadn't sent for you, told you to come, you wouldn't have come. Am I right to assume that?'

'Oh, sir! Of course I'd have come, anyway. Of course I would.'

Penworth looked from his eyes to his lips, and back again to his eyes. The glance was bold and quick, as sudden as the fall of a hawk from its hover. Charles instinctively moved his head, and the blood flung across his cheeks.

'Come here,' Penworth said deliberately. 'You silly young ninny.' His regard was big with anger. 'I sometimes think,' he said, 'that you're a danger to this School, Fox.'

He let Charles go out of his hands, and laughed.

'You have the vanity, too, to talk about love—and girls—you do, you! With a face...'

He stopped himself. Charles stood helplessly, while tears of rage filled his eyes, and became tears of misery; they fell and he was unable to move to conceal them. His breath choked in his throat.

'I don't talk about it,' he cried, with shame and misery and ebbing anger tearing at him.

'Oh, yes you do,' Penworth remarked lightly. 'Kindly don't contradict me like that.' A voice was asking clearly

241

and curiously in his mind why he was doing what he did. He shook it aside as he would at that moment have shaken aside the hand of any mendicant. It came again; it was Charles's voice.

'Why do you say this to me? Is this why I was to come and see you? You were my great friend, and now you say this to me, and you don't even know what it means. I wish I had never come here. I wish I had never been born.'

Penworth swallowed, determined to look unconcerned before such childish hysterics; but he could not see the anguish he had brought into the boy's face without seeing also that it was as true as his own pretended coldness was false and cruel. Yet the pain he watched gave him a great surge of—was that pleasure, then, that overpowering sense of elation, and self-pity? Was that pleasure?

He regarded Charles for some minutes, saying nothing, noticing the curve from his averted head to his neck and shoulders, and the way those shoulders shook, almost as though he were being whipped. Then he stood up and turned once more to the window, enjoying the curious sensations of his secret shame and elation, and above all enjoying now that supreme and most godly power, the power to comfort when his dramatic sense admitted comfort.

It was some time before the silence in the white room was broken. When Charles spoke, his voice came steadily.

'Mr. Penworth, I'm sorry. I'm sorry if I've made you angry. I didn't mean to, sir. It was just that I felt so unhappy coming back here, and looked forward to seeing you; that was all I did look forward to. I didn't know you'd be feeling wretched. Even in form this morning—I thought it was just—just you, and I thought it was just a sort of pretence and that you didn't really mean what you said, sir.'

Penworth followed his dramatic sense, and turned round. Charles was confused to see him smiling. He had expected further reprimand, spoken to make his difficult apology seem only right and apposite, spoken rather stiffly as though to any boy, and to be followed by a brief dismissal. To see, instead, the old smile of friendship and interest made him wonder what would happen next. His attention was so concentrated that he could not smile himself.

'They call me the Bad Penny, don't they? Well—It's all right, you needn't give them away—perhaps I am. Always turning up. He that turneth up—a stone…He that turneth up the stone of my heavy humour finds a worm beneath.'

He laughed pleasantly at his thought.

'It's all right,' he said again. 'You needn't frown like that over what I mean. Or do you see it? Perhaps you do— you of all people, Charles Fox. The long and the short of it is, Charles, that nothing in the School's prospectus, or curriculum, gives me the right to treat you as I like to, and do. Mr. Jolly will tell you that it's a bad policy for a Master to make a boy an especial friend, just as it's bad policy to be everlastingly hard on a particular boy in class. Mr. Jolly will tell you, if you care to ask him, that especial friendships are bad for the Master's disciplinary powers, and not fair to the boy; they hamper him in his efforts to assume his rightful social status as an ordinary member of our happy community. So, Charles, I do wrong to you, and I do wrong to make you the slave of my humours—or to be willing to make you. Now you shall choose: whether do I continue

243

for the next eight or nine weeks to coach you in here, or whether do I inform Mr. Jolly that my time is too much occupied, and ask him to free me from the arrangement. Now choose.'

He leaned against the window-frame, put into a gentle humour again by the pleasing sound of his own words, and by his certainty of how the boy's choice would fall. Self-confidence had returned to him with the affirmation, during these last minutes, of his own singular personality; and when he was assured in self-confidence his desire was always to be kind. He watched Charles.

'Well, sir,' Charles said hesitantly. 'If you would— would you mind, just until the exams are over, going on as we were?'

'I should be glad,' Penworth replied with amiable frankness. 'You are doing particularly well. Come here, old thing.'

He put his arm round his shoulders in the old way of friendship, and rocked him gently from side to side.

'You look tired,' he said, and he closed his fingers in the ruddy curls and tilted his face far back. 'Yes, you do look tired. You've worked too hard. And,' he said slowly, as though piecing together the thought as he spoke it, 'I believe you feel too hard, too. I believe you do. Your hair, now, is said to be the colour that indicates an excitable nature. Let me have a good look at you. There.'

He held him away, gripping his shoulders with his broad, strong hands.

'An excitable nature. A good nose, though; a nose suggesting will-power, or determination. Same thing.

Same thing? I wonder. Anyhow…Eyebrows rather thick—
concentration. But eyes too dreamy even for a youth, and
a mouth too soft, altogether too soft and generous, not
sharp-cut. Eyes and lips like yours are a nice combination
in a boy, I must say! You might have been an artist; but
I don't think you will: you're not hard enough. So, if you
feel too deeply, I don't know what you'll do. And God help
you, anyhow.'

He let him go, watching him.

'Now—am I not nice to you? What do you think of
my summing-up? The temperament of an excitable girl
combined with a very masculine strength of will and a
masculine mind…It's no good, Charles; you'll get into
awful messes. But I expect you'll get out of them too. What
do you think?'

'I suppose you're right, sir,' Charles said. 'I don't know;
is it—is it always possible to tell from a person's face what
he's like?'

'Ah, now that depends upon the teller. Just as if you
were a small depositor. And you needn't laugh at me like
that. You see—an excitable nature, as I said. You're laughing
from nervousness.'

He taunted him affably; and as he did so he was
startled by a thought that irritated him suddenly in spite of
himself and made him wonder whether something in their
relationship had not been resolved that afternoon, so that
now certain desires of his, stale desires once warm, begotten
of a loneliness of which he must make himself master, were
assuredly hopeless. He cursed himself for having shown his
feelings as he had done earlier, and made a determination.

'You've worked too hard this year, Charles,' he said. 'I shall have to keep an eye on you when the examinations are finished. Life will be easier for you then, and for me and all of us. You can come and read poetry to me in your spare time. There'll be lots of that.'

'Oh, I should love to, sir.' Charles's expression was dubious, yet flattered. 'You've been so very kind to me; if it hadn't been for you I don't know what I'd have done. Honestly I don't, sir.'

'You talk as though it were all over and done with,' Penworth said abruptly. 'Anyhow, that remains to be seen.'

He sat down, lost in thought for a minute.

'Now, let's get things clear. When do you have to go and run races; what afternoons?'

After Charles had gone he leaned back in a sort of exhaustion, rubbing his face slowly with his broad palms. Again a mood of discontent had gone from him: he had exorcized that devil with a little witchcraft, in his own way. But now he found himself disturbed, not by discontent but by the residue of the last half-hour's emotions. It would have suited his mood to have called the boy back into that little room, so that he could talk to him and look at him, seeing his words reflected faithfully and with a richer dramatic colour in the young face over against him, while the afternoon went coldly down into blue evening. That would have eased his heart of the ghosts of those stale longings which now troubled it, and which were made more persistent by the present languor of his mind.

Listlessly he considered his future life. At twenty-five,

with a Master's degree in Arts, a choice knowledge of musical literature and of the masterpieces of his own language and two others, and an intelligence not frequently to be met with in this strenuous new country, he was still nowhere. There was in his mind a growing suspicion that a school teacher, whatever grace his qualifications might have, was a person of small importance in himself. Such a man by beginning to teach came to believe, when he observed the clumsy ignorance of his scholars, that wisdom lay in books. And as a teacher he was at the bidding of those he taught; his mind was a widow's cruse for them to suck at without being failed; but, he thought, the quality of the oil would not change.

There was another way of failure, which he himself hardly yet perceived in thought, though it was hinted in the growing disease of his moods and the unreasonable way his emotions sprang and ran. He had come from a country rich in traditional beauties of thought and practice, and calm in the knowledge of its heritage. His own mind and intelligence were nourished at that rich fountain, Oxford, the left breast of England, close to England's heart; there he had clung and sucked till he was full, his ear against the heart beating beneath, his fingers on its placid pulse. Knowledge and understanding flowed into him, and gradually he was raised, through imitations and then through voluntary exercise of choice, into a young perception of the beauty of thought and truth. He was, with the consent of his own heart, fitted out for life, and likely, by the quality of his mind and nature, to make a place for himself in worthy estimation.

Then, prompted by God knew what conceit of his young ego, he had left England for this land. It was infinitely more foreign even to his imagination than would have been a European country where men spoke a foreign tongue. It was to him the very end of the earth. The language was his own—almost his own. He found that his own ideas of culture, of behaviour and of conduct were considered right and unarguable; that good manners were the same, and that the complexities of social relationships, though relaxed a little, perhaps, as was only natural in a country with a semi-tropical climate and a cosmopolitan history, were in form unmistakably English. Here he had come, ready to open the treasure-chest of his mind and share out its endless contents, keeping for himself, above all else, the esteem he would earn and the authority in certain things with which esteem would by degrees invest him.

And already he had failed, and dreams were crumbling. For, under this surface of promise and willingness in which even a century or so had planted and germinated seeds of culture, and sometimes a being of full genius, he was being made aware of forces beyond his comprehension, powers of the earth itself that would corrupt and conquer his mind; powers that were so untamed and untamable that they would tear down the curtain of his intellectual worth and rudely lay bare the poverty of his soul's strength cosseted within. These giant subtle forces were no mystic emanations of open places, no genii lurking only in the vastness of an unknown and untroubled continent; they were the very daemons of men's minds, in cities, in homes—in schools where the childhood of the nation was nursed, and where he, come armed with gifts of rich knowledge and charm of nature, was to be shown that his own race, which like a bold adventurer he had left to cross three seas, was old, old—that its traditions and cultural beauty, faced with these crude world's-end forces, were like the encrustations of decay; popularly beautiful still, yet old with the preserved and waxen impotence of a very old man who cannot die. And he himself, the envoy of his own choosing, would in time be made a living sacrifice to the colour and the light and the human brutality of a country that had no use for him otherwise.

These things he did not see, as he sat limply in his chair, with the sour, dry odour of ink and paper in his nostrils, and a mild benison of tobacco smoke unseen in the fading light. The air on his fingers was cold without penetration; he let his hands lie still, clasped on the polished wood of the table, while he considered without emotion how little he had yet done. Yes, it seemed that if you were a school teacher you were no one and got nowhere.

Had anyone told him that as long as he remained and all his life he would be a puppet on strings in this adopted country, just as were the others of his kind who at first seemed to triumph and were pushed aside at will by the unseen hands, it would have caused him to smile. In believing he knew himself and his work as well as a young man may he was right; but he knew nothing of the power which could move untroubled, regardless of one man or of a nation, choosing its initiates and sacrificing them again to itself at the hands of the mob it swayed. He had forgotten that the most beautiful and perfect things had always been

249

chosen by his ancients for sacrifice. He would never belong; and although those were words he said to himself often enough, he said them with complacency as well as with bitterness, and did not understand their deepest meaning.

I shall leave this place in the end, he thought. When I get away from this School, I shall grow again. It's the School that confounds me. I was not meant to be a teacher in any school.

He returned to thinking of Charles, and considered with sober disquiet his warm desires, complex, multiplied, and ceaselessly relevant to his awareness of the boy. Passages of the *Phaedrus* haunted his mind also, and after wondering over them, he leaned across to his bookshelves to draw out a thin volume, beautifully printed in the most perfect Greek type he had ever seen, almost beautiful enough to rob the words of their fullest worth of meaning, encouraging the eye to break them up and taste the characters like pomegranate seeds clustering in them.

Reading slowly aloud, he heard also the voice of his mind translating.

To pass on from these obvious thoughts—let us next consider what good or what harmful effects upon your fortunes it will be natural to expect as a result of the companionship and tutelage of a lover. To all, and to the lover himself most of all, it must be clear that he would hope for nothing more deeply than for the beloved to be deprived of those treasures most dear, most precious and most holy to him. Gladly would he see him bereft of father and of mother, of relations and of friends, in all of whom he observes that censorious and obstinate opposition to his enjoyment of the traffic with his beloved which he desires above all things.

He stared through the page, frowning faintly. At last, with an effort, the focus of his regard brought back to his waiting mind the words.

Furthermore, if a youth possess property in gold or other such substance, he will seem the less easy of conquest, and less easy of control, that conquest having been made. So it cannot be otherwise but that a lover will grudge his chosen one the posses-sion of fortune, and rejoice greatly in its loss...

Over the remaining sentence he lingered gravely.

Nay, he would even have him remain as long as may be without wife, or children, or home, such is the sort of his desire to gather for ever the fruits of his own enjoyments.

Coldly he remembered that girl the boy had told him of; and this memory brought back the faint aversion he had felt as he listened to what he assured himself was a senti-mental account of meaningless calf-love. His eyes strayed to the opposite page, stepping down from line to line until they were held by a phrase, and he read again.

251

...the object of this passion has, furthermore, at all times and among all men to beware of censorious observation...to listen either to difficult and excessive praises, or, as is equally probable, to unbearable condemnation, from his lover's dark caprice... as surely, when his desire is grown stale, will the lover be until death a traitor to him upon whom with promises innumerable, yes, and with oath and prayer...

He let the volume sink and close between his fingers, and stared at the fading white of the wall, while the light from the windows behind him grew faint, and into the House beyond his door sounds of life returned. Sport was ended for the day. They were changing, plunging under the shivering chill of the showers; he could hear them shouting, and follow the ring and echo of their hilarious laughter, the slaps of hands on chest and flank under the water, the sharp whip-crack of flicking towels. Somewhere out there was that lad whose face and voice had troubled him many times in many months.

Yes, he thought, I must leave this place. It's the School that confounds me. But before I go...

Leaving that thought uncompleted, he put the slim book carefully back into its own slit of shadow in his shelves.

September had eluded them like a dream; before they knew it, the gales and madness of the equinox were gone, and October enveloped life in its brief balm and calm before the rigour of summer began. Suddenly the earth was revealed to them in all its delight and newness. In the darker grass pink flowers and white flowers came out, threepenny stars with six points that shone for a time in the warming sunlight. The days were lengthening, mysterious now with spring's virginity and promise; the cold nights were shorter, brilliant in moonlight green or the dark silver of starlight, cloudless, windless, frosty and serenely still. That stillness was of the whole earth, that lay quiet like a woman woken from sleep into a dream of new consummation.

Charles was for some days at the mercy of that halcyon languor. The air swam with bees and light, beyond the windows; he could breathe the breath of flowers, Cape lilacs clouding purple and white against the high sky, roses from the Masters' garden trailing their ripe sweetness through the cold corridors among motley odours of books and dust and cedar flakes on the floors; and a perfume of grass warmed by the sun lying on the lawns. He was suddenly aware of his own weariness. It would not last. Masters were patient with their classes; they too felt the season's serenity sucking at the marrow of their bones, though they did not feel it with such swooning keenness as did those young adolescent creatures on whom they smiled. Charles felt the heavy, sleepy warmth in his knees and back, and struggled in vain against its drugged dominion of his mind; but little by little its weight was eased from smothering him, and with a renewed and happier energy he went to attack the last weeks of the year's study.

November was perilously near, he thought. The first despair of his return had gone, leaving him apathetic to everyone about him, as though he had wakened from a sleep, from the reality of a dream. And indeed, looking back always upon that last holiday, it did seem dreamlike to him, with all a dream's reality and irrevocability. Like a dream the girl's face haunted him, making the daylight less bright, as though through a veil he saw it, and lighting the darkness of night and sleep with something warmer than moonlight.

They had said, informed by some wisdom beyond their years, that they would not write to each other. In all their encounters they had been made aware of the tyrannous impotence of words; to have addressed himself to her in words written would have satisfied his necessity as little as the hunger of a child is satisfied by a voice that would comfort it. He recalled her voice, and her eyes as she said it; he looked into her warm, quiet face, and thought that to-morrow she would be gone, and in two days he too would be back within the confines of a place where love was as incommunicable as any dream. For a while, in unhappy silence, they were afraid; they dared not look at one another, and the cool brilliance of the waning afternoon came between them like a parting. But, when he said that this was the saddest part of every day, looking out over the illimitable, pale afternoon spaces, they were together again, though their hands had not yet touched; and then they said that they would not write, but would wait till the summer holiday brought them into each other's sight, and see what life should give them.

'I might see you at the Oval,' she said quietly. 'We go; all of us. I might see you there.'

He looked at her in silence.

'It won't matter,' she said, after he had been thinking about it. 'No one will know. We can look at each other. Only we will know.'

When they were parting, with the rusted wire of the fence already between them, neither could think of any last words to say. They held the wire in their hands, but, by the absence of expression in their faces, they might have been judged strange to one another, and unaware each that the other was there, so deep was their concern in the immortality of that moment, behind their shoulders the east and the west were pale with sunset, and the air lay coldly upon them.

When their lips met, to kiss now for the first time, it was as though that were also the last. Her lips were cold; he did not know what spell was upon them, but knew only that neither in this nor in any other parting would there be a farewell.

Charles, after the first day's distresses were over, settled himself to work with stubborn will. His apathy towards outward things arose from the thin unreality with which his mind invested them, and not even to Penworth did he become fully alive. Nevertheless, they began studying again at once, and Charles found that three weeks before the examinations he had completed his classics set books and flogged his mind through the course in Mathematics. There remained three weeks for revision. The seventh of November was a Monday, and on that day examinations would commence in the gymnasium, cleared of its movable fittings and invaded now by an orderly army of small tables and chairs marching in long lines towards the tiered gallery at the south-east end. The fact that they looked like an army was Old Mac's only consolation in such a complete defeat. During this regular yearly eviction he would prowl interminably, and his eyes ceased to twinkle, and became harassed.

With Penworth, Charles began again at the opening chapters of Latin syntax and accidence, skipped through the earlier ones, and gradually became slower and more concentrated as his memory of the work warned him. In his two modern languages he was easier. He took to rising early in the mornings so that he should have an hour before the breakfast bell in which to go over with great care the later mathematical rules and examples, trying out his memory of each one and confirming it with exercises of his own invention. Three weeks before that perilous Monday the form was given sample papers set for other examinations. When Charles found that he had done only indifferently, he felt a clutch of fear and helplessness, followed by sudden exhaustion. He went out into the sunlight of the parade ground, where boys were walking about in pairs and groups and alone, laughing, arguing, kicking their heels and running about for the joy of being alive. Many of the youngest, to whom examinations were revealed in the healthy light of careless scorn, mocked their elders for such seriousness; some of these were carrying books open in the sunlight, reading aloud or silently. Saunders, who had sat once for these examinations, was marching about by himself, audibly repeating certain set lines, giving no meaning or expression to the words. He caught sight of Charles standing still with the morning in his hair burning darkly, and called to him.

They were aloofly friendly now, making no emotional move towards one another, but not uneasy together.

'Here,' Saunders said, 'hear me through this, will you? This bloody English paper's getting on my nerves.'

There was to be a final grammar paper following that break.

'Go on,' Charles said. 'I think I know it, but you say it, and I'll find out if I do or not.'

He listened gravely to Saunders's gabble, and was patient and unmoved over his muttering pauses. Never did Hamlet's most famous speech sound so like the feckless wanderings of a mind insanely decayed. Saunders was an honest fellow, without even a conception of vanity of the intellect, and his one desire was to have the thing word-perfect; time enough when the paper was under his hand to consider what the words meant.

'Well, that's all right,' Charles said, giving him back the book. 'But don't you think it's risky to do it right at the last like this?'

'Oh, I don't care,' Saunders said. He began to kick the grass with the toe of his shoe, his hands deep in his pockets. When he did look up it seemed to Charles that his eyes were embarrassed.

'You're quite a decent chap, Foxy,' he said.

Nervousness of coming examinations, in which he had once failed, broke down his abrupt, instinctive reserve for a time, as it did that of many. Friends and others sought each other out at odd moments, in the brief, intense community of fear, came closer than any laughter could have brought them, and afterwards pretended to have forgotten it all.

With arms linked they would walk up and down in the afternoon sunlight or the warmer light of morning; the more sensitively shaped found private places where they could sprawl together at ease, finding a relief from fear or uneasiness in the comfort of each other's expressed affection. Charles, who had begun to regard these aloof couples enviously, was aware both of the impulse and of its transience. He turned, now, and Saunders fell into step beside him. Clearly, after such generosity of commendation, it was for Charles to speak first.

'I don't know whether I'm decent or not,' he said with a laugh. 'I do want to get through these exams, though.'

The situation between them, withdrawn from the peril of embarrassment, rested comfortably. Saunders began to talk at ease, and they involved themselves in argument over the comparative difficulties of French and Latin, until the distant clamour of the bell cleared the field. They had walked far, and were obliged to turn and run back together.

It was at this time that the friendship between Charles and Mawley became something sure, to which they both resorted. Mawley was an easy talker, frankly boyish and without shame, but with Charles there were always reservations. He had certain moods now of sudden, foolish gaiety irritating enough to those who did not know him, when he would laugh a lot and make bad puns in imitation of a Master whose reckless extravagances both in and out of form were well known to everyone. Mawley, careful of his ankle still, could not join in sport that year, which was very injurious to vanity; but Charles's gay moods were a compensation in their own way, as were his far more frequent inclinations to silent, curious listening. He seldom spoke seriously for long; but sometimes he did talk about Penworth, struggling even as he spoke to make plain to himself the young Englishman's strange manner. He was concerned to think that it was his own fault that a friendship between them was failing to achieve that understanding on which permanence depended; but to suggestions that there was more in it than friendship he was for a long time unwilling to listen.

'I never know where I am with him now,' he said. 'That's all. That other business—it's finished—it never started, anyhow. How could anyone...I mean, you can be friends with a man without that. Can't you? I don't know. It's beastly to be touched, I think.' He looked surprised. 'At first I didn't realize. I didn't mind, I suppose; never thought. Why do you say there's more in it than just friendship?'

He heard Mawley's explanation in silence.

He would listen to the talk of others less reticent than himself, with a sort of embarrassed fascination, as though he were an intruder among secrets that did not concern him but of which he must know, of which he must be sure.

'I think it's ridiculous,' he said angrily, describing how he had come stumbling upon a couple of lads closely communing in a hidden place, one drowsy Sunday afternoon. 'What do they do that sort of thing for? Behaving like a lot of girls.'

That was the only time he spoke of girls in a tone of contempt.

The two of them walked to and from the playing-fields together in that lovely weather, talking wisely of many important things; but of what was most frequently in his mind he said nothing then, although, unlike most of the inquisitive and inexperienced among the boys, he made no effort to let his dumb surprise seem instead the weighty silence of knowledge unspeakable. It was a wonder to observe how little he did know. Most revelations he received as a hungry man receives food, silently, from need, not greed. At times, frowning fiercely to get a true grasp of something, he would make a guarded remark, that it was strange, that he might never have known...that it 'made a difference'. That noncommittal phrase he now used frequently. It bespoke a mind continually awakening to its own innocence.

'Well, it makes a difference about Mr. Penworth, what you say. But it doesn't seem fair to him. You don't know for certain, anyhow. I mean, he's such a lonely sort of man, and it's probably just that.'

What he really was thinking was by no means evident. Perhaps only of his own loneliness earlier in the year, and that other loneliness which now would await him at home. His mother's manner, her seeming intention of defending him from dangers he could not perceive nor credit, troubled him, and in this slight alienation from her he intuitively found an alienation from his home itself, and felt, for all his defiance, that he must be somehow culpable. Because of this confusion, this inevitable stormy prelude to his own affirmation of self-hood, he was more and more inclined towards work, wisely recognizing the insidious anodyne distilled in a mind wearied with being forced. It was easier to lose his identity with its particular problems in the impersonality of study than to submerge it, as another would have done, in the minutely developed social life of the School. For the sake of peace in leisure hours he tried to be interested; he would willingly have convinced himself that his House mattered above all else and that he was necessary to it; but the unreality persisted, and his self-deceit was plain to him. To Mr. Jolly, who now and then let it be seen that he was aware of him by appearing before him suddenly and asking him what he was reading, with a stare of scholarly unbelief, he looked as to a father, and made great show of enthusiasm over House affairs; but Mr. Jolly was not so much in Chatterton now, having removed himself and his books to the empty, echoing house dedicated to the use of Headmasters, where no doubt he communed sceptically at times with his predecessors and imagined 'the fools of fellows' who would live there when he was gone; and Charles, who well knew how little he himself cared, was not often put to the necessity of deceiving him.

The year was not to be thrust aside from his mind easily, nor its effects so lightly evaded and shrugged away. To one great and one lesser purpose he was sworn now by his choice, his undertakings and his experiences; and so deeply was he sworn that it was, as always in youth, impossible to look into his own future with the eye of imagination, for life as he observed it lacked all perspective, and he could not see it save as colour and imminence, light and shade. One great and one small purpose haunted his days: beyond the examinations was the summer holiday; and in the summer holiday, already there attending him, was Margaret.

Many times, in that weakness of will coming at the day's end when work was put by, and his mind had relaxed, he thought he must write to her. The desire to see even her name on paper became gradually as powerful as a passion in him, and he set it down secretly in Greek characters, and put it in his pocket, as though it were a charm of magic certain to bring the fulfilment of every unspoken promise he remembered and imagined. This silence seemed unbearable as it then concealed her from him. He dreamed ceaselessly at night, in hours of sleep without depth; but there was regret only, and no comfort, in the broken enchantments of his dreams, and with the morning light waking him he remembered of them little save that fair peace and immobility he had known in her, and the unsmiling concessions which in dreams she made to his tumult of desire and fear. Such memories, broken as they were and potent in their suggestion of all the dreaming he had forgotten, filled him with grief and determination; but there was no comfort in them.

So in those last weeks, strict against himself in keeping silence, he came to find once more a sort of consolation in his hours of work in Penworth's room. Penworth himself was beginning to show in his face and voice the strain of the year's endeavour. His eyes were tired, and more unwilling to be kind, and in his classes he talked little, sitting silently bowed over his book above the room where a feverish murmur of application echoed the sound of bees outside in the sun. But to Charles he now remained the same always and made no gesture; his friendliness did not turn sour, and whatever went on in his own mind was concealed there, beneath an aloof gravity of manner which was what the boy most needed to lubricate the hot working of his brain. He spoke of little now but the work in hand; only at times, when perhaps his day had been calmer and the signs in his forms reassuring, he would lean back in his chair, look out through the window into the paling, late sky, and discourse in the old way upon learning, or poetry, or the obscurer delights of whatever music he happened to have in his mind. Then, in the energy of a chosen enthusiasm, his voice lost its accent of tiredness, and took colour into it from what he discussed.

'The year,' he remarked once, 'is a parabola. We are on the downward swing now. It sometimes reminds me of the best works of art. You can feel it in the air, at this time; we speed down the curve. Perhaps if it weren't for the life here, I wouldn't notice it so much; but it fits in with what I'm used to—down, down, October, November, December—Christmas and winter and the dead end of the year. In England that's how it is.'

He thought about it, and it confused him subtly.

'Here, after all, you're on an upward swing really, outside these walls of artificiality. Spring, with summer close behind; outside that's what it's like. But in here we move towards a close—you know, you get that in the middle of the third movement; a sudden restatement of a theme..."Remember what I said at first" sort of thing. You know what I mean?'

'You talk,' Charles said, 'as though you were dying—no, no, not dying; but something. As though you were going away.'

Penworth looked at him in a quiet speculation, without speaking, for a minute or more, observing the question in the steady hazel-coloured eyes that regarded him, the frown between their dark brows. Then he reached forward for his pipe and tobacco, and began to fill, rolling the tobacco to a wad in the palm of his left hand with the outer edge of the right hand; and still looking at Charles. Then, as he glanced down to adjust the bowl so that it would receive the fill easily, he replied:

'I am going away—that's right.'

They looked at each other.

'Why?' Charles began. 'Why—oh?'

For the first time, with a sharp and conscious emotion, he strove to imagine his next year at the School, and saw, not himself but, Penworth's absence, as though it were a positive phenomenon. Somebody else would sit in this room, behind this orderly table; some other man's books and prints would replace these. No more was he to be gladdened and amused by the arrogant fullness of Penworth's gown as the young man strode into a classroom, still with that elasticity of knee and shoulder which he salvaged from a life now past; no more to see that pleasant, condescending smile, as, having reached the dais, he swung round suddenly, smoothly, to confront a class alert with the expectancy his entry had aroused. No more would he see such small, important dramas as that measuring out the days; and no more might he look forward with pleasure to hours like this hour, secure in this small white room with its immaculate bed and its soft odour of tobacco smoke well enjoyed, of books, ink, paper, and wood, seeing opposite him the familiar beauty of the eyes that knew him so well, hearing the quiet voice, full of praise or scorn or mild laughter, to which he had so willingly paid respect.

'Oh,' he said, 'I am so sorry. I don't know—it won't be the same here, without you, sir. I'll feel quite different.'

Penworth, lighting his pipe, glanced up secretly under his brows and laughed with pleasure, but shook his head in half-mechanical denial.

'Nonsense. You'll make plenty of other friends. I've told you, next year won't be like this. You'll have far more time, and you'll be able to live some sort of a life of your own, and get to know what the other fellow is thinking. That's more important than anything I can teach you.'

'It won't be the same.' Charles put his own meaning into the words. He looked up, smiling. 'I don't know how I shall manage to work without your help, sir, now. You've helped me very much.'

'That's what I'm paid for. And anyhow, it's been great fun. And furthermore you can have too much of help; you must be able to stand by yourself. Don't imagine that the work is beyond you; you happen to have more intelligence than the average, that's your trouble. And in the end it's the very opposite to a cause for doubting yourself.'

Charles said nothing, rubbing his hand backwards and forwards along the edge of the table whose corner separated them.

'Don't, of course, tell the rest of them yet,' Penworth said after a while. 'You have a right to know. I'm going—for the sake of other people as well as for my own. I want a change, that's chiefly why. What I shall do I don't know; but at any rate I shan't be here. If I stayed too long I'd simply get—stale.'

Charles nodded.

'Even a schoolmaster,' Penworth said, 'leads a life of his own at odd moments, you know. You do know...'

'Oh, I know, sir,' Charles said nervously. 'I know—it must be pretty terrible here. I used to think how nice it must be to be a Master—free, and all that.'

'I may be mistaken,' Penworth said slowly. 'One never knows. I may be trying to escape from my own self, from something I never shall escape by running away. To go may be a coward's way out—leading simply to other cowardices. But I must go, before I can find that out for certain. For each one of us life's chiefly a matter of trial-and-error proof, you see.'

He talked easily on, and Charles, as he listened and watched his pale, expressive face, thought of the coming year, and of the year after it. It was not himself he saw, for he was still visualizing only Penworth's absence from the familiar scene, and feeling as one feels when a picture has been secretly taken down from a wall, leaving a characterless wide space behind which looms, a memory of the eye itself, the shadow of what was once there, affronting the gaze with the faint melancholy of so much strangeness...

Penworth had moved suddenly, and was standing beside the chair where he sat. It was a swift movement, calculated, not clumsy, and it took Charles by surprise. He looked up as the other's pale face came down above his own. Trying to move and unable, being walled by the side of the table and by Penworth, he felt almost like laughing. He was held by the shoulders, and did not know what to do.

'Now,' Penworth said in a low voice, urgently. 'Now, Charles. Before we say good-bye for good.'

The pupils of his eyes were dilated, as though by anger, or fear. Charles stared into them, afraid, and unable to rise under the hands resting on his shoulders. The way those words were spoken had frightened him; the beseeching tone of a voice used always in command, in careful, interested but dispassionate explanation, alarmed him more than any anger would have done. He felt the blood drain from his head and face, and with an effort restrained himself from crying out. Penworth made another sudden movement, and had him strongly, gently by the wrists. Automatically he stood up and drew back.

'Let go,' he said, and the surprising steadiness of his voice gave him courage. He heard the other's breath, coming and going quickly. Outside that room the afternoon was placid and still.

'Let go, please,' he said again firmly. 'Please don't do this. It spoils everything.'

What he meant by that he did not afterwards know; but it caused Penworth to laugh shakily.

'You talk like a damned schoolgirl being seduced.'

'I'm not a girl,' Charles said slowly, 'even if I do look like one.'

That was difficult to say, but it had the effect of making Penworth release his wrists. He stepped suddenly back as his weight came free, and the chair fell noisily. They heard the sound of steps approaching through the changing room.

'Don't make such a row, you little fool,' Penworth said.

He spoke with a bitter scorn; but he said nothing more, sitting down on the bed and putting his white face into his hands, breathing unevenly. He looked like one who had escaped a vicious, uncontrollable danger, without knowing by what means he had escaped it.

The whole thing had taken no more than two minutes. The steps crossed the hall outside, faded, vanished, while they listened. Charles, trembling now with the release of tension, stooped blindly down and set the chair upright, by the table where it had been before, where he himself had sat, listening to that cultured voice talk easily to him of life and beauty. He stood staring at the chair, not knowing what to do or how to break the spell of what was a perfect conclusion for them both.

'Better go,' Penworth said at last with difficulty, still pressing his hands to his face, his elbows on his knees. That position was so strange, so dramatically out of character, that Charles felt tears come into his eyes. He went to the door, and did not hesitate to open it and go out. On the way up the stairs he thought he was going to be sick, and hastened his steps; but in the upper bathroom, a place of sure solitude at that hour of the afternoon, nausea gave way to the misery of reaction, and tears blinded him. He leaned against the wall at the end of a row of basins, and, as Penworth had done, hid his face in his hands.

But even in the sharpness of that misery he felt, surprisingly, a great coolness of relief, as though a decision had been made for him, and as though at last he were in an open place here, with a free wind blowing in his face, and his vision clear before him.

During those days of examination the first heat of summer came westward like the waves of a tide rising over the hills. Passing a long morning alone at the far end of the parade ground, waiting for dinner and an afternoon sitting, Charles was surprised to see the grass already dry where it stood up golden from the hardened earth. October had worked with sweet secret poison, and a week of heat would reveal the final dryness at the heart of all free, untended growth. In the misty gold of the tall grass, wild oats drooping ripe against the sky, sorrel turning purple and brown and hard on the red earth, cicadas had, as it were in one day, reached their swooning full chorus, and rushed the trembling light with a sound like blood heard in the ears. The whole earth and all nature sank into a still swoon beneath the eternal ravishment of the sun, and the ceaseless, passionate susurrus of the insects gave sound to the heat, as already mirage was giving it a shaking visibility, clear and refractory like water. Charles felt once more the bite of it on his skin, the dull strain in his eyes; dry and brilliant, as brittle as glass, light lay on all things, and now, scarcely at the middle of November, October's mysterious spring, with all its gentleness and drowsiness in the mean of beauty, seemed never to have been; the earth lay swooning, the day marched like an army, and in the illusion of the windless grass sang the myriad cicadas.

Lying on the hard ground, he smelt the earth and the warped dead leaves. Tough, hardy grasses, slippery and matted like hair now, had ripened their transparent pods of seeds hurriedly; they were the fruit of those pink and white threepenny stars, the only reminder and proof that they had ever shone in the balmy October sunlight. Looking carefully into the tiny maze of shadows beneath the silken strands, he could still find seeds not yet baked by the sun. They were sweet and bulging with juice, so full that between his teeth they cracked and burst like minute grapes in March. Above him the sky arched, enamelled dry and bright. No cloud troubled its mighty concentration. It had not yet the bleached pallor of full summer, but winter's depth and the hazy velvet of spring were already gone from it, and its cerulean sweep was glossy and hard.

There was a great vigour in life, a kind of muscular tension and the urge to do. The sun thrust like a sword into all things, but to men's bodies it gave an electric and galvanic impulse. Charles found it difficult to keep still, as he lay with the lacy shadows of blue leaves falling on his head and shoulders. He was restless, with a deeper restlessness than the melancholy compulsions and regrets of spring. As vividly as though he might turn his head and see it, the vision of his home stood by him, dazzling white between shining camphor laurels and the black green of the tapering cypresses. The sunlight flung back from the walls, and in doorways and under clipped eaves black shadow stood like unpolished stone, impenetrable and cool to the eye. Jimmy had been watering the lawns and gardens at dawn; now the heat of late morning drew up an invisible vapour from earth and water, and filled the vibrating air with perfume from the hot, wet grass. Beneath its banks the river seemed to lie still in its bed, a green glass holding images of the trees that hung in great motionless green cumulus, sunk heavy upon their white trunks. There the air was warm and sweet with the rotting water-levels of winter floods. Snags thrust up above their brown reflections, snakes staring into the sun's eye out of their mirror, drying and crusted with their own watery decay, but hard as iron beneath, and slippery to the swimmer's naked foot...

The imperative ringing of a bell, struck quickly at first and dying out in slow repetitive monotony, flicked open his eyes and made him sit up. Before him stretched this landscape which his own homesickness had made unsympathetic and more than strange; it swept flat from the foot of the red, burnt slope, lying out towards the river and the shimmering trees. It was not his own; he knew it, but it held no secrets and no dreams of his, no memories and no power to console. It was alien, as there against the hard bright sky the burning brick of wall and tile, brilliant, dazzling in the sun, was alien to him.

He got up and walked towards it.

After dinner, when another bell called a summons to the examination room, he took a clean handkerchief and went with others to an outside tap to soak it. The stream of water was cool, but the earth, as though already thirsty, drank it glittering as quickly as it fell and spread. They took turns at the tap, or went into the downstairs lavatories from nervousness or caution. A big grass-fly with huge eyes and glassy wings settled on the hot metal of the tap, and began its steely mechanical chirr and tick. Several made an attempt to get it, but Charles had been quicker; he took it away struggling powerfully within the cage of his closed fingers, and threw it with force into the sky. The sun sucked it up, and it was gone.

For most this was the last day. The English paper rounded off all, and even the clannish, clumsy modern science students, whose bugbear it was supposed to be, faced it happily.

The big room was full, and reasonably cool. Outside, easily to be seen and admired through the wide-flung side doors, light swam with the sound of bees, and troublesome odours of drying grass and the earth by dripping taps came slyly in. Life was unreal, but beautiful and full of promise; the day itself, not yet seeming to move in afternoon's decline, could be felt in every movement of hand and arm and knee, and when the eyelids were closed a heaviness like sleep weighed dangerously upon them. Up at the front of the room a boy slipped down fainting in his seat before the papers were distributed, and two of the supervisors, serious-faced undergraduates from the University earning a little money to help them through the coming year, laid him out on the dusty floor and put a borrowed wet handkerchief over his face. Heads craned to see who that was; some dared to whisper, after cautious glances towards the supervisors' tables, where sealed packages, awful with difficulties unrevealed, were being opened. When the folded blue slips were given out, a minute before the hands of the clock-face pointed dramatically to two hours after noon, the boy who had fainted rose unsteadily, gripping the edge of his small table, and sat down in his chair. The serious, silent undergraduates walked back along their aisles to the end of the room, where a tension of silence made the movement of eyes and hands and faces seem as sharp as sounds. Work began. Heads were bowed, and pens whispered their secret, trivial confidence to the white paper.

Charles saw Margaret suddenly, among the great crowd that seethed and swam like an ocean about the edge of the wide green Oval. He had been thinking of her since he arrived there, before the luncheon interval; standing in the sun with a few others, their faces all shadowed sharply by the hard edges of hat-brims, he had thought continually of her, consciously and with a deliberate attempt at reason; he had been aware of her face, the only face there known to him, long before she was there in person; and it was without surprise that he now saw her in a group of girls and boys clinging to the warm shade of one of the pavilions; she was staring straight ahead as though just now she did not hear her companions laughing and chaffing among themselves in the noisy interval between two races.

He at once moved across to the shade, to be near her. Nothing need have prevented them meeting now, he thought; nothing in the world need keep them apart, even had not all the Schools mingled together, boys and girls and their parents, with teachers, men and women, bereft now of authority's meaningless personality, looking like anyone else there. Into this sweep of grassy land, spread out like a fan from the length of the Oval's westward curve, they seemed to have been tipped like tumbling, various-coloured seeds. Nothing need have prevented these two meeting here and speaking for a moment. In the flushed stillness of her

273

face he looked as well as he might from where he stood. She was inconspicuous, leaning there against the weathered stone foundations of the pavilion; no one would have singled her out among so many full-breasted, neatly dressed girls, unless she might have seemed strange in not laughing and talking excitedly as the rest laughed and talked, and for having no least light of expectancy in her face.

But to Charles she seemed to stand there alone, as though all that had been between them and all that would yet be, all she had said, all she had heard him say when they were alone together, was now making only her alive to his eyes. At this final memory of her he felt suddenly weak and tired; he wanted to sit down, or even to go away where he could not see her standing there, so that he might not remember, with this quick and terrible conviction, all their intimacy. He felt afraid, as once before, coming secretly upon her in the sun, he had felt afraid.

He wanted to go away, but found that he could not. Minutes must have passed; the tumult of noise resolved itself and concentrated into a high burst, an explosion of cheering. The teams were taking the field again. Over the cobbled mass of heads stretching to either side he saw them run out smartly, ones and twos; his own School's colours forced a recognition from his mind as he watched.

The cheering rose again, died down, became a shrill murmur of talk. The runners were going to their positions. He turned away from the brilliant green with its white figures and marks, and saw Margaret looking steadily at him. A silence fell at that moment, so unexpectedly that their meeting glances might have closed a door on the day;

but it lasted only until the thin crack of the starter's pistol broke it into a sigh that became a terrific shout, a roar, a scream of multiplied and varying exhortation. The Schools were urging on their own, their chosen ones.

With a glance back to the young people she had been with, who were in a dancing frenzy now, she came across the trampled turf towards Charles. He could hardly bear to watch her coming; he frowned in an effort to stop himself from turning away. She was beside him, looking towards the field. The race was a long one; in his ears their tumult swelled incredibly.

'Look,' she said, with her lips so close that he could feel the touch of the word on his cheek. 'Look, there's something I must tell you. Can you hear?'

He nodded. 'Yes. But can't we go away from here? Behind the stand...'

They walked quickly round the end of the pavilion into the full glare of the sun.

'There's something I must tell you,' she said again. Her voice was troubled, but in that light her lips and eyes were calm when he looked at them. Only in the hard clasp of her gloved fingers together was there a hint of tense purpose.

'I knew I should see you,' he said quickly. 'I couldn't wait. You weren't here this morning.'

'No. The first afternoon race. But...'

'Wait a minute,' he said. 'Is it something terrible? Because if it is I can't bear it. You know what it's like. This feeling's gone on too long. I've worked too hard; anyone will tell you that. I feel I can't bear anything. If we were at home, if only. But...I can't bear it. I feel as if I'm going mad—something; I wonder do you know. Something's going to happen. That's what I feel. Not only you—not that; but a thing hanging over me, something terrible. Ever since the last day of the examinations. I caught an insect and—no, no, not that. It hangs over me, I mean, and yet I feel empty, and I wanted to see you, Margaret...'

The words rushed from his lips, tumbling over one another as he stammered them out. She looked into his white, twisted face as once he had looked into hers, when they stood in the rain and she spoke with just such wretchedness and passion.

'Don't,' she said. 'Don't feel like that—for heaven's sake, Charles! I shall see you soon. I'm coming down. Don't let yourself go like this, Charles, for your own sake. We shall be together down there.'

Her eyes were dark with frightened compassion. She took his hand in her gloved fingers, and pressed it against her. He felt his body relax at her touch.

'Is that what you were going to tell me?' he said. 'No. There's something else.'

'It doesn't matter,' she said. 'It can wait.' She leaned against him, her shoulder and arm touching him for a moment.

'You'd better tell me,' he said at last. 'We haven't much time. I'm sorry I let myself go; but you know—I— I've not been able to feel happy since you went away that last time. And all this term's work, and Mr. Penworth... And Mother writing strangely. I felt as though there were nothing left, not even you left. And now when I see you I see it's—it's you that's made me like this. I can't forget you. I can't. It's so easy to talk, Margaret, to say the words; so useless.'

She turned her face away so that it was hidden to the lips from him, but he could see her lips trembling before she put up her hand to cover her mouth, as though holding back a cry.

'I can't talk to you here,' she said. 'But I must tell you. I feel like you do, and nothing makes any difference, never at any time. Nobody knows—even if they see they don't know. But here I can't talk. But I must. Listen, Charles.'

And, while they stood together in the sun, behind the backs of the crowd sloping away below them, she told him that her sister and brother-in-law were taking her to England with them at the end of January, and that she was to be sent to a school in Switzerland, a place whose name sounded like Neufchatel when he thought of it afterwards.

'I don't understand,' he said. 'How long? How soon will you come back?'

He now saw by her face that it was this she had had to tell him; he saw that she did not know of any return.

After a time he asked her, 'How long have you known?'

'About a week.'

'What did you say?'

'What could I say?' He saw the remembrance of her passion in her eyes. 'I said I didn't want to go. I begged them to let me stay, got down on my knees. What was the good? They said I didn't know—it would be all right once I was gone. Elsa said I'd love it after a while, and that she knew how I felt.'

She looked at him again, as though beseeching him to let her cease.

'She was surprised, I could see. Elsa is like that—it's what she always wanted, herself, to finish at some school in Europe—to learn French and...and she's being kind, she thinks. And I suppose she is really. Oh Charles. How can I, oh, how can I?'

'Is there no hope; no possible chance?'

She shook her head.

'I tried. I tried everything. You can guess. But Elsa wants me near her. You see, she—she can't have any babies, and she's always had me, and so she thinks of me like... like that; because she's much older than I am. So she won't let me go.'

He looked at her hard, trying to think; but nothing seemed to be happening, as though his mind were asleep while with open eyes he regarded her face, where grief for herself and grief for him stood whitely, and her expression was frozen in her eyes.

'Nothing seems to have any meaning now,' he said slowly. 'We don't understand older people, I suppose.'

She said passionately, 'We! They don't understand us. What do they care? We belong—they can do what they like. We don't matter. Oh, I've thought it all out now. Bessie—my Aunt—she said that day I did as I pleased. Do you remember? Well, I don't, and I never have. I couldn't then. I wanted to run out and get away; and I wanted to take you away too. And instead I just walked out with you, not thinking I'd say a word, till something, being with you, so close, knowing it was you, really there—that made me. I could have touched you. You're the only person I've ever been able to talk to, and I don't suppose there'll ever be another.'

'How could I forget?' he said. 'I shall never.'

'Perhaps,' she said, 'we shall both forget.'

'It's not true,' he mumbled between stiff lips holding back all real outcry. 'What? How could we? But it's not true—all this.'

'Can you wait?' she said at last. 'Till I come down, Charles?'

Her soft voice broke at that; she put up her hands, with a woman's gesture of hopeless self-defence, to hide her face from him, and a dry, gasping sound shook her whole body, harsh and choking. The sunlight beat furiously on them. Charles stood waiting, incapable of feeling anything, either of pity or of self-pity. Here were all his memories, his flimsy dreams, the experiences of the whole year—come to this: a standing together in the heat of the sun, with hearts and lips and eyes dry, tearless, robbed even of the assoiling weakness of emotion, barren and without shame or pity. He could look at her and feel nothing. Her grief, colourless, speechless, was unlike the day with its hot cloth of gold pouring over them.

'Wait,' she said brokenly. 'Don't go for a minute. Charles. I want to tell you, Charles—I—Oh, wait till I come down. The week after the Schools break up. Wait till then. You'll see. I want to show you, please Charles. Now go—it doesn't matter if you do or not, though. You can have me to take with you.'

She began to laugh, wildly and quietly, behind the clumsy protection of her gloved fingers.

279

He walked away, and, going down towards the Oval's edge, lost himself, as he thought, among his own sort there; but her voice followed him, as though she were talking on and on, brokenly and unsteadily and unheard.

That night there was great argument in Hall about the day's sport. When the team came in, judiciously late, a charitable yell of cheering, like a stale, self-conscious echo of the afternoon, rose and gripped the roof and shook it. They stamped and howled, carried away not by triumph but by the deep, angry excitement of sharp disappointment; this was a last chance to give fierce expression to their feelings, and they took it, and there was a sound of hysterical applause pressing upon their own ears, intoxicating them.

Up on the dais the Masters frowned and smiled at once, deprecating and pardoning such a devil's row, because it was in the order of the day. Mr. Jolly stood up, tall and stooped; his eyes glanced slyly from side to side, and that lock of hair gave him the mildly dissolute look of a weary reveller. Brushing it aside without hope, he cleared his throat and growled until they were silent.

'The team did well,' he said hoarsely, 'and I know you're all as proud of them as I am. If we didn't win the shield this year, it's not because our men weren't all triers, who put up a splendid performance that deserves the highest praise. Next year we're going to see to it that we do win. This year—to-night—we can be proud of the best efforts of our best men, who have played fair and deserved our sincerest congratulations.'

As he sat down, there was another tumult of cheering;
everyone felt better, and so they could give themselves up
again to that interminable discussion and argument which
characterized their age and spirit, as though the strenuous,
savage emotions of the day had left them untouched and as
fresh as they had been at breakfast.

'Good old Maxie...'

'By Christ, did you see that finish, when...'

'If that chap Hall hadn't beat the gun, we'd have won
the open...'

'They're a dirty lot of bastards, all that mob are.
When...'

They shouted across at one another, in a madness of
excitement relived, of races won and points scored. The
older voices were riddled by the squeals of the small fry,
who, a year before, would not have dared to open their
mouths in laying down the law of it all, as now they dared.
The School was theirs; it belonged to them all, a possession,
a boast, an idea; it was no tyranny of stale and accursed
textbooks, but a window-display of muscle and bone and
sinew and the achievements of these. The desire to conquer
and to destroy, translated into countless curious channels,
gave a dangerous edge to their words, and shone in their
lively eyes like a knife, in this hour. The incipient moral
conscience of adolescence made many offer the gesture of
fairness to the others, to the victor whom they hated, and
to the other vanquished, for whom their contempt knew no
measure; but still they raged in a frenzy they could not have
understood. It was no shield they had fought for, nor an
ideal; they had longed after the right which victory would

give them—the right to destroy, if they wished, what they had vanquished.

Penworth, glancing every now and then down the Hall when conversation became too difficult at the long table, marvelled at them and thought of his own youth at school, trying to remember whether there had ever been a scene such as this, realizing that there had not. It could not have been so. There was not this fury and violence. What could this be? He might call them 'little savages', ironically, in the Common Room, and pass over it with a laugh but there was more in it than that. They had not the supreme innocence of savages. This was no mob-hypnotism; even in their massed excitement they kept their individuality clear and separate, turning upon one another just as readily as they turned with one another. Three times now since he had been at the School he had seen this performance on this night, towards the end of November, as though it were some unconscious ritual. Summer's iron hand was closing over this mysterious country, and they seemed to feel it, though not with his weariness, and to need just such an opportunity to fling themselves together wildly. He could see the flushed, untidy faces of boys facing him at the nearest tables; each one seemed, like a drunkard, to have forgotten all but himself, the raging, struggling core of his own world.

He sighed. I shall be glad to get away, he thought. Boys are such wretched little animals. It's the School that confounds me.

Outside, the night was cool and windless. He excused himself to Mr. Jolly, and left the table.

At the end of the flagged path where he stopped to light his pipe, cupping his hand round the bowl and the matchlight as though there were wind, the Chapel towered into the sky, pale and monumental in the night. The great west window glowed faintly round the screen behind it, a colour of pale honey, and other light shone through the arrow windows set in the right tower. There was a muffled humming sound from the organ, like bees underground. He walked that way slowly, loitering outside the doorway to smoke his pipe for a few minutes while he stared at the darkness of the lawns and listened. There was a half-moon that shed no light. Within the Chapel the organ murmured and chanted; the stone of the porch moulding under his hand was warm still, and he let himself believe it vibrated in an accustomed sympathy with the diapason. In spite of the brightly-lit uproar he had just left, which still came to his ears without intruding, the night seemed peaceful to him. There was a great air of calm, now that the sun had gone, as though the earth were waking from its swoon and listening with him to this buried music that vibrated elusively under his hand on the stone. Beneath all sounds, the night was peaceful, and still; cool air lay against his forehead and cheeks.

Inside the Chapel, however, the air was warm, dusty and slightly stale. But that stream of music pouring down the narrow stairway, spilling out on the dim black and white marble squares of the vestry floor like the yellow light itself, was cool, sublimely without passion. Jones had a habit of going through the organ preludes and fugues for an hour at a time. He thought he would wait.

283

He crept up the stone spiral way and sat down on a step near the top, holding on to the hot bowl of the pipe in his pocket. The fugue went on, insisting and insisting with different voices in its argument; it grew up, mathematical, perfect, black and white in its lordly simplicity; it built up an architecture of sound like peace in his mind, an edifice into which his consciousness could enter as he had entered the Chapel, listening to the inspired dictations of the music.

Ah, he thought, if only this were all of life, to listen and to believe. But a moment afterwards he was smiling at the youthfulness of such a wish, and reminding himself that this calm elation, free of all desire to do, was one of the resting-places, where a man stopped and sat down, and from which he must rise and go on, refreshed but never contented, consoled but not fully at peace.

When the fugue was ended with a triumphant shout from pedals and keybanks, he stood up. The organist was sighing after the energy of his playing; there followed the felted rustle of pedals and a faint clicking of stops pushed in. He went up the last few stairs.

'Oh, hallo,' said Jones, his thin face shining in a smile, glistening with sweat, glittering as the organ light flashed across his spectacles.

'Hot work,' Penworth remarked.

'Hot but good. I shall never get tired of these—whatever else...' He stroked the pages with his hand. 'Never.'

'I suppose you know I'm off as soon as term's ended?' Penworth said.

'No! Your own idea?' Little Jones looked at him eagerly. 'You're not going Home?'

'No, unfortunately. I wish I were, in some ways.'

'So do I. In fact, you know, I think I will.' He spoke as though his own decision surprised him. 'Impossible to work properly in this country, Penworth. And then, my wife...'

He took his glasses off and began polishing them with a piece of silk. Penworth was leaning glumly against the organ, glancing round over his right shoulder to speak without unfolding his arms; his eyes searched the gloom towards the altar. Jones looked up from his polishing, and then looked down again.

'I can't work here,' he repeated mildly. 'I think I'll have to give notice, and go back at the end of next term. Trust to luck, you know. After all, even an organ billet in a village...'

'Yes, I know,' Penworth said bitterly. He took his lower lip between his teeth. England in summer. Oh God—the beauty of it all, and the peace. 'Go while you can,' he said. 'If you stay as long as I have you'll never get away.'

Their quiet voices woke no echo in the vault or the nave. Jones looked down dispassionately at the cloth he was twisting and rubbing; his eyes were strangely naked and helpless without their glass screens.

'Go while you can,' Penworth said again, 'or you'll find it's too late, like I have. The only escape I can make is to get away from this confounded School.'

'You see,' Jones said absently, as though he had not been listening, 'as long as Helen's there I could go. I wouldn't be surprised if it was some sort of idea of that kind—subconscious, you know—that made me let her go back alone. By the way,' he added with mild irrelevance, 'there's one chap in this place, that lad Fox, who may do quite well. He's got a weird and wonderful sort of understanding of music although he doesn't know much about it yet. I wonder if you could tell me what he's like in class? He's a nice chap—very serious yet, you know, but he'll get over that. I wonder what his other work's like.'

'Oh—he's all right,' Penworth said. 'The same in class as he is with you: understands more than he knows. Got a good brain. It's strange you should mention him. I think he's the only one of them all I shall be sorry not to go on with. He's a bright spark. The others smoulder, and if you don't keep blowing on 'em they go out.'

'He's the best of my lot,' Jones said darkly, 'but he doesn't practise enough. I've been at him. I'd like to have the teaching of that lad. He looks as though with the proper sort of handling he might do something good. Most of them think music's a confounded nuisance.'

'He might,' Penworth said, 'but I sometimes doubt it. He's too soft; he wants a bit of good hard badness in him. The good stuff's there—if he doesn't get it knocked out of him. I'm glad he's interested you too. Music may help him a bit, later on.' He spoke with gloomy detachment, remembering something now ended. 'It's done me a lot of good, I know that. And a lot of harm, I sometimes think.'

'Look here'—Jones was suddenly earnest, eager, like a child—'do go and get your fiddle, Penworth, and let's go through some of this stuff together. How about it?'

He stood up in his eagerness to persuade. Penworth turned about from his leaning position, shaking his head.

'I've got about four dozen papers to mark between now

and to-morrow afternoon. I'm afraid I can't do it. Sorry. Music would knock me out for the night. Otherwise...'

The little organist looked sad.

'It's a pity,' he said. 'It would have done us both good. Like a purge, if you know what I mean. Nothing like Bach.' He sighed again.

'Nothing,' Penworth agreed.

'Are you sure you won't?'

'I can't manage it, old man, really.'

On the path boys passed him. They were still arguing across the cool darkness; their voices rang out clear and sharp. Somebody called out from the distant porch, and an answer came floating back. They were all about him in the darkness, not knowing he was there. In the black night they were not so excited; arm in arm they walked about, talking always. There was no evening study, and until prayers they would be free to go where they chose. Happy, sudden laughter, disturbing in its night mystery, bereft of the image of a distorted face, lingered behind him, out on the wide unlit parade ground, as he walked towards the main building to get the papers from his cupboard in the Common Room. A sense of his own loneliness, a passionate envy of them, hurried him on through the darkness towards the light; taking advantage of his body's fatigue, it weighed heavily on him.

In the white solitude of his own room, he sat down in the chair, took his face between his hands, and cursed the country and his own weariness. Before him, the tidy pile of papers mocked him; the uncultivated, gross handwritings were like boys' faces scorning him with twist and flourish, muttering in secret illegibility things whose meaning he could not grasp, as though they alone knew and were germane to the deep cause of his discontent.

I came here, he thought bitterly, with a certain knowledge of myself. I was confident. I had what few men of my age have in this damned place. And now, where is it? Is it my own growth, or an intellectual cancer, or what? What is happening to me, here, now, to-night and every night and every day?

Trying to get hold of the problem sanely, he groaned aloud, and buried his face in his crossed arms so that no light should beat redly behind his closed eyelids. That helped not at all. Thoughts crowded confusedly into his mind, and a sea of faces, as many as the hosts of insects making the night tense with their sibilance, rose like a tide before that inward vision from which no grateful darkness this side of sleep could ever free him. Was that insects? It might be, he thought, the sound of my own blood in my head. And all the faces were hot and untidy, and had their mouths open to shout, to argue, to laugh in the darkness with a mysterious, challenging laughter, dangerous, secret.

'Sleep after sunset,' he muttered suddenly, staring at his clenched hands white over the knuckles. The imperfection of the spoken phrase charmed him faintly, like poetry, with all that was not said; he imagined sleep coming into the mind as night came to the earth, after the setting of the sun consciousness. When he had thought of this for a while, he grew happier, and smiled, and at length took up a pen stained with the bronze green of dried red ink.

When it came out of the ink-well it was as darkly red as though it had been dipped in blood. He looked at it, turning it this way and that in the light as he would have turned something precious, dipped it again as his thought went forward, and after a moment put it to the paper to draw a line through a word, and wrote his comment, thinking with relief that this was the last time he would be faced with this sort of task.

It's the School, he thought; that's what's the matter with me.

After a week of days which time seemed almost to drag backward, the end of the term and of the school year did come. Speech Day, with its ceremony, its giving of shiny prizes to nervous, self-consciously victorious students, and all the flutter of light dresses on the lawns and in the Chapel, the women's soft, pleased voices and exciting unfamiliar laughter, the faint unease of fathers and elder brothers, went by like a dream. The Headmaster, making his speech from the dais in the Hall, touched on the year's tragedy which was also, he said—clearing his throat and roving his eyes with sober slyness from side to side—the greatest tragedy that could ever happen to a Public School as a School, and to every individual boy belonging to it. People were particularly still while he mentioned, with an expression of emotion which many perceived to have been feigned, the name and attributes of his predecessor, going over each good quality in a low, audible voice whose hoarseness was too familiar to the boys to seem remarkable. Most there had already forgotten, and this passage had a little of the drama of surprise for them, and made the day more happy in their memories.

'You will understand,' he said, 'the grave and difficult task that faces any man who finds himself called upon to conduct a great School such as this. If, like him who was the friend of me and my colleagues and the chief trustee of your children's early lives, such a man is in bodily pain, suffering yet compelled by his own faith-keeping to go forward, longing for rest and unable to rest, the strain may become greater than any of us here can understand. But if that is so, and if such a man in the end gives beneath it, we can feel only a deep compassion—when it is too late—and wish that we might have given every help and every thought, before it became too late. Remember in your prayers that man, who made the School to a great degree what it is to-day— an institution of which we, its governors, must always be proud, and of which you, as members of its society or as parents who chose it for its high and honourable reputation, must be proud also, as long as it remains to gladden your memory and welcome your every return...'

Charles, listening dully, felt again that sense of personal loss which had so long ago shaken him. He watched Mr. Jolly's distant face against the brown of the panelling. Standing up alone, tall and grey in front of the averted faces of gowned and hooded Masters at his back, he continued his year's report; and as he stood there, speaking with proper weight and pause, not worrying about his notes but roving his eyes slyly from side to side, there was in his mind the vision of himself standing and speaking, just so, at the end of the next year, and the next; until he too should be made absent from that assembly, by age or death or some such release, while some other man, unwilling perhaps like himself but at the bidding of such as his own discomforting will and wisdom, would take his place, another actor playing this part, another leader wanting only leisure, rest and a final freedom from the perilous loneliness of authority.

When that part of the afternoon's ceremony was completed, and the year's prizes given, tea was served to visitors. The School had come to the end of its year. This hour was one of release, into the greater bondage of free responsibility for some, but for most into that much-dreamed-of time, the seven weeks of summer holiday leading them from December swiftly over Christmas into a new year. The spirit of friendship smiled among them all; sentimentally they took leave of Masters and of one another, and the excitement of their voices was now without unkindness, for in that hot, cloudless, long-declining afternoon they were given what they fiercely desired, freedom and individuality, the liberty to go. With that desire appeased, they could afford to be kind.

Charles walked up the covered way alone, for the last time that year. In the spontaneous happiness of all those with whom he had lived there was an overtone of triumph now that drew responsive echoes from the unhappy bewilderment within him. The air of parting had no weight in his mind; he felt satisfied to know that for some time after this day he would walk these floors no more, and see nothing of the glass and wood of this genial prison; but he faced the holiday, as something stark and positive, with uncontrollable tremors of foreboding. The black promise, that had

291

rung like far thunder in his mind ever since that day when the examinations ended, was now to be fulfilled by life with a wave of the hand; and so—farewell. He was in no mental state to do deliberate battle with his own misery; by no careful and constructive architecture of thought could he sort and build up the material of the future into any credible structure. In the landscape of things certain to happen, one empty fact gaped like a chasm into which with a rush of cold wind and a bursting heart he was being hurried by the days.

As though he were still waiting to hear a known sentence of death pronounced upon himself, he remained inwardly frozen save for the interminable quick beat of his heart against his ribs. Day after day, from the time of that brilliant sports meeting, he had seemed to wait. In his mind, keyed even now to a defiant, unreasoning optimism, a constant, mechanical thought insisted that life was lovely and good, and so would remain; but though he might nod his head as he heard it, and make himself smile and talk and move about between the lines of each day's relaxed routine, his consciousness bent its whole scrutiny now upon the shape of bereavement. If he could have done so, he would have cried out against whatever trick of life had put into his hands something which, before he had discovered what it was, was irrevocably withdrawn; but it was not yet in him to cry out against life, for his childhood had been a happy one, and now his unhappiness was only eased because it became too great and swollen, and his mind again and again slid away from it, too tired to hold it longer even though it was the only reality now in a sea of incomprehension.

Of this incomprehension Penworth partook in his mind. After some hesitation he sought him out in his room, before leaving the House and the School with his bags. There was doubt in him as to whether he should do this, for, as he now felt, any passage of emotional stress would very likely break his carefully devised resistance to all outward demonstration.

Penworth, however, received him calmly enough, as though they had been slightly acquainted for some time.

'Hallo. You off already?' he said. He had taken off coat and waistcoat, collar and tie, and his short sleeves were rolled above the elbows. Charles, embarrassed because they had had no informal meeting since that day just before the examinations, noticed how white and solid was his neck above the gaping edge of the shirt top. In that room there was already an air of adventure and departure foreign to his memories of it. Their eyes met.

'Yes,' he said, 'I'm going.'

'Don't look so miserable about it,' Penworth said. 'You've played your first game with life—and won it. Haven't you?'

'I don't know, sir,' Charles said. 'There's more than...'

'Oh yes.' He was lightly ironic. 'There are other games. For a young man in love I should say you don't look as pleased with yourself as you might.'

The sense of strain between them, and the feeling that he was being derided now by one whose derision he had never known, gave Charles the hardness he needed; but he could not go yet. They stood still. Penworth had been packing books; the hollow lid of a wooden chest flung itself back expectantly against the edge of the bed, and a litter of volumes lay on the cleared table. It was hot, and there was much busy dust.

'Great things, books,' Penworth said suddenly, following his look. 'You always know where you are with them.'

'Yes,' Charles said. There was some importance in the words, but he could not resolve them. He turned to Penworth again, ready to hold out his hand and say farewell. There was a bitter taste about this; they were clearly separated already, and he wished it had come about in some way less difficult, so that he could have spoken easily, and in the certainty of being fairly heard. As it was...

'Look here,' Penworth said, 'what are we standing here for, like this? There's nothing left, I believe, but to say good-bye. I am right, am I not?'

'I suppose so,' Charles said. 'Only—it's a pity it happens like this, after all the...'

'Your choice, my friend. There can be no other way; and I don't think I myself am exactly to blame for it. Do you?'

'No, sir. It's all my fault. But—oh, I ought to be able to explain...'

'Does it matter?'

The words were spoken calmly. For the first time Charles saw clearly where life was leading him, and in a brief illumination of understanding perceived what part Margaret played in this miserable conclusion in which she seemed not to be concerned. As a friendship this had failed; but now it had made him as hard as a man—harder than

Penworth, who was looking at him as though he divined his thoughts, looking with something like his old quizzical understanding. He began to go to the door, wishing to stay no longer.

'Don't go, Charles.'

Penworth's voice was friendly now. He was holding out both hands, as though welcoming someone long absent from him.

'Don't go like that. I know what you feel. I know what it's been like for you, this year. I ought to; I had a lot to do with it. You had to choose, didn't you? Well, you've chosen, and I admit your choice—from your point of view—is right.'

Listening to the dispassionate humility in his words, Charles felt something like triumph, a strange feeling, surely irrelevant to this certain parting.

'Well,' he was saying, 'that's all there is to it now. But'—he came forward and took Charles's hands and held them loosely—'I would not have you go like this. There's no reason why we shouldn't part as friends. Is there?'

They stood looking at one another steadily, until Penworth's regard wavered and shifted.

'No,' Charles said, choking over the words. 'No, there's no reason. That is, if you feel there's not. I don't think it's been your fault, though; honestly I don't. But you see— she—it's as though it's her fault. Hers, and of course mine, I suppose. And now I don't care—whether it's her fault or not. I don't care. If I could tell you, you'd understand.'

His eyes were full of tears. Penworth drew back and leaned against the table, grasping its edge firmly with both hands. His voice was calm enough.

'I understand that,' he said easily. 'You've made your choice. It was in you to make it. And now you must stick to it, and stick it out. But, listen to me.'

He held his look with his own.

'Try and see things in some sort of perspective. That's been your trouble all along—you can't do it. Don't be more unhappy than next year, say, will advise you if you look into it. I know it's difficult…even though I don't know, and certainly don't want to know, what's going on between you. From now on your life's your own concern. I can't help you. Nobody can. But we can still be friends if you choose. It seems, by the way, that most choices are yours.'

He laughed.

'Doesn't it? It does. So if you choose we can be friends, Charles. I won't be here any more, so it will be easier than it might have been. Life altogether will be easier for you this coming year—in so far as work is concerned, and in other ways, of course. Even if I'm not here it doesn't mean we can't be quite good friends, does it?'

'No, sir,' Charles said.

'Well, cheer up, then.'

He moved to the bed, kicked away the wooden chest, and sat down.

'Come and sit here for a minute, till you feel ready to face the world. Use a handkerchief freely; I don't mind.'

Charles sat down by him, and in spite of his misery, triumph was still lively within him. After a while he could smile and they could talk, not indeed with that former feeling of intimacy now lost to them, but freely and in increasing unconcern.

'I'm sorry to be such a fool,' he said at last. 'I suppose it's the excitement and all that.'

'Glad it's all over now?'

Charles hesitated, looking up through the open window at the sky, hearing the innumerable, excited sounds of reunion and departure.

'I'm glad about the School,' he said at last. 'But home's different now. I don't know: my mother's different. We don't seem to understand each other as we used to.'

Penworth's fine eyes regarded him steadily, in silence. Aware of the look, fearful of once more venturing into that realm of personal conflict now closed to them in speech, he said nothing, and Penworth, after the short silence, turned to other things in a way that seemed strange but was now to be a rule.

When at last Charles could restrain himself no longer, and must go, they stood up together, and at the door their hands met and clasped.

'Well,' Penworth said, 'I'm like you—not sorry to leave here. But don't forget, we write to one another sometimes. A bargain?'

'A bargain.'

'And don't forget, either, that this mustn't be an end, but a new beginning.'

The look in his eyes, of one still grappling with the awareness of defeat in all defeat's isolation, made Charles turn quickly and walk away without looking back.

Those words remained in his mind, when he left the School that afternoon, and during his first long week at home.

He too was now isolated, until she came. The words had more deep and immediate significance than Penworth could have supposed when he said them, with that keen smile driving creases into his cheeks and making his grey eyes more beautiful; they applied so clearly to the conviction of his own heart that he came to think he had uttered them himself with the defiance of despair. This mustn't be an end, but a beginning. Not an end...

He communed with himself day after day, doggedly and desperately. There was no one he could speak to, now, when he most needed to set his mind moving forward, out of this coil, towards some purpose. The brilliant days reflecting in water and air, the flowers that Jimmy—shrewd Jimmy, who knew the ways of all flowers—had caused to bloom everywhere, mocked him, as his own body, his pale, dulled face mocked him from the water he stared into before he broke it. To be unhappy among all things that had taught him happiness was like seeing a sneer on the lips of someone dearly loved. It lay contrary to the fury of reason in all desire. The fear of losing what he did not have dragged at body and mind. He knew his mother was watching him, but would not meet her eyes, and could not care what else she saw, knowing that what she saw her own alienated will would interpret in the interests of alien feelings.

In a helplessness such as he had never known nor imagined, he went through those few days, waiting for a final pronouncement in action of what her words had already told him.

A note came for him from her, at the end of the week. He felt frightened and sick when he saw it, though he had never looked on her handwriting before. Studying with fascinated distress the characters of his own name on the envelope's whiteness, he tried to think what was inside, trying to imagine something that existed in her mind but still, even in that moment, had no existence for him. He knew what was written, and was trying to remember. No, no—he did not know. The handwriting was uneven and without marked character, like that of women whose hearts are generous and deeply swayed, to the confusion of their minds. He looked most carefully at it. No trace of scholasticism had shaped that C or that clumsy F. *Charles Fox.* He looked at it, surprised to think that that brief and definite description meant himself, meant his body and the tumult that was his mind; and as he thought of this he saw her hand resting on the paper under the pen, making these marks.

A note inside the envelope said with the rapidity of thought:

Elsa and John are going away for Christmas for a week, but that's all. After that I have to come back to start getting ready. There is nothing else, I must go, but I will be down there for a week with you anyhow.

And then, like a futile crying aloud:

Oh Charles if we had never known one another that day you would be happy now and it would be so easy and for you too. Do you wish we never had?

He laid it flat on his table. A green light, like sunshine refracted by sea-water, came softly into the room beneath the faded canvas awning pitched outside above the window. In this light the stumbling handwriting looked illusory and kept escaping him. After he had been staring at it for some time, watching it vanish and reappear, he heard his mother calling him from the foot of the stairs. Folding the sheet, he put it carefully into the torn envelope and went down.

'Come and help me, son,' she said. 'There's that new bed to be laid out; I can't decide. Jimmy says it should go between the coach-house and the wall. You have a look.'

She went out into the blind brilliance of the morning with him, pulling on an old shapeless hat of straw to keep the fury of the sunlight from her face, and perhaps to make it not unnatural that he should not see her eyes. She was glancing about as she talked, but not at him. The white look in his face half an hour ago, when he came in with the mail that one of the O'Neills had left at the outer gate, had alarmed her, and she knew that her alarm must not be revealed to him—not yet. After months of absence from him during which she had found it hard to write as she had written at first, when all was well between them, in the new knowledge that her quiet command of his affection in obedience was now put in peril by what she could not yet control, she was determined to say nothing to him of that girl until he spoke; and even then she had not thought what to say. All her life it had been clear to her that the emotion of every moment dictated its own happiest expressions.

Meanwhile, walking with him out into the sun, she was satisfied that for the present he should be unhappy and alone with her; and she spoke easily of small things. They had considered the placing of the bed for new roses, and to please him she was agreeing with his own suggestion, when Jimmy joined them, wiping sweat from his brown, creased forehead with the back of one wrist. His blue eyes under sandy brows were bright and interested.

'No, Mist' Charles. Not there, lad,' he said mildly, having in his turn surveyed the position Charles had liked.

'Why not?' Charles, ready now to be at once defiant of all opposition, of whatever importance, spoke almost angrily. For no reason at all he was determined to hold to what he had suggested.

'Why, because of the weather, ye see. It comes that way.' Jimmy waved his pipe at the hard, flawless sky in the north-west. 'Put 'em as you want, and they'll get the worst of it, lad.'

She was looking from one to other, smiling. Charles closed his lips in a way new to her knowledge of him; she saw it, and caught the sudden anger in his eye.

'It won't look right,' he said impatiently. 'You go back as far as the hedge, and you'll see what I mean.'

'The weather,' Jimmy repeated with mild, imperturbable certainty. 'You can't go against that, Mist' Charles.'

'Well,' he said, 'I don't agree that it ought to go that way. That's all.'

'Jimmy is right, son.'

His mother's smiling words, contradicting what she had said a minute earlier, ended the matter. He turned away abruptly, and was going towards the house, to escape from the fire of the sun and from a fresh sense of open conflict which was intolerable to him. As he walked between beds of brilliant, hot flowers, watching his inky shadow cling like a pool to his feet, her hand touched his shoulder and she was there beside him, smiling still, but without triumph.

'You silly fellow,' she said. 'Jimmy meant nothing.'

He saw that behind her smile was unease and unhappiness, and made an effort, as they went inside, to show a contrition he did not quite feel.

'I'm sorry, Mother. I know quite well it doesn't matter which way the bed goes.'

She pressed his arm against her. In the house, blinded securely against the day, there was a deep coolness that smelt faintly of polished wood and flowers and books. They went together to the long front room.

'Did you have any letters?' she asked suddenly.

'Yes.'

'Oh. Nice?'

'All right—yes, quite nice.'

'I just wondered. Do you write to Mr. Penworth? You don't speak of him now as you used to.'

He had won back composure and recovered sufficiently from his first shock of surprise to be able to raise his head and smile.

'I haven't yet,' he said. 'I will though.'

She knew, before a sudden intensification of reserve in his voice and face, that she had not the courage to ask what she so keenly wished to know.

'Nothing's wrong, is it, darling?' she said at last. 'You're just over-tired still, I expect.'

'No, nothing's wrong.' He was swinging himself from side to side, balanced on his heels.

'Oh, son, don't do that. It takes off all the polish. What are you going to do with yourself?'

He stopped swinging about, and with a new determination drew near and sat down on the arm of her chair, looking into her upturned face. She was calm; she bent the flimsy hat of straw between her hands idly, returning his look with a look more questioning.

'I don't know,' he said. 'But on Sunday I—I promised Mrs. McLeod, that is, I promised Margaret last time I'd take her to the big pool this summer. Could I have some lunch? Would Emily mind?'

He had almost said 'Would you mind?' but caught himself from it in time. She looked away, shaking her head.

'I'm sure Emily wouldn't. What would you like?'

'Just something easy,' he said with relief; for he saw how much he had feared her spoken opposition, and now it was past, her consent given, part of the unknown future known and assured to him. She was sighing faintly; her hands ceased moving in her lap, and lay still. He was on his feet again, hearing her sigh, thinking it a sign that all was not yet certain.

'Well,' she said lightly, 'I'll see Emily about it now. After that I must write some letters.'

She stood up, and without another word, without smiling, left him there. He saw her expression of sorrow, and went up the stairs slowly, longing for but in despair of present repose and an easing of this mad strain between them, and determined at the same time that no weakening of his own should ease it. When he was in his room again, he lay down on the bed, breathing heavily as though he had been running.

She was watching, he thought; she knew—she has known all the time. That was why she called me down. She wanted to see, to be sure.

He closed his eyes and pressed his clenched hands together, in an effort to think. In itself her knowing mattered nothing to him; but he feared the difficulties between them when she tried, as he knew she would try, to be kind without desiring to be kind. A cold compassion flowed in him. Trying to be kind, when they could not even speak to one another! She never knew what to say. There was nothing to say; no words between them now would ease either him or her. She would lie awake thinking what to say, and never be able to say it so that he could understand; and so they would remain like this, like enemies.

Afterwards, he thought, when it's all finished...

The thought came like a cool wind into the hot fervour of his mind. When all was over. There was to be an end, then? He dropped his hands on the blue coverlet, letting his fingers relax and fall open as though all strength had gone out of him. From shoulder to heel he felt his own weight stretched out on the bed, relaxed, heavy, unable to move. If he had been asleep he could not have lain more heavily or more still.

The bed bore him up; he looked at the ceiling, and saw above him the girl's grave face gazing down into his. She was always there now. But an end—he could not picture it. He wondered what it would be like, and what was to pass between them before then. How did one say good-bye? That was a word which somehow they had never said. It was as if they had superstitiously avoided it, in a primitive suspicion and fear of all words. I would not close a door after her, if she went out of a room. Good-bye would be a door closing; blankness drawn across her face, her body, her hair, her arms and hands and all, as though after that she could exist no more. He saw it happening. He said the word aloud to himself. 'Good-bye.' It had no meaning, he thought angrily; two syllables hinged on clattering consonants, with as much power and as little meaning as has a key with which you lock a door; a formless thing with sorrow and relief for its secret.

He did not want to lose her, yet already she was lost to him.

Who started it? he thought. Neither of us. Or was it I, and is this a punishment? We have had nothing from it all but this. We did no harm to anyone; we have done nothing except be alone together.

His mind returned again to that first long look between them, when from almost nothing had been created something that now, under the compulsion of desire, retrogressed its first appearance to reveal an origin in the heart of time itself. It seemed as though each had held the half of a secret, and as though by the eternal impulse towards unity those halves must come together and they with them, so violently that life had seemed to end there, not begin. Afterwards came the unrecognized clamour of the flesh, and inevitable confusion; life thrusting towards fulfilment when a greater fulfilment had already been encompassed.

Some understanding of this laboured to be born in him, but he could not find words for what he was sure he knew. He entered again and again into the endless brevity of that look between them, until he imagined his own figure and hers, marble, without consciousness and beyond motion, turned each to other under the August sky. Her passionate confessions of knowledge were, it seemed, as nothing when he remembered that. Even their one cold kiss was like a gesture made without thought, lacking consequence, a common admission of perfect sympathy in understanding.

She had said, 'Wait till I come down...You can have me to take away with you.'

He shivered, and wished he had not left her there laughing behind her gloved fingers. She had more under-standing than he had. There was something she knew; the words, now, were tremendous with promise. She must know. She had spoken like that, impetuously, out of some irresistible conviction, as though she had a woman's years. 'You can have me to take away with you.' The words seemed strange to him, like the feckless words of a fool; but she had said them consciously, deep-sunk in each word, as though they were the brief statement of a matured philosophy.

A fanatical blindness of thought made him fail to see the import of them. I can't get there, he repeated. I remember and remember, and it seems as though every-thing has already happened. And still I want her.

That afternoon he went down to the river and tired himself with swimming. Relaxation came with weariness. When his body was exhausted by the thin, unresisting fresh water, he dragged out into the sun, and lay face-downwards until the heat stupefied him, and all the images in his mind became slow and vivid, poised between waking and sleeping, like the most vivid of dreams. All that afternoon he remained there, lying in the delicate shade of the leaves of great Chinese bamboos that rose stooping high into the pale sky, curved and motionless. He lay so still that the leaves and stems of grass branded a complex red net of pattern on his arms and legs; the water dried away; ants came out of the grass, crawled over him, and fell back into the grass again. Laboriously the sun shifted over to the west, and the still air was a little easier, cooled here by the water in which every overhanging spray and leaf was mirrored with eternal perfection. After some time, finding the leaf-shadows gone and the sunlight crawling danger-ously up his legs and bare back, he staggered to his feet and dropped into the water again. It was cool enough to make him gasp a little. He crossed to the far bank and crawled on to a log that ran down into the water; there he perched, and the tiny dragon-flies, ruby and sapphire, came and perched with him, on the brown rotted trunk and on his bare knees.

From the platform Emily called to him; there was tea made. She peered out from under the droop of a towel flung over her head. In summer she put a towel or an apron over her head even at sunset, as though while ever the sun was above the horizon its light was personally dangerous and malicious to her uncovered. He waved, and watched her climb up the rough stair cut into the bank. Life would go on, with balance and purpose underlying its confusion, as long as there was Emily to call people to drink tea in the late afternoon.

That night, and all the next day, he kept himself so employed that thought was held at arm's length most of the time. In the evening of Saturday, when the sun was dropping down out of the world in a blaze of rusty, hard light, angry and powerless, he set off for that part of their boundary along which the railway line passed towards the south. His mother, who now kept herself quietly aware of his movements, saw him go, without a word; and as he went out the garden gate and down the drive between the old, friendly pear trees whose upper limbs held the red light like velvet, he knew she was looking after him, but did not care. When he had closed the white gate behind him, he turned to look at the sun, as he was used to do. It must be, he thought, after seven, and the evening train came in soon after half past. He would have to make haste.

For a few minutes he ran headlong after his lean sliding shadow. Then all at once, jerking to a halt, he sat down in the warm dry grass of a bank at the edge of a field. It was, after all, useless to go off like this simply to see the train she would come by. His breath rushed fast and dry from running; the warm grass, full of crickets and singing insects mad with sunset fever, smelt as sweet as flowers in that still air. Far away the tops of the blue hills were on fire with the last of the light; the sky was white behind them. Looking at them now, he remembered speaking of those lonely men who came down, in summer evenings when work was done, to watch the evening train go by. Mad, he had said they must be; and now in his way he was akin to that madness. They came down to see and hear a proof that the world still existed beyond their solitary shacks; he would have gone to assure himself that the world he knew had not suddenly contracted to the sharp limits of his own thought. After all, it was a kind of madness, such as is visited upon the lonely ones of the earth.

He sat in the dry grass, and the evensong passion of the insects seethed about him like an invisible ocean stretched from the horizon in the east to the red west. His hair had been on fire, and the flame went out in it quickly; light was going up into the sky, going out. Night must fall.

To-morrow, he thought, to-morrow. Only this night between now and then.

High over him the sky was as pale as moonstone, without a cloud; pale as though a veil of fine gauze had been drawn over it, serene and illimitable. When the sun had set light lingered in the warm air, and soon he could smell the earth's evening exhalation, like a long sigh released, underlying the intolerable nostalgic sweetness of the dry grass stretched for miles under the evening. He got up and walked through the fields towards home.

A murmur on the face of the silence arrested his hand as he was about to open the drive gate, and he stood still, listening, his hand still resting on the white bar. It was the evening train going in.

The low rush of sound swelled faintly, lying on the silence like the stroke of a pencil across a printed page, cancelling but not obliterating. When, after what seemed an unusually long time, it faded out and he could hear nothing but the stillness, he opened the gate and went through. The sound of his feet on the road of the drive was sudden and loud.

That night Charles slept heavily, as though some strong drug had been given him. In the morning, when he woke an hour after sunrise, he remembered no dreams. A leaden heaviness of fear seemed to tear his heart downward on its strings, but the pulse of excitement fluttered moth-like in the cold palms of his hands. He put on his clothes with irrelevant solemnity, as though he had been a condemned man dressing for execution; shoes without socks, a blue shirt, grey trousers, such as he wore on any summer morning—clothes that could be slipped off hurriedly and without thought by a pool's edge, flung over the courteous arm of a tree, forgotten; clothes that clung briefly to a wet body, and dried in the sun, forgotten and kind.

At the breakfast table on the veranda he ate rapidly, with simulated appetite. His hands were beginning to tremble whenever he stiffened his wrists.

I must get out of this, he thought angrily; get away and get it over, whatever it is.

With great strength of relaxation, he held himself still until his mother had finished. As always, she ate slowly, methodically, seeming not to taste the food at which she looked with mild surprise as she put it to her lips. He thought how ridiculous is the human face taking in food— the raised eyebrows, the drooped, careful lids, the hungry width of the mouth opening as the head and shoulders lean forward possessively over the plate, crouching and sure. Turning from her face to the day so that his eyes should not discomfort her, he saw it hard and bright already through the holes in an old creeper that hung its curtain of dark outward green from the veranda eaves. There was still that flowery magic smell of sun-bleached grass, sweet on the air; and the air in their shadow was cool, for Jimmy had been watering lawns and gardens at sunrise, and now the morning heat sucked up vapours of water and earth, and dried the wet leaves.

'Son!'

His mother's voice, mild and tired, sounded a note of urgent warning. He looked round from his frowning stare.

'Don't do that. It does look so ugly.'

'What was I doing?' he asked.

'Biting your nails. It's such a bad habit, darling,' she pleaded mildly. 'You've never done it before. Only since you came home this time...I don't know what's the matter with you.'

He refused to reply to her last words.

'All right,' he said, and added, inanely, 'It's not as though I'm hungry.'

I am hungry, he thought, I am, I am. In another way.

She was looking away from him, and her hands, that were usually so still and sure, that had comforted him so often with their quietness, now trembled as she fidgeted surprisingly with a spoon.

'You'd better go early,' she said, and her voice was as unsure as her hands and wrists. 'You can't make the girl follow you about when it gets too hot. Though no doubt she—she would.'

She had made a show of speaking lightly, but the words brought him to his feet in one movement; his face went white, and he opened and closed his lips once, before he could reply.

'How dare you say that, Mother? How dare you? She follow me! Why—why—Oh! I follow her, if that's what you want to know. Yes, I do. And I will, I will, I tell you.'

She was startled by the passion with which he spoke, by the dark flame of anger and fear in his green-brown eyes. Unable for some seconds to reply, she made a small, helpless movement with her hand. He saw it, and sat down suddenly.

'I don't know what's the matter,' he said in a voice that trembled. 'It's been like this ever since I told you. I wish I never had—I've wished it ever since.'

'Oh, God,' she said quietly, and began to cry, her face still save for an incessant trembling of lips and eyelids.

'I know,' he said. 'I know. You don't think I care what you feel. But I do.'

He was ashamed of an impulse to laugh, to laugh hysterically in her face, to shake his fist at her and tell her to cry; an impulse to increase and swell out his own suffering to breaking-point and release.

'I often wonder,' she said brokenly. 'For such a long time...Ever since you went to School you've been different.'

He said quickly, 'Well, you made me go, didn't you? I never wanted to, and I've never liked it.'

'Of course you had to go.'

'Then...'

'But that's not the point.'

'What, then?'

'You've changed in another way.'

'Yes—started to grow up.'

'You're not grown up yet, my child,' she said. 'Don't think it.'

'All right,' he said. 'You want to keep me not grown up, I think. Can't I live my own life now? I always used to, and you didn't mind then. Why do you mind now?'

'You don't love me any more.'

'Oh, I do!' he cried, exasperated.

'Then don't go away from me to-day, son.' Her voice pleaded with him. 'Don't go. Stay with me to-day.'

Slow tears filled his own eyes.

'You're mad,' he said. 'You're mad to say that.'

'All right,' she said, suddenly looking up, her eyes bright. 'That—girl. I know...'

'Don't,' he said. 'You don't understand. You make me feel you've never been young.'

'You're wrong,' she said, so that he could hardly hear her. 'You're terribly wrong and unkind. Perhaps I understand better than you think. Perhaps that's why...'

She could not end it.

'Why what?' he said wildly.

'Perhaps that's why I don't want you to get mixed up with any girl at your age.'

'Mixed up! Mixed up!'

'You're young,' she said, averting her face. 'You don't know—it's impossible to know the risks. Believe me, son, I'm only thinking of your happiness. And it's so—so—hard.'

'Happiness,' he said. 'Would you like to meet her? Would you like me to bring her here?'

Her hand went suddenly to her breast.

'No doubt she would come,' she said.

'Would you like her to?'

'No.'

313

The look in her face made him unable to speak. They sat still, passionately regarding each other now, and it seemed to him that the restraint of decency and good manners she had taught him had been by her thrown violently aside. Words choked in his throat and dissolved there into bubbles of breath. He was frightened of himself, now that all pretence was away from them.

'Damn you,' he said.

Rising, kicking back his chair so that it fell with a sound startling after the quietness of their voices, running along the veranda into the house, he thought furiously, I shall regret that for the rest of my life. And he did not care. If she called after him he would not answer. There was one being on earth whom he wanted to see now; all others were enemies, madly against him. If she called he would neither hear nor reply.

She did not call. At the foot of the stairs he took up the knapsack already packed by himself, and for some moments stood perfectly still in the dim coolness of shadow there, his breath quick and dry, his mind suddenly arrested so that he could not move. The image of his mother's face bitterly accusing him, of Penworth saying good-bye, of himself moving between these two, and then a startling image of the girl to whom he would go turning her face up towards his, held his mind and body in a petrifaction of terror and triumph...

At last, in a sudden relaxation, he sat down abruptly on the lowest stair, as he had sat outside Penworth's room that cold night and heard the dramatic passion of the Cesar Franck sonata for the first time. He remained there for a moment. The house was strangely still, as though listening with him. Rising as abruptly, he shouldered the straps of the knapsack, and went out by another door into the hot golden day, through the green, still orchard red and purple with shadow and sun on the earth, towards the stables beyond, where the mare was waiting for the saddle.

When he was gone she had remained sitting quite still, the grief of her defeat holding her rigid there with her elbows on the white cloth, her hands clasped and trembling, her eyes turned sideways towards the garden, where day rioted already like a madman loosed. Through the holes in the creeper's curtain, bonfire salvia twenty yards away blazed defiance at her, redder than any flame would have been in that still, tempestuous sunlight, red as blood above its emerald leaves.

The tears dried from her eyelashes and her cheeks. She found herself thinking, I don't like that salvia. I shall never plant it again.

By the time Charles came to the new farm his fear was a rage of terror, his hope an equal rage of desperate determination. He did not know what he was to do with these two dangerous and unwieldy weapons. When he leant down from the saddle to open the gate, he drove back the sign of conflict from his face, and it went in deep like a poison, making him numbed and unnaturally calm.

It will be right, it will be right, he repeated in his mind; and those two weapons, over-big for him to use it seemed, clattered together inwardly in a boiling silence, while a part of consciousness, remote from all stress, stood by smiling and observing him.

'I should have been here before,' he said to Mrs. McLeod when she opened the wire door to him.

'Och noo!' she murmured, 'y'ken sh'only arrived yesterday.'

Her eyes slid round on him with that same elusive concealment of mockery, and with something else also, some flash of suspicion that justified his guardedness. He had manufactured a lie to act, on his way hither, and that look confirmed him in it.

'Oh—I thought—oh well, that's all right, then,' he said, forcing relief into his voice, and lightness. 'I've been all the week getting used to being home again.'

All the week waiting for this moment, he thought, and ached with the fear still surging in him. Clearly she too was watching him. He did not care.

'It seems a long time,' he said.

He did not realize that neither of them had spoken Margaret's name, though she must have been very vividly present in the thoughts of both of them.

'Do you think she would come out somewhere and have lunch?' he asked with admirable casualness. 'It's pretty hot; still, she might like.'

Mrs. McLeod leaned forward into the dark doorway leading into the inner rooms of the house.

'Meg,' she cried, 'here's a young man come jus' noo, speerin' after y'. Come and see what.'

She turned round to him, her face serious now, and secretly unsympathetic.

'Y'ken they're taking her away t'England,' she said, and the bitter concern in her voice now seemed accusing and guarded, though her eyes were full of a surprising pity for him, and her face sad at the thought of her own loss. She appeared to know that he knew; he thought she sighed as she went back to her table by a window over which a blind was drawn low, and the light fell on her arms and hands moving firmly in their work. He could say nothing. 'Ye'll take guid care o' her,' she said firmly, with her back to him.

'Yes,' he said, 'I will. Of course.'

The tone of her voice, guarded, almost as though warning him of himself, made him again realize that their world held more than their two selves, and that others were to be affected by her actions also; and this realization drove him dumb, until suddenly Margaret came in, and he must speak.

'I thought you'd—I wondered if you'd perhaps like to come out and we could have some lunch,' he said with some difficulty. Mrs. McLeod clattered things on her table without looking round.

'I'll come,' she said, and looked at him. Her direct, dark glance was like a look of uncontrollable rage. He did not recognize it or know what purpose lay behind it.

'She does as she likes,' Mrs. McLeod said pleasantly. 'Don't you, our bairn?'

'Yes,' the girl said. Her voice trembled, and again he met her look, direct and dark from the depths of her eyes, and again it seemed as though she were struggling with a rage of fury she could scarcely control. He remembered how

317

she had spoken, when they were together on the afternoon of the sports meeting, of what people said about her doing as she liked; she had been in passionate disagreement, and he wondered whether that was the reason for her startling look as she said 'Yes'. But the dramatic stillness and fury of her glance gave him the sensation of having seen a cover lifted from a cauldron of something so hot that it could not move, like molten metal, though it was liquid. He wanted to look, but he wanted also to step back, as a man does at the sight of a thing dangerous and not altogether controlled or calculable. This had happened to her since he saw her last.

'Well,' he said, 'shall we go soon, before it gets too hot? I don't want to drag you round in the heat too much. We'll go to the big pool, if you like. It's always cool there.'

'All right,' she said. As she went out he called to her down the length of the room.

'If you're reading something, better bring it. It's not much use doing anything lively now.'

'What d'ye mean by "lively"?' Mrs. McLeod asked.

Unconscious of her mocking smile, he answered gravely, 'Well, running about and doing things that make you hot.'

'Eh, when I was a bit of a thing like Meg we didna mind making oursel's a bit hot, forb'e! I wouldna say it was just wi' running about, y'ken.'

He did not hear her. He was wondering still about that incomprehensible look; it was the expression of one in pain or fear, or the anger of a furious purpose. That there had been no quarrelling he was certain; no one could quarrel or be angry with that cheerful big woman. Was it against himself, then? Perhaps he had done wrong to come like this. But after that note; after that last futile outcry on the paper? It could not be against himself.

The morning was very still. From beneath the fig trees outside, heavy now with huge leaves and swelling fruit, a lazy clucking of fowls came to their ears. The mare was in the shade; from time to time she stamped a hoof at the flies, standing there motionless in the strong black shadow of the tree. The light swam like water, shaking and eddying as it consumed outlines so that they seemed to melt. Charles leaned against the door-post, aware of the quiet, the small sounds, and the day's still power. He could hear the light secretly vibrating into a mirage shimmer.

'May I leave Julia?' he asked presently.

'Ay, do,' she said.

'I can get her when we come back,' he explained, unable as he was unwilling to imagine anything of that return; knowing only that it would be late.

'Put her in the calf paddock jus' noo,' she said. 'Y' wouldna leave her tied a' day?'

'No. That'll be splendid then. Thank you.'

He walked out into the sun, glad to be gone for a time from the feeling of difficulty and unhappiness that hung, a different, subtler shadow, in the doorway. While he was hauling off the saddle, smelling the hot leather above, the hot sweated padding beneath, he thought, At home, and here too. As though someone were going to die. (He could imagine no more terrible suspense than that of waiting for a death.) The feeling of conflict became clear

319

in his mind, as clear and sharp as the ring of the stirrup irons clashing together when he heaved the saddle into the crutch of the tree. Julia shook herself with a little thunder. Taking the rein, he led her out to the small paddock, where old barren plum-trees were growing in broken rows, two or three together, giving a scattered, illusory shade in the burning day. Such a conflict was quite foreign to his memory of home and this country; coming away from the School he had wanted urgently to leave all warring externals behind him, as he had always done; and now he found he was still under their power. His mother was watching him just as the Scotswoman watched him and Margaret. She herself was changed, it seemed. The look of rage in her eyes, the look of a runner who sees the end of a race and is in a fury to be done—that was a look he had never seen in anyone's face before. He could not understand that she had a purpose now, for he himself had none; the separation they were approaching had already robbed him of every energy save that of hope, which, facing a future undefined by any certainties, knew not how to run.

In the passionate sunlight he felt calmer, and regretted the way he had spoken to his mother. The sun on his head like a hand, burning through his hair; under the thin blue stuff of his shirt he could feel its prickling bite and pressure. To see the mare free, rolling on a patch of bare ground as though she knew she had a day of freedom, gave him a new assurance; he imagined the curve of the day up to noon and down the afternoon hours, seeing himself alone with Margaret, unrestrained by any compulsion save that of her presence, gladly obliged to look at her as though no increase of time were to drive a wedge between their bodily nearness.

I do not feel young, he thought, and yet I know I am. So is she. If we were only a little older, perhaps it would be...

He thought of her clearly, supposing that she felt the same helplessness, whose essential passivity made life seem to have run mad about them. Yet the way she had looked at him, and something else in her now, defied his under-standing. He wished it had been winter; summer was too strong, and had a purposeful confusion in it. In winter, in those inspired August days, they had been so single in their mind, turned so much outward to one another, that conflict had no room in the happiness that crowded the hours. Now she was changed; from him she had turned into herself and her own being. The rage in her eyes was a fury of self-concentration like that of a woman being possessed bodily, with all her will and might, at the end of a long-denied desire.

He lifted the knapsack he had put down by the door, and slung the straps across his shoulders. Inside the kitchen, dark coolness touched his face; when he could see clearly he realized that no one was there. The woman's voice came to him from the depths of the house; the words were indis-tinguishable; after listening with stretched attention for a minute he let his breath out and was easier. The rise and fall of the tones had seemed calm, reassuringly normal, like Julia's heavy roll on the hard ground, like the motionless shadow of the twisted plum-trees. He sat down on a corner of the long table, waiting, still uncertain of what the Scots-woman thought of him now.

Presently they came in together.

'What a time you take,' he said, pretending to be merry to conceal the joy and distress that each new sight of her touched in him.

'Have y'everything you'll be wanting noo?' Mrs. McLeod asked him; and he answered, 'Yes, everything' looking at Margaret. She was fastening the leather thong of a sandal across the bare instep of her right foot; her raised, bent knee, from which the edge of the red skirt fell down, was white in that dim light, and the skirt was as red as blood. The colour fascinated him. One long plait of hair brushed across her arm as she bent her head.

'Off you go then,' the woman said, 'and if ye're late home there might be no supper, jus' mind.'

She smiled at them, not as easily as she had been wont to do, and with a shadow of doubt in her blue eyes. They did not speak.

'Eh, look at yon fire all out!' she exclaimed, and ceased to smile, and turned away to make it. Charles was surprised; it had not been lit. They called good-bye to her from outside the door, and her voice achieved cheerfulness as she warned them to mind the sun and snakes in the long grass.

When they were some way from the house, walking along a bridle-path by the bed of the trickling stream, he wondered aloud what was the matter with everyone.

'It's as though we'd done something wrong,' he argued slowly, tracking down his thought. 'My mother looks at me as your aunt does at you. Watching all the time—just as you watch a young puppy to see it doesn't hurt itself.'

She said nothing. The brim of her wide straw hat cast

a shadow down her face, and in it her eyes flashed momentarily as she looked at him. The soft straw let in tiny points of light that lay like a powdering of stars on her skin. Once more, catching the movement of her eyes, he was aware of the tensity of some purpose he could not grasp.

'What's the matter? Even you...'

Her hand touched his and was gone; sought it again and held it. He noticed how hot were her fingers.

'Is it my fault, then? Have I done wrong?'

'Wait,' she said. She seemed breathless. The shadow over her face contrasted so strongly with the light that when he looked he could not be sure of what he saw.

'Am I going too fast?' he said.

'No, go on. I'm all right.'

The narrow bridle-path would lead them with the trickle of the shrunken brook to where it joined another stronger stream, pouring its thread of water into the deeper current between high banks. Down that larger stream they were to go, to where it gathered into a broad pool, shallow above a floor of white sand, with deep water at the lower end where, over smooth rocks, it spread and fell and continued its course, glittering in the sun with no suggestion of the lovely coolness of its current. The thin brook they followed was one of its hill tributaries; its water was famous in that district, and for much of its course it lay in their land, meeting lower down the slow river in which Charles bathed. There was always green grass by it; and again and again, following its wanderings, you might come upon hollows in its rounded banks, worn deep by the hoofs of beasts going down to water between the enclosing trees.

But the big pool was higher up, and Charles knew that no one ever went there. It was his own place, and he had his own name for it; it knew his pale reflection as it knew the summer, and he could bathe there, naked and alone at his leisure, all day, scarcely aware of the cool tree shadows moving from west to east across the white sand beneath them; for the whole place was cool and in shadow, a haven in a scorched and burning land; from the lower edge, where the rocks were, arose the ceaseless ripple of the escaping water, quietly hypnotic and full of sleep in the smoky heat of afternoon, and at night melancholy and sweet, complaining in the vastness of night's silence like one lonely voice. Only then could be heard that strange rhythm, elusive, esoteric, deep-seated, intensely secret, that running water has for a continual surprise and mystification of the ear; the most haunting of all night sounds.

As they walked, apart now where the path was narrow, he listened for her step behind him; but the soles of her light sandals were soft, and made no sound in the red dust. He felt, while he could not see her, that she was there, urging him on, and he wanted sometimes to stop and look at her; but the heat was like a wave bearing them, too strong, too urgent now for pausing. Better to go on, he thought, and get this part of it over. Sweat lay warm on his forehead already, and prickled under his arms and on the backs of his hands.

'Am I going too fast?' he asked again. 'We're not far away now.'

He looked back over his shoulder. She was there, near as he had imagined her; when she saw him looking she shook her head. The fury of the cicadas steamed harshly on the still air, and above them, patterned by blue leaves, the hot, pale sky arched over the emptiness of day.

'Listen,' he said, stopping abruptly. 'That's the morning train going out.'

She too stopped, but not soon enough to save herself from coming against him. Her hand, lifted to protect her body, grasped his bare arm, and she looked up. He had never seen her look like that; her face was flushed and grave, with a frown darkening her grey eyes. He put his other arm about her, easing the strap of the heavy knapsack.

'Smile,' he said, after they had looked at one another with a look like speech; and she tried, but could not, so that her face looked frightened and unhappy, as though she might cry. He had never had her as closely as this, and he was surprised at the firmness of her body within his right arm and against him, for her voice and her looks were soft.

'Let us go on,' she said, waiting for him to release her. He felt her tension against him, even when he pressed back her head and kissed her mouth that returned his kiss urgently, even when her eyes were closed and she seemed eagerly to dream. So he moved away from her, and they walked on, breathless indeed now, and troubled anew by the terrible willingness of the flesh, and the mysterious purpose of its desire.

The thread of water on their right hand grew stronger, forming itself into little pools under the low banks, glittering mercilessly in the sun where rocks and the roots of trees thrust up and teased it. The sound of the train had gone, and once more they were alone. That rushing murmur of sound, with its memory of time and a world of humanity, must have thrust them together for those few moments; when it was gone and forgotten they could go on, thinking only of themselves, and silent still from the strange experience of that embrace. In some way he knew she had desired it; to him also it was like having drunk cold water and gained from it new bodily energy, to walk on through the blazing day. How much she had desired it he did not wonder; he had cause enough for thought in the memory of his own kiss's hard and solemn urgency; that was new, and seemed to have come from the new darkness of his inner sensations running downwards in a heavy current into his thighs and knees.

When at length they came out from among the trees, the full sunlight struck them like a blow from a giant hand. There was one field to cross; a sheep pad, almost hidden now because it had not been used that year, led them diagonally over, up rising ground where grasshoppers shot away from their path and sped furiously through the shaken air, unseen but audible. At the top of the rise, which had been a near horizon to them, they could look down over the silver grass to a fence, and beyond the fence to one more steep slope above which the bulging, motion-less tops of trees showed against the sky.

'There is the river,' he said. 'Don't stop. It's too hot.'

They went quickly down the sloping ground, and at the bottom of the dry hollow he paused to help her through the fence, and got through after her. The wires were hot in his fingers, as though they had recently known the fire.

'You'd never think,' he said breathlessly, as they fought up the last slope against the day, 'that there—had been—any winter. Would you? February—is worse—even.'

She was in front. He put his finger-tips in the small of her back as once he had been taught to do, and felt the straining of muscles there as he helped her to climb. The trees climbed with them, on the other side; from the crest of the rise they could be seen, complete and perfect, solid green cumulus low above the thick white pillars of their trunks. There was a sly gleam of water visible through the twisting lower branches.

'There,' he said gladly. 'Down you go. Thank God.'

He could not pause at the shadow of the first trees, but must walk down to the edge of the stream. Looking into that limpid movement, cool in the green shadow, he forgot the day, and the fierce sunlight. It was dim there as it would have been in a room from which all direct light was shut. The heads of the low, thick trees met above the water; his own face peered back at him, green-white, and he looked through the mirrored eyes to the soundless stir and shift of the sandy bottom, where all sorts of small disturbances were for ever taking place. In the middle the current was strong.

At last he said, 'Isn't this worth it? Isn't it?'

When she made no reply he looked round, for he wanted her to be with him in his sudden overwhelming relief and content. There she was, stretched out on the thin dry grass at the edge of the white sand. Her face was whiter than all; the hat brim, fallen loosely back, let him see it clearly now. It was sickeningly white, and the closed eyelids looked dark. He sprang up.

'What is it?' He believed she had fainted.

'I knew,' he muttered, putting his hand under her head. 'I knew I shouldn't.' But she opened her eyes, and said she was all right again. He was on his knees beside her. The look of anger, or fear, or whatever it had been, was gone now from her eyes and mouth.

'Don't look like that,' she said. 'It's all right. I've been feeling like this—a long time. It's nothing.'

She sat up, but soon lay back again, never taking her eyes from him. The skirt, red in the shade like blood, lay across her thighs. He felt the stuff with his finger-tips. It was a kind of flannel, soft and dry to touch.

'This is not the place,' he said quietly, 'but we can stay here if you like.'

'The pool, you said,' she reminded him. 'No—we'll go there.'

'It's not far. But rest now.'

He remained kneeling beside her, looking down, and while his eyes explored her still face, he thought how heavy her head had been on his open hand, how cool and alive the hair his fingers pressed.

Everything we say, he thought, seems like an empty pretence. Words now were only nervous sounds emptily concealing something. He had spoken last, and the brief phrases repeated themselves quietly in his mind, as meaningless and as measurable as a clock's ticking, but, like the sound of a clock, urgently suggesting something immeasurable. He wondered if she were thinking as he was. Her face was as still as sleep; only the trembling eyelids told him that if he spoke again she would hear. The full, pale curves of her lips were without shadow or movement. In her throat the cord of an artery rose and fell, heavily, slumbrously under the skin, as though it had a life of its own apart from the mute stillness of her face; and on each side the plaits of fair hair led him downwards with their unreal involution to the near-defined offering of her breasts, round and larger than he would have imagined them, and very proud. They too seemed to have a life of their own. He closed his fingers hard in the sand.

Some minutes passed without movement or speech. Beyond that sanctuary of shadow and sand and flowing water the day marched upward, leaving them alone; the air, dry and warm and sweet with the flameless burning of grass, shook without ceasing, as though in the grip of some huge, triumphant passion, and glistened afar off like water swimming above the earth. Everything took on unreal motion; the trees in the distance quivered from root to top as if in a moment they would dissolve and melt into the air; posts and rails trembled with the same illusion of movement as have objects seen under flowing water, and along the line of high ground the filmy grass, sucked upward by mirage, swayed unnaturally tall. But under those trees, whose rounded heads shut out all the sky, it was cool, and every outline, the girl's face, her ankles, her gentle hands, his own knees pressed upon the sand—all was clear and very real, like figures suggested upon an artist's canvas. The blue of his shirt, and the blood-red splash of her skirt, made bright colour in the cool green and white of that seclusion, walled in by the white tree-trunks and the rising ground behind.

At last she opened her eyes and looked into his, smiling, capturing all his thought.

'That was wonderful. I was awake, but I seemed to dream you were there.'

'I was looking at you,' he said.

'I know. I wanted you to.'

She moved her arm, and her hand lay limply on his knees. He felt its warmth burn through against the skin.

'Isn't it lovely,' she said. 'And oh—Charles! it does seem as if it will last.'

'Yes.'

'It does. I don't think about it. Do you know how I've been longing for this—to be with you in this place? Such a long time. It's summer now. Only a few months—a year ago I didn't know. Now I know.'

Her hand moved and came to life. He felt it so sharply, with his whole consciousness, that the small quiet stir of fingers and wrist was almost unbearable.

'I know,' he said. 'And usually I don't like summer; yet now it somehow fascinates me.'

'It makes you hot all through? Does it? Warm all the time, from inside?'

She raised herself slowly on her elbow, leaning towards him.

'That's what it does to me now,' she said, hesitating in a sudden eagerness. 'Now. I can't remember before. All sorts of new things I notice when I'm with you.'

Her voice was warm, as though she were waking from sleep. His knees remembered where her hand had been.

'Charles. Just for these few days…'

Her smile implored him, and answered for him when he could not speak. He continued to look at her steadfastly, feeling that he had never clearly seen her before this hour; and it seemed to him that indeed he had not, though what he saw as a change in her was, unknown to him, an awakening of a part of his consciousness hitherto restlessly asleep. He perceived her to be, in the glow of her physical being, desirable.

'Not for these few days,' he said in a low voice. 'Time—time is—it's all different now, Margaret. I know what I didn't know before.'

She took his face between her hands, leaning so near that he became lost in the wide, dark dilation of her pupils, unnaturally large and containing small reflections of himself held by her hands.

'Do you know too?' she murmured. 'How can I know you do? How can I be sure you know, Charles? Oh, Charles.'

'I think,' he said, 'I'm just beginning to see you as—as I should have done before. Now it's too late.'

'No, no,' she cried passionately. 'It's not. It's not.' But when he asked her what that meant she turned her face away without answering, as though she had said too much, and wished him to forget her words.

'It must be,' he said, suddenly made miserable by his awareness of a situation he could not fully understand. It seemed that something was moving with inexorable leisure to a close before he had realized its event; and, as if a nightmare landslide were upon them, he wanted to take her, alive and willing, into the stricture of his two arms, not for her protection but for his own futile comfort at a time when protection was not possible. The knowledge of that futility, suggested by his perception of some irrevocable conclusion, made him stay still, looking at her averted head with a sense of loss already accomplished, and of the poverty of all speech and movement.

'There's a way,' she said at last, in a dry strangled voice. Her throat and all he could see of her face were slowly flushed; but she did not move nor look towards him with the deliberate effort of defiance he might have expected after her words. With his eyes on the trickle of sand between his fingers, he thought he heard her say something more.

'What did you say then?'

'I said...oh, what's the use! It's terrible to go on talking like this.'

'I can't help it,' he said helplessly.

'It all takes so long. And it's not *us*—is it? We're not really like this.'

She turned to him again with that same eagerness.

'We're not, are we? Charles? We're together all the time. Talking is just horrible.'

'Well,' he said, 'stand up and see how you feel. We could go down.'

He stood up, and, taking her hands, felt her weight in his own as she rose. There they remained facing one another, until, without seeming to have moved, she was near and he felt her breasts soft and strange against him. Their eyes were almost level.

'What are you going to do?' she said. 'Will you go and bathe? I can feel you're still hot, and your shirt's wet.'

'Will you go in?'

She laughed breathlessly. 'We have nothing to wear. Suppose...'

'No one will come,' he said quietly. This was easy— more easy and right than he could have imagined. He could not know that the ecstasy of that August afternoon had constricted his mind more than anything following, more than any other encounter, and that now, in physical contact with her, there was a promise not of repetition but of some solution and easing of the constriction. All he knew, as wave after wave of unknown rhythms mounted in him, was that this, this touching and perceiving the firm reality of her flesh, which no garment could conceal, was what for so long he had desired. It was this he had feared to lose, and had thought, even a few minutes past, to have lost already. The other, the discovery of her in his most inward being, would never be lost.

But he could think now of no future, for the urgency of the present forced his vision to see only her and the transparent water laving their two bodies with its flow.

'Let's bathe,' he said with finality. 'Then we shall be cool, and have appetites for food. Come, I'll show you.'

They went down along the low firm bank of the stream. Grasses spilled over into the water, combing free a pattern of ripples that faded and were for ever renewed. The water-smell lay on the air they breathed. On their left the trees grew more widely, and great bold patches of sun threw shadows as they passed, and were gone. After a hundred yards or so they were in deep shade again; the sun was high overhead; day neared its climax, and the air burned, shrill and dry, glittering over the yellow silver of the grass-land.

Under the trees the brilliant cruelty of noon was unreal to them. At last he stopped and showed her.

'There. You stay here; you can't be seen—see, you're shut in a room. Go quickly into the water and wait for me. I'll go over the other side. Float down. That's what I always do.'

She watched him take off his shoes, roll up the bottoms of his trousers and cross, most of the way on a tree-trunk lying diagonally out from the bank there, half-sunk, with the water rolling silently over it. When he was gone, and the low echo of his voice saying 'All right now' had left the air more still, more expectant than before, she took her clothes off as though in a dream, dropping them on the sand by her, calmly, quickly, apparently without thought.

When she was naked, she looked down with an expression of surprise waking in her face, and a warmth of colour rose from her breasts to her forehead, a colour of perfect shame. She ran the palms of both hands slowly over her body almost to her knees, carefully, as if to assure herself of its shape and reality. The heavy silken plaits of hair lay against the powder-smooth skin when she rose from stooping. She began to look about her, clasping her hands together with an unconscious expression of anguish. Something, some change of thought, perhaps some remembered knowledge of herself, seemed to have made her hesitate. After appearing for some moments to be in a grave uncertainty, she bent down and took up her garments, which she held in her hands, looking at them with that wakening surprise in her face once more. Then she began to put them on.

When Charles came down with the voluptuous current

he did not see her, until her voice, quite close to him, said softly, 'How white you are! As white as—me.'

She was on the shelving bank a few yards away, staring at him steadily with a look of faint surprise. He could not understand why she had not come in.

'I couldn't,' she said. 'It wasn't that I didn't want to. I couldn't.'

She stepped into the water and came out near him where he crouched forward, sitting on the harsh sand of the floor. The water rose to her knees; she drew her skirt away from it and leaned forward to touch his shoulder and back with her hand. It made him shiver. He watched the slowing current curl away from her knees in a thin, shadowy wake. She took her hand away and put it to her lips. She was smiling.

'I could splash you,' he said. 'I could pull you in.' He caught her hand as she let it fall by her side. 'You make me wish I hadn't come in, now. It's not so nice alone.'

'Well, I'm here,' she said, and she put her hand to his own lips, and pressed it there. He breathed the perfume of the skin, as once before he had done, closing his eyes so that he might see all. His wet fingers clung to her wrist. Her expression of surprise softened and became a look of unutterable compassion, but this he did not see. She gently withdrew her hand from his.

'I must go out,' she said.

He opened his eyes.

'All right. I shall too. Go up and wait for me.'

She was gone. The ripple and splash of water as she moved away across the current grew faint. He was glad she was gone, now; but a greater intimacy, full of confidence, had come to them in those few minutes. Even if he relaxed and was content to be alone, he was content, too, that they had been there together like that; it gave his thoughts the comfort of accomplished security. He must have been shaken by a wish to touch her, to see her wholly, for his hands felt empty, and he gripped them and wrung them under the water, and looked at them, conscious of much of their purpose, and suspecting their part in the expression and confirmation of love.

On the farther bank he dried his hands in the grass, rubbing the slippery dead blades between flat palms. The scorching air did the rest. Within a few minutes he was clad again, and there was a sort of relief in the touch of the warm garments on his cool skin. He went to cross the stream again, with the knapsack on his shoulder and his shoes in one hand.

Through the low leaves showed the red splash of her skirt, a living colour like new blood. He went across. Sitting on the sand, with her back curved and her knees drawn up, she was fastening the sandal strap across one instep. He remembered the same pose in the kitchen—how long ago was that? Surprised by the length and whiteness of her leg at the back above the knee, he looked away, as he meant his mind to turn away at present from too searching a thought of her. Self-consciousness was new to him, and he was ashamed.

The water and his innocent nakedness had made a stranger of him, and when she stood up, throwing back her head to shake her hair away, they looked at one another searchingly. He was in such a dream that he stood without speaking, wondering not if this were so but if there were any truth in any of his memories of that previous life, that stood like shadows at the edge of his consciousness of her. She looked at him as steadfastly, her hands hanging open by her sides, her lips apart. A sort of exhaustion grew heavy upon them, as though they might fall down. At length, dragging himself free, he spoke.

'Shall we go down and have something to eat—now?'

They were both hungry, and that seemed surprising enough to be laughable. Side by side they followed the stream round; under the trees by the pool, white sand curved to a low mass of rock, and the shade was intense like the sunlight outside. A reflection from the open water in the middle was not able to reach in to them.

'I'd never have thought it could be so cool,' she murmured, stretched out face-downwards in the sand, her cheek on her hands, watching him; and he told her that this was the coolest place in the world, in summer, but very melancholy in winter, and very dark. He showed her the smooth bed of sand on which they rested.

'This is all under water. That's why it's so smooth and even. No marks are left.'

With a twig he wrote her name in the white surface.

'Leave it there,' he said soberly; and because his thought was evident to both of them, like an intrusion of the world they were forgetting, neither spoke, and they took their food in silence. He did not taste what he was swallowing, after that.

Later she went to the edge of the pool for water. When they had drunk of it, and poured some out in instinctive libation to the lonely spirit of that place, they moved near to one another on a common impulse, and lay close together. Her head was in the hollow of his arm, against his side; he could touch her breasts and her cheek. They remained silent, looking up at the roof of leaves, beyond which the hot metallic sky shone unseen. The stream was splashing and sleeping among its rocks at the lower edge, but now they could not feel any relaxation of sleep in their bodies or their eyes. Out there the day poised triumphant, at its height and fullest power, careless of this final conquest it made within them; the singing insects were mad with light, and the air stretched to a perilous tension, ready to split and shatter, ready with the whole world to burst into flame.

'Charles,' she said.

She raised herself upon one elbow, so that her face was above his own. She was the day. Her dry, soft fingers touched his lips, his cheek, his forehead, and strayed again into his hair, dully caressive. She was looking down, bending over him, but not seeing him; he trembled to know the heavy relaxation of her lips, swollen and parted with the blind concentration of love. A measureless knowledge in her gaze made him close his eyes; he wanted to cry out, but her hand was over his mouth, holding him silent.

In time he put up his arms, to undo the green ribbons that swung at the ends of her heavy fair plaits; and at last, like a silken fall of cloth, her hair spread free, shutting in their two faces. They could not smile now, nor speak, not even to say each other's name that was loudly in the mind of each. The day had too sure a power over them; though they might evade it in cool shadow, they were a part of its triumph, and it forced them together, encouraging them with the illusion that what they did they did by the blind volition of their own single will. In its cruel majesty it echoed mockingly her one cry, that was a cry of relief from a long tyranny.

Mawley kept some of his old note-books. Their cheery words in time became unreal, and suggested faintly an enchantment of life impossible to believe in, after the passing of some years. They were enthusiastic in their assurance that the summer of that year was as hot as the devil— 'a record heat!!!' The carefully mature, consciously cultured handwriting mentioned this two or three times during passages written in December and January and February; very blithe passages telling of happy holiday affairs. Hope, which Penworth called '*cette original*', the smiling deceiver, must be amazed at the sad futility of making early notes on life and people; only the wish, the green thought, the unreality of a suggested enchantment evolved by time, are preserved in such apish, facile jottings, whose very abundance condemns them afterwards. Nevertheless, these coy pages held still some reminiscence of that swoon of the blood, swoon of the brain, sharp swoon and weight of the burning air, which curdle somnolently in the flesh, making all movement heavy with effort, and coaxing the lover of such summer weather to lie in the white-hot sand and listen to the thunder of waves at his feet and the cease-less secret of gulls of wind in his ears.

He had written that in February Charles was in 'a very interesting condition'—a happy expression that seems to have been unhappily applied this time, though it does give some hint of how changed he was from the ignorant and remote angel he had seemed when, a year before, his mother left him at the gates and walked away through the thick hazy heat of late afternoon to catch her train. There was not much dramatic interest in him then; but between then and now he had seen something of life as he was to live it, and had made his first and greatest decision affirming his own manhood. But in one way he would not alter: for he had not the fatal power of being satisfied, and his love of life therefore was conscious and intense. His mental processes, of self-analysis and objective reasoning, also altered little, and remained a sort of torture to him when he considered his own short-comings and the incomprehensibility of the rest of the world. It appeared, however (though this the optimistic note-book failed to record) that whereas before the holiday he had been often miserable and discontented for all to see, now whatever he had of discontent was the surface measure of some inward reconciliation of wish with wisdom, of a decision made and irrevocable.

Mawley afterwards insisted that at this time he knew little enough of him; but Mawley's memory was always clear enough to represent a picture of him coming in through those gates to begin another year of obedience and of work. His face was pale and thinner; he had never liked summer, though, as he said, it fascinated him, and now in his eyes a look of labour tried to conceal itself beneath that mask of defiant indifference which you could imagine him unhappily assuming during all the journey up from his home to the city, from the city eastwards to the School station, from the station along the dusty private path to the dark gates sweating in the heat.

It was like him to say no word of greeting to Mawley, letting best welcome reach out in the sudden brilliance of his smile, and to speak at once of something in the life he had now returned to from the oblivion of weeks of absence.

'I want to get the bed next to you, Mawl. Do you think I can?'

This was the final gesture of friendship, in those days, for it made a claim of spiritual equality. They went to see. He said nothing in the oven-heat and steamy shadow of the covered way, but in the first changing room beyond it, where the brassy afternoon sunlight suddenly set his hair afire, he turned his head quickly.

'I must say I'm glad to see you off those crutches.' And, on a sequence of thought impossible to follow, 'It'll make a difference not having Penworth here.'

He explained, climbing the stairs, that it would be in a way easier.

'But I'll miss him. You will, too, I know. He liked us both as much. I wonder what he'll think of our mean passes.'

There was a letter for him in the rack at the top of the stairs. Mawley mentioned it when, after putting hat and suitcase on the locker between their beds, in sign of possession, Charles was ready to sit down and talk. His face was always pale. Now it went so white that the green pigment in his skin showed. He looked as though he might have fainted, and, instead of walking down the dormitory at once, he leaned heavily on the top of the locker, with his eyes closed. Mawley said the handwriting was unmistakable.

He looked, and sighed as though he had escaped a danger.

'Penworth? Oh—that's good. Why didn't you say? I'd better get it, hadn't I, before everyone sees it and my name's dirt again.'

But instead of going, even then, to the stair-head, he sat down on his new bed, exhaustion coming when restraint had been unlocked. His hands hung limply from the wrists over the neat bed's edge.

'God, I'm tired. This summer's too much. As though I've been trampled on all night, when I wake in the morning.'

He said it had rained half the time while he and his mother, taking a holiday which she had needed as much as he had, were down on the southern coast, and that he had had a good time there—quiet, but good. By that, it appeared that he had been left alone, freed from the intolerable antagonism which he could not understand. What he had paid for this freedom was hard to guess.

At last, hearing other people coming, he got up and went for the letter, muttering something about having forgotten. There was a look of mild surprise in his face.

The symphony in three movements was opening; the air of expectancy had broken with the familiar sound of feet and voices in the class-rooms beneath, in the bathrooms, on the stairs, and a division of life into two parts, the known for them, the unknown for those timid newcomers without background or social rights in older scholars' eyes, of whom a year before, to the day and hour, Charles had been one. Now there was an invasion of Dormitory C, where he, as a second-year scholar, had a right to live if he chose. He came back with his letter; two or three other boys, laughing at some comfortable crudity of wit, were following in a group. Their round cheeks had flushed red with the heat, and were sleek with sweat; the skin about their lips looked by contrast white, as it would do in the sudden lividness of anger. Charles took no notice of them. He sat down to read. Mawley, watching his face, saw the familiar easy tears come into his eyes and brim and tremble on the lower lids. When he looked up his smile was brilliant. It was plain that even now he was not thinking of Penworth; but all he said, as he rubbed his eyes with the back of his hand, was, 'Do you remember what he said in the dormitories? "B is B, and C is C, and never the twain shall meet." It always amused me. I don't know what made me think of that. It's some misquotation, I think.'

Mawley remembered, more readily, that anything that moved him deeply had always the power to command his tears. It was not Penworth's letter, surely, that had done this. His state now was reminiscent of early convalescence; but of the mind, not of the body.

'Here, read it yourself. I'll unpack this case,' he said, holding out the open sheet of creamy thick paper.

Penworth's writing, as delicate and incisive as only a man's can be, was almost a self-portrait: its scholarship was warm, not dry, and it lived choicely on the page, suggesting in the individuality of each character much fluent penning of Greek running script.

'My dear Charles,

'A word with you on your return, since we are to be friends. My gratification at your pass may only be equalled by the content you should now enjoy, and it should, you know, be outdone by your determination to go on as you have begun. Te saluto—sed non moriturus!

'Pas du tout. I am conscious rather of being on the eve of a new night not without its moon and stars, nor lacking promise of the day to follow. (Aliter (Anglice)—Life's good-oh, and as a musician, master-pupil-cum-anything else that may be, I am finding myself easier with myself.)

'One of these evenings, lordly in my not-always-to-be-praised independence, I suppose I shall return to haunt the precincts, and shall walk leisurely up the covered way to Chatterton. Looking round from Cicero (In Catilinam, I think?) in prep. at the insulting, improper sound of voices, you will perceive me with Mr. Waters in the shadows outside, looking in; but I shall not gloat. Nor shall I commiserate. Whether you understand it or not, I shall probably envy. You will find one day how much you have that I have not and have not had.

'How is your heart? Changed at all? I dare to ask as a friend—never as a mentor. Let things happen as they will, Charles, and enjoy whatever joys there are in loving. You may come to an end; but—if you are very lucky—you may come instead to a beginning. I hope you do. How do I know?

I don't. This is the schoolmaster's wordy peroration, which is let off at random, in the hope always of striking a spark somewhere, in some darkness. Let it be no more than that; and remember that even in love you have my good wishes...now. Once it might have been otherwise.

'*This note, ended perforce by the arrival of the afternoon's first pupil, coming down the garden path, is just the beginning of a beginning.*

'Tibi,

'*Christopher Penworth.*'

Mawley finished reading, and folded up the letter. The air was quieter outside; February days in Australia become tired before sunset. From the Chapel path and the front courtyard and the green lawns all about, a rise and fall of voices sounded cheerfully, and the husky tones of pigeons and doves, falling from the orange-hot roofs, were by contrast fictitiously peaceful. The day was tired, and Charles, susceptible as always to changes of that sort, was aware of its exhaustion in his own limbs, and its melancholy of decline tightening his throat.

Mawley, on looking up, observed that instead of unpacking he had remained sitting on the edge of his bed, his face expressionless like that of one who thinks steadfastly of something past and irrevocable, upon which great happiness had once depended.

Text Classics

Dancing on Coral
Glenda Adams
Introduced by Susan Wyndham

The Commandant
Jessica Anderson
Introduced by Carmen Callil

Homesickness
Murray Bail
Introduced by Peter Conrad

Sydney Bridge Upside Down
David Ballantyne
Introduced by Kate De Goldi

Bush Studies
Barbara Baynton
Introduced by Helen Garner

The Cardboard Crown
Martin Boyd
Introduced by Brenda Niall

A Difficult Young Man
Martin Boyd
Introduced by Sonya Hartnett

Outbreak of Love
Martin Boyd
Introduced by Chris Womersley

The Australian Ugliness
Robin Boyd
Introduced by Christos Tsiolkas

All the Green Year
Don Charlwood
Introduced by Michael McGirr

They Found a Cave
Nan Chauncy
Introduced by John Marsden

The Even More Complete
Book of Australian Verse
John Clarke

Diary of a Bad Year
J. M. Coetzee
Introduced by Peter Goldsworthy

Wake in Fright
Kenneth Cook
Introduced by Peter Temple

The Dying Trade
Peter Corris
Introduced by Charles Waterstreet

They're a Weird Mob
Nino Culotta
Introduced by Jacinta Tynan

The Songs of a Sentimental Bloke
C. J. Dennis
Introduced by Jack Thompson

Careful, He Might Hear You
Sumner Locke Elliott
Introduced by Robyn Nevin

Fairyland
Sumner Locke Elliott
Introduced by Dennis Altman

The Explorers
Edited and introduced by
Tim Flannery

Terra Australis
Matthew Flinders
Introduced by Tim Flannery

My Brilliant Career
Miles Franklin
Introduced by Jennifer Byrne